HEIR'S REVENGE

RETURN OF THE AGHYRIANS BOOK 4

PATTY JANSEN

CAPRICORNICA PUBLICATIONS

GET FREE EBOOKS

DID YOU KNOW?

Heir's Revenge is also available in audio. Visit https://
pattyjansen.com to find out more.

1

THERE WAS a light in the yard next door.

Ellisandra stopped halfway through pulling the curtains shut and peered into the snowy dusk, where the grey buildings of the city faded into the murk of mist and falling snowflakes. The yard of her house was already covered in a good layer of snow, gilded by the glow from the windows downstairs. The wall that surrounded the yard had acquired a white cap, as yet undisturbed by the wind or the creatures of the night. On the other side of the wall, a snowy expanse stretched to the ruin of the house next door. In amongst the broken and fire-blackened walls stood a storm light, its flapping flame casting long shadows in the snow and on whatever remained of the walls.

That was odd. There hadn't been any activity at the Andrahar house for years. Why would someone come out to the ruin in the middle of this weather?

Behind Ellisandra's back, in the comfort of her upstairs room, the ladies of the theatre committee still chatted, accompanied by the chink of spoons on porcelain. The smell of sweet cakes hung in the air.

"Oh, no I don't think we should do that," Aleyo Hirumar was

saying. "I think everyone will be quite upset if we change the ending of the play. I know I would be."

"How would you stage it then?" asked Tolaki Telimar.

"As it is supposed to be. As it was written." The indignation dripped from Aleyo's voice.

Ellisandra should go back to the group and help Tolaki convince Aleyo to be a bit more adventurous, but now she spotted a man in the Andrahar yard, a tall figure shrouded in a thick long-hair cloak. The light glinted in his curtain of hair. It was typical Endri hair, past the shoulder, silver-white, sleek, straight and loose. He wore knee-high boots with a strip of fur around the top, all very traditional, and very upper class.

According to the stories, the Andrahar family had been very traditional right until the moment that they decided to betray their home nation and leave. They had lived in Barresh since she was a little girl. Ellisandra was too young to have remembered the fire that destroyed the house or any of the riots and that treacherous trial that went before it, in which the family smeared Miran and tried to ruin the nation's reputation by trying to implicate it in criminal activities.

With his gangly appearance and fluid motions, this man next door was too young to be one of the four Andrahar brothers. Who in Miran still wanted to work for that family? No one she knew at any rate. No one local.

But the hair . . . she had heard jokes that the first thing Endri did when going to live in Barresh was cut their hair. Long hair was a pride thing, especially for the men. There was a saying that hair symbolised a person's ties with Miran. When a man moved away and kept his hair long, there was a chance that he might come back.

Behind her, the ladies of the theatre committee had gone quiet.

"Anything wrong, Ellisandra?" Tolaki asked.

"There's someone in the yard next door."

"Oh, let me have a look." Aleyo pushed herself up and hurried to the window. She pushed her face to the glass, shielded from the reflection inside the room by her hands.

"There is, too." The window fogged up where her mouth was.

Now Tolaki also came to the window, and peered into the darkness over Aleyo's shoulder. "I see him. Probably just a groundsman."

"In this weather?" Ellisandra said.

"Doesn't look like a groundsman to me," Aleyo said. "Look at his hair. That's pure Endri. It's gorgeous, too. And who would employ a groundsman for a ruin like that anyway?"

Good points, both of them.

Even Sariandra had come to watch. But Tolaki and Aleyo were blocking the window, so she stood further back, looking forlorn and lonely in that dour dress of hers.

"Who do you think he is, then?" Tolaki asked, frowning at Ellisandra.

"No idea. Never seen him before."

"Do people still come to look at that ruin?"

"Very, very rarely. I don't think I've seen anyone there for years." The last time it had been a local surveyor. She tried to remember when that had been, but couldn't. Long ago. Possibly longer ago than she thought, because she remembered Father standing behind her looking out of the window and Father hadn't been able to do anything that remotely looked like "standing" unassisted for a long time.

Aleyo put on her conspiratorial voice. "What if we discovered something? I mean, no *normal* person would be out there in the dark in the middle of this weather. What if they're finally selling up but don't want anyone to know?"

That's what everyone had thought last time, too.

"No," Tolaki said. "Last I heard, Isandra Andrahar said that they'd sell the house and office 'over my dead body'."

"Maybe she died," Aleyo said. "She has to be pretty old—"

Ellisandra protested. "Not that old, I don't think."

"Well, if she died, then those sons of hers wouldn't care a bit about the house." Aleyo stuck her chin in the air. "I mean, it's not like any of us would want them back. I don't understand why they kept the house like this for all those years. The office, too, right in the prime locality downtown. Has to be worth a fortune."

Ellisandra thought she had an explanation. "Maybe they never sold because they didn't want any dirty Mirani credits for it." There was not much they could do with those outside Miran, not legally anyway. Not that it had ever before stopped any rich family from selling their house and leaving Miran for good.

Aleyo added, "Or maybe they were waiting for land prices to improve."

Tolaki laughed aloud. "Only to have seen the prices drop to a tenth of what they were when they left? Serves them right. We don't do selling for a lot of money here. We don't want foreigners to buy our houses."

Aleyo snorted. "Yeah, the Andrahars were arrogant, greedy pricks, even when they still lived in Miran."

This statement met with sage nods, even from Sariandra who had said barely a thing.

Oh well, no time to dwell on it. Surely the guards would keep an eye on this stranger. And no doubt he'd be gone soon and she'd never see him again.

Ellisandra pulled the curtains shut and sat down, meeting the eyes and mousey face of Sariandra Bisumar, who, failing to get a glimpse of that strange man, had returned to her seat. She sat straight-backed, clamping both hands between her knees covered by that grey-pink dress that looked too dour for her young face. It was loose in the chest, too, as if the dress had been made with the hope that her womanly shapes would fill the flabby bits of fabric. But if she remained as shy as she had tonight and never touched any cakes, then that was unlikely to happen.

Ellisandra addressed her now. "Sariandra, I haven't heard what you think. What should we do about the ending of the play?"

"Oh, I . . . um . . ." She averted her eyes and tucked a strand of hair behind her ear. Her cheeks grew red.

"Do you think that if we perform this for the council, that people like your father would be upset with us for changing the story a little bit?"

Sariandra nodded, her eyes wide. "You propose to change the ending of the play. That's not a little bit."

Aleyo nodded sagely. "That's what I've been telling you. Didn't you hear that story that a councillor once walked out of the performance of *The Redemption of Jilan Ilendar* screaming because the lead actress wore a modern buttoned-up dress instead of a lace-up one? That's the sort of attitude they have. It's got to be historically correct."

Ellisandra let her shoulders slump. "Yes, but the other ending is terrible. It makes us sound like cruel barbarians. No one today would kill prisoners when they're harmless. It makes me sick. And then the way all the councillors in the play sing while stepping over bodies, holding hands and singing of great glory. It's awful."

Sariandra looked down at her hands. "But it's the way the play goes. It's traditional. You can't just change it."

Aleyo continued nodding through all of it, her mouth kept in a prim line as if she knew *everything*. How annoying.

Ellisandra said, "I wish the council had picked a different play for the opening of the Legislative year. We could have done *Midwinter Fair*, or *The Days of War* or anything, really. Why did they have to choose *Changing Fate*?"

"To remind us of the glorious days of Miran," Sariandra said.

Everyone looked at her in a *You-have-got-to-be-kidding* way. But Sariandra wasn't kidding, not even a little bit. Her young face was dead serious.

"Um. Would you call it glorious to kill defenceless prisoners?"

"They were enemies. They invaded us."

"They were captured and could not defend themselves. They had already been punished."

"Times have changed. People didn't have much food back then, and they couldn't afford to keep enemies alive. It was a normal thing to kill them. Good even, because if you killed them, they could never attack you again."

A cold feeling of horror crept over Ellisandra's back. How could she say this with such a demure, detached voice? What was worse, how could she think that an attitude like that was even remotely acceptable? "Yeah, like they could kill all Coldi, all billions of them. The people back then couldn't even put a vehicle in the air, let alone fly it to Asto to begin killing all of them." She cringed at Sariandra innocent face—she really didn't understand this, did she?—but seriously this type of attitude frustrated her so much. "We are not in those times anymore. There will be children in the audience for the performance. When I have children, I don't want them to think that this is all right."

"My father will want the play to be performed as is written. Sorry if you don't like it, but that's what you asked." There was a hardness in Sariandra's tone that belied her shy appearance.

An uneasy silence followed in which Tolaki looked at Ellisandra, wide-eyed in a *You-said-what-to-the-High-Councillor's-daughter?* way.

Ellisandra poured herself tea to cover up the embarrassment. Sometimes she wished she could shut her big mouth. Only sometimes, though.

Then she continued, "I still can't understand why anyone would choose this play, let alone for the opening ceremony of the legislative year. This play hasn't been performed in the great hall for years."

"That's probably why they've chosen it," Sariandra said.

"But why? The ending is horrible. Usually the plays have a message of hope or a new beginning. They're telling the people, *Your council is looking out for you and making things better.*"

Aleyo said, "Um, I don't think the council consciously chooses the play for the message. It's just that most plays *do* end with a message."

"Yes, it makes the people feel good. Why choose this one?"

"Well, we can't change that, it's the council's decision" Aleyo said. "And I agree with Sariandra. We should perform it with the original ending. It's a very heroic play and the council probably had reasons to choose it, if only those reasons were that it hasn't been performed for a long time."

And that's what it all came down to. Reasons. The council always had Reasons, and everyone would run, and then when it was all done and someone said, "The way you wanted it done was so much work," someone from the council would come back to them and say, "Really? I had no idea. Why didn't you say so?" And the whole thing would have been so much easier if only people hadn't taken the council's Reasons as law.

Ellisandra met Tolaki's eyes, knowing that her best friend shared her abhorrence for the needless violence in that last scene.

Tolaki shrugged, her eyes sad.

Yes, it was probably too late to voice her objections, and she could think of plenty. There would be children in the hall, and it was not a play that showed either behaviour suitable for children or displayed morality suited to children.

Times had changed. Many plays remained beautiful and poignant tales of love and war. This wasn't one of them.

And then to think that she'd been keenly awaiting the council's decision on a play for what would be her signature performance, her last production before she married and possibly her last ever as stage director.

And what had they given her? *Changing Fate*. Really?

Someone must hate her very much.

She'd seen a performance of it when she was young and the only thing she remembered was how in the last act the soldiers on the stage killed everyone. She didn't understand the reason and, having read the play later, she'd seen that the reason was weak, except *we hate foreigners*, and that was a sentiment that Miran was very good at these days.

She remembered that a family friend was in the play and had lain face down on the stage. Only she had been too little to understand that it wasn't real, and she'd started screaming. Her mother had to carry her out of the hall, to the great annoyance of the surrounding audience.

She sighed. There was nothing she could do except accept the inevitable. "All right then. Who and what do we need?"

She put the sheaf of paper with the play's text on the table.

"Let's have a look at the notes." Tolaki picked up the cover sheet and read aloud. "*Changing Fate* is the story of the two lovers, who are on the eve of their betrothal—seriously, who wrote this? This is ancient. Who even says 'betrothal' anymore?—when the Invasion occurs. The play starts on the eve of the delayed ceremony, except Mariandra has second thoughts. She has become tempted by the sweet-talking Rana, the leader of the Coldi negotiators who demand the return of the soldiers that were taken prisoner after the Invasion."

Most importantly, there were three main roles. Jihan Ilendar and Mariandra Tussamar made up the central couple, with Rana the antagonist. Typically, Rana did not come with a last name, or clan name as Coldi used. Though having been a negotiator, it would have been something high, like Palayi.

"Ellisandra, what do you think of giving the part of Jihan Ilendar to Keldon Nirumar?"

"Sure." Keldon was one of their few male professional actors. A golden boy, suitably vain and self-conscious to qualify as a lead performer. He'd love the role.

Tameyo Harumin was suitably infatuated with him to be cast as Mariandra. Liran Telimar usually took the role of the antagonist. She disliked the thought of having to "kill" him, even in theatre. She liked Liran. He was neither vain nor self-conscious and very down to earth.

The other lead parts were easy to allocate. The Endri class paid for the theatre, and it supported a small group of full-time actors who took the main roles. Any roles underneath those had to be assigned in a certain order according to the seniority of the actor within the theatre. When that was done, they could look at filling the places of lesser roles with volunteers.

While discussing names, all Ellisandra could see was that final scene where Mariandra is rushed "to safety" by her fiancé while the body of her lover is on the ground amongst those of the prisoners he tried to free.

Ellisandra had never left Miran, and had seen a Coldi person maybe once or twice, but she couldn't imagine that they would be impressed with this retelling of events. As far as was known, an event like this had happened, and it had marked the end of the Coldi attempt to invade Miran. That in itself was a miracle, because Asto had both the vast population and the technology to wipe Miran out within a day. *They* didn't see Miran as an enemy, even if Miran saw *them* as such.

They discussed costuming and stage props, which she would have to get built. They had teams of builders for that, and it was Ellisandra's task to deal with those.

Through all this, Ellisandra felt increasingly uneasy. There were some plays that she didn't like as much as others, but the more they talked about it, the more she knew that she hated this one with every fibre of her being. Unable to change that horrid ending —and Sariandra was right about it, the council *would* object—she could only do one thing to show her displeasure. And they wouldn't like it.

Tolaki said, "You're very quiet. What are you thinking?"

Ellisandra licked her lips. She spoke thoughtfully. "I'm thinking that if the council wants *Changing Fate* produced faithfully, we give it to them faithfully."

Aleyo smiled and nodded.

"What do you mean?" Tolaki asked, because Tolaki knew her a lot better than Aleyo did, and she would know that there was a different meaning behind those words.

Ellisandra continued in that same slow voice. "That last scene in the play is a blood bath. Blood baths are not heroic or glorious, or in this case, even necessary. But the council wants a blood bath. So we give them a blood bath."

The girls all frowned at her, and it seemed to be dawning on Aleyo that she wasn't going to like this.

"When all those prisoners are killed, 'in the name of the glorious nation,' that must have been a horrific scene. Dead and dying people everywhere, screaming, and blood everywhere."

Now Aleyo's face displayed a *I'm-not-quite-sure-I-like-where-this-is-going* expression. Good.

"So, let's have blood. We'll use dye, or we'll go to the abattoir and get real blood and we'll put it in little bags that the actors can burst when they're 'fatally injured' and fall on the stage. By the time Jihan and Mariandra join hands over the bodies of the dead prisoners, there will be blood on their clothes, on their hands, on their shoes. There will be blood on the blunt swords that the actors will be using. There will be blood dripping from the stage."

"Eew. That's disgusting," Aleyo said.

Ellisandra was happy to see that her face had gone pale.

"The play is disgusting. It's full of death, most of it unnecessary. The council wants death? We'll show them so much death that their stomachs will churn. They want the play performed as it was written, historically accurate? Let's give it to them!"

She spread her hands.

Aleyo said, "I'm not sure if that sort of thing was intended. It's about heroics and glory in battle."

"There is nothing either heroic or glorious about that scene and we should not depict it as if is."

And that was maybe why the council wanted it performed: to show how the times had changed.

All three girls looked at her with wide eyes. No one said anything for an uncomfortably long time.

2

D URING THE REST of the meeting they managed to avoid the subject of the play's final scene. There was plenty to discuss that did not divide opinions, so it didn't matter. Ellisandra was convinced that if she turned up with a clear stage plan, the others would see that she was right. People would be shocked, and they would see that war was horrible and would be grateful that Miran was a much kinder place these days. They were no longer at war, so they could afford to be.

The women divided the workload within the committee.

As usual, Ellisandra would look after the building of stage props, Tolaki would deal with the cast, Aleyo would handle advertising and sales, as well as the music, and that left Sariandra with the job of costumes, which, she said in a quiet voice, suited her because she had done some dressmaking.

Ellisandra told her sternly, "You are supposed to buy the fabrics and decide what needs to be made and in what style. The actual making of the costumes is not your job. It's that of the seamstresses."

Sariandra nodded, wide-eyed.

When the meeting was over, Ellisandra asked Tolaki if she would like to stay for a chat, but Tolaki shook her head. "I can't,

I'm sorry. I told my mother that I'd help her with the guest list for the wedding."

The guest list, of course, had to be written out by hand by a calligrapher, and seeing as so few people still took calligraphy education, calligraphers were expensive and hard to get, so anyone with any artistic ability did it themselves. Tolaki was quite handy with a pen and ink.

She met Ellisandra's eyes, and Ellisandra cringed inside. That wedding that had her friend in a flap was *her* wedding to Tolaki's brother Jaeron.

She smiled awkwardly. She shouldn't forget how big a deal it was for Tolaki's family to marry into the only Foundation family still left in Miran. Some people still thought that kind of thing was important, even though the Foundation families had mostly lost their status.

"I'll be so happy once you live in our house," Tolaki said, touching Ellisandra's shoulder.

Ellisandra thought, *Only until you get married yourself* and she would be left by herself in the house with people she barely knew: Jaeron and his parents.

What would it be like, to be alone in a bedroom with an adult man she barely knew who had only one thing on his mind? What would it be like to be undressed by him and touched in places where no light ever came?

She had agreed to marry Jaeron far too long ago, back when she wore her hair in tails and getting married seemed so far away that it would certainly never happen.

She had chosen Jaeron because of the nifty posy of flowers he had given her, a round ball of pinks with occasional white ones, which seemed an utterly stupid reason to determine who she'd live with as adult.

Father, of course, had chosen the candidates, and they were all from families he approved of. The choice she'd been given, facing three terrified young boys in the official dining room downstairs, was a farce.

She'd been too young by many years to make that kind of decision.

What if she hated being married? What if she hated him? Would she be like the embittered wife of *Midnight Folly*, carrying a hammer around the house in case her husband became violent when he returned home late at night?

Aleyo left with Tolaki, and Ellisandra and Sariandra watched both of them striding down the veranda steps and disappearing into the snowy night.

Ellisandra drew her cloak closer around her. Tonight would be a cold one. Already, her breath steamed in the night air and the long winter hadn't even started properly.

The light from the street lamp just outside the gate cast Sariandra's face in sharp relief. She was fiddling with something in her pocket that produced a bluish glow that silvered her fur mittens, sleeves and her face.

'What's that?" Ellisandra asked.

Sariandra showed her the thing. It was a disk-shaped object made from brushed metal, rounded and flat, and it fitted neatly in her mittened hand. Apart from the oval screen, it had three dark-coloured buttons, all marked with foreign characters printed underneath in fluorescent paint. Coldi, she thought. They wrote from right to left.

It was odd that Sariandra would have this. The council went out of its way to make it clear that they frowned upon imported things, especially Coldi-made technology. Why would the High Councillor's daughter be using this?

'This is how I let my father know that the meeting has finished."

'Does that go straight to the Exchange?"

'It does. See here." She pressed something and the tiny screen came up with the text *Miran Exchange Local Network*. In Mirani. That was something at least.

'Is there a local network for everyone? I thought only Traders used it, and only with special permission."

"There is a network. It's not used a lot, mostly because you can't get the readers anywhere in Miran."

No, she bet not, because imports of off-world technology were severely restricted with the boycotts. Other entities of *gamra* would rather die than sell technology to Miran. Miran would rather die than admit it couldn't make the technology within its borders and allow imports.

"My father gave this to me so that I can let him know where I am. He will of course replace it with a Mirani-made device once when we start making them." She looked prim, as if she believed what she said. How old was she?

"Is it necessary to let him know where you are every moment of the day?"

"It's so that he can come to pick me up. The streets are not very safe for a girl walking alone at night."

True. "But you could have walked with Tolaki and Aleyo."

"They don't live in the same street."

"No, but they live close."

"My father prefers me to be absolutely safe. There are robbers and maramarang after dark."

How odd. The streets were not that unsafe. Yes, there were robbers, but not so much in the Endri quarter of the city. It used to be much worse, but the council had sent a big group of vagrants to work on farms near the coast where they wouldn't be in anyone else's way.

There were maramarang at night, too, lurking on the rooftops and peering down with their beady little eyes and flapping and stretching their wings. However, they didn't normally come down to street level until everyone had gone to bed and the streets lay deserted. They were more interested in raiding rubbish bins and attacking inert people, like sleeping beggars, than moving ones. It wasn't that late yet.

Sariandra slid the thing back into her pocket.

Very strange.

After an uncomfortable silence, Ellisandra asked, "So, what did you think of the first meeting? Do you think this is something you would like to continue doing?"

Sariandra nodded. "If my father says it's all right."

"Isn't working with the theatre what almost every Endri woman does? Or music, or teaching? Your father should have no problem with that."

"I guess not . . ." She sounded hesitant.

What was it with this father of hers? Did she need approval for everything?

"Do come to the meeting tomorrow. We'll talk about costumes and we need someone to sort through all the actors' individual text sheets. I don't know when this play was last taken off the shelf, but usually after a play has had its last performance, the actors return their texts, and they get piled into a mess that's badly out of order and may have parts missing. We need to sort through and make sure that each actor gets the right text."

Sariandra nodded, still wide-eyed.

"If you have any trouble with the costuming, let me know, and I can find someone to help you."

"I know a fair bit about traditional dresses. I worked for merchant Ranuddin until the shop closed." Until the man's prices caught up with his business, his age caught up with him and no one in his family wanted to continue the business.

"I never saw you in the shop."

"No, I was in his work room at the back. As seamstress."

That seemed an unusual position for an Endri girl, but never mind.

From the darkness at the edge of the yard came the familiar squeak that signified the opening of the main gate.

Sariandra peered into the snowy night. "That's my father."

The High Councillor himself? Even if he thought it necessary for his daughter to be picked up, why didn't he send one of the domestic staff?

The figure that crossed the yard was certainly tall enough to be Asitho Bisumar, and when he was closer to the house he proved that Sariandra was right. He came up the veranda in large strides, stomping the snow off his boots and then nodding to Ellisandra as he entered the pool of light that surrounded the lamp at the front door. "Good evening, lady."

"Good evening, High Councillor."

He wore his High Councillor cloak with golden chain and glittering medallions that denoted several orders and positions in government. His face was narrow, even for an Endri, and his nose long and straight. Ellisandra was unsure of his age, but his hair had gone past that stage where you couldn't be certain if it was still blond or had lost its colour. It was pure white, neatly combed and trimmed at the ends.

He smiled to his daughter. "Enjoy yourself?"

"Yes, I get to look after all the pretty stage dresses."

Ellisandra hadn't quite broken to her that the dresses from that period were not very glamorous. Coming out of the invasion war, the people back then had no access to pretty dyes from the coast, and the designs were usually drab and functional.

Asitho patted his daughter's shoulder. "I'm sure you'll do well. *Changing Fate* is an impressive play, and I'm sure you'll do it justice." His very pale blue eyes met Ellisandra's. "You know, the last time it was performed, I was a youngster and fancied myself an actor. I applied to be cast as Jihan Ilendar, but they let my cousin have it. I guess I'm still not over that. The selectors probably did Miran a favour." He laughed, a hollow sound. "I love the drama of that piece. It's a very under-appreciated work, and I don't understand why it hasn't been performed for so long. I was of the opinion that this would be an excellent time to mitigate that situation, don't you think?"

"Um, yes." Did he mean *he* had chosen it? Ellisandra cringed inside. And here she had been complaining about the play to his daughter. Really smart move, bigmouth that she was.

"As theatre director, I'm sure you will understand the deep nuances and the many layers of the play. The writer was pure genius. I wish the names of these writers were more widely known, even if they did work for the council. He fully deserves the credit for this masterpiece. I'm very much looking forward to seeing it performed once more, and I'll be proud that my daughter takes part in it. Thank you for accepting her into the committee."

Ellisandra met the penetrating gaze of those creepy, almost-white eyes. She had the feeling that he could see straight through her, that she disliked the play, that she had decided to use the ending to make a point. Many layers? How many layers of death and violence did he want?

The door opened behind them.

"Elli, can you—oh!" That was Enzo, Ellisandra's older brother. He nodded a respectful greeting. "High Councillor. I didn't know you were here. Do you wish to come in?" He was almost as tall as Asitho Bisumar, but gangly in a way young men often were.

"I was just here to pick up my daughter." Asitho smiled. "Thank you for the offer, but I wouldn't want her to miss out on tuition." Sariandra cringed visibly. Asitho continued to Enzo. "I got your message and I will be in touch about the discussions regarding the proposed plans at a later date."

"Thank you for listening to us."

"Well, someone has to listen. What you say interests me, but I need to look into it a bit more closely before I can make definite recommmendations."

"I'm looking forward to it." Enzo hesitated. "The law debate is the day after tomorrow, so that the full council can approve it as soon as the voting season starts."

Asitho Bisumar winked at him. "I know. Don't worry. I will look into it."

Enzo bowed. "Thank you, High Councillor."

Asitho put his hand on his daughter's shoulder and they walked through the yard. Enzo went inside immediately, but Ellisandra watched the pair of them disappear into the snowy night. Asitho a big, furry shape under his cloak, Sariandra much smaller, walking slightly in front of him. The main gate squeaked and fell into the lock.

What was that all about?

I'm sure you will understand the deep nuances and the many layers of the play.

What rubbish. She had studied the ancient plays and knew all about nuances and layers in the classic plays. This play was barbaric, that was all that could be said about it.

But did she really want to draw out the gore and violence and upset those men in power? They obviously saw something in the play that she did not. Maybe she should try to learn what it was before shooting down her reputation and drowning her career in a sea of fake blood.

3

SARIANDRA HAD first come to the theatre about a year
ago. Ellisandra remembered that well. She sat in the stands
with her mother, a timid and thin woman who looked
young enough to be her sister.

At first, Ellisandra had not known who she was, but Aleyo had
pointed out, not-so-subtly, that this was the High Councillor's
family, so Ellisandra had gone to introduce herself, and offer
Sariandra a job in the production, because that was why she was
here, right? That question had resulted in one of those awkward
silences that so often happened when Sariandra was concerned,
like she never knew what to say, and she'd rather say nothing at all
than talk to all these women who had worked in the theatre for
years.

When the position in the committee had come up, there was an
unspoken assumption that Sariandra would fill it, being who she
was. Normally Ellisandra didn't have a problem with that. Tolaki's
father owned the theatre building, so it would be perfectly reasonable for him to expect that Tolaki sat on the committee.

Tolaki was so much fun that they'd become best friends.

But this girl was different.

Thinking about this made her feel a little queasy. Up until now, the committee had been so much fun despite Aleyo. But that was when Gisandra was still part of it. Gisandra overshadowed any of Aleyo's complaining. Loud, with infectious laughter and never too serious. Unfortunately she was now far too pregnant to bother with the theatre. She wouldn't be back after her child was born, either.

And damn it, this play wasn't anyone's definition of *fun*. It was deeply serious, tragic, horrid and someone had chosen it for a reason.

That reason was certainly not to let Ellisandra's last year with the theatre be an easy one.

Same time next year she would be married to Jaeron, and he would want an heir as soon as possible. Apart from the theatre, the Telimar family managed the commercial block and shop rents. There was lots of property involved in their family wealth. Lots to inherit.

With the wedding set for the long spring, this time next year would have her looking like a balloon, staying inside most of the time, receiving only close friends, groaning every time she got up from her seat, and saying that it wasn't much fun. At least those were all the things Gisandra did. The price of being a highly-valued fertile Endri woman.

Ellisandra walked across the veranda, hugging herself against the cold. All her life, she'd assumed that she'd grow up, get married and be happy, but Mother had been dead so long that she remembered no good examples of how to be married happily. At least she thought Mother had been happy. Although apparently, Father had always had a penchant for chatting up or making inappropriate advances on pretty girls because she remembered her parents arguing about it in a hush-hush kind of way.

That was a scary thought. She had no idea how to be in a successful marriage. Certainly she wasn't supposed to obey Jaeron's every word, like Enzo expected? She could refuse Enzo, because he was her brother and an annoying prick, but her husband?

So many uncomfortable thoughts.

She'd better go back inside and check on Father. She glanced over the wall at the ruin next door. Of course the light was gone by now and the man would be safely inside one of the guesthouses. Snow had already covered up his tracks so that only the faintest depressions of footsteps remained. It was as if he had never been there.

Enzo came out of the living room the moment she shut the front door behind her.

"Elli, can you—"

"Has anyone brought Father his tea?"

His face went blank. He blew out a breath through his nostrils and turned around, shutting the door to the living room behind him with a more vigorous thud than necessary.

Yes, Enzo. I have responsibilities.

Why did he always assume that her life revolved around him?

Ellisandra climbed the stairs. The first room to her left was her father's. In the hallway, she took off the loose vest that she was wearing and hung it over the hook outside the door. The dress underneath had short sleeves and was too cold for the weather, but the bodice drew tight around her upper body, with no loose folds of fabric to grab. Then she rolled up her hair, drew a couple of pins from the secret pocket at her waist and pinned down the bun.

As soon as she opened the door, she braced herself for the too-warm air with the cloying smell of soap that usually hung in the room.

Her father sat by the hearth in his chair, his hands, old and gnarled, on top of the blanket in his lap.

He looked up when she came in. "Oh, there is my dear daughter again. The only one in the house who still comes to visit me. Unless they need something, of course."

"Didn't Darma come in to give you your medicine?"

He frowned, his old face creasing into deep canyons. "Which one is she again? A girl came in but I sent her out again. I said I wanted Lina."

"Father, don't be so hard on Darma. She's coming to help you."
Lina had left years ago. She'd been the last of the old servants to
go. She'd cried when handing in her resignation, but she said she
just couldn't take it anymore.

"I don't like this new girl."

Ellisandra sighed. He was not making life easy for the staff.
"Let me look at you."

She dragged a chair over to the fire, while fishing up the face
cloth from the table next to his chair. The waft of air that enveloped
her stank so much that she had to hold her breath. He'd dirtied
himself again.

She'd have to deal with that later.

First his face.

This dry weather made his eyes water so badly that the tears
ran down his face. It looked as if he'd been crying although he
would lash out if anyone asked him what was wrong.

She softly dabbed the cloth on the paper-thin skin. The area
under the eyes had already gone raw with the constant wetness. It
would only get worse during the coming season.

From amongst the jars of pills, ointments, bandages, and
syringes in the medicine cabinet against the back wall, Ellisandra
went to get a pot of salve. She sat on her knees and applied it to
her father's skin. His eyes, mellow and cloudy, followed her
hands.

It was part of her daily ritual, putting cream on that dry skin.
She'd cried a little when they'd had to cut his hair recently. She
could still see the white ponytail on the floor. She'd picked it up
and put it in the drawer against the back wall, and hadn't been
able to bring herself to throw it away.

While her hands massaged the old skin, she chatted about the
theatre. "We have a new member of the committee now. Sariandra
Bisumar."

"Hmph. That Bisumar girl has too big a mouth for her own
good. You know what she said to me?"

"I found her very quiet." He was confusing Sariandra with

Mikandra Bisumar, Sariandra's much older half-sister, who at one stage had told him off for leering at her.

Secretly, Ellisandra liked that story. Apparently, after Mother died, Father had tried to find a new wife. Mikandra carried the curse of Endri infertility and was unsuited as first wife, but could make, as they said, a *nice plaything for a man who already had a family*. Mikandra, however, had other thoughts about it, bless her heart.

If rumours were true, she was now married to Rehan Andrahar in Barresh, but seeing as it would be his first marriage, and the inheritance of the Andrahar family was a mess, Ellisandra wasn't sure that she believed that story.

The truth easily got lost in gossip. Miran drowned in gossip, especially about what was going on with its former citizens who now lived elsewhere.

When she finished putting salve on Father's face, she wheeled his chair out of the room into the bedroom they had modified as a bathroom. When Father could no longer easily walk down the stairs, Enzo had declared that the bottom floor of the house was not to be turned into a hospital. So Ellisandra had, at great expense, employed a builder to add piping and a washbasin, all specially made so that the wheelchair could get in and that one person could bathe her father alone. Because Father tended to make leery remarks if he'd had a bad day, that someone was usually her.

It was warm and stuffy in the room, with that same strong smell of soap that made her feel queasy, not because it smelled bad, but because of the hint of bad smells that it masked.

It was hard work, getting him to stand up from the chair, which he could do very well, but usually made a point of being difficult about. Then she had to pull off his pants and peel the dirty underclothes off him. She chatted about the committee meeting while doing this.

Sometimes useful things bubbled up from his muddled memory, but today, he wanted to know if Gisandra Tussamar was still in the theatre and Ellisandra told him—not for the first time—that she'd married and was expecting a child any time now.

And he said—and it wasn't the first time he'd said that either—that he always thought that she'd be the first of Ellisandra's friends to be married "because of her big tits."

Oh, it was going to be one of those days, was it?

When she leaned over him, he grabbed her wrist in a surprisingly strong grip. He pulled her in his envelope of bad breath and smell of soap, shit and stale urine.

His hoarse whisper chilled her. "Show me your tits."

"Did I tell you about the plan I have for the play?" Ellisandra pulled at her arm. For a man his age and with his poor health, he was surprisingly strong, but she managed to get her arm free. Her heart was thudding. He wasn't strong enough to be a threat to her, at least she didn't *think* so, but this behaviour frightened her. This leery, disgusting creature was not the father she knew growing up. And it seemed to be getting worse. No wonder they couldn't keep any of the servants they employed for him.

She chatted nervously about the theatre or some other thing, she didn't even know what.

When she had to bend over him again, she made sure that she was careful to stay away from that right hand that still retained surprising strength.

Oh no, he wasn't a cripple, not at all. He just enjoyed the attention.

He now grabbed the cleaning cloth, but she had become used to that, and had a supply of them ready, so she just picked up another one. The only thing was that she'd just cleaned his shit-covered backside with it and he was very sensitive to getting stomach infections. He would gnaw his fingernails sometimes.

"Give that to me, shall we?" She pulled the cloth out of his hands but then had to wash his hands with water from the basin on his other side, while avoiding being grabbed again. That was why she always wore dresses with a tight bodice, because once he'd torn all the buttons off a looser dress. She had screamed and then he'd stared at her in her underwear and started crying *what have I done?* That was so awful, she never wanted to go through that again.

Sometimes, he would go really clear-minded, as if someone had snapped their fingers and the haze lifted for a short while.

Washed and dressed in clean clothes, she wheeled him back to his room, where Enzo was waiting, seated on the couch, leaning forward with his elbows on his knees while clasping his hands together. As soon as she came in, he rose.

The goings on in the bathroom had left her hot and sweaty despite the cold weather. Enzo looked clean, aloof.

He nodded to his father and wrinkled his nose.

Ellisandra wanted to shout at him, *Yes, I know he smells of soap. You try to keep him clean.* But that would only make him angry. She did *not* want him to be angry because he threw things and then she would have make sure they were all cleaned up, too. And maybe the servants would say that Enzo was going the way Father had, and she did *not* want any of that kind of gossip.

So she said nothing.

She parked the wheelchair in front of the fire, passing Enzo who didn't move out of her way to let her get through. Oh, how she longed to tell him to *fuck off*. One day.

While she had been in the bathroom Darma had come in to bring dinner, so Ellisandra dragged a chair over to the fire, put the tray on the table next to her father's wheelchair, covered his chest with a napkin and proceeded to cut his bread into pieces which he could pick up and put in his mouth with his crooked and gnarled hand. One thing Father genuinely hadn't been able to do for a long time was control the fine movements of his hands, so eating was a messy business.

Enzo snorted and sat down again on another chair further from the hearth.

He began in a tense voice, "I'm doing this for you, all right?"

"Doing what?" This sounded like it was going to be one of his manipulative power schemes.

"Working hard, making sure that we're in good standing with the high council, making sure you have nothing to wish for at your wedding—"

"Why don't you just tell me what you want?"

She could really do without his *I've got it so hard, why don't you run for me when I tell you to?* rant.

He said nothing, which probably meant that whatever he wanted to say to her wasn't something he thought Father should know.

"Can you talk to me when you've finished here? I don't have much time."

"We have all night."

"The Citizen's Group is coming tonight. I need something. Why are you . . ." He spread his hands and rolled his eyes at the ceiling.

"I'll look into whatever it is you want. After I've finished here."

"Let Darma do it."

"Just be patient, all right?"

With a sigh, he sat back on the couch.

Father's hand trembled. He spilled some soup on his face. It dripped onto the cloth, and Ellisandra wiped the rest off his chin. She held the cup to his mouth, making an effort to keep her hand still. Why had Enzo let himself be roped into joining a Citizen's Group? All they did was spread gossip and fear. Spy on other people, the rumours went. After friends or family members joined Citizen's Groups, suddenly the council or guards knew about things that family members did that the council didn't like. They got warnings and were quietly told to stop doing whatever they were doing.

Who was Enzo trying to impress by being with this group? Was being in the council as the family representative not enough?

Slowly, Father ate his soup. Enzo fidgeted. Ellisandra wiped Father's chin whenever his hands shook too much to keep the soup on the spoon. The fire crackled in the hearth.

After a long silence, Father said, "Do you know that the last time *Changing Fate* was performed was the night before Nemedor Saterin was elected as High Councillor? He was the one who had the biggest decision in choosing the play. I don't think most of the councillors like it very much. In fact, I don't either. To be honest, it's an awful play."

His eyes were clear when they met hers. "I told him so, but he just laughed at me and ordered the play performed anyway. It was very meaningful, he said."

This was the father she knew and loved, the tiny shard of normality in the decrepit chaos of his mind that kept her going.

Was he trying to tell her something?

4

WHEN FATHER didn't want to eat anymore, Ellisandra wiped his face and his hands and took the tray outside. Enzo followed close on her heels, and when she closed the door, he asked, "Why don't you let Darma do this?"

"She snipes at him and doesn't do the job properly. You know last time when his skin got covered in rashes because she didn't wipe his face, and he came to the theatre like that and Ariandra Hirumar commented on it at the Ladies' Ball, and next thing I knew I was a bad daughter neglecting her father? Well, I don't want that again."

"Then we get someone else. You know I don't want you doing this, Elli. We have servants for this work."

"He scares them all away. We burn through servants like straw. Some of the ones we've lost were quite good in all their other work and I would have loved to have kept them. It's not them, it's him."

"Tell him clearly that he shouldn't say inappropriate things to them."

"You don't understand."

"I don't need to understand anything. It's plain bad behaviour.

If he grabs Darma through her shirt, then this is what he gets. It's his own fault."

"No person I pay to be in this house should have to deal with Father's bad behaviour. He doesn't *know* he's doing it."

"That's rubbish, Elli. They're excuses. He's done this all his life. Never known to keep his hands to himself. No one should have to put up with it."

"It's too late. If I don't feed him and wash him, he's going to go hungry and will sit all day in his own shit. Do you want that? Do you want your children to do that to you when you're old and you can't think properly anymore? He's your father, too."

His face tightened.

Ellisandra started down the corridor. "I'm going to grab something to eat myself."

"Wait." He held her back by the sleeve of her dress, his eyes intense.

Here it came, the reason why he'd been hovering around her.

"I need some figures, and I need them before the property commission of the council sits tomorrow afternoon."

She looked at him, meeting his eyes, his sharp face and thin mouth. His eyes were light blue, like those of most Endri.

"What sort of figures?" The back of her neck pricked with suspicion. He was asking this right before he was going into a Citizen's Group meeting? "Why are you asking me?"

"I only want to know how many credits the Tussamar Traders paid the Ilendar family for their nephew's house, or if they paid in some other currency."

"Only? That information is in the Accountkeepers' system." The currency system that kept track of all Mirani credits—tirans—and that was the domain of trusted users who had to swear under oath that they wouldn't share information with others.

"Yes." He gave her a penetrating look.

"Oh no, you're not asking me to do that. Yes, I know I've got access because of the theatre's finances, but . . . No, Enzo."

"Only one figure and it's many years old. Is the old Ilendar even still alive? Let me have a look. It's important."

"I don't even know how to get into that part of the system if I wanted to, which I don't, and if I did, they could track information I requested, and know that it has nothing to do with the theatre and—" She raised her hands. People had lost their jobs over things like that.

"Aw, come on, Elli, you're my sister."

"Yes, but I also run the theatre and I have to protect our integrity. I have sworn on Foundation Law that I would keep financial matters private. The theatre is a Trusted Employee, and we cannot do illegal things, not even for our family members." She knew that no one cared about Foundation anymore, but Takumar was a *Foundation* family, the only one of the five original families still left in Miran and she wanted that to have meaning. They were meant to uphold the law. "What do you need this for, anyway?"

"For council business." His expression had gone stiff.

"Then you should get this information through the council. They can legally request it." Was he sure he didn't mean Citizen's Group business? They had no legal status and could not ask for the information.

"The Accountkeepers told me that I can apply for the figures, but it's going to take too long. We're preparing major changes to ownership laws. I need this information."

"And what do the Tussamar Traders and their house have to do with ownership laws?"

"It's not about them directly. It's about the sale."

"Then what about it? Can't you get the information through the normal channels? Why not simply ask them?"

"No, I can't. Come on, Elli, it's important."

"Why is how much someone paid for a house important for a law you're debating in council?"

He backed away. "Hey, whoa. I asked for a single figure. I didn't ask for the inquisition. It's for the good of all of us."

' Let me get this straight. I am expected to do something I'm not supposed to do and you can't even explain to me why?"

"It's law stuff. You wouldn't understand."

"Try me."

"There isn't the time now. Some of my friends are already here. For crying out loud." He rolled his eyes at the ceiling. "I understand where you're coming from, Elli. Really, I do, but you should let go of those romantic notions of honesty if you want to grow up and play our games. Because people in power are not honest. I'm telling you this out of concern for you. I deal with these people every day in the council. The people in power all help their friends and family, too. They use every last bit of all the resources they have, legally or illegally. When you get handed a gift like access to the Accountkeepers' financial system, you don't just let it sit there and stare at it. You use it. Everyone knows that you'll be doing it. It's part of being in power."

She gave him her best *really?* stare.

"Your family will be the most important thing in your life, your only support when things go wrong. I don't even know if you've noticed, but things are likely to go wrong in the near future. Haven't you seen all the empty houses that belong to Endri families that they can't sell? Our whole economy and financial system is based on set proportions of Endri and Nikala in Miran. Those proportions have become seriously skewed. So many of us Endri have left. The Nikala won't keep living like this, when we no longer have jobs for them, and some of them are starting to go hungry. Which is why, for as long as we're still in power, you should always think of the future of our family. One figure, Elli. It's about the future of our family and Jaeron will benefit quite a lot, too, if this law goes through."

She said nothing.

"Don't you want to live in a nice house?"

"I have no doubt that Jaeron has already bought that house." She knew that for certain, through Tolaki, but it wasn't supposed to be public knowledge.

When she still didn't answer his question, he said, "Fine, but don't tell me that I didn't warn you."

He turned around thundered down the stairs and went into the living room. Ellisandra followed at a slower pace.

Brothers!

When she entered the downstairs hall, Darma was letting someone into the house. The man came into the foyer, took off his boots and cloak and chose a pair of house shoes from the rack. Then he came into the hall.

"Elli." The deep voice was familiar, and so was his angular face with strong chin. He wore his work clothes, a black tiyuk leather jerkin with gold clasps, done up all the way to his chin against the cold.

"Jaeron." She smiled, feeling a bit awkward. He looked so official, like he was still strutting around the commercial district talking to tenants and arranging maintenance works to his family's many commercial properties. She slipped her arms into her vest, but her skin was still sweaty and the fabric stuck to her, with the result that she couldn't pull the collar where it was supposed to sit. Her hair, too, looked like she'd been standing in a storm. She quickly pulled the pins out and let her hair tumble out of the bun. "I'm sorry, I'm not very presentable."

"You're always presentable to me." He gave a stiff little bow.

"I . . . didn't know you were coming. I would have . . . made sure that there was tea and biscuits." Biscuits were good. They would sit by the hearth in the living room in the chairs that faced the little table. He would eat the biscuits and compliment the cook and then they would talk about cooking and wasn't the season for fish good this year and my, the snow is early this year. Stuff like that. Those were the kinds of discussions that started with biscuits. Although she did still feel very sweet and sticky from the committee meeting, and a little bit queasy after dealing with Father.

"It's all right. I'll come another time to talk to you. I'm here for your brother."

"Oh?"

"I'm sorry to disappoint you. We're having a meeting, and Enzo suggested that it be at his house."

"He didn't tell me you were coming."

"It's not really something you should worry about, just boring council matters that we're discussing. Much less interesting than the theatre, I bet."

Was Jaeron part of the Citizen's Group as well?

It was one thing that her brother was in one of these spying, male gossiping groups that weren't exactly legal. Citizens Groups were said to be responsible for several cases of thuggery where some business owner was ruffled up, usually at night after closing up his shop, and demands were made. Most of the stories were vague, but Ellisandra knew that the groups did the dirty work that the council couldn't legally do themselves. Mainly, they dealt with silencing dissenting voices.

The idea that her future husband was in a Citizen's Group made her feel sick.

'I hear you're staging *Changing Fate*."

'Yes, we are."

'Now that piece is a challenge, if ever there was one. Much more productive than trying to change laws, politics and boring things like that. Now, I must go, or your brother will be cross with me."

Another stiff little bow and he went into the living room.

Ellisandra looked at the perfect veil of white hair dancing over his leather-clad back.

She didn't *think* they were deliberately hiding anything from her; it was just their usual *women-shouldn't-be-in-politics* attitude. Fine. She hated politics anyway, but why couldn't they at least answer her questions? She wasn't stupid.

There was a lot of politics in theatre, after all.

A small noise behind her made her turn around.

Father had somehow wheeled himself out of the room,

wormed himself from his wheelchair and stood on top of the stairs, holding onto the railing with trembling hands.

"Father!" She ran up the stairs and grabbed hold of his arm before he could topple face-first down the stairs. It wouldn't have been the first time that had happened either.

She took him firmly by the upper arms, feeling again how frail and thin he was. "What's wrong? Why didn't you call me?"

"I may be an old man, but I'm not entirely crippled." His eyes were clear of the fog that normally clouded his mind. She realised that he'd started an episode of clear thinking just before she left the room, when he reminded her how long ago *Changing Fate* was last performed. How much had he heard of what Enzo said to her?

"There is no shame in asking for help. It's much better than hurting yourself. What do you want me to get for you?"

"I need to go down."

"I can bring up to your room whatever it is you want." She glanced down the yawning gap of the stairs with a deep-seated *no way* feeling. She didn't know if she had the strength to get him down. He hadn't been downstairs since last spring.

"No. I have to go down and talk to these young men. I didn't give Enzo my council position to break down the laws we spent years building up."

5

FATHER WAS NOT to be dissuaded, so Ellisandra helped him down, careful step by very careful step. He was too busy not falling down to answer her questions and trembled with the effort, but as she already knew, his hands retained surprising strength and he seemed very determined. She was hoping that halfway down, he'd change his mind or he'd forget what he wanted. The discussions between him and Enzo about politics never ended well. But when they were finally in the hall, he was as determined as ever to go and *give the young men a history lesson.*

Their voices, heard through the door, fell abruptly quiet when she knocked.

She opened the door into the warmth and firelit glow of the room.

"Elli?" Enzo sounded annoyed.

His friends gave Ellisandra and Father suspicious looks, including Jaeron, who frowned at her in a *I'd-have-thought-better-of-you* way.

"Father insisted on joining you." And Father was still the official head of the family and couldn't be refused.

Enzo jumped up from the chair by the hearth that had always been Father's. Ellisandra shuffled with him through the room.

Apart from Enzo and Jaeron, there was Diantho Hirumar, who was a cousin of Aleyo's, and one of the Tussamar twins, she didn't know which one, Raedon, she thought.

The pungent smell of menisha brew hung in the room, and a carafe of the orange liquid stood on the table. It was half-empty, too. Jaeron balanced a glass on the armrest of his chair. Raedon held a cup of the liquid, which he swirled in a "challenge me if you dare" way. So that was why they didn't want tea.

Ellisandra disliked it when men drank. They'd get loud and shout a lot, and sometimes they'd fight. Traditionally, brew was only served in the bathhouse for social occasions when people would sit around in the steaming water and talk, but more and more young men used it to prop up their gatherings.

At meeting her eyes, Jaeron's mouth corner moved up in a most unconvincing smile. The other two young men looked, of all things, at Father's stubbled head with expressions of disapproval. Yes, she'd ordered it shaved to save herself and the staff from the agony of having to wash and comb it. Father sat in his chair all day, and he used to get this massive knot at the back of his head and would fight anyone trying to comb it out.

Endri men could be so funny about their hair. Women were allowed to put their hair in a bun, but the men had to wear it loose. Cutting a boy's hair was a punishment. Cutting a man's hair was like unmanning him.

Ellisandra made sure Father was comfortable and that he had a cloth to wipe the right eye that kept weeping. He wanted tea and *none of that rubbish that you youngsters drink* while eying the carafe on the table, so she said she'd ask Riana to bring him some. Then she bowed and left. No one spoke until she had closed the door behind her.

She hesitated with her hand on the door handle, wondering if she should listen. Father was speaking, but his voice was too soft to understand the words.

Then Enzo's voice came loud and clear through the wood of the door. "That is a very old-fashioned view that doesn't apply to today's situation."

Father replied, his voice more firm this time, but she still couldn't hear it well enough to understand all of it. Something about old laws, about Foundation and honour.

"I don't agree. Literal interpretation of Foundation Law is something of the past." This was one of the other men, she didn't know who.

Father said, "That proposed law means that you are dismantling all the safeguards that were instated in the past. We've been through this before. Families defaulting on their responsibilities or doing outright criminal things. Bribery and other financial shenanigans. No, I know that you're too naïve to believe that this can happen, but it has happened, and it will happen again. When it does, you want to be able to remove councillors, even High Councillors. Foundation was instated exactly because there was too much concentration of power and money in too few hands. Endri and Nikala are not masters and slaves to each other. According to Foundation—"

"Father, Foundation is dead! It's been dead for years. No one takes any notice of those old laws anymore. All the Foundation families except us have left town. That's why we're changing it."

"It is not about the families. It's about the structure."

"The structure arcane. It relies on honour. And you know what honour means? It means gossip. As long as people don't gossip about you, you can get away with it. There is no enforcement. It won't work. It isn't working."

"Because young men don't have honour anymore."

"And whose fault is that?"

"You have no respect for the older generation, young man. If you did, you wouldn't argue for these crazy deals. No, the Nikala and lower Endri class won't understand it. They only see Foundation Law's impediments to their power. But this is not about power."

"It's about making Miran work."

"Son, you're so far under their influence, you don't even see how this can never work. Nemedor Satarin and Asitho Bisumar are not men who have Miran's best interests at heart. They want to keep their fist on Miran's credit system as a means of keeping citizens dumb and isolated. As a means to make themselves rich."

"They're stopping us from being invaded by foreigners."

"The foreigners are not the problem! As if there are any foreigners who'd even *want* to come to Miran. We have a problem right here in our own council. These men are trying to break down laws that have worked for generations. They are doing this with shady means, using standover tactics with Citizen's Groups, to intimidate people into agreeing, to profit for themselves."

"We do not. We're reforming an arcane system that doesn't work and hasn't worked for years."

"So changing credit laws to enable all Endri families who have left Miran to get big payouts for unused credits they've accumulated isn't selfish? Who's going to pay for it? Do you even understand the system before you try to break it with your shady activities?"

"There is nothing shady about what we do."

"Trying to con your sister into giving information she isn't free to give isn't shady? Heavens! Where did I raise a son like that—"

"I didn't do that."

"Yes, you did. I was there, and I heard you, although you love to discount me as just an old man and a fool. I'll tell you something, because I've seen this all before. The council members are all in each other's pockets, and this law is only going to make that worse. There is no good in a system that does not allow a measure for appeal and that places no controls on the top level of government. No matter what Asitho Bisumar and Nemedor Satarin say, it is a bad idea and if you don't see that, I have failed as a father."

"Father, for once just listen to us. We need urgent action. Yes, we've been planning to change the laws for some time, but just recently, something else has happened: someone has started taking credits out of the Ilendar account."

"Well, hmph, they're entitled to use it."

"The Ilendar Traders' account, Father. They don't live in Miran anymore. They can't spend money unless they're spending it in Miran. We haven't yet found out where that money is going, but there's been quite a lot of it spent."

"What of it?"

"Do you know how much money sits in those accounts?"

"Money will be freed and put back into circulation. How is that a bad thing? Worry about the important things."

Ellisandra turned away from the door. Although she'd heard most of these arguments before, there seemed to be a new bite and urgency to them. This was bigger than the older generation against the younger one, often framed in terms of tradition against modern ideas. This was about Foundation. Why was Enzo so worried about the Ilendar account? They might not live in Miran anymore, but it was their money and they should be able to use it. Why was it a problem that someone had been spending this money?

In the dining room, she found her younger brother Jintho at the table, looking at papers spread out over the table in front of him. He was scribbling on some documents and another untidy stack lay next to him.

Riana had made an effort to set the table, but had to leave the plates to the side where his papers weren't.

He looked up and smiled at Ellisandra when she came in.

"Just as well Enzo is busy." If nothing else, Enzo would throw a fit if the table wasn't set properly.

Ellisandra sat down, and Riana came in and put a plate of soup in front of her. She put Jintho's in the middle of the table, and she unloaded a bowl of steaming, freshly-baked fish bread from her tray as well as tea.

Jintho picked up a pale bread roll from the bowl, and promptly dropped it.

"Ow, that's hot!"

The roll tumbled over his paper.

"You're so impatient, Master Jintho," Riana said. "Wait until I bring the tongs."

Ellisandra said, "Can you bring some tea to Father? He's in the living room."

Riana turned sharply to her, eyes wide. "With master Enzo and his friends?"

"Yes, he is. Give the tea to me and I'll bring it if there is a problem."

"Master Enzo told me not to disturb them."

"I told Father that someone would bring his tea. They won't mind if you come in to do that. If they do, come to me and I'll make sure Father gets his tea."

She swallowed. "Certainly, mistress."

"Riana, Enzo does not rule this house."

"He as good as does."

"That still doesn't give him the right to scare you."

"Master Enzo gets very angry."

"If he does, send him to me."

She swallowed again, nodded and left the dining room. She would have to talk to Enzo about this—again. Seriously, did so many servants leave because Father leered at them or because Enzo scared them?

Ellisandra studied the papers on the table. The closest sheet was a form of some sort. Official name, date of birth. Jintho had even listed his birth name *Iztho*. It used to be such a popular and common name in Miran, but after the betrayal of Miran by Iztho Andrahar, a lot of parents had renamed their young sons. The only young men still named Iztho were those Mirani who had left Miran at that time. Her father had just never made the name change official.

Looking back on that time, the signs of his failing health had been clear for a long time. Just no one had ever noticed that his forgetfulness could have a cause that would get worse with age.

"What is all this paperwork anyway, brother?"

Jintho started stacking the papers. Some of them were folded at the corners or had stains across them. "I'm applying for a commercial licence."

What? "What happened to becoming an artist?"

He looked up sharply. "You ask me that, you, who have told me time and time again 'to get a real job'? You can't have it two ways, sister. Look at me, I'm applying for something that isn't an art project. Why aren't you happy?"

"It's a bit . . . sudden. I thought that the bathhouse had contracted you to do a mural."

"I can do the mural *and* apply for a commercial licence."

"All right." Except it wasn't all that long ago that he'd argued anything that paid him a regular salary would be *selling his soul* and interfere with his creativity. It had been a big argument, too. Enzo had gotten involved and the two had almost come to blows.

She wasn't going to go there today. "What's . . . changed?"

"Nothing. Just me and some friends are thinking about setting up a shop."

"Thinking." She tried not to sound sarcastic.

"Yes."

"Not actually doing?"

"Well, we'd have to find somewhere to rent first."

"What would you be selling?"

"Clothes."

She couldn't help it, but started laughing. "Clothes? I mean— look at you."

"What about me?" He spread his hands. He was wearing an old shirt that he'd had for many years. Frequent washing had faded the red dye into a kind of grey-red. At least Darma had recently patched the holes in the elbows.

"You don't look like someone who sells clothes."

"I wouldn't be selling them. I'd be designing them."

"And who'd buy these expensive clothes? Merchant Ranuddin

couldn't keep his shop afloat, so why should a couple of young men with no experience have any more success?"

"Come on, Elli. We could use another decent place to buy clothes. The closing of merchant Ranuddin's shop has not left us with many choices."

"But *merchants* open shops." Since when did he ever buy clothes anyway?

"Does the fact that I'm Endri mean that I can't be a merchant?"

"No, but what do you know about running a shop? About pleasing customers and getting stock and pricing? Merchant children grow up with this stuff. You didn't."

He spread his hands in a melodramatic *Jintho* way. "You're right. I grew up with absolutely *nothing*. One older brother to occupy the council seat. One older sister to devote her life to the arts. No business to manage, no occupation to fill. My existence is pointless."

She sighed and looked at the papers. Another one of his schemes indeed. Started on a whim, poorly researched, poorly thought-out and abandoned a few days later. *After* he'd paid the application fees of course.

She could be made to agree with him on the pointlessness of his current life, but whose fault was that anyway? There were many opportunities to find useful employment, if only he could stick out completing any training or mentorship.

Why did she have such a stupid family? Father made an idiot of himself by making inappropriate advances on the female staff, Enzo was a women-don't-know-anything-and-can't-do-anything arsehole and Jintho took the concept of *whinging, entitled, lazy loafer* to new heights.

"How was the committee meeting?" At least he always seemed genuinely interested in her work, one of the very few people in the family to display this curious phenomenon. He also came to the theatre performances whenever he could.

"I don't know," Ellisandra said while sipping from her tea. "I asked Sariandra Bisumar to join us, but I'm not sure if that was such a good idea."

"Why not?"

"If nothing else, I'm afraid she's going to side with Aleyo and be all traditional."

"Being a Bisumar, does that surprise you?"

"Guess not." Ellisandra shrugged. "She's young. I don't mind a little bit traditional, but there is no need for her to enforce her father's opinions."

Jintho met her eyes. "Why do you think she's on the committee?"

Ellisandra shrugged. "Most Endri young women spend some time in the theatre. There's nothing unusual about her wanting to join. Being the daughter of the High Councillor, I could hardly put her in the orchestra, right? Nothing wrong with that."

"No, there isn't. But how well do you know Asitho Bisumar?"

"Well enough to know that her life can't be that easy." Which was polite speak for *Asitho Bisumar is a complete prick*. After his first wife and two daughters had run out on him, he remarried so quickly that all kinds of rumours circulated about him. "I guess I felt sorry for her." Sitting there in the stand next to her mother, Sariandra had looked forlorn and shy.

Ellisandra knew the price for ignoring the daughters of high-profile councillors, so it seemed like a good idea to ask her into the committee, to make her loosen up a little.

Jintho shook his head. "Asitho is an obsessive control freak. His wife and daughter can't do anything without his approval—"

"I know. She had a kind of device on her, a Coldi-made thing, that communicates directly with the Exchange and lets him know where she is—"

He gave her a sharp glance. "Be careful of that thing."

"Why? It was only a reader of some kind."

"It records things."

What? "You mean spying?"

He nodded.

"Why would she do that? We're in the *theatre*. We don't discuss anything important, just plays and stage props and dresses—"

"You don't discuss the politics of the plays? All of the classics are highly political."

"We don't—" Hang on, she had just loudly voiced her low opinion of a play chosen by the council, and argued with Aleyo and Sariandra about changing the ending.

Not only that, but Asitho had wanted to see Enzo, and Enzo had pressured her into giving him details she wasn't free to give, and those details he needed for new legislation . . . for which Asitho wanted to see Enzo.

She stared at her brother, a deep chill coming over her. "But . . . why?"

"Because Asitho Bisumar doesn't trust anyone."

Riana came back into the room with the tongs for the bread and a platter of beans which she set on the table in the tense silence.

"Thank you, Riana," Ellisandra said, her mouth dry. "Has Father finished chewing a piece off Enzo yet?"

"I helped master Enzo take him upstairs. That's why I took so long bringing the tongs, I'm sorry."

Well, that was something at least. Probably Enzo had taken the first available opportunity to get the old man out of the room. Likely, too, Father's clear-minded moment had faded as fast as it had come.

"Sorry you had to do that, Riana. You could have called me. I would have done it."

"You deserve a break from that leery old man. You're a pleasure to work for, Mistress."

Jintho snorted.

"You're a pleasure to work for, too, Master Jintho." She moved to place a plate in front of him. "But really, it's not a good idea to put all these papers on the table where they will get dirty with the food. Master Enzo wouldn't like them being on the table. If he comes—"

"I don't think he'll come." Ellisandra thought of the carafe of brew in the other room.

"But he hasn't eaten, mistress. I worry about him. He's much too thin."

"He's a big boy. He can look after himself," Jintho said.

Riana walked out of the dining room again, leaving Jintho and Ellisandra in a cocoon of silence. Suddenly, she wasn't all that hungry anymore either.

6

A T THE END of the hallway, next to the formal living room, was a large room where few people came these days. It was a large echoing space with an elaborate mosaic floor. The room itself had been added onto the house when Father was a boy. It was a round stubby tower a bit over two floors high. It had a domed ceiling adorned with murals where a spear of light traversed the dusty air. Two days a year, it would fall exactly on the metal plaque in the middle of the room.

Ellisandra and Jintho used to sneak in there as children and run around the middle of the hall-like room, stamping their feet as hard as they could and listening to the echoes.

A gallery level ran along the sides halfway up the walls. All the walls on both levels were lined with shelves which contained thousands and thousands of old books. They were wooden shelves, too, custom-made to fit the curved walls, from wood imported from the coast.

In his working life, Ellisandra's father, Geonan Takumar, had been the head librarian of the Miran library. The function of that library was not only to hold a collection of works of public importance, but also to document and hold records of council proceedings and laws. She had been a little girl when the council, under the newly-elected High Councillor Nemedor Satarin, had decided that recording meetings in large books was arcane and had move the entire system to the Exchange. The books were to be destroyed.

Her father had been so upset about it that he had taken a lot of the books home. She remembered them being delivered to the house, and remembered being told off by the maid for playing on the boxes which were temporarily stored in the laundry while this room, which had been built as a ball room, was turned into a library. She remembered the smell of those books when the boxes were finally opened and their precious content placed on the shelves.

She could still see Father looking at her with his wizened face. His long silver hair had been beautiful in the way it fell over his shoulders lit by a shaft of sunlight that pierced the room from the windows in the little tower in the very top of the domed roof. He sat at his desk and she stood next to him on her tippie-toes, wanting to know if there were any pictures in all those books.

There weren't. They were all boring books. Father berated her for saying so.

"You have to understand this well, daughter of mine: Takumar is a Foundation family. You will have learned at school that the five families came together on the hill where the Foundation monument now stands and negotiated and signed an agreement that would shape Miran and would give both the Endri and Nikala rights and responsibilities. That was the first meeting of our council. The decisions of all those meetings were recorded in these books. They're written down in ink on paper. No one can erase ink on paper, unlike this silly system the council wants us to use. These records are here for eternity. I will keep recording them for as long as I can, and I hope Enzo will continue to do this after me."

"But why?" she had asked, as children were wont to do.

"Because we're a Foundation family. In that first meeting, the heads of the Takumar, Ilendar, Andrahar, Calthunar and Velisar families agreed to be protectors of a fair Miran. These books are our records. This is where the fairness can be tested. Now

Nemedor Satarin, who isn't even Endri, wants us to record our meetings on a foreign system that is dependent on foreign technology. The worst thing about it is that details can be changed afterwards. They tell me that there is a timestamp that can never be altered, but I don't trust it." He pointed at the book in front of him. "This is indelible ink on paper. Their way is nothing more than squiggles on a screen. You turn off the screen and the text is gone. More importantly, even, who else can read it? It's a *foreign* system. Nemedor Satarin says he's convinced it's secure. I don't believe that."

In hindsight, Ellisandra was surprised at how much of this she had remembered and understood. She had been quite young. It had made a big impression on her: Father standing up for something he thought was wrong. Father had many faults, but this wasn't one of them.

Today, the room was cold and dark. Darma would light the fire in here only occasionally to dispel the humidity and the worst of the cold, but she had done that a number of days back, and now it was cold enough that Ellisandra's breath steamed in the air.

She crossed to her father's old desk that sat in the middle of the room and turned on the lights with the switch in the corner of the desk. Pinpricks of greenish light flicked into being around the walls. Those lights were the only concession to modern technology in this house. Father would not have oil lights near his precious books. To be honest, Ellisandra far preferred the warm glow of oil lights, even if they could not be turned on with the touch of a button.

Now then, where would he have put the books she wanted?

She slowly turned around, looking along all the shelves behind and to the sides of the desk and all those books on the gallery level above her. The place was much neater than she remembered it being when Father still came here a lot. In those days, there would always be stacks of books everywhere, and also some dust because Father forbade the staff to dust and clean in the room when he was working on something, which was most of the time.

She found what she was looking for in the most obvious place: right behind the old-fashioned desk stood three fat leather-bound books with *Foundation Law* embossed in gold letters across the back. Underneath in small letters, it said *abridged version*. The full version required almost a room of books.

She slid the books off the shelf, piled them on top of each other and carried them to the warmth and comfort of her room where Darma had lit the fire and where traditional oil lamps spread soft light. That cold light cast by those light pearls was just awful. Someone had told her that it was the only type of light used in Barresh, and she couldn't imagine it.

She kicked off her house shoes and curled up in the big chair by the fire. The text of the play beckoned to her from the table and seeing it brought a stab of guilt. Really she should read through the play and make a list of what stage props they needed and in what act, and start thinking about the larger pieces, and the orders for materials that would need to go out as soon as possible, and look in the store inventory to see what they already had that they could re-use, and . . . But she could do that tomorrow. This to-do about Foundation Law made her suspicious. So, Enzo didn't want to tell her, huh? He and his friends thought that women were too stupid to understand law and politics, huh?

Well, *he* had obviously never directed a play and didn't have a clue how much politics there was in Mirani theatre, even in dividing up the roles. And he obviously underestimated her.

She opened the first book. The first couple of pages contained a long index of subjects covered in the three books. The section dealing with *Ownership and Property* would be in the second book. So she took that and opened it at the indicated page. She scanned the page until she found a section that dealt with housing and land.

Foundation families: According to the original Foundation document (section 1.1.A) ownership of land or fixed assets, including but not limited to, dwellings, commercial or service premises, shall be determined by the families designated in Foundation, or their agents. Ownership by

these families carries the responsibility of maintenance and the employ-
ment of staff for this aim. Ownership carries the right to derive an income
from the property, but this income cannot be derived from the sale of the
property itself—Cross-reference with Section 1.1.A: Foundation families
shall be responsible for the maintenance of general services from which
they can draw wages but nothing above reasonable living expenses—

She put the book down, frowning. Did she understand it correctly that anything owned by a Foundation family could not be sold at all?

That was odd.

If so, why had the Velisar family sold their business? Why had the Ilendar family sold their house to the Tussamar Traders? Why—

Wait. The Andrahar family had *not* sold their house and business for all those years since they had left Miran. Everyone had wondered why, and maybe this was it. Maybe now they knew that the council was about to change that law and had sent someone to . . .

To what?

Clearly no one had cared about the enforcement of this law for some time. Ever since she remembered, the Foundation families had always sold properties, if usually not their main residence. But that was because they were living in it, right?

She couldn't imagine that influential people like the Andrahars would let themselves be restricted by this law if no one enforced it.

The next paragraph went on about the details of what constituted profit from a sale. In the margin, Father had written, *Personal residence: claim as a business.* So that was a loophole by which they sold property anyway? Because somewhere it said—she leafed through the book to find it—that Foundation families were free to conduct businesses in the same way as other families.

She wondered if this applied to all Endri or just Foundation families. Also the book said nothing about the sale to or from people outside Miran. Rules about that would have been added much later.

She would find references to those decisions in Father's notes, because they would have been taken after the start of the *gamra* boycott. And this was why there were so many empty Endri houses. Those families had been unable to find a loophole to sell their house. The market for houses had collapsed as well. The only people who could afford those houses were other Endri, or some of the upper merchants, and there weren't enough of them.

People often complained about the many orphaned accounts from families that had left Miran. Mirani tirans were tied to land ownership and could not be exchanged for foreign currency or spent outside Miran. When a family left, their money was taken out of circulation, and, according to some, the sheer value of unused credits in these accounts was starting to become a problem. But because the tiran was linked to land ownership, it was next to impossible for the council to increase the number in circulation, because it would play havoc with the livelihood of too many people, unless the council declared accounts held by people outside Miran void, and compensated those families in a different way. But that made it certain that those families would never return to Miran, and would cost the council a whole lot of foreign money it didn't have.

So why did these men think she was too stupid to understand that?

When Ellisandra left the house the next morning, the snow had blown into big fluffy banks in the yard. The groundsman Karit had already shovelled a path from the front door to the gate as was his first task in the morning, but judging by the low scudding clouds with that typical leaden greyness that heralded snow, he would have to do it again later today.

A pathmaker was just coming up the street, a low flat sled drawn by two shaggy-haired tiyuk. The animals held their heads close to the ground and strained in the harness while pulling the heavy load uphill. Steam blew out of their nostrils. Both the animals were mature males, with the horn plates on their necks and the typical dark mottled pelt.

The driver was one of the herder nomads who came to the city during winter when pastures were covered in snow and the townsfolk had lots of hauling or snow-removing jobs. The woman sat huddled in her cloak, showing only the top half of her wind-blown wizened face surrounded by thick fur. She wore no gloves.

Ellisandra waited on the side to let them pass with much snorting and cracks of the whip.

Except the sled wasn't a pathmaker, which in hindsight she could have told by the fact that it seemed too heavy for the job. On the flat tray at the back lay a multitude of building materials: metal beams, bags of cement, resin sheeting, big packs of insulation wool, and stone blocks, a lot of them, quality building stone, too. Two young men sat on this pile.

The sled went past and stopped at the gate of the Andrahar house. Someone opened the gate from within with a clinking of the metal chain against the bars, and the sled turned into the yard with much cracking of the whip.

Well, that was odd.

Ellisandra followed it uphill, stepping in its tracks.

The sled had stopped in front of the ruin of the house, and the driver was speaking to someone wearing a thick hooded cloak who might be the same man she had seen yesterday, except he had his back turned to her and the hood covered his hair.

The two young men were now unloading the contents of the tray into an area against the wall—and out of view of her bedroom window—which had been made free of snow and covered with a sloping canvas roof. In the shadow of this roof stood additional piles of bricks and cement. At the far end of the shelter stood a table and a couple of chairs near an outdoor stove with flames lapping over fresh firebricks. Two other men sat there, huddled within their cloaks, and a third was stirring a big pot steaming on the stove.

Only a few walls were still standing of the old house, made of fire-blackened limestone bricks, the same material used in most of the Endri houses. It was quarried from the coast and cost a bundle to be brought all the way up to the city. She'd heard that there had been much resin board and even real wood in the house, which had contributed to the severity of the fire. She had been a baby back then so remembered none of the scandal which had started with the betrayal of Iztho Andrahar and the Two Day War in the enclave of Barresh.

Over the years, vagrants had broken into the place and removed every single thing that could be of any use or sold, including loose stones, roof tiles and bathroom fittings. After the original fire, there had been two more fires, but for the second one the only available fuel had been a squatter's shack and its contents. You would not think a shack would burn that well, but there were rumours that the old man who had lived illegally in the ruins had set his own shack alight because he grew too nervous of guards finding his illegal liquor. That liquor certainly burned well.

But now something had changed that she couldn't have seen from her room's window.

On the side of the ruin that faced away from her house, there were little yellow *posts* in the snow, with string tied between them.

A group of men came up from behind her. With greetings of *Good morning, lady,* they walked past Ellisandra and into the yard. They looked like workers, all of them dressed in coats and thick trousers.

If she hadn't known any better, it looked like these people were going to rebuild the house, with the tent and the table—for the plans—and the stove and the materials.

But why would they do that? The house had not been sold, or everyone in town would have known.

Then a cold chill: was this possibly the reason why Enzo had wanted to get access to the council's financial system? To check if the house had been sold recently?

And also: how in all of heaven's name had this stranger been able to get the men to turn up while there was snow on the ground? Builders never worked on snow days.

It didn't look like anything was happening here in a hurry, and she really needed to get going on finding people to build stage props, so she started downhill, a little reluctantly. Curiosity was one of her worst vices, and she'd much rather go back upstairs to peek at the goings on from a safe distance.

By the time Ellisandra had reached Miran's central square, it had started snowing again. The first thing she always noticed when she came here was the round, flat-roofed library tower at the top of the council steps. It was an old thing, not particularly straight, and originally built as a jail. When Father worked as Miran's chief librarian, he used to have an office on the top floor, at the end of a dark and curvy set of stairs. From the tiny window up there you could see all over the square and the commercial district. Father used to have to lift her to the windowsill. She could still feel the pitted stone under her hands.

She walked past the Foundation monument, a pentagonal platform with a post on each corner, looking sad and forlorn today. During nice days, school classes came out here to be told of Miran's history, or there would be weddings in spring when the monument was decked out in mountain flowers and the couple were asked to join hands over the central point of the monument where that first council meeting was said to have happened.

These days few people had their weddings at the monument, but hers next spring would be one. Most people considered a wedding at the monument a quaint thing to do. Not even Nemedor Satarin's daughter had married at the monument last year. At the time, Ellisandra had just started thinking about her own wedding and had asked him why not, because the important weddings were always held at the monument.

He'd smiled at her. "As a member of a Foundation family, yes, I understand that you'd like to adhere to the old custom, but frankly, Foundation has never meant much to me or my family."

She'd thought long about whether that remark was a barb. Nemedor Satarin, of course, was Nikala, a property merchant. He had long survived in the council by acting as if he were Endri, as upper merchants were wont to do, but of course he wasn't, and Foundation wasn't as important for Nikala as for Endri.

Secondly, recent discoveries in science had made the history of Miran an uncomfortable and confusing subject.

For a fair while now, some people outside Miran, most of them in Barresh, had declared that the Mirani Endri people had come from Asto when that world had been struck by a giant space rock. They declared that the Endri were almost pure descendants of people they called Aghyrian, the human species that had given rise to all other humans and that had been thought lost.

People in Miran had scoffed at that theory for a long time, but then a group of those Aghyrians had come to town and taken blood samples. Ellisandra remembered that. They were mostly black-haired, paled-skinned but dark-eyed people. They were tall like the Endri, but she didn't think they had much else in common.

They'd published the results in one of the *gamra* bulletins, and most people, some Endri even, accepted that they were right.

The new version of history was that Miran started not with two tribes coming together on the mountain pass, but with a ship full of government officials selfishly fleeing Asto when destruction was imminent, leaving behind all their citizens. Those historians had even gone way up the highlands and discovered the cave and metal fragments which might have been the remnants of the ship. There were many people, some historians, too, who didn't believe this, but all agreed that the metal was non-Mirani.

People didn't like it. The new information upset many ideals: of the purity of Mirani blood, of Asto as the ultimate enemy, of the unique construction of Foundation, the agreement between the Endri and Nikala people that described each of their tasks and responsibilities.

Historians hung onto their version of history for as long as possible, looking more like quaint old men with every passing day. The healers in hospitals and others who had taken part in collecting the data argued for the research. The historians argued against, based on flimsy arguments peppered with the word *tradition*. The argument went on forever. It was silly and stupid. People turned off and ignored it. Schools cut back on their teaching of Foundation, because teachers disliked having the arguments repeated in their classrooms. In the process, the truth got lost. And people lost interest in Foundation, because every time someone mentioned the word, a fight broke out.

The blocky shape of the market building stood on the high side of the square. In the gloomy overcast light, the warm glow of firelight spilled out of its many entrances. Inside, merchants were setting up their stalls, talking to colleagues, clutching steaming drinks.

The smell of cooking wafted onto the square.

The markets were still quiet enough that all the merchants greeted Ellisandra as she walked between the stalls. Most of the ones on this side sold food: wonderful warm fish bread, different types of flours, beans of all sizes, dried fruit and other preserves, fresh, dried and salted fish, fish meal and other fish products.

Most of these stalls surrounded an open area with tables and stools, where the hubbub of talk mixed with the clangs of cooking pots and the hiss of frying pans, where steam billowed from soup stands and where just about all merchants in the hall seemed to be sitting and talking and having breakfast before the start of the trading day. A huge fire burned in an open metal dish, and people stood as close as they found comfortable to warm themselves.

Ellisandra's appearance caused a string of nodded greetings of *Good morning, lady*. The only women here were merchants' wives and daughters. They were all Nikala. In fact, Ellisandra bet that she was the only Endri woman to come here on a regular basis.

The men she had come here to see usually sat on the other side of the fire, or stood around a clustered collection of notice boards, checking out the latest job offerings. Lately someone had even set up a screen, although the handwritten notices were always the most popular.

Ellisandra took such a notice out of her pocket. She had written it last night, sitting in her comfortable chair by the fireside. Normally, jobs were in such short supply that the men would besiege her and walk with her to the board so that they could be the first to bid for the jobs she had on offer. Today, she made it to the notice boards without a single follower.

That was strange. She clipped the notice *builders wanted* onto an empty peg and turned around. Still no one.

That was really strange. Where were all the regular construction workers? Not near the fire. Not near the stands. Not even at merchant Almarin's fat-fried fish stand.

Ellisandra felt stupid. She'd never come here and found herself so utterly . . . ignored. She strolled around the cluster of noticeboards, glancing casually at the jobs posted. Most were for domestic positions or workshop hands. Seriously, was Asitho Bisumar hiring even more grounds staff? His yard was not that big. What had happened to the previous ones?

While she was at it, why were all these men watching her?

Those men over there at the fish stand, and the ones near the fire, and the one on the opposite side of the fire.

Why had no one come to her to ask what sort of people she was looking to employ? The men knew her. They knew what she was doing here.

Heart thudding, Ellisandra walked down the line of noticeboards and stopped close to a group of men who were discussing one of the posted jobs, pointing at the notices and arguing about pay rates.

"I wouldn' work fer that," one of the men was saying. "What's he think he is, wanting a fellow t' bust his gut fer nothing but beans."

"Yeah, he can keep his beans. I hear they make a person fart."

Their mates all laughed.

"It's serious, man," the first worker said again. "I'd be getting less than my pa did ten years ago working fer th' Andrahar family. Everything costs more. Can youz see th' problem?"

Nods all around. "Those were th' days."

"We're getting less and less fer doin' th' same work. This whole thing scares th' pants off me."

"Me, too. What's goin' t' happen when all th' old families who paid decent money are gone 'n we get left with a whole bunch o' pinchpennies who's out t' screw us?"

"Yeah, like that old merchant Tamarin who was wanting t' get th' whole lot of us t' work fer th' price of one. They jus' keep screwing us 'n screwing us, until we have t' give in 'cause we need t' eat, 'n any money's better than none."

"Yeah, th' council is all about bein' equal 'n that, but things don' look too equal from where I'm standing. I din' mind th' Endri. Most of them, at any rate. I did th' job, they always paid, 'n they fixed anything wrong with my house, 'cause it belonged to them. With these people, they want us t' pay rent, *and* they pay less than half what I got before, and they don' even fix th' leaking roof."

Sounds of agreement all around.

"Th' council's forgettin' one thing. Endri 'n Nikala were never equal. Nothing in Foundation says they ever were. Foundation gave us things t' do. It gave them things t' do. Put it all together, and that's Miran. Endri and Nikala aren't equal. And not bein' crude 'n all that, but though I can fuck an Endri girl all I like, she will never have my child."

A burst of laughter went up from his mates.

Ellisandra's ears burned. She ducked as deep into the collar of her cloak as she could.

"Better be careful now, eh?" one of the mates said.

"What?" The maker of the crude comment turned around and his eyes widened as they met Ellisandra's.

"Oh." His face went red. "I'm sorry, lady. I din' mean—I mean

. . . I'm sorry. I wasn't talking about youz, or anything . . . Um. Can't I help you with anything?"

Ellisandra had to do her best not to laugh. "Yes, you can help me, actually. Is Loret not here today?"

'Oh no, lady. They's all got a job t' do. Wen' out early this mo:ning, too."

Damn it. "Are any other builders here? I've got some urgent wo:k for you. We're staging *Changing Fate* and I need the stage props to be built, with a moving stage. I will need about five to six people."

The announcement was followed by an awkward silence. Normally, they'd be happy and would say things like, *Sure, when do you want us to start?*

Not today.

"Did I say anything wrong?" Her heart thudded. What was go.ng on?

One fellow said, "I don't know that you'll find it so easy t' get people. Many of us were just hired t' do a job." His name was Nissa, and he was an experienced carpenter. He'd worked for her before, with Loret, and he was competent, punctual and reliable. She didn't want to have to find anyone else.

"Must be a big job?" Construction was normally quiet during the snow months.

"A strange fellow came in here yes'erday—"

His mate cut in. "Not jus' a strange fellow. A foreigner."

"Lemme talk, ya goof. I was gettin' t' that part."

"A foreigner?"

"Certain as I'm standing here, lady. I mean—he looks Mirani, but he isn't. Never seen him around here. He speaks well, but very old-fashioned. Fer his age, I mean."

"Who is this foreigner?"

"You'd know, lady. He's up there where youz are, rebuilding the traitor's house."

"The Andrahar house."

"That'd be the one."

"What's his name? Where is he from?"

"He din' say that, did he? Before youz ask, he din' say why either. 'S all a big puzzle, that is. But he's payin' us all two tirans a day, so nobody's complainin'. When I told her, it was th' first time th' wife has smiled at me for about a year."

Ellisandra's head reeled. *Two* tirans? For a building job? No wonder these men were not interested in her measly offering.

Damn it, what was she going to do now?

7

THE GIRLS of the theatre committee were meeting again that morning, so Ellisandra had no time to solve the problem of a shortage in good workers. It was a fair walk to Tolaki's house, where they were meeting, and she had to walk very fast—because running would be unladylike—and still came late.

The maid opened the door to her and let her into the hall.

The house was smaller than hers and, being newer, it lacked some of the older features—like those small ornamental windows in all the interior doors that often rattled, let in cold air or even fell out—and had a more compact and practical layout. That meant it was warmer, cosier and looked less like some high-ranking councilor's office.

Tolaki ran in from the living room the moment the door shut behind Ellisandra and rushed across the hall, sweeping Ellisandra in a hug. "Oh, here is my sister-to-be!"

"You're acting like I haven't seen you for years. I only saw you last night."

"Yes, but that's such a long time ago."

Ellisandra laughed. "Is anyone else here yet?"

"Yes, they're all here. Aleyo has almost eaten all the cakes."

Aleyo called from the living room, "She has not!"

Tolaki giggled.

"I'm sorry," Ellisandra said. "I've run into some trouble. You know Loret and his team of builders?"

"Yes. They're good."

"We can't have them."

Tolaki's eyes widened. "Why not?"

"Because someone hired all of them, and a lot of other builders, too."

"But it's winter!"

"I know. No one understands it. You know the man we saw yesterday in the Andrahar yard? He is *rebuilding* the house."

"What? Why?"

"No one knows. I had a look in the yard this morning. He's got a big tent sent up and a camp kitchen and he's had a lot of building materials delivered. The builders don't know why he's rebuilding either. But it means that we're stuck for good people to help us out. I don't really know what to do now."

"I'll go over there and tell him that the men are yours," came a male voice from the dining room door.

Ellisandra gasped. She had not seen Jaeron approach. He stood in the doorway, his arms crossed over his chest. He wore his black oiled leather suit in preparation for a day of work. His hair hung loose over his shoulders, immaculately trimmed and combed. His eyes met hers in a penetrating gaze.

Ellisandra protested. "But they're not really my workers. They are free to—"

"I won't have my *wife* coming second to some kind of blow-in foreigner."

"He got the workers fair and square. I was just a little too late to—"

"There is no *fair* in this situation. He's a foreigner, and he'll be paying the men in foreign currency. I bet they like that, but it's illegal."

"Well . . ." She was a little taken aback by his abrupt stance.

Nissa *had* said that they were paid in tirans—and a lot more than the theatre could afford.

Jaeron continued, "I'll go and see this fellow tomorrow morning. I'll bring Enzo and Raedon in case there is trouble."

There *would* be trouble if Raedon was involved. "That's not necessary. He's probably just an employee for the family."

"I don't care if he's Asto's Chief Coordinator's son. Those men work for you. And that is all there is to it."

"Please, just let it rest. I'm sure we'll solve it in some way. It's probably a good idea for me to train a few back-up builders anyway. In case—"

"Be quiet. I will not hear that from my future wife."

"Hear what?" She looked into his hard face.

"I will not hear apologies and excuses to settle for second best. You are of the Endri of Miran. We pay for a lot of these Nikala people's houses, for their services, for their health care. We pay them so that they will work for us, not for some stranger to poach workers from under our noses. That's the last I'll hear of it."

If he'd been Enzo, Ellisandra would have told him in no uncertain terms that she could look after herself and didn't need babysitting. Enzo would expect that sort of thing from her, because she told him off a lot, especially when he was being a pompous dick. But Jaeron was her future *husband* and she couldn't possibly make a scene before they were even married, and in the household that he would expect to lead, in front of Tolaki and the family's domestic staff.

So she said nothing, but she went into the living room with her fists balled so tight that her nails made little crescent-shaped impressions in her palms.

By the time Ellisandra came home, she knew for certain: letting Jaeron talk to the stranger on her behalf would *never* do. He'd even said he'd take Raedon Tussamar. Jokes used to go around that if

you wanted to start a brawl, you invited Raedon Tussamar. He
might have calmed a bit now that he was married, but one thing
she knew about a confrontation between those two men and the
stranger: she did not want to be the stranger.

And damn it, what had he done to deserve that?

Given people jobs, fed them and started rebuilding a house. No
wonder Miran had such a bad reputation within *gamra*.

She looked over the wall into the yard from her bedroom
window. It was almost dark, and everyone had gone. The sled had
left, and she couldn't see the canvas shelter from her position,
although a faint glow radiated into the yard from somewhere
behind the wall where she'd seen the camp kitchen set up this
morning. He wasn't still working there, was he? It would be much
too cold.

But as she stood there with her breath fogging up the glass, a
single man walked through the yard with a measuring tape. Every
few steps, he crouched in the snow to add another line of string to
the network of posts and string that she had seen this morning and
that had since that time spread to this side of the house. A flapping
storm light silhouetted his tall figure.

The workers had already done a lot: knocked down a couple of
the half-burned walls, removed damaged stones, put up a couple
of metal frames. Snow had been cleared away from the site. Most
workers used snow as an excuse not to work. With the amount of
snow that fell in Miran, that was guaranteed to make for a lazy
lifestyle. There were many jokes about how nothing was ever built
in Miran because snow stopped work for most of the year.

But clearly they had no trouble turning up for work if the pay
was high enough. Think of all the projects workers could finish if
only they worked when there was snow. She wondered what else
this man had said to the workers to get so many of them to
show up.

She had an idea: she'd go and talk to this mysterious man
herself tomorrow morning. Maybe she could come to an arrangement about Loret and his group, because the thought of Raedon

Tussamar going out there made her shiver. This man might be mysterious and no one might know who he was, but that didn't justify sending thugs.

For one, he'd done a decent thing by paying his workers well. And he'd managed to do in one hit what many years of commerce in Miran had been unable to achieve: to get building work done on a snow day.

When Ellisandra pushed aside the curtains in her room the next morning, she found that the morning had dawned bright and clear. That didn't happen very often in Miran, especially not in winter. The view from her window now stretched all the way to the summit of the mountain they called "The Watcher", its snowy slopes crisp and clear against the sky. Light from the two suns beat down on the fresh snow, making it glitter like thousands of tiny gemstones. The shadow of her house in the snow was sharp, with a blue-tinged double edge. A set of tracks ran through the yard where two maramarang had chased each other. You could see where their wings had brushed the snow and where one of them had taken to the air, while the other one had climbed onto the rubbish bins.

Activity at the Andrahar house was in full swing, a most unusual sight in winter. Another delivery sled had turned up, this one with just a single stack of stone blocks. A couple of men helped the nomad boys unload.

The stranger stood talking to the sled's driver. Today, he was wearing a black leather outdoor suit similar to the one Jaeron wore. The sunlight made his hair glow. It wasn't *quite* as silver-coloured as that of Endri men. His hair had a yellowish tinge to it.

Ellisandra went down to the dining room, where both her brothers sat at the dining table having breakfast. They had been talking but fell quiet as she came in and sat down.

Enzo had a reader next to his plate and flicked through a couple of pages without reading. Jintho glared at him.

"Did I disturb something?" Ellisandra asked.

"No, I was just about to leave." Enzo picked up the reader. He fixed Jintho with a hard stare before leaving the room. "You will come then?"

"I'll see."

"The fuck you will. I can't plan anything with half-arsed promises. You'll either be there or you won't, you limp dish rag."

Jintho glared at him. Enzo turned on his heel and left the dining room, slamming the door behind him.

"What was that about?" Ellisandra asked while taking her usual place.

"I guess you've seen the activity next door?"

She nodded. Jintho's room was on the same side of the house as hers.

"What about it?"

"Well, apparently the Exchange has no record of this man entering Miran, and no one has any idea who he is and where he's come from."

"Someone could go and ask him." Jintho probably wouldn't appreciate that she was planning to do just that as soon as she finished breakfast, so she said nothing about it. When she told him later what she'd found out, he would be more understanding.

"The guards *have* asked him, but they can't find anything to pin on him. He's clean, unknown to them, has never been to Miran before and they have no reason to cross-examine him."

"Has that ever stopped them before?"

"Not if the visitor is someone of low status. They seem to think that he might be a spy or some kind of bait."

"What do you mean?"

"Like the previous cases where either Asto or Barresh have tried to infiltrate Miran. The pattern is well-known: they send a single person who is quite high profile. This person does something illegal and gets arrested. The next thing all of *gamra* is up in arms about it because 'Oh, no. Miran has done something bad again.' Then the next thing there is a raid or highly publicised escape of some kind. Like, the Andrahar trial, Amandra Bisumar's departure from Miran, the raid on the council supposedly to 'free prisoners', forgetting that these people were here by their own will. We know about these tricks. They're only doing it to prove that we are stupid or to prove to all their member entities that yes, Miran is still bad and still deserves to be boycotted."

'What does that have to do with you and Enzo that you were just talking about?"

Jintho's mouth twitched. He averted his eyes.

"Jintho?"

"He wants me to join the Citizen's Group."

"Not you, too."

"That was my thought. It's bad enough that my brother and future brother-in-law are involved."

So it was true, Jaeron was definitely in the Citizen's Groups. Ellisandra shivered.

"Your fiancé reckons that the guards are being too soft. He's asked Enzo to help him question the guy next door. Enzo wanted me to come."

"No. Don't get involved. I don't want Enzo to get involved either, especially not with Raedon Tussamar. He's trouble."

"You try tell Enzo that. He's convinced that this foreign man is some sort of spy and that the Andrahar family are planning a last-ditch attempt to scuttle the laws they want to change in the council."

"Is this visitor a member of the Andrahar family?"

"As far as we can track, no. The guards have looked at his pass. His identity checks out. He's even got a chip. It checks out, too. He's from an influential family in Barresh."

"So, he works for the Andrahar family? They can't come back here without having their heads removed, so they send someone who passes for an Endri to do whatever the family plans on doing

with the house. I don't think it would look very good if an innocent worker was attacked."

"That's what I said. But Enzo wants to rough him up just to
make sure, and see if they can scare him into leaving."

"Does he need to leave? That's exactly how Miran gets its bad
reputation. If we ever want to climb out of this isolation hole,
we've got to stop attacking the few foreigners that are still stupid
enough to come to Miran."

"That's what I told him, too, but . . ." He spread his hands and
let them fall by his sides.

"And? Are you going?"

Jintho shrugged. Looked down at his empty plate. "I don't
know that I have much of a choice. Enzo has to sign my application, as the family's heir."

"Application?"

"For a commercial licence."

So he hadn't abandoned the idea yet.

"Don't look at me like that, sister. I know what you're thinking,
but this shop is going to happen."

There was a kind of desperate tone to his voice that she had
never heard before, but he would tell her nothing more, and she
really had to leave if she was going to talk to the man and be at the
theatre in time.

8

ELLISANDRA LEFT the house after obtaining a promise from Darma that she would bring Father his breakfast. Hidden deep within the warmth of her cloak, she stepped onto the porch. Clear weather meant that it was colder than usual. The air had a strong bite to it that made her wish that she had brought her scarf.

With the crisp air came a flood of bright light, both from Ceren's suns and the reflection from the layer of cloud that blanketed the lower-lying areas. From the top of the steps to the porch, she could see those clouds between the two houses on the other side of the street: filling the valley below the city with a hard-edged and incredibly bright cloud deck. The sky above was the deepest blue imaginable and both suns, a hand's width apart, shone brightly in the sky. The morning sun was the white one and the evening sun the yellower one underneath.

The gates to the Andrahar house stood wide open, and Ellisandra walked through unchallenged. A large group of workers stood in the shelter of the tent, many of them with their hands wrapped around steaming mugs of soup. How many people could this guy afford to hire? There had to be at least twenty.

The wonderful scent of hearty soup drifted through the yard. The cook stood under the shelter, stirring a big pot on the stove. A chunk of meat hung over an open fire, dripping fat onto the flames. It was still pink on top, and would certainly take until midday to cook.

The midday meal.

Behind the stove stood a closed tent or maybe two tents, interconnected dome shapes of light grey fabric.

A young man came past with a tray and asked, "Lady, can I give you a warm drink?"

Ellisandra was going to refuse, but the smell of the soup was heavenly.

She accepted a boiling hot cup and walked slowly towards the house while cradling it in her hands. The heat seeped through her mittens.

The builders had made pretty good progress so far. They had put up the metal frame and a few young men were stacking stones for the first layer of walls. All their faces were familiar. As Ellisandra walked past, there were polite nods and mutterings of *Good morning, lady* and *Nice day, lady*. Did she see a twinge of guilt in some of their expressions?

She found the stranger talking to Loret under the shelter of the canvas. They stood looking at the plans pinned on the table. The stranger was at least a head taller than Loret, who, as a typical Nikala man, had a short and wiry build with strong arms and shoulders. Being middle-aged, Loret was perhaps a bit softer around the waist than most, but the stranger's presence dwarfed him.

The stranger wore his hair loose, like a very proper Endri man. Like most Endri men, he wore golden loops in his ears.

As soon as he spotted Ellisandra, he crossed the yard and came to her. He was even taller than Jaeron, and definitely had an Endri way about him, even if his eyes were . . . light brown. The colour of sand in the bottom of the river and creeks.

Well, that was . . . really strange.

"My lady, can I be of assistance?" His voice sounded oddly formal, but perfectly Mirani.

Ellisandra felt ridiculous even for coming here. He paid the men two tirans a day, and he employed a cook to feed the workers, too. There was no way she could compete with that. The men would be working in a desperately cold and clammy theatre and would have to make do with cold bread rolls, for half the pay.

"I was . . . curious. I went to the markets yesterday to hire workers, and it seems that you have employed them all."

"My excuses, lady. They did not mention that they were taken."

"They wouldn't have been taken yesterday, but the theatre production happens every year, and every year we hire the same men who are good at building stage sets. There is quite an art to it, and these men have experience." She met Loret's eyes briefly before he looked away.

Oh, he'd known very well that she had been about to come to him, but given how much the stranger paid, she wasn't sure she could blame him for taking this job either. It was likely to go on for longer, too.

"You work for the theatre?" There was interest in his voice.

"Yes, I'm the director."

"Of the Mirani state theatre?" His eyes were intense. That colour was so weird.

"Yes, I just said so."

He bowed. "My excuses, lady. I did not mean to interfere with the theatre. Also, I haven't introduced myself. I'm Vayra Perling Dinzo."

What sort of name was that? "My name is Ellisandra Takumar."

"From the Foundation family?"

"Yes."

"You live next door." It was not a question.

"I do." How did this guy know all these things? She glanced at her house over the top of the wall. Her window was nothing more than a dark rectangle. It would be next to impossible to recognise people from down here, wouldn't it? A chill went over her back. She had never considered that anyone could look into her room from here, because there had never been anyone to look. Come to think of it, why was his Mirani so good?

"How come you know me? I haven't seen you before."

"That is because I haven't been here before. It is my first time in Miran. My excuses if I gave the impression that I've been studying you personally. That is not true. Of course, a lady like yourself is well worth knowing, but the reason that I know where you live is that I've studied the layout of the streets and I know which family lives where."

Did he always speak stiff and formal like this? "So you're here to rebuild the house?"

"Correct."

"But why? The Andrahar family can't come back to Miran."

"They're not coming back."

"Then why are they rebuilding the house?"

"They are not. I am. The house is mine."

"Yours? What about the foreign investment laws? What about . . . You can't sell anything to people from outside Miran."

"I know. I also know that according to Foundation Law, the Andrahar family can't legally sell the house, but they can give it away, and that's what they did."

Give the house away? Suppose they could. She didn't think the law said anything about that. "Why would they do that?"

"They're not using it."

"But why you? Um, I hope that's not an impolite question."

"Not at all. I've known the family for a long time. They became our neighbours in Barresh when they fled. I was a toddler, the oldest of five, and fascinated with the older children next door."

She frowned.

"Miruhan and Iztho, Taerzo's twin sons."

"Taerzo is the younger brother, isn't it?"

"Correct. The twins were always playing in the yard so I often climbed over the fence to join them." He smiled. "I was often bored and lonely, so I liked coming to the family. There were always people in the kitchen, talking about all sorts of interesting things. Three of the brothers were Traders, and they always had interesting travel stories to share. I liked looking at the aircraft in their back yard. Whenever I had to come home, my parents always had to drag me away from there. My parents thought it was a good idea if I learned Mirani, so Isandra and sometimes Rehan were my teachers. Later, Isandra ended up joining the Barresh council, and I did a lot of work for her, mainly translation and legal work. When none of her sons wanted to return to Miran, she gave the house to me."

Just like that, huh?

"What are you going to do with it?"

"I'm going to rebuild it exactly to the old style, with the entrance porch, the coloured glass windows, the floor mosaic, the correct slate roof tiles that were all stolen, the painted tiles in the bathroom—"

"You seem to know a lot about it."

"They told me what the house used to look like, and I made a model based on their instructions and pictures that exist of the house. I will fine-tune it now that I've been able to take measurements."

"Is that what all the yellow posts are for?"

"Correct. I'll show it to you some time."

"That's really nice, but . . ." *you're barging into the middle of a political fight that's partially about keeping foreigners out of Miran.* "What are you going to do with the house?" He couldn't possibly live there.

"I'm doing this for my mother. It will be a present to her."

This was getting ever more strange. "Your mother is Mirani?"

"No, she is Aghyrian, like me."

"You mean . . ." Aghyrians were the people who had originally fled from Asto, and were the forefathers of the Endri. She saw why she had mistaken him for an Endri man last night.

"Doesn't your mother already have a house?"

He smiled. "She does, but she's going to move here, but she doesn't know that yet." He winked. "Don't tell her."

This was the strangest thing she had ever heard. The very few foreigners who had lived in Miran when she was young were long gone. His mother might be younger than Father, but why would she want to move to Miran if she wasn't Mirani? He had to be either really bold or incredibly naïve. Did he know anything about Mirani politics?

"Well, um . . ." What could she say? If she told him what people thought about foreigners, would he laugh in her face or feel offended?

"I'll tell you the story about my mother, one day."

One day? She studied his serious face for signs that he was joking, but she saw none. "How long are you planning to stay?"

"At least until the house is finished. After that, who knows?"

There was another awkward silence in which she was dying to tell him that if her brother and his friends had anything to do with it, he wouldn't even stay that long, but telling him so felt like betraying her brothers. They were right: who knew why he was really here and what he wanted? It was best not to get involved.

"I'm really here because I'd like to come to an arrangement with you about my workers."

A slight frown.

"The ones who normally work for the theatre during this time of the year. I don't want to take them off you, but the theatre is lost without those men. We have about two months to get the production finished, and I don't think I can train replacements, as well as give them time to build the stage props, before the date of the performance. Is there a way we can share? It won't be for all that long."

His frown deepened.

"I know that you employed them fairly, but I have a theatre production to complete, and the council won't be very happy if it's not done to their standard."

"I guess they wouldn't be."

"I mentioned that you had hired the men I needed, and a couple of young men told me they'd sort it out for me. I don't know what they're planning, but I know who's involved and it's unlikely to be pleasant." She cringed. Next he would ask for Raedon Tussamar's name. He would probably know who he was, too. "I know these men, and I know that they can be very aggressive. If I could make a deal with you, that would stop them—"

"If I let you have these workers?" He completed the sentence for her, and smiled at her.

"Yes. Pretty much." She blew out a relieved breath.

He smiled, fixing her with those eerie sand-coloured eyes. "You're much too nice and honest to resort to blackmail."

Yes, probably. But if she didn't come to some sort of arrangement, Raedon would turn up, and Enzo would rope Jintho into doing stupid things. "Well, that's the deal. Because these men really exist and they will cause you trouble."

"I have no doubt that they exist. There are always those who would resort to thuggery if they can't get what they want in an honest way." He gestured at the men in the yard. "These workers chose to work for me. I pay them what I think is a fair rate and I feed them. I had a long list to choose from, a very long list. If there is some sort of rule that prohibits me from hiring them, why did none of them bring it up? Why, indeed, do they turn up here without looking over their shoulders? They sure like to work here."

It's amazing how money will do that to people.

"I'm sorry, I didn't mean to offend. I didn't say they should stop working here. I asked if you could spare the men who normally build the stage for me and let them work for me until the stage is built."

"How many of them would that be?"

"There's four or five of them. I won't need them all the time either. It's probably enough if they could just come in the mornings or afternoons."

He looked out over the building site. A group of men had

already started mixing cement and were getting stones ready. He nodded, once. "All right. I wouldn't want to impede the Mirani theatre. So what is this play about?"

"We're playing a classic Mirani work called *Changing Fate*. I guess you're not familiar with it."

"Actually, I am."

She frowned at him.

"It's the play where Miran takes charge over its fate and ousts the invaders. The one that follows from *The Invasion*. From what I believe it starts out with a scene with three vagrants sitting in the streets while a group of Coldi prisoners of war are marched into prison."

"Yes." She was impressed. "Have you ever seen it?"

"Not a live performance, no, but I would love to. Do tell me when and where this play is on and I'll come to watch."

With all the dignitaries from the council there? "Um—I'm not sure if you'll be able to—"

"All plays put on by the council are free, are they not?"

"Yes. Yes. But it gets very busy." Not half as busy as she would like, and the size of the audience was becoming smaller each year. There were days that all seats in the grand hall had been filled up on Theatre Day, but that was before she was born.

"Well, I shall be there early, then. Now, do tell me which are the men you would most like me to lend you for this marvel of culture?"

She couldn't help chuckling. "Do you always talk like that?"

He frowned at her. "What do you mean, talk like that? What is wrong with the way I talk?"

It occurred to her that the way she'd brought this up was not very polite. He'd done nothing to justify ridicule.

"Well, obviously you're not a local. But excuse me. I should be complimenting you on your Mirani instead. I mean, it's not as if we get a lot of visitors." Her cheeks burned with heat. "I'm sorry."

"It's all right. I didn't expect a grand welcome." One corner of his mouth moved up. His eyes met hers, and the corners crinkled with a smile.

Her blush intensified. That should teach her to keep her big mouth shut.

She glanced over the wall at her house. What if Enzo or Jintho saw her here, or Jaeron? They had said not to go here. They had said they would handle it, and her bumbling would only prove that they were right.

"Um, mister?" This was a male voice behind her. Ellisandra turned around. A council guard had come into the yard, a Nikala man wearing the council-issued grey cloak with the red and white Mirani crest embroidered on the chest.

"Yes, how can I help you?" Vayra said.

"You're the guy in charge here?"

"I am."

"You're going to undertake a major building project. I have to inform you that you need a licence for that in Miran." His Nikala accent was barely audible.

"I have a licence. Wait." Vayra dug in the inside pocket of his cloak and pulled out a small card. He held it under the guard's nose.

The man frowned. "What is this? I can't read it. You'll have to have it translated—"

"It's Damarcian. It's a licence from the Masterbuilders' Guild."

The guard's frown deepened. "You're a licensed Masterbuilder?"

"Correct."

"I will . . . have to get someone to verify that."

"Sure. I understand."

"You will also have to submit building plans to the heritage committee—"

"It's not necessary for rebuilding a structure exactly as it was. The council's rules are that only new structures have to be approved."

The guard glanced sideways at Ellisandra in a *Did-you-tell-him-that?* manner. Ellisandra shook her head.

The guard went on about building regulations and Vayra seemed to have an answer to every problem the man could bring up. Ellisandra had the impression that he knew more about the rules than the council worker did, and although the council worker seemed to get more frustrated, Vayra's calm manner never changed. It reminded her of the Trader jokes, which usually involved Traders remaining absolutely calm while the world exploded around them. She didn't even know if Traders actually did that or if it was a myth. She had certainly never seen them do it. There were so few Traders left in Miran. Just the main branch of the Tussamar family and a few other minor Endri families.

It didn't look like the conversation between Vayra and the guard would end any time soon, and the girls would be waiting for her at the theatre, so she turned around and made for the gate.

"Wait, lady!" Vayra called after her.

She looked over her shoulder.

"Where do I tell the workers to go?"

Ellisandra frowned.

"You wanted to use their expertise, and I understand that. Your project will probably not take all that long, so I'm happy for the men you need to work for you in the afternoons. I just want to tell them where to turn up at midday."

The council worker frowned at her in a *does-he-always-talk-like-this?* way.

"Let them come to the theatre. They know where it is."

"I will tell them that. It is a pleasure to meet you, lady."

"Thank you."

He returned to his discussion with the council worker, and Ellisandra made her way out of the yard.

She stopped at the gate.

Work at the site was in full swing. Men were hauling stone blocks on sleds. Others were hammering away old stones. Still others cleared away snow. Given their usual unwillingness to do anything during snow days, this activity was incredible. Vayra must treat them exceptionally well.

He and the council worker had gone to the shelter of the canvas tent, where they studied the plans on the table. Vayra gestured and the council worker pointed.

Vayra looked up over the man's shoulder, and met Ellisandra's eyes. He smiled.

A chill went over her back. Hadn't her brothers and Jaeron told her not to talk to this man?

9

MIRAN'S STATE THEATRE was a stately building in the commercial district. Flanked by some of the most prestigious shops, the building's imposing façade dominated the streetscape. A set of broad marble steps led up to the main entrance: two large doors each custom-made of a large panel of resin. If you stood close up, you could see the hundreds of layered grass stems in the resin. Someone would have built each door with resin poured over layer upon layer of carefully-arranged stems.

Ellisandra by-passed the main entrance with its echoing and empty foyer and grandiose-looking arches with little painted animal heads.

The staff and actors had their own entrance at the end of an alley that ran down the side of the building. Via the door under the porch, she entered the theatre's dressing rooms, now all dark and empty. Mannequins with old costumes lined the walls like silent sentinels to times past. There were little signs on the wall next to them, indicating which famous actor or actress had worn the costume for which performance. Ellisandra passed all of these and went up the stairs.

Her office above the dressing rooms had a little window

through which she could see onto the stage. The curtain would be pulled shut during performances, but was always open for rehearsals. A couple of people stood on the stage. One of them was Tolaki, two of the others were the lead actors in the play. Keldon Nirumar was such a typical ladyboy. Mirani men took pride in their hair, but he had explained to her at length that he washed his every day with the spawn of some kind of fish that made his hair shine. Most Mirani men wore small golden hoops in their ears, but his hoops were huge, and had tiny jewels set into them that glittered when he moved. Most Endri men had tattoos, usually of the family crest, and mostly on their shoulders, normally hidden under their clothes, but he had green tattoos all over his upper arms and his shoulders and into his neck.

Tameyo, who played the role of Mariandra, looked very plain and classy in comparison. She was from the upper Nikala class and always had great trouble getting her curly hair to remain straight if she played an Endri role. She would often comb her hair with a heated brush in between acts, but this dry weather did it no favours. Flyaway curly strands danced about her head.

Both she and Keldon held a couple of sheets of paper, from which they read while acting out the actions described. A number of other people played the crowd, although they were not the ones who would do it on the day of the performance.

Classic plays were usually melodramatic, so there were lots of hand gestures and speaking directly to the audience. The onstage crowd would react to all these gestures with exaggerated responses: opening their mouths for surprise, putting their hands over their eyes for fear.

Seen from here, without the sound, it looked rather ridiculous, but this was typical of the classical plays. There was even a small modern theatre group who wrote their own plays that often mocked the silly over-reactions of this "crowd" and made fun of the actions. Their performances were hilarious. Pity that so few people paid to see them.

Ellisandra went to put a firebrick onto the fire and dragged her chair over to the hearth. Seriously, was she getting soft or had this winter started earlier than ever?

Through the door into the next room, she could see Sariandra seated at a table drawing on a big piece of paper. Flowing dresses —with laces, not buttons—long capes, wide men's trousers. Sariandra might be shy and a spy for her father, but she seemed to know what she was doing.

Everything was going to plan so far. The most important test would be if Loret and his team would turn up in the afternoon.

Ellisandra went to work, leafing through the text of the play to check on everything the men would need to build. Of course she should have done this last night, instead of getting caught up in checking Foundation Law.

The first act took place on the steps of the council building, and they'd need to build a façade with a door. The second act was set inside the council assembly hall. She'd only need a frame for hanging a painted sheet depicting the inside of the hall. But she would need chairs and benches, although they came from the stores. The third act took place in the dungeons. It would need a foyer with a fake tiled floor, with cell doors with bars so that the prisoners in the cells could all look into the foyer. It was a fictional locality, since the real prison didn't look anything like that. It had dank corridors and closed doors, low ceilings and roughly-hewn stone floors.

She wrote setting notes for Loret. In the years he had worked with the theatre, he had become very good at making fake stone walls out of cement-soaked cloth. He could even make them look old, with dabs of paint that resembled sludge and stains.

She hoped that Vayra would keep his word and let the men go.

When she finished with the notes, she went to the theatre's library, a dark and cold, low-ceilinged room off the corridor that led to the actors' entrance.

In between the many racks with storage boxes, each containing texts of plays, she found the play's texts in three boxes that looked like they hadn't been touched for years, except for a couple of recent fingerprints on the very dusty lid of one of the boxes. Those would have been Tolaki's fingerprints from getting the texts she was using on the stage right now.

Ellisandra carried the first of the boxes to a large table in the middle of the room, and tipped the stack of paper onto the table-top. The last time these scripts had been put away, some of the sheets had gotten folded. A mountain scorpion had eaten a hole into the bottom corner of the box, and had chewed a neat bite out of the corners of the bottom sheets. Those papers were also covered in the creature's black droppings.

Ellisandra went to get the other two boxes and tipped the contents of those onto the table, too. With the last one, a scorpion scuttled over the table and jumped off the edge before she could squash it. She ran after it, but it disappeared under a shelf.

Wow, what a mess. She should find some money to get someone to dust these shelves.

She spread all the texts out over the table. Tolaki would have the master text upstairs on the stage. Ellisandra started sorting the papers into individual parts.

One of the actors had made extensive notes in the margins. The handwriting was rather old-fashioned, but she could figure out that this was the female lead, the woman who had played Mariandra.

She flicked to the last few pages with that horrible scene of death. The scene description said:

All the prisoners are dead on the floor. Jihan enters the stage from the main entrance to the foyer. He steps across the bodies and opens the door to Mariandra's cell.

JIHAN: Will you forgive me, my love?

Mariandra comes out of the cell. She steps over the body of Rana and does not look at him.

This was the part of the play that was just all kinds of wrong.

For most of the play, Mariandra was strong and defended the prisoners and Rana who had come to negotiate for their freedom. He spoke very little Mirani and was being cheated and lied to by everyone. He was perhaps naïve, but a sympathetic character. She helped him, and they fell in love. Their shared love felt natural.

How could someone go from being a lover to not even looking at their body in such a short time? What had the hero done, except kill defenceless prisoners, that justified her coming back to him?

In the top margin, the actress had written:

This scene symbolises the death of the relationship between Miran and the Coldi. It signifies the start of an independent Miran. The scene has a deep symbolic value that needs to be brought out in the acting through the triumphant exit stage of Mariandra and Jihan.

Fancy that. If even the actress needed to remind herself to be cheerful, then there was something wrong with the script.

At the very bottom of the stack that had tumbled from the boxes, she found the book of author's notes. It was a plain-covered, slightly frayed very old little book that didn't give the appearance of having been opened since it had been printed.

Some of the pages were stuck together with scorpion droppings. Someone really should do something about those pests.

Ellisandra leafed through the pages that she could open. She would have to take this home and unstick the pages so that she could read through it. Many plays had these books, which were usually artistic instructions from the author. It was often the only hint at the author's identity, because the plays had been commissioned by the council of that time, and it wasn't customary for the author's name to be known.

Changing Fate was the second play in what the scholars called the classic period of Mirani theatre.

The Invasion was the beginning of that era where plays reflected real and often violent events rather than re-told romantic mythology.

Historians referred to the period as the time when Miran lost its innocence.

Prior to the invasion of Miran by Coldi, the city had been prosperous, free of foreign influence, blissfully ignorant of both the existence of other worlds and the people on them. Miran had been run much like a city-state back then, because travel to the eastern coast or western agricultural lands was overland only. It was difficult and took days. The mountain tiyuk were good climbers, but were ill-suited to warmer climates.

There was no need for travel and there was little trade between the various settlements: Miran, Estevan in the highlands, Bendara in the west and Kesilu on the east coast. The city still fitted inside the walls, the Nikala worked the fields, the Endri provided them with houses and protection, and the council debated the arts and building projects.

And then one day, the sky filled with flying machines, bringing Coldi warriors from Asto, raiding Miran for riches and food with space machines and space technology. The people fought back, but many were killed. Miran lost more than lives that day: it lost its isolation, its innocence and much of its pride. Afterwards, it had hastily developed technology but according to some, its pride had never fully recovered.

The great writers of that time had poured all their emotions into these texts, and at the time, their main emotion was anger. *The Invasion* told the original story, and was compulsory viewing for all school students. This was the theatre's most-performed play. It was where Mirani children learned what Asto had done to them and why the Coldi should never be trusted.

Changing Fate came immediately after *The Invasion* and was a combination of a love story combined with a vengeful streak of violent retribution. The combination was odd, didn't add up to a coherent plot, and the only person whose character was seriously affected was the female lead, who had a change of mind about her lover.

The antagonist Coldi prisoner wasn't much of an antagonist. One, he was in prison for much of the play and two, he seemed nice and civilised.

Maybe that was the problem with the play: It did awful things to people who, according to modern understanding, hadn't deserved it.

Father had said last night that the play had been last performed the night before Nemedor Satarin's election to the High Council. Nemedor Satarin might have had a hand in choosing it this time, but no matter how much Ellisandra tried to think of a special reason why that had been done, she couldn't find one.

It was much later when Ellisandra looked up from her work and realised she had forgotten to take her midday break and she was so hungry that it made her dizzy. All the scripts were now sorted in little piles around the perimeter of the table, ready to be tied up and given out. Some pages were missing, but nothing problematic that couldn't be copied or resupplied. She'd ask the printer to take care of that.

She was also really cold.

On a little desk in the corner of the room stood a reader hub. It was an oddly modern piece of equipment in this stuffy room, tucked away in the darkest part of the building, as if anti-technology people would come to look for it. She turned the reader on and fired up the link to the council printer, which held copies of all significant texts. She quickly ordered copies of the needed pages. With a bit of luck they would be delivered later today.

Upstairs in the office, Sariandra still sat in the room next to Ellisandra's office, bent over the table drawing designs for costumes. On the stage, Tolaki and the actors had stopped rehearsing. They sat in a circle with food trays between them.

Ellisandra called to Sariandra, "Come on, let's have something to eat."

"I'll just finish this," Sariandra said, still busily drawing.

Well, if nothing else, she was a hard and independent worker.

Ellisandra left the room and went down the stairs. Soft tones of music rose up from the downstairs stage assembly hall, where she found Aleyo conducting the theatre orchestra. The group held about twenty players: harps, lutes, bow-harps, horns and trumpets, flutes and drums. The part they were practicing was the sweeping and familiar rhythm of the Lovers' Dance. Now there was a piece that was often played in bars and at parties. She didn't realise that it came from this play. Fancy that, the dance was of Mariandra with Rana.

Ellisandra stopped to listen. The music did not quite fill the space of the backstage hall. It was thin, insecure. The drums were slightly out of time, the lead harp missed an entry, followed by an ugly discordant note.

"No, no, no," Aleyo called.

The music stopped.

"The flutes are too early again. First the drum goes *dum, dum* and then the harp comes in, and then the flute solo."

The lead flute player said, "Wait, it says here we have two bars and two counts rest."

"Three bars," Aleyo said in her *Seriously?* voice.

The woman squinted at the page. "So it does, too." She was one of a couple of players who used to play in the state orchestra, but were now too old for the relentless practice or whose hands were too sore to hold their instruments for long periods of time.

The woman scribbled on the music and then gave her pen to the younger woman next to her. A couple of others were also making notes.

There was a lot of work still to be done here. It might be an idea if some members of the orchestra got glasses. Or maybe they should just retire and let the younger players have a chance to play. Maybe they should play by current ability, and not by past accolades, but try to get *that* past the council's arts committee.

Aleyo clapped her hands. "Everyone ready? Let's play that part again."

Ellisandra took the opportunity to slip past the group in the darkness and curtained partitions of the backstage area, while the uncertain tones of the flute solo drifted through the open space.

Every time when starting on a new play, she managed to forget how the orchestra was always a weak point in every production, and how hard it was to keep good players and how they looked like they were not going to get the pieces ready until the very last moment.

The group of actors still sat on the stage talking and laughing. A tray stood on the stage in the middle of the group, but it only held a few crumbs of bread.

"There she is," Tolaki said.

While Ellisandra crossed the stage, the people in the group turned around. Apart from Tolaki, there were Keldon, Tameyo and Liran, who played Rana and whom she hadn't yet seen, and also the theatre's caretaker. They sat at the very edge of the stage, facing someone who stood in semidarkness amongst the seats for the audience: a short and slight man with a sharp face, wearing a felt uniform with the insignia of the Mirani council embroidered on the chest.

High Councillor Nemedor Satarin.

He stood straight-backed, with his hands, free of jewellery, on the back of a seat. His cloak hung over the seat next to it.

Every time she saw him, Ellisandra noticed how small and light-built he was. He was from the upper merchant—Nikala—class, and in the style of the army commander he had been, he kept his hair cropped very short. He had a sharp-nosed face with thin lips and penetrating dark blue eyes.

He nodded a greeting. "Lady Ellisandra." The military decorations on his chest glittered as he did so.

"It's an honour to have you pay us a visit, High Councillor." Her heart thudded. Why was he here? The only time he ever came into the theatre was during performances, and then only to the important ones.

"Excuse my presence. Don't let me interrupt your normal preparations. I'm very excited. It's a delight that after so many years, the theatre is performing my favourite play. I found your direction of *Saving Grace* last year most interesting, so that's why I personally chose this play. It's challenging, but I'm sure you will find a way to make it new and refreshing."

The little smile on his face, a smirk almost, brought a wave of anger.

She was hungry. It didn't look like there was any food left and she was not in the mood to smile about this horrible play. His favourite? Seriously? Challenging?

All these men were playing with her. Don't do this, you can't do that, don't talk to that person. So they went, *let's give her this play and see how she jumps.* Well, she was going to jump. The play was badly written and everyone knew it.

She knew how to do that ladies' smile that was the equivalent of his patronising smirk. "I have some plans for this play that will make it unforgettable."

His eyebrows went up. "Now you make me curious. Do tell me about these plans."

"It will be a surprise for everyone. It will be shocking and controversial, and you'll still be talking about it for years to come."

"Very, very interesting. I'm looking forward to it."

She spotted Tolaki looking at her with an uneasy expression.

Nemedor Satarin continued, "Well, it looks like that is under control, so you can spend all the time doing costumes and stage props and music." He glanced at the entrance to the backstage area.

Could he hear the orchestra's rehearsal from here, or how long had he been listening and watching?

"We're working on the music," she said, trying not to sound grim, but her heart was thudding. If a non-musical person could hear the trouble, then they did have a serious problem. "We have time. We'll get there. It will sound beautiful on the day." If only she could find better flute players. Maybe she needed to shake the orchestra up. Like *that* was something to look forward to, on top of all the other things that needed to be done.

The awkward moment was disturbed with the sound of heavy footsteps.

Loret and his men tromped onto the stage with heavy thudding of their sturdy work boots.

"Good aft'noon, lady. Here we are, as promised." He'd taken his usual crew of three younger men. Selip, Dojat, and she kept forgetting the name of the other one.

Loret bowed to Nemedor Satarin. "Good t' see youz here, High Councillor."

"Greetings, Soldier." Nemedor Satarin had a much more friendly smile for Loret than for her. "I see you are doing well."

"Better 'n ever. Haven't forgotten th' army, High Councillor."

"Didn't I tell you? Once a soldier, always a soldier."

"Too right, commander. Glad t' serve youz." Then he turned to Ellisandra. "Where d'youz want us t' start, lady?"

"The plans are upstairs in the office. Have a look at them, I'll be up there shortly."

Loret and his men tromped back off the stage, hammers dangling on the back of their belts.

"Strange time for them to turn up for work," Nemedor Satarin said, in a semi-offhand tone that she didn't mistake for chattiness.

"They're also working on another site." She suspected that he knew this already.

"They were offered other work while everyone knows that you use them for the theatre?"

"Their employer didn't know that."

"That is no excuse. I am aware of the situation with the foreigner at the Andrahar house. Allow me to say this, lady. I think that you should have referred the matter to a councillor. As a lady of the Mirani Endri, you absolutely should have priority over this foreigner. The workers should know that, too. In fact, I am disappointed in them. Mirani interests should always come first. They should not have been offered this job."

"The foreigner didn't know any of that. He seems to have a robust project, and he makes the men very happy. We came to a compromise—"

"And they are not happy working for you?" His expression was penetrating.

"I can't pay them as much as he does. He employs a cook, too, and they get free meals. I can't do all those things."

"You shouldn't have to buy the men's loyalty."

"Loyalty doesn't pay their bills." And it was due to the current council that there *were* some bills. In the past, the Endri would have provided everything and the Nikala's wages were paid in food and housing. This council had introduced rent.

"So what is he paying them?" He fixed her with an intense look.

'I . . . don't know." Seriously, what was this about?

"You know that the workers are paid more than you can pay, but you don't know how much?"

Damn it. "Someone mentioned two tirans a day."

He whistled. "That's not bad for hauling a few rocks. Where do you suppose he gets the money?"

"I don't know." She glanced at the backstage entrance, desperate to get out of here.

"You were seen talking to him this morning."

"That's when I arranged that the workers could come here in the afternoon." She took a step back. He was standing far too close for her liking, and his expression had an intensity that made her afraid to breathe. "Surely the guards have asked him all these questions?"

"They have, but he's an evasive fellow. He will answer a question in that old-fashioned way of speaking of his, and then later you'll realise he hasn't answered that question at all."

That was not how Vayra had come across to her at all. If anything, she thought he'd been too open and naive. "I didn't have a need to ask him any questions other than about the workers."

"I understand, lady." He retreated a step, and the intensity of his gaze let up a bit. "Did he seem to like you?"

What?

"My apologies for this rather intrusive question, but a female smile may loosen information from him where a guard's badge does not." He winked.

What, what, what, seriously? "Well, I have no reason to see him again. I—"

"Then you could *make* a reason. Say, you wanted the workers for longer than half a day—"

"But I don't."

"That's insubstantial. I tell you that you want the workers for a whole day, so you go over to the house and ask him. It doesn't matter if he says yes or no. The important part is that you'd get to talk to him. You get to bat your pretty eyelids at him and he'll answer your questions, like who he is, how he entered Miran, why he's here and why he's rebuilding the house."

Ellisandra felt sick. "His ID card should give you that information."

"Oh yes, but we have the information from his ID already. He's Aghyrian, from Barresh. His name is Vayra Perling Dinzo. He was born in Barresh and lived there all his life. His parents are high-profile people in the Barresh Aghyrian community. His father Daya Ezmi used to be Chief Councillor of Barresh. His mother Anmi Kirilen Dinzo is one of the buried children of Asto. They're both Aghyrian. Apart from his high-profile parents, he's had a most unremarkable life, but incredible academic credentials. He's got a legitimate Masterbuilder's licence from Damarq. He completed the Masterbuilders course while he was studying *gamra* law and studying for his Trader licence. Three degrees in one, and not ones that normal people can combine."

"It seems you know a lot more about him than I do already." She seriously did *not* want to agree to be a spy.

"Yes, but we don't know a couple of important things. We can't track how he entered Miran. We have no idea what he wants. We don't know who he's working for."

"You think that he's going to tell me those things?"

"Lady, it is amazing what a pretty female smile will do to a man."

"Jaeron's not going to be impressed." With increasing sickness, she realised how *that* situation would bear resemblance to the dreadful play they were performing.

"Jaeron knows. He approves."

Was he serious about that? "I'd like to talk to him about it first." Because the last time the subject of her talking to another unmarried man came up, Jaeron had berated her for hugging Keldon Nirumar onstage after her last successful performance. And Jaeron had not even been at the theatre. Keldon Nirumar, a ladyboy, for goodness sake, why would he think there would be anything going on except friendship?

And she was *so* not going to go there again.

"Certainly, lady, I understand. It would be very advantageous for both of you if you could provide me with that information. Your husband-to-be would like to move to a more senior position in the council, wouldn't he?" When she didn't say anything to that, he continued. "This foreigner will have done something illegal to enter Miran. The sooner we can pin something on him, the sooner we can be rid of this spy. Let's fight spying with more spying, shall we? You will be my special weapon."

He laughed, but Ellisandra could not have felt less like laughing.

10

THAT ENCOUNTER left Ellisandra so disturbed that she forgot what she'd come down for. She only remembered the lack of food and her empty stomach when she was halfway back up the stairs and she met Sariandra who was on her way down.

"If you're going down for the midday meal, don't bother. They've eaten all the food."

Sariandra made an O with her mouth. She looked disappointed.

Ellisandra grinned. "It's the actors. They never have enough to eat." The reality was that it was freezing cold in the hall, and after a full day of standing on the stage, she always ate lots as well.

"Are you hungry?" Ellisandra asked.

Sariandra nodded.

"Let's go and buy something then."

Sariandra's eyes widened. "But my father didn't give me an account code to use."

And she had none of her own? How old was she? "You don't need an account. I'll put it on mine."

"But I can't let you . . ."

"Don't worry about it. Get your cloak."

Sariandra stared at her.

"Come on, go."

"Yes, yes." She ran upstairs while Ellisandra found her cloak. Seriously, what sort of home did this girl live in to be so frightened?

"Where are *you* going?" Aleyo asked. She sat at her conductor's chair while the members of the orchestra took their midday break. Her tone was disapproving. Aleyo tended to sound like that.

Ellisandra shouldn't let it rile her so, but the fact was that it did. She was hungry, she was cold, she was still shaken by Nemedor Satarin's visit. Aleyo complained about so many things while having so few responsibilities.

"We're going to buy some food. You lot ate everything."

Aleyo gasped and clamped her hand over her mouth. "Oh, I thought you'd already eaten. I'm sorry about that."

No, she wasn't, and she probably hadn't even asked if everyone had eaten yet. It wasn't the first time that it had happened, either. She put on a prim voice. "We'll just go to the shops. We'll be a little while. Good luck with the orchestra."

Aleyo turned around without a word. Good luck indeed.

Sariandra returned wearing her cloak, and the two of them left the theatre building through the side entrance. Walking through the alley to the main street, Ellisandra had no idea what to say. Had Sariandra been anyone else, they would have chatted about the play, gossiped about Nemedor Satarin's visit, or would have vented about the orchestra. With this girl, there was no knowing where that information would end up.

Since when did the theatre become this distrustful?

They talked a bit about the weather—that was always a safe subject, even if winter weather consisted of snowstorms and snowstorms and oh, did you hear about the snowstorms? So yeah, it was not a very interesting subject.

On the main street, they turned downhill towards the busiest section of the commercial quarter. In the shops and stalls on both sides of the street, trade was in full swing. People lined up in the shops, mostly Nikala workers or servants. Street sellers advertised their wares and tried to stop potential buyers in the street. As two high-ranking Endri women, Ellisandra and Sariandra's presence caused a few strange looks and raised eyebrows.

On the corner, where the main street met the major side street that led into the Nikala residential quarters, was a grandiose old building built from white bricks. It had decorative granite columns with carvings of flowers and cornices bearing carved leaves and trailing vines. The arched entrance provided access to a large indoor space that held a number of businesses over three gallery levels.

The ground floor of the central part of the building consisted of a large covered courtyard where shoppers sat at tables surrounding open fires. Unlike the similar area at the markets, there were proper chairs with cushions and blankets and waiters walked around collecting people's orders.

Ellisandra chose a table closest to the fire. She sat down and rubbed her hands while Sariandra took the chair opposite her.

A waiter rushed to the table. "Can I take the ladies' order?"

Ellisandra ordered tea, bean soup and fish bread.

"It's quite warm here," Sariandra said while wrestling herself out of her cloak.

If Ellisandra hadn't already known Sariandra's status, her high position would have been evident from her magnificent cloak. The heavy, glossy and mottled tiyuk fur came from the prime males in the herd. The nomads rarely killed an animal like that, because it was worth much more to them in breeding fees than they could ever make selling the pelt, and the price of the fur reflected that fact.

The collar of the cloak was held with an elaborate gold clasp, and the lining of the hood looked like pure fur-tail felt, which was made in a laborious process from the fluffy seed heads of a plant that grew in creeks.

"Don't look at me like that," Sariandra said.

"I'm just looking at your cloak. It's beautiful."

"Thank you." Spoken without any enthusiasm.

There was a small, painful silence.

"How are you going with the costumes?" Ellisandra didn't really want to talk about work, but she had run out of remarks about the weather, and remarks about clothing seemed to be out of bounds as well.

Talking about *work* would be more productive than *the weather*, but it all felt so stiff and horrible. When she came here with Tolaki, they'd be laughing about . . . well, things. It didn't matter what. Just trivial stuff. Gossip or other "women's talk" as Enzo would call it.

Sariandra explained what she had been doing with the costumes. She said that the books she had on her desk belonged to her half-sister Liseyo whose name came up frequently in the theatre, because she had been very talented when she was caught up in her older sister's involvement with the Andrahar family which led to both of them moving to Barresh as part of that family.

"They're beautiful books about historical clothing. I used the pictures to draw the costumes. Tell me what the budget is for fabric then I'll tell you what I need." Her eyes shone.

"You really enjoy dressmaking, don't you?"

She nodded. "Father didn't like me working in merchant Ranuddin's shop and I think he was secretly glad when the shop closed, but I cried the whole night when I heard the news. I can't believe no one has reopened it in all that time."

Ellisandra thought the shop had been over-priced and thought that the merchant was a bit of a leery old man, but she guessed he did know a lot about high-end fashion. "What do you suppose has happened to all the workshop equipment?"

"It's all still there, collecting dust, as far as I know. Ideal for someone to take it over. But none of his sons were interested."

"The entire building is still owned by the Andrahar family, isn't it?"

Sariandra nodded. "There are still some tenants upstairs but the bottom two floors are empty now. I don't understand. They could easily rent out the space."

The building in question had become an eyesore with the shop at ground level boarded up and the upstairs office windows gaining more and more dirt with every passing year.

The waiter came and brought tea and a large plate of fish patties that were so hot that they steamed. Ellisandra took one and bit a piece off. The salty taste exploded in her mouth.

"Get stuck into them, because they get cold very quickly."

Sariandra picked one up daintily between thumb and index finger and bit a piece off. "This is very nice." She looked around the courtyard. "Nice place, too."

"Haven't you been here before?" She couldn't imagine that, since merchant Ranuddin's workshop was just up the road.

"No." She blew on the white flesh inside the fish patty.

"Didn't you ever have a break at the workshop?"

"We always ate inside. The merchant provided the food."

Ellisandra had found that a lot of businesses did that, and the staff would sit around a table and discuss work. Midday was always an excellent time to find someone in a business.

"How come you worked there? It's not something one of us would normally do. Were there any other Endri in the workshop?"

"No." Sariandra took another fish cake off the plate. "Are you sure you don't want me to pay for this?"

"Look, next time we come here, you pay, all right?"

She nodded, not looking convinced.

"It's all right. It will happen. We come here a lot."

"I thought the theatre staff would feed us. That's what they told my mother."

"They're supposed to, but sometimes there is no theatre staff on duty, or they forget or, like today, you don't get any. There is never quite enough, and those actors always eat so much."

Sariandra smiled, uneasily.

"You have never done anything like this before, haven't you?"

She shook her head. "No. I wasn't quite expecting . . ." She shrugged and clamped her hands in her lap.

"Is there a problem?"

"I promised my father that I'd stay in the theatre and not talk to strangers."

"Am I a stranger?"

"No, but . . ."

"But what? When you finish drawing, you'll have to go out and buy materials, and you'll have go to the stores to sort out accessories. You can't just hide in the building."

Sariandra nodded, nervously.

"Do you want me to come with you?"

"No. I'll be fine." She looked at her hands.

"Do you actually *want* to be in the theatre? Because if you don't then—"

"Of course I do! I want it more than anything." Her eyes glittered. She looked away.

Whoa. "Then what is the problem?"

"There is no problem. I'll do everything exactly as you say, even if you want to use blood and ripped clothes in that last scene. I'll do it. You'll be happy with my work."

"Are you afraid that your father won't like it if we make the last scene gory?"

"He won't."

"Tell him to blame me. Tell him I told you to do it."

"He'll force you to resign."

"It's my last year anyway. I'm getting married. Anyway, we're not doing anything wrong. For the purists, we'll be performing the play more accurately, because it must have been horrific." She shivered, remembering that all of the Mirani classic plays were based on real history. Vaguely, she remembered some to-do over Coldi people wanting to visit the simple unmarked cairn that signified where those prisoners had been buried. She remembered there had been an application to the council by Asto to put up a plaque. She didn't think there was one on the cairn, but the last

time she had been to the cemetery had been after her grandmother's death, a long time ago. Burial horrified Coldi people, apparently. They wanted their bodies to be burnt. "If we perform the
play as I propose, the audience will know how I feel about the
play. They'll know how all the women and the artists of Miran feel
about violence in the name of glory. About the glorification of
violence, about striking people when they're already down." Her
voice had risen during her speech and people around them looked
over their shoulders.

And then another thing. "You're recording this, aren't you?"

"I'm—what?"

"That thing you showed me yesterday. It records what I'm
saying, doesn't it?"

"It does not."

"Then why are you carrying it around with you all the time?"

"I told you, because I can get into contact with my father. He
wants me to be safe. I know you don't believe me, but I don't care.
No one ever believes me. Everyone thinks my mother and I are
stupid or something."

"I don't think that at all—"

"You do, and even if you didn't, I don't care. It's none of your
business anyway." Her cheeks had gone bright red. She picked up
her cup and cradled it in both her hands. They trembled.

Whoa, what was going on?

Sariandra drank, which possibly made her cheeks go even
redder. Ellisandra took the last fish patty, which by now was
almost cold. She ate it anyway, for the sake of having something to
do, but the fish had gone dry and lost most of its taste.

"I'm sorry," Ellisandra said after a lengthy and very awkward
silence, although she wasn't quite sure what she had to be sorry
for. She wiped her fingers on her dress. "Look, I don't know what
is going on, but I didn't mean to make you feel that we think
you're dumb, because it's not true and we don't think that at all.
It's just that . . ." She spread her hands. "In the committee, we are
also each other's friends, even Aleyo, never mind she can be *really*

annoying at times. We gossip, we laugh and talk about silly things." She let her hands sink to her lap. Sariandra just looked at her.

"If it makes you feel any better, invite some friends to come on the committee."

Again, there was no reaction.

Ellisandra sighed. She rose and put on her cloak. "Let's go back."

They walked back to the theatre in silence. Aleyo and the orchestra had vacated the large backstage room, and someone had dragged tables into the middle where a merchant had spread out rolls of fabric. Sariandra went to talk to him, while Ellisandra continued upstairs. She stopped at the door, glancing at Sariandra's designs. The device Sariandra had shown her yesterday lay on the table.

11

WELL, THAT made her feel like a profound idiot.

On the other hand, if Sariandra didn't have the thing with her, then why hadn't she said so? Wasn't her father supposed to know where she was at all times?

Come to think of it, he knew. The device would be telling him that his daughter had been in the theatre all day.

Damned if she understood this.

She went upstairs to her office to find that while she was out, the printer had delivered a pile 'of paper, which was on her desk. Reprints of the missing pages in the individual actors' parts. She'd go and insert them now so that she could hand out the texts.

On her way back downstairs she met Sariandra coming the other way. She walked past and into the drawing room without saying a word.

Ellisandra felt awful. Whatever was going on with the High Councillor's daughter wasn't her business.

But then again, imagine having a father who demanded to know where you were every moment of the day.

Demanding *not to talk to strangers*. Strangers being anyone he did not approve of. Maybe she *was* a stranger in that definition. An independent woman, not afraid to speak her mind, with no man in her life who could tell her what to do.

Until she married.

That was a thought that kept coming back.

She wished she had more confidence that Jaeron was going to share her outlook on marriage, but all signs were that he was going to be traditional and expected to lead the household and tell her what to do. The fact was that, having lived with her brothers, no one had told her what to do for quite some time. And she'd probably dislike it if someone tried.

A very scary thought.

And somehow that explained why every time she thought of her upcoming wedding, her gut knotted with nerves. She'd be a bad wife. She talked to *men* other than her husband. It wouldn't be long after their wedding that rumours would start to flow about how she talked back to her husband and how she tried to tell him what to do. People would laugh behind their backs. She was fine with that because people always laughed behind your back when you ran the theatre and you put something in a performance that they didn't like, but Jaeron wouldn't be fine with it at all, because he had his business and that was *serious* and bad gossip wouldn't make him look good at all. People would tell him to *have a good talk to his wilful woman* and *beat the notions out of her*.

The old family matrons usually said how a child or two fixed wilful women, but to be honest, she wasn't sure if she wanted to be fixed. Or if she wanted her life to descend to mothers' gossip circles, where the only subjects of conversation concerned children and what they were or weren't doing at what age.

It will be different once you're expecting, Gisandra had said, but honestly she couldn't see why it made any difference at all.

Already, the men were always trying to steer her away from political discussions or treating her as if she had no interest in what went on in Miran. Once there had been women in the Mirani council, but now there were none. Once even there had been a woman High Councillor, but she now lived at Hedron.

And no matter what Nemedor Satarin said, she couldn't believe that he had really asked Jaeron if she could use her charms to get information out of the foreigner. That was just wrong in so many ways. From now on, she was going to make all effort *not* to talk to the stranger anymore. Then she couldn't betray his trust and couldn't get into trouble with Jaeron for flirting with another man either.

Although the latter disturbed her on another level, but she seriously wasn't going to go there either.

Downstairs in the library the stacks of scripts still lay on the large table. She inserted the reprinted sheets in each set as needed. These she tied with a ribbon to which she attached a card with the actor's name. They would be responsible for the text while they rehearsed and would need to return it in the best possible condition afterwards.

By the time Ellisandra completed sorting out and tying up the scripts, it had gone dark.

She had meant to apologise to Sariandra, but when she came back upstairs, she found that the High Councillor's daughter had quietly finished her work and Ellisandra had not noticed her leave. Well, bummer. It was absolutely vital that the theatre committee work as a team, so she would have to patch something up tomorrow, although what form that patching up would take, she had no idea. Whenever she and Aleyo had a fight, they'd go and buy tea and cakes, sit by the fire and laugh about stupid things. It happened quite a lot, and it was a wonder both of them weren't as round as barrels. Sariandra didn't seem to know how to laugh and be silly.

Having already tried the tea and cakes thing, what could she do to make her relax and simply be *friends*?

Ellisandra grabbed the quaint old book of notes for the play—more to read—and put it in the middle of the table before she left the theatre. She walked quickly through the snow-covered streets. A lot of workers had finished for the day and many of them hung around the open fires at the markets where the food stalls were doing a roaring trade.

The streets, too, were still quite busy despite the darkness.

All this was in stark contrast with her house, where it was warm, but where the dining room was deserted.

It was rare that Ellisandra had tea with both her brothers, and it had become more common that she had it alone in the kitchen while Riana bustled at the stove, or did the day's washing up. Today, she was kneading dough. When Ellisandra came in, she wiped her hands on her apron and went to pour tea.

"I'm sorry mistress, but dinner will be a bit late. I had to cook sweet cakes for master Enzo's visitor."

"It's all right." She was hungry and cranky, but there was no need to snipe at Riana.

"Where is Jintho?"

"He's gone out." She pounded the dough with flour-covered hands. "I worry about master Enzo, mistress. The friends he has scare me a little sometimes. They drink far too much."

"They do."

"I'm worried that he might do something with this group of his that will get him into trouble."

Ellisandra sipped from her tea. "Raedon Tussamar isn't someone you want as a friend."

"Do you know that the rumour says that he was meant to go to jail, but his uncle bought him out?"

"I'd heard something about that. Wasn't that for kicking an old vagrant?" That was supposed to have happened at the square, where a group of vagrant men usually came together in the boarded-up entrance to merchant Ranuddin's shop.

"Yes, but his uncle went and bought the man a cloak and he withdrew his complaint."

"For a cloak?" She met Riana's eyes. "That seems a very small payment." The court would certainly have asked for more.

"The man was afraid, simple as that." Riana punched her fist into the dough. "He didn't want to push his point, and didn't want it to go to court at all. That boy is bad news. The drinking is bad news. That group is bad news. I told Kalit about it and he said, 'If he's going to be in one of those groups, maybe we should start looking for another place to work.' "

"No, Riana. I don't want you to go." They'd already lost so many servants because of Father.

"I don't want that either, mistress, but my man, he's afraid. He worked for the Dolisar family and he was glad to be out of there."

That family had started the vigilante movement that had later become the Citizen's Groups. *For the good of Miran*, they said, to stop subversive elements taking hold in the city. In practice, the groups were full of angry young Endri men wanting to impress councillors so that they could fast-track a more powerful position in the council. They did this by providing the council with all kinds of information about Miran's citizens that the council couldn't get through legal means. The groups had no official status and, when things went wrong, when leaks, break-ins and illegal access issues were discovered, no official protection from the council either. That was how these men ended up in jail. Or how their families ended up buying their sons out of jail.

She wanted Enzo to leave the group. He was the Takumar family heir. He should start acting the part.

Ellisandra finished eating and then took a tray upstairs for Father.

In the hall, the door to the living room was closed, and now she noticed the unfamiliar cloak—heavy and mottled—and similarly high-quality boots. The faint sound of voices drifted through the door.

If she was not mistaken, the visitor was Asitho Bisumar. He had said yesterday that he wanted to speak to Enzo.

Hopefully Enzo was aware of the methods the man employed, that he'd be recording every word said in that meeting, and playing it back whenever it was most inconvenient.

Maybe not. Maybe he reserved the spying devices only for his daughter.

She stopped at the door and leaned close to it.

"I'm afraid that it's only the start of our problems," Asitho Bisumar was saying. "I need to arm-wrestle the Accountkeepers to find out just how much was in those accounts, but I'm certain that it's enough to create a serious problem. I would appreciate any help you could give me."

"I told you I've already asked her, but she went all proper and lawful on me, and she was right, so I couldn't argue the point."

That was about him asking for access to the council's financial system, wasn't it?

"Hmmm," Asitho Bisumar said. "We need to approach this in a different way. Is there something she wants?"

"Well . . ." Enzo hesitated. "You got me there. She's getting married in long spring, but to be honest, I've not heard her talk about it in a way that suggests she's looking forward to it."

"A nice house would be something she'd want."

"Jaeron's already bought a house."

"Surely there has to be something."

"Yeah . . . You know, I think she would be interested in a position in the council."

"What? In the assembly? I thought we were done with women having notions of running the country."

There was a silence, in which Ellisandra was afraid that they could hear her heart thudding through the door.

"I'm sorry. You asked what she'd want. My sister is a pretty happy person. I don't think she wants anything badly enough."

"Then we *make* her want something."

Another uneasy silence.[1]

Then Enzo said, "I feel she might help if she can be informed what it's for."

"Tell her of council business?"

"That's what she asked, and she was pretty insistent about it, too."

"I think, young man, your sister has slipped from your control."

The tray was heavy in Ellisandra's hands, and any moment she kept standing here someone was likely to come past and see her snooping at the door. She badly wished for some excuse to go into that room so that she could scream *I heard that!* She wanted to make it clear that she wasn't a slave they could control, and oh, that she wasn't interested enough in politics that she wanted to go into the council, although it was intriguing that Enzo thought she would. Most importantly she wanted them to understand that she didn't think it was fair to be asked to do something against the terms of her contract with the theatre without knowing what it was for.

While she was at it, she hated how the council was making changes to the law important enough to get Father all fired up, but no one would tell her what they were, because *politics was boring* and women weren't supposed to ask or be given answers.

Maybe politics was boring, but these men were deciding the future in her name.

She was getting really angry about this.

Getting angry in this slow, simmering way was not good, because it made her do things she later regretted. She had been in that state when she had yelled at Enzo about Father—because she was angry about his indifference to his own father. The slow anger was the reason why she planned to make the last scene of the play gory—because she was angry that the council's art committee never asked the women of the theatre what play *they* would like to perform. And because Nemedor Satarin was playing games with her.

It was a type of anger that led to stupid acts, deliberately planned and meticulously executed. Things that left old folk tut-tutting and shaking their heads. Things that made her a *wilful* woman.

Maybe she was a wilful woman, and maybe she should just accept that. The things she'd just heard Enzo say about her made her feel *proud* of Enzo, never mind his stupid friends and the stupid Citizen's Group and the fact that Enzo seemed to be trying too hard to please Asitho Bisumar.

Clearly, they *really* wanted to get into that financial system without anyone being able to track their visit. And that brought her to her second-worst vice: curiosity.

Slowly, Ellisandra carried the tray up to her father's room.

He sat in his usual chair by the fire but, unusual for him, he turned his head and cast a sharp glance at the door the very moment she came in.

"It's only me, with your dinner."

His shoulders slumped as if he'd been holding a straight-backed and upright position for too long. He'd been expecting someone else?

Ellisandra crossed the room and put her tray down on the little table next to him, but when she went to sit down, she noticed that he clutched the fire poker in his hands. "Father? What is the matter?"

"War is coming." His eyes were wide. "They will fall from the sky in flaming ships. They will kill all of us."

What had gotten into him? "No, they won't. Believe me. Give that, before you drop it on your toes." He'd done that before, too, and, being old and frail, his toes were likely to break, and Ellisandra could *really* do without Healer Eydrina Lasko telling her that her father's eyes should be rinsed six times every day—six times!—and he should be made to get up at least three times a day to walk around the room.

The healer was welcome to *try* and tell Father what to do, and besides, where would she get the time to do all those things? She was a theatre director, not a nurse. And it was not as if they hadn't tried employing a nurse either.

She prised the fire poker out of his white-knuckled hands. It normally stood inside the wall recess that held the firebricks, and as she put it back, she wondered how he had managed to get his hands on it. He must have been pretty determined.

"You're mistaken." He pointed at her, his hand trembling. "Did no one tell you, child? There will be a second invasion, and we'll all be killed. We had no mercy on the Coldi prisoners and they'll have no mercy on us."

Where did this come from? He'd been reading the text of the play? "Don't worry, we're here to protect you. It's been a long time since the invasion. Like us, the Coldi will have stopped these barbaric acts." When he was like this, disagreeing with him only made him worse. The best thing was to pick out one bit of his statements, somewhat agree with it, and slowly change the subject.

"War is coming! Their spies are already amongst us."

Only today, that didn't seem to be working. "War will come if you don't eat your dinner." Ellisandra broke the bread into pieces for him.

He was too agitated to eat much and kept trying to get up. "I have to go. The spies are already here. Look out the window."

"I know about the young man rebuilding the Andrahar house. We are keeping a close eye on him."

"No, look out the window!"

Ellisandra went to do as he said, but apart from falling snow, she saw nothing out of the ordinary. The builders had put up two additional frames and sleds had delivered more blocks of stone, which stood in neat rows, all with a cap of snow. There was no one in the yard at the moment, but a faint glow of light came from the shelter against the wall, which was invisible from here. Was Vayra still at work?

"Yes, I see what you mean." She sat down.

Father had either calmed down or forgotten about what had spooked him so much. While he ate, she glanced around the room for clues for why he was so out of sorts, but she found none. After he finished, she wheeled him into the bathroom and washed and changed him ready for bed.

He had never been of sturdy build, but now he was so thin that she feared rough handling would break his bones. She'd been told that old people could break bones just from sitting.

It hurt her to see her strong father so frail and no longer with it.

But for the time being he was warm and safe, and when she tucked him into bed, he put a paper-skinned hand on hers.

"You're my girl. You'll always be my girl."

She kissed him on his forehead. "Good night, Father."

At the door, she realised she was crying. Who would look after Father when she had moved into Jaeron's house?

In the downstairs hallway, she bumped into Enzo, who was just coming back from the door, presumably after having let Asitho Bisumar out.

"Do you know what happened to Father?"

Enzo frowned deeply. "What do you mean what happened? What's wrong with him?"

"Something scared him out of his wits. He was talking about war and spying."

"I have no idea."

"Did you see him at all today?"

Now he looked defensive. "This is not going to be one of your lectures, is it?"

"*One of my lectures?* He's your father, too. I could be forgiven to think that you don't care about him at all."

Enzo stared back. He *didn't* care, but she was still trying to get him to say it out loud so that she could then take it to the Lawkeepers and get the inheritance of the house transferred to her. Because whoever the house belonged to, Father would stay in the house, and that way she got to care for him after she married.

"Don't worry about the old man."

"I do worry. Who will look after him when I'm gone?"

"There will be someone to look after him. I think I have my wedding plans sorted out."

She gaped at him. That was the first she heard of it. "You're getting married?"

"I thought I just said so." He seemed smug about it.

"Who is this woman?"

"I'll announce it when it's ready to be announced."

Then another thought. "You're willing to subject your *wife* to Father's groping?"

"She'll come with experience." He gave a smug smile and went upstairs.

Ellisandra continued to the kitchen with the tray. Her head was reeling. Ever since he had so publicly rejected an offer from the Tussamar family, everyone had assumed that it would be a long time before he married.

If Enzo wasn't joking—and he did sometimes tell deliberate lies about things like this just to see how people reacted—this house would soon belong to him and his new wife.

Jintho sat at the table in the kitchen, eating soup. He met her eyes and smiled.

"Brother. Riana said you were away." She crossed the kitchen and put the tray with Father's dinner things on the bench.

"Change of plan."

"Oh?" With Jintho, changes of plan often meant that he or one of his friends had a run-in with their family.

"We were going to meet at Milohan's house, but his parents decided to stay at home so we decided to forego the meeting." Milohan's parents, of course, were very traditional and highly disapproved of their son's arty friends.

"You could have had the meeting here."

"And run into Asitho Bisumar instead? No, thank you." He laughed a hollow laugh.

"What *are* you doing? What is going on? Is this still about the shop?"

He nodded.

"Is there a problem?" She didn't know what to think about the fact that he hadn't forgotten about it yet.

He spread his hands. "Is there anything that *isn't* a problem? Enzo thinks I'm crazy—"

"Well, then he isn't the only one."

"Yes, but I could sweet-talk you into signing my application, but you are not the one signing."

She put her teacup on the table with a clunk. A good amount of tea sloshed over the edge. "No, I'm just a stupid woman!"

His eyes widened. "I didn't say—"

"Yes, you did, and so does everyone else. We can't tell you about politics, because you're a woman and therefore you can't possibly be interested. We want you to flirt with this man, and your fiancé is going to be as jealous as hell, but this is all right because you're just a pretty face, and this guy is going to tell you everything about himself just because you're a pretty face."

He stared at her. "Who said that?"

"It's about the guy next door. I'm sick of it. Either tell me what it's about or shut up! I'm not just a pretty face."

"But you *are* very pretty, sister."

"Shut up, shut up! You don't get it at all, do you?"

The door to the dining room opened, and Darma appeared in the doorway. Riana and Kalit were behind her.

Ellisandra looked from her brother to the workers. She rose from her seat with such force that her chair fell over, and she strode through the room, pushed herself between Darma and Kalit and ran to the stairs.

Riana called after her. "But mistress, your dinner!"

"I'm not hungry anymore."

12

E LLISANDRA RAN into her room and slammed the door
behind her. She stopped a few paces into the room, her
chest heaving with deep breaths.

Why was everybody in her life so infuriating? Why did they
talk about her behind her back? Why did they act like she was
stupid?

She strode over to the window and yanked the curtains shut,
then stuck her head between them to look outside. The glow from
the shelter behind the wall was clearer from here. It was a greenish
kind of light, a puddle in the darkness.

She thought of how she'd met the stranger there this morning
—Vayra, she should call him by his name. He turned out to be
pretty smart, and yes, he would probably tell her more than he'd
tell the guards if she turned on a pretty smile.

But you know what? She wasn't going to do that. She was not
the kind for pretty smiles and girly giggles. And certainly she
wasn't going to do that to deceive someone, never mind that he
was a foreigner and could probably not be trusted.

She let the curtains fall shut again. It was really a pity about her
temper and dinner, because she was quite hungry. This silly
behaviour of hers would mean that she'd have to get Riana out of

her room later tonight to fix her something, and that would just be embarrassing and cause more gossip. She could already hear Gisandra's mother.

That Takumar girl is much too free. She just says anything that comes into her mind. That's going to cause her problems when she marries.

Yes, probably it would.

Poor Jaeron.

Or poor her.

Asitho Bisumar had hit his first wife. That was why she had run out on him. Was that what these men were telling each other when they met behind doors that were closed to women? *If your wife is wilful, then bring her into line with threats or violence?*

That little word, *wilful* was really starting to make her feel sick.

But most importantly, these men were doing something to Foundation Law, and they were doing it in her name. Enzo was going to vote for it as the holder of the family's seat in the council, and she wanted to know what he was voting for.

She sat down in the chair by the hearth and grabbed the fire poker. Stabbing the firebricks until they fell into a hundred-odd little flaming pieces always made her feel good. The fire rose to a roaring inferno when she did this, and the heat warmed her through.

So, Enzo had trouble naming a thing she wanted that could be bought with money.

She wanted the house in her name, so she could continue to care for Father. No money involved there, because the house already belonged to the family.

She wanted Jintho's shop to succeed, crazy as the idea seemed to her. Jintho badly needed something to go right for him. No money involved there, either.

Thinking about shops, she wanted the shelves of all the shops in Miran to once again be full of interesting things. Fruit from Barresh, clothing from Asto, other items, big and small, from all over the place. She wanted people to be able to buy technology that the council always said Miran would develop, but which hadn't happened for the past twenty years.

Why did no one accept that Miran was a traditional, agricultural nation, which did not have enough people to develop technology that wasn't years behind what everyone else in *gamra* was doing? At least not without help from people from outside Miran, and probably not even then.

That was it: she wanted no money or material things or anything for herself. She wanted the boycotts lifted.

That required the council to vote in favour of dropping restrictions on foreign visits and foreign settlement and investment, and opening their records to *gamra* inspectors. It also required allowing some *gamra* investigations regarding things that had happened in the past, most notably a group of foreign people that had occupied a disused wing of the council buildings. Had they been prisoners? Had they lived there by their own will? This needed to be answered.

Like any of those things were going to happen.

She picked up the law book that still lay on the table from last night. Somewhere in there were rules or safeguards against a minority of families gaining too much power. Somewhere, there were rules about things Foundation families could do that seemed archaic, but had gotten Father so wound up that he'd risen from his wheelchair and walked down the stairs.

She leafed through the pages. There were three extremely thick books with tiny print on the thinnest paper she had ever seen. What were her chances of finding these things before the voting happened?

Father would know, if he had a clear episode, but he'd just had one, and they were usually days apart.

She skimmed past pages to do with criminal behaviour, reading snatches of text.

Once the verdict has been reached, the judge shall have the final word in the punishment. The judge can only be contradicted in cases of capital punishment by the heir of a Foundation family as evidenced by the Foundation token.

That was interesting, but Miran had done away with capital punishment many years ago. Not to say that no prisoners died in jail, but that was supposed to be accidental.

And what was this Foundation token? It wasn't the first time she'd come across the term.

Hang on. She remembered a trip to the library with school when she was little. She'd been an idiot during that trip, by the way, boasting that her father worked in the tower and that she'd already been to the library so very many times—what a cringe-worthy big-mouth moment that had been.

During that excursion, the teacher and a guide had taken the class into some rooms where she had never been before—which a boy named Hiran really liked rubbing in. Seriously, why did she have to think of this now? This was so terribly embarrassing. She had been such a precocious piece of shit as little girl.

It was kind of dark in that room, with a small pool of light in the middle, where there was a glass cabinet. Inside, on a bed of red fabric, lay four silver chains with on them, near-identical pendants made from a simple river stone encircled by a silver band with tiny characters engraved.

The Foundation stones. Each used to belong to a Foundation family, but they had all been handed back after some scandalous event—which she couldn't remember. There were, of course, five families. She was sure there had been four stones, or maybe there were five? Had the teacher said anything about it?

Damn her stupid memory. She'd been much more preoccupied with the embarrassment inflicted by a classmate.

Someone knocked on the door.

Ellisandra snapped the book shut. "Yes?"

"Elli?" That was Jintho's voice.

Ellisandra sighed, put the book on the table, rose and went to open the door.

Jintho stood in the corridor holding a tray with a plate that held a couple of bean patties and oven-roast bread dripping with fragrant herb oil, her favourite.

She stepped aside to let him in. The wonderful smell of food followed in his wake.

"You're hungry, sis?"

"How did you guess?"

"You are really very bad at tantrums. You should look at Enzo more closely. Maybe he can give you lessons." He carried the tray into the room and put it on the table.

Ellisandra snorted and took a big bite from the bread.

Jintho poured two cups of tea, put one on the table near her and took the other one while sitting down in her visitor's chair. "I'm sorry, by the way. I didn't mean to upset you, you know that. You're my favourite sister."

"Not to mention your only one."

He managed to look put out, and then grinned. "Come on, Elli, you can't stay angry if you tried."

"Not at you, I can't, but . . ." She sighed. "Do you have any idea what part of Foundation Law the council wants to change?"

He looked taken aback. "But you wouldn't . . ."

"Be interested in politics? No, I'm not, but something is going on and the only thing I'm asking is for someone to explain what it's about. I'm not dumb and I hate it when everyone treats me like I am."

He let a short silence lapse. "No, I never said you were dumb. I'm sorry, Elli, if I've given you that impression. It's just that—"

"Women are not supposed to ask about politics."

His cheeks went red. "Um. Yeah. That's pretty much it." He looked at his hands. "Pretty stupid, really. Amandra Bisumar was one of the best High Councillors Miran has ever had. Chased out because she had a Coldi lover."

Ellisandra nodded. She knew the story.

"Anyway, if you want to know about Foundation Law, you'd have to ask Enzo—"

"Who won't tell me, because I'm a woman, remember?"

"True. I don't have a clue, to be honest. I don't much care about politics."

And that, precisely, seemed to be the problem. No one cared. "Maybe we should start caring. I gathered from Father that it's something to do with safeguards, and responsibilities of Foundation families. My best guess is they're going to dismantle some safeguards that give Foundation families power over the council. They're going to compensate those families by allowing them to sell their houses or land, or to compensate them for not having been able to sell their property up until now. It's going to cost a lot of money, but they're hoping that they will be free of constraints placed on the council by these laws, which I understand are ancient and have been mostly forgotten."

Jintho stared at her. "And you ask *me* what was going on? You know twice as much as I do."

"I'm only guessing. You know what I think, Jintho? I think we should try to find out what this is about."

"You should go on the council."

It was the second time today that someone had suggested the same thing. "Why does everyone keep saying that? Enzo already has our seat. I very much doubt he'd give it up for me." In fact, the world would end before that happened.

"No, but there is the public section."

"You mean . . ."

"I mean the way Nemedor Satarin entered the council. Being voted into a seat."

"Stop dreaming, brother. All the people in there are Nikala merchants. Why would anyone vote for me? They'd just say that I'm already represented by my family."

"Why would they vote for you? The same reason you want to get in. Because you're a woman and half the Mirani population are also women?"

For a moment, she could see herself standing triumphant in the council assembly hall while people cheered. Then she shook her head. "I don't know how you do this, Jintho."

"Do what?"

"Not only do you get all enthusiastic about your own outrageous schemes, you manage to think up schemes for other people and get *them* all enthusiastic about it."

"Schemes?"

There was so much pain in his voice that she already regretted having used that word. "You know, about opening a shop. Or, for that matter, importing sweets from the coast, or wanting to buy up farms for investment . . ." She counted off on her fingers. She had meant it as a joke, but the pained expression didn't disappear from his face.

"Elli, I'm serious about the shop. I'm going to have to do something to make an income. I can't keep living here anymore." That desperate tone, she knew, too. He'd go into one of these moods on a regular basis.

"Just keep living here while you're looking, all right?" That's what she always said.

"This isn't like any of the other times." He shook his head, his expression distant. Ellisandra wondered if she should ask what was the matter, but whenever she had done this before, he'd always come up with a long story about some trivial concern. Jintho was full of self-doubt. One time a merchant had told him that he disliked the artwork in the bathhouse and he'd spent days moping over that. He had already put on his moping face.

She wasn't in the mood for moping. "By the way, do you know anything about Enzo getting married?"

He gave her a sharp look. "No. It's the first time I've heard. Is he?"

"He says so."

"But what he says and what he ends up doing aren't often the same thing."

"That's true, but I can't see a reason for him to lie."

"I don't know, Elli. Enzo speaks to me as little as he speaks to you. He sure would have mentioned a wedding to Father—"

"Father would have told me."

"Really? I think he's getting worse all the time. There are hardly any moments where he thinks clearly anymore. All he can remember is his bitterness towards Enzo, because he doesn't agree with Enzo's political direction, but often he can't even remember what that direction was supposed to be."

Painful as it was, that was true, too. She considered briefly that Enzo's announcement might have upset Father so much that afternoon, but on other occasions that someone had done something that upset Father, the facts twisted by Father and the stories from other people in the house added up to a complete picture. This was not one of those times.

13

A FTER JINTHO was gone, Ellisandra threw another firebrick on the fire, dragged her chair closer and went back to the book of Foundation Law.

As soon as she opened the pages and the musty smell of the unused book hit her, she felt sleepy. The intense cold of the theatre always made her tired, something she didn't usually notice until she sat at home by the fire and her cheeks glowed and her hands pricked with sensation coming back into them.

She forced herself to read the first page. The section that detailed ancient Foundation Law wasn't very big. It was the exceptions and amendments that had been made afterwards that made the law books cumbersome. Sections like the one she'd been reading before Jintho came in. She'd lost where that was, and although the information was interesting, it was not what she needed. Obviously, she wasn't going to find the section dealing with safeguards by leafing randomly through the pages, so she was going to start right at the beginning.

Across the first page was written in big letters,

Foundation Law

Underneath that, in smaller letters,

*To aid and guide the harmonious co-existence of the people of the cave and
the people of the mountain.*

That's what they used to call the Endri and Nikala, with the
Endri being the cave people. They'd always been known as soft
and delicate and unsuited to hard work.

She turned the next page.

Section 1.

*It is recognised that the location of the pass and the adjacent valleys,
known as Miran, was first settled by the cave people. It is recognised that
they built the first dwellings and ploughed the first fields. Therefore, by
designation of this law, they own the land and the buildings on it.*

*It is recognised that the mountain people work on the fields and
within the walls of the town, that they deserve compensation for their
work. They deserve sustenance, accommodation and care for as long as
they remain on this land or in the buildings.*

*It is recognised that these two halves make Miran. That one is incom-
plete without the other, and that the other is unsafe, hungry and cold
without the one. This is law.*

Ellisandra knew those words off by heart. Every Mirani child
learned them at school. When she was young, Foundation was the
heart of every Mirani organisation and decision. Both peoples had
their tasks, and the Endri's task was to *give the workers housing and
food and care for their sick and their leisurely well-being.* That was
where the theatre came in and why so many Endri women worked
in the hospitals.

Did children still learn Foundation?

Of course, because the mutual responsibilities rendered the
society almost without money, nothing in Miran was worth
anything except when traded with another Mirani person. The Endri
were rich only within Miran, and unless a family sold outside Miran
—which a fair few used to do before the boycotts—there would be

little wealth and money that could be taken out of the country. That was the main disparity within the Endri class. Some of them *could* leave because they had real money. Many of them could not. That was what the first conflict in the council, the one that had resulted in the Foundation families being ousted from the High Council, had been about. That was what almost every conflict in Miran was about: imports and exports that undermined Miran's unique economy.

She turned the page and arrived at a description of the composition of the council—then consisting only of Endri. The High Council had originally consisted of a representative of each of the five Foundation families, and each had been given the right to veto decisions made by the council. She could imagine that situation had soon become unworkable.

The Calthunar family was the first to go when their main heir remained childless. According to the stories, he was a strange character who became involved with a young woman who was later murdered. In one of the most public cases in Miran, he had been convicted and sentenced to death. But because a section of the council didn't believe his guilt, there had been a delay in his sentencing, during which someone had let him escape. Who had done this, and whether the family line was still alive, was one of the great mysteries of Miran.

When he had gone, only four Foundation families remained. For many years, the Andrahar, Ilendar, Velisar and Takumar family representatives had made up the four remaining seats in the High Council. Everyone got on relatively well, the council was mostly in agreement with each other and no one had ever used the right of veto.

However, the distinct power imbalance increasingly caused tension. Andrahar and Ilendar were both Trading families, incredibly wealthy both inside Miran and out. They viewed the Invasion as quaint history, because they had Coldi colleagues, friends and even lovers, and sold handsomely to Asto. They saw no need to keep adhering to the most important Mirani pastime of hating

Asto and the Coldi people—not that the Coldi saw Miran as of enough importance to hate them back.

The Velisar and Takumar families had been much more traditional, part of the Mirani barter economy whose wealth only held in Miran and who had no interest in allowing foreign influences and foreign money—which, to be honest, was something people would have to accept eventually if they wanted a better life.

Ilendar and Andrahar wanted to introduce a proper currency.

Velisar and Takumar argued that a currency would encourage investment from outside Miran and it would breach Foundation Law.

The argument went on for so long that the resulting stalemate had lasted more than a year, during which the council had not been able to make their normal decisions. There was claim after counterclaim from the High Councillors, each of whom demanded that the others left. Eventually a councillor got them all to do something illegal based on a technicality and managed to dismiss the High Council. The Foundation family heirs couldn't work together anymore. The High Council broke up and became a body elected by the people out of a list of candidates put forward by the existing council. It was not much later that the Nikala were allowed to stand for election because it became clear that the Endri population was in decline through infertility in many of the women. And about thirty years ago, the public section had been instated, thirty seats that were open to anyone, Endri or Nikala, and decided by general election. Most of those seats were held by Nikala, because Endri were represented by their family heir.

But what about the old laws?

Did anyone still have the right to veto? Did Father still have it, or Enzo?

What were the rules surrounding it?

She flicked to the later pages of the book, but there was so much small text on those pages and the language was all so dry that she stared at it without reading anything. She was too tired for this. There was too much to absorb in these books for her to do it within just a few days.

Maybe she should ask Father about the veto right. He enjoyed being asked questions. Whether his answers were correct was another matter.

~

But when she lay in bed, she couldn't get to sleep. Thoughts churned inside her head.

Enzo's comments on what she wanted, and his and Jintho's suggestion that she might want to stand for the council really got her thinking. It was all very well to keep saying that she wasn't interested in politics, because that was what the men wanted her to say. But the council was where the decisions were made, and if she was interested in those decisions, then she supposed she *was* interested in politics.

The book of Foundation Law told her that any Mirani of adult age regardless of family status could stand for the public section of the council, which made up a third of the general assembly. Membership of the public section was determined by vote. Voting wasn't compulsory, and most Endri didn't bother, because they felt that the public section was not about them.

This was also how Nemedor Satarin had come in, because back then many Endri had a thing or two to say about his rise in popularity and might have bothered turning up to vote against him had they known how long he was going to stay and how powerful he was going to be.

Since coming to power through the Nikala vote, he had unified people behind him. The fact that he'd made a solid stand against outrageous accusations against Miran by foreign interests had been a huge help. Miran was proud. Rather than comply with invasive investigations, they'd put up with boycotts. No one dictated to Miran what to do. And predictably *gamra* had reacted with its own boycott, so that no one could buy any of Miran's produce either.

The trouble was that the mutual boycott had hurt Miran much worse than it had hurt the rest of *gamra*. And that over the years information had come out that some of those accusations hadn't been so outrageous after all.

So, considering all the facts, she supposed that proposing the removal of the boycotts meant . . .

Standing against Nemedor Satarin.

Damn it. That thought scared the hell out of her. Go out there and publicly nominate herself? Run campaigns for next year's election? That was too much right now. She had the play to organise, Father to look after, a wedding to get ready for. She'd reconsider going into the council later . . . when she was married.

As if Jaeron would let her do anything of the sort. Who was she kidding?

No, the best time to declare, and run a campaign, would be when she'd finished the play and had properly upset the entire council with her interpretation of it, and if the people showed any sign of understanding the message behind her interpretation. If they wanted change. If they were ready for a fight.

That was a big if.

If she stepped into the role, there would be no easy solutions and no second chances. There might be no easy life and no marriage either.

That was just way too scary to contemplate.

But she owed it to Miran to do *something*, because she'd hate herself for the rest of her life if the council made a bad decision and she'd had the opportunity to try and stop them, but had done nothing.

~

It was still dark when she rose, got dressed and went to eat breakfast in the kitchen. Riana was already up, re-kneading the bread she had been working on yesterday.

"You're up early, mistress."

"Big day at the theatre. A lot of work to be done." She tried to be matter-of-fact about it, but was unsure if she came off convincing. Riana tended to have a pretty good sense for when something was up.

A layer of snow had fallen thick enough to create a small measure of chaos, even in a place where water only fell as snow, and where big snow mounds were a fact of life.

As he usually did on big snow days, Kalit had risen early to shovel a path to the gate, but so much of it had fallen that he was still hacking with the snow pick to make enough room for the gate to open. While he jiggled and pushed the gate, Ellisandra took the snow shovel and shoved as much of it as she could away from the entrance.

"You shouldn't be doing that, mistress. Go back inside where it's warm."

"I need to get out, and I'm a healthy girl, so let me just do this for you while you sort out the gate."

Both of them shovelled and chipped in amicable silence. Ellisandra got nice and warm from the work and it helped her take her mind off her troubles.

While she was working, a lot of people came past. A path one sled wide would have been cleared by snowploughs on tiyuk sleds before dawn. It seemed unusually busy in the street, even when accounting for further clearing sleds going up and down to widen the cleared path. Each time, the scoop at the front pushed more snow aside. This, of course, got progressively harder the more snow had been removed off the central part of the street, so a few tiyuk nomad men had come with a snow press and were busily working the mounds into neat compressed blocks. These were piled along the sides of the street to be picked up later. The joke went that moving snow around was a major business in Miran.

In addition to this, it looked like there was some to-do at the

Andrahar house. A group of builders stood around in the street talking to each other and someone with a sled full of materials had stopped at the gate, presumably because the snow hadn't been cleared enough for him to get into the yard, but by the looks of things, people were working on it.

It was amazing how many people this one man employed. There were even some guards chatting with all of them. Good. The guards would give the council the information they wanted, and she wouldn't have to spy anymore, much less confront Nemedor Satarin about not wanting to do that.

By the time she arrived at the theatre, the morning sun had just cleared the horizon. It was later than she had wanted to come in, but fortunately still before anyone else turned up for work. She opened the back door—why had she never noticed how much it creaked?—and changed her shoes in the foyer. It was cold and empty here without anyone around. Her footsteps echoed in the empty halls, and the mannequins with the old costumes looked like they might come alive, as if they were spies that would tell everyone about the thing that she was about to do.

She went to the corner of the library, to the little desk from where she had sent the requests to the printer, and turned on the reader. The screen lit up with soft greenish light that was characteristic of light pearls.

She sat down at the desk. In the drawer she kept a small book with instructions on how to access all of the theatre's different administration systems. To find each section, she had stuck in little tags that indicated where a new section started. She opened it at the Financial System tag.

Normally she would access this system at the end of every month. She guessed that checking funds available for buying materials was a valid reason for looking in the system at this time, and it wouldn't arouse suspicion, she hoped—though she normally wouldn't do it.

When she finished looking at the theatre accounts, she hesitated. On the screen was a list of other accounts in the Accountkeepers' credit system, the ones she had sworn to keep confidential.

With her head turned to the door, she held her breath, listening out for footsteps. There were none, so she typed *Ilendar*.

A list of accounts came up, mostly of minor Ilendar families.

The least active accounts were usually at the bottom, and she didn't find the Ilendar Traders account there. She scrolled back to the top, and there it was. Last accessed three days ago.

She checked over her shoulder again. Her hand hovered over the screen. This was not right. She shouldn't be here. When she had made the confidentiality agreement, she had signed that she would respect the privacy of others.

It was still respecting privacy if she told no one about this, right?

She selected the Ilendar Traders account.

A wall of figures came up. Ellisandra stared at the page while her mind worked out what she was seeing.

Money. Staggering amounts of it. Transfers of huge sums. From Tussamar Traders for the sale of a house, about ten years ago. So Enzo had been right about that.

Also for other things, less clearly specified. There was no amount less than a hundred thousand, most vastly more than that. And to think that Loret and his men considered two tirans a day a very good pay. Heck, she considered it a good pay. Her entire yearly theatre budget was only about two thousand, and that was plenty, because most things were cheap.

Wow, she had no idea that Traders were this rich. Even richer than she thought because when they left Miran, they had abandoned this money.

It was very clear from the account when they had departed Miran, too, because transfers had stopped abruptly.

And then, three days ago, someone had taken out a smaller amount. The description of the transfer said *maintenance*, the account where it had gone was that of a business in Miran that sold building materials. This was followed the next day by another withdrawal entry called *rentals*, with a company name she didn't recognise. The next line was for a domestic supplies store for *plates, cups, pans, cutlery* and a hefty payment to a supplier of food, as well as a generous payment to the animal markets, presumably to pay for the use of sleds or pack animals.

By now, she was almost certain that this was Vayra using the account.

Well, that was one problem solved.

She couldn't see what business this was of anyone's, certainly not the council's. The privacy of Endri families was to be upheld. If the Ilendar Traders had wanted to sell their house and the Tussamar Traders wanted it, then no one needed to know how much money had changed hands. She gathered the council wanted to know the amount so that they had an idea of the market value of property that expatriate Mirani Endri had to be compensated for, but that was no reason to break trust. Without a better explanation, she certainly wasn't going to give them that information.

While she had been in the library, people had arrived for work. The foyer inside the door was a mess of outdoor boots and molten snow, and someone had taken off with the pair of house shoes that she usually wore. The only pair left was much too big and the heels dragged on the ground when she walked. That earned her some raised eyebrows from the members of the orchestra as she crossed the downstairs hall.

Tolaki and the actors had ensconced themselves in the upstairs hallway, because *It's not as cold in here as on that stage,* but the room was cramped and the group was in the way, especially since they had to speak loudly in loud projecting voices, and because they had to be able to hear each other over the sound of the orchestra which was rehearsing downstairs. Was she imagining things or was the orchestra missing players? If they didn't start to improve quickly, this was going to be a problem. Where could they find a couple of good players, especially since the state orchestra had their own very busy winter programme?

"Hey, Elli, what was all the to-do at the Andrahar house?" Tolaki asked.

"I don't know. Was anything going on?" It had been very busy, but she'd seen nothing unusual.

"There were a lot of people standing in the street. I walked past and someone said people had stolen things from the site last night."

"Had they? I noticed all the people, but no one said anything about what they were doing there. I don't walk in that direction, and I was already running late so didn't have time to go for a chat."

Tolaki chuckled. "Isn't that typical. You have the best seat in the house, and you still miss it. You can see everything from that window of yours. I bet you could even have seen who had done it."

"Well, I sleep at night. The house next door is not that interesting." Besides, she had looked, and had seen nothing that warranted further attention.

Ellisandra went into her office, threw a firebrick onto the fire for all the good that would do in this draughty building, drew her cloak and scarf close around her and then sat down at her desk. She started sketching the stage designs so that Loret and his team could start to work on them when they arrived. She shut out the noise from the actors in the corridor and the music from downstairs. Having grown up in a household with two brothers, noise didn't bother her overly much. Her pile of drawings grew steadily, and it wasn't until mid-morning when Tolaki came in to warm herself by the fire that she realised someone was missing.

"Have you seen Sariandra?"

"No." Tolaki said, and then frowned. "I thought she'd gone to market."

"She would have asked me for the accounts if she had." And

her father might not have approved of her going to the markets alone.

Ellisandra went into the drawing room. Sariandra's workbook lay open on the table. Across the pages were sketches of men and women in old costumes in exquisite detail. "Have you seen this?"

Tolaki came into the room and looked over Ellisandra's shoulder. "Oh, wow. This is really amazing. Did she do these?"

Ellisandra nodded. "Apparently she used to work for merchant Ranuddin."

"Really? I've never seen her around here." And Tolaki knew almost everyone in the commercial quarter, either through her family's business, or because she spent a good amount of time outside with the actors, rehearsing and advertising the plays.

"She said the merchant used to feed his workshop workers and she never went outside at midday."

Tolaki frowned. "That doesn't sound like merchant Ranuddin. He's a pinchpenny and would be all too happy to let his workers pay for their own meals. In fact I know they used to go out."

Ellisandra felt sick. She had more or less told Sariandra to come with her yesterday. Sariandra had gone upstairs and deliberately left her reader thing on the table. She had been nervous and jumpy, not because of anything Ellisandra said, but because she was afraid that someone would report it back to her father that his daughter had done something as silly as go out for a meal at midday.

Everyone said Asitho Bisumar was a control freak. Why had she not seen the signs?

She stared at the beautiful drawings, her heart pounding.

Could it be that someone had reported that Sariandra had gone outside and mingled with strangers, and now her father kept her at home?

That was just awful.

Deep in her heart, she desperately didn't want to see Asitho Bisumar again, but there was only one way to solve this: she had to talk to Sariandra's family.

The Bisumar family was not one of those considered the core Endri families of Miran. They lived on the very high side of town, in the quiet area between Ellisandra's house and the old city walls. It was a nice area in which the houses were more modern, but smaller and closer together than where she lived.

Today everything was covered under a thick layer of snow. The main Endri families employed groundsmen whose task it was to clear snow, stamp it into blocks and leave it in the street for the sleds to collect. In the minor Endri quarter, yards were too small to justify a groundsman, and because the houses were closer together, the spaces between them acted as snow traps. There were huge mounds, most as yet uncleared.

Asitho Bisumar's house looked very tidy in comparison, with snow swept out of the yard down to the tiles. Someone had spent a lot of time doing this. Where had they put the snow?

Lights burned in the rooms to the side of the door. When Ellisandra knocked, there were footsteps and the door was opened by a very old and very bow-legged man. She hoped he wasn't the one having to clear the yard.

He gave a quaint little bow. "How can I help the lady?" He used old-fashioned language that acknowledged her status as a member of a Foundation family. Funny that, coming from a servant to someone who wanted to abolish that special status.

"I'd like to see Sariandra and talk to her father, if he's at home."

"Certainly. Come with me."

He preceded her across the hall into a door directly opposite, which turned out to lead to the dining room. It was warm in here, and the family sat at the table for the midday meal, Asitho at the head, his wife to his right and daughter to his left.

"Master, there is someone to see you."

As soon as Ellisandra entered, Sariandra's eyes grew wide.

"Lady," Asitho Bisumar said. "Do sit down. Do you want some tea?"

Ellisandra had just drunk tea at the theatre, but it would be impolite to refuse.

The bow-legged servant bustled with a cup and the teapot, making just enough noise to dispel the uneasy silence.

Asitho's wife looked young enough to be Sariandra's sister. Her name was Ielandra. If Ellisandra remembered correctly, she was from a minor branch of the Ilendar family who had dissociated themselves from the Ilendar Traders, one of the first Traders to leave Miran.

There were all sorts of rumours surrounding the marriage, including that because Asitho's first two daughters were infertile, he'd arranged that she would share his bed on agreed nights and he would only marry her if she fell pregnant. At the time, she'd been an adolescent, and had been very slight. The birth had damaged her so much that she had never fallen pregnant again.

The woman had a thin and narrow face, in which her eyes looked unnaturally large. The only time Ellisandra had seen her was when Asitho brought her to the theatre for performances. Sariandra looked more like her mother than her father: thin, large-eyed and shy.

"I missed you at the theatre today," Ellisandra said, feeling the penetrating gaze of Asitho on her and doing her best to ignore it.

Sariandra's cheeks had gone bright red. She looked at her hands which she held folded in her lap under the table.

Asitho said, in a definitive tone, "My daughter needed some time to think."

What was that supposed to mean? Ellisandra continued to talk to Sariandra. "I was concerned about you. I looked at your drawings and they are really good. I'd like you to make those costumes."

"My daughter has some important decisions to make," Asitho continued as if Ellisandra had said nothing.

She turned to him. "Any decisions that are so important that she cannot take part in the theatre production?"

"My daughter has a wedding to plan."

Sariandra let her head hang further. A tear ran down her nose and hung there at the very tip.

Wedding? What sort of odd situation had she walked into? "Please. I don't need to know any of the details. I just want your daughter to come back and help us in the theatre, because we'll be stuck otherwise."

"Someone spotted my daughter in the eating house at the Civic corner yesterday."

"That was my fault, I—"

"I was given assurance that she would be provided with food by the theatre company."

"That is what normally happens, but yesterday the food ran out, so I asked her to come with me. If that was the wrong thing to do, my apologies. I didn't know." Heck, this had to be the strangest family she had come across.

He nodded. Whether it was an agreement or acknowledgement she didn't know. "You said my daughter's work was good?"

"Yes, it is. It's very good. She knows a lot about period costumes and knows all the details. She will be an asset to the theatre. If you're concerned about something, I will personally make sure that she is looked after in the way you want."

He thought about that for a while. "Your personal guarantee, right?"

"Yes."

"Your guarantee that she won't mingle with people from outside the theatre?"

"If that is your wish, yes." Not that she could see why, but that was another story.

He met her gaze squarely and she returned the stare of those pale blue eyes. If this was how he treated his family, no wonder his previous wife had walked out on him.

"Maybe my daughter doesn't want to work for the theatre anymore."

"Maybe we shouldn't talk over her head. Ask her."

"My daughter does not deserve the option of answering questions."

Sariandra's cheeks grew even redder.

What the hell was going on here? Ellisandra had to bite her tongue. If she hadn't needed Sariandra so badly, she would have shown him a piece of her mind, and it wouldn't have been a very nice piece, either. "I will guarantee that she doesn't leave the theatre anymore, except with one of us on theatre business. Can I point out that she *was* on work business yesterday. We discussed the play."

His lips twitched.

"It's not going to look good if she is to withdraw from the production now. We have enough trouble already finding the right people." Like good musicians for that blasted orchestra. "I can't afford to lose anyone. This is for the council year's opening. The play is a favourite of Nemedor Satarin's. He's been watching our rehearsals."

He blew out a deep breath. "You promise?"

"Yes, I promise. And I'd like to take her back with me right now. The production isn't too far away and we really can't waste time."

He laughed. "And I'm wasting your time."

Oops. Her cheeks grew hot. "We are a theatre company. We don't have parties, we don't go out. No one drinks at work. We don't discuss politics. I'm about business. I need the play to be performed. I need costumes to be made."

"You amuse me. All right. Take her. But if anything happens to her it will be on your watch."

"I'll take the risk."

"Can I go?" Sariandra asked, her wide-eyed gaze on her father.

"If you wish."

Sariandra shot up from the table as if she had been sitting on a spring. She ran into the hallway, simultaneously wiping tears from her face.

Ellisandra followed after having made polite farewells. In the hallway, she was almost swept off her feet by Sariandra's hug.

"Whoa, whoa, calm down."

"Thank you, thank you. I want to go back so badly!"

"Well, be quiet now. Let's go."

Without speaking much, they put on their boots and cloaks, walked through the yard to the gate and into the street.

"Thank you so much for coming. I'll be grateful forever. I thought he was going to lock me up, and—"

"I don't know what is wrong with going outside for something to eat or why he kept you home. I'm not sure I want to know or that you should tell me, but you can stay at the theatre for as long as you like." Then she remembered something Asitho had said. "Are you getting married soon?"

"Yes." The joy vanished from her eyes. Her shoulders slumped.

"Did you know that when you came to us?" How old was she anyway? Too young to be married, Ellisandra thought.

"No, it was only recently arranged." Sariandra sniffed.

Ellisandra put an arm around her shoulders.

So, here was another girl being married off to stop her from being wilful. And being wilful in Asitho Bisumar's house obviously justified being married off to the first available candidate.

14

ON THE WALK back to the theatre, Sariandra chatted about dresses and fabrics and in fact wouldn't shut up, so that Ellisandra suspected she didn't want to be quizzed about what had been going on at home. But her cheeks were red and she seemed happy and Ellisandra didn't need to know any more. She knew what older men did to their daughters when they failed to obey. The fact that she could see no bruises didn't mean that there were none. The fact that Asitho's former wife was a very timid woman who had felt so desperate that she had seen no other option but to leave was another sign. Everyone knew that he was a hardline manipulative bastard.

To be honest, she didn't understand why Nemedor Satarin was happy to have this arrogant, controlling prick in the High Council. She thought better of him. She thought better of all the other councillors, too, but obviously, they were standing by while all this had gone on. They'd even promoted Asitho Bisumar to the High Council *after* his former wife had made no secret of how he had treated her. Come to think of it, did Sariandra's mother ever leave the house? Were their lives worthless just because they were Endri *women?*

Damn it, she was getting really angry about this. That slow-burning anger that got her into trouble.

It started to snow again, a heavy drift of fine snowflakes that whirled in the wind and added to the snow banks already on the lee side of walls.

In the draughty halls and passages of the theatre, it felt like it was only marginally warmer inside than outside. A couple of men walked past carrying wire webbing of the type that Loret would hammer to constructed frames. He would then cover these with fabric and spread cement over the fabric until it resembled an old wall or rock face or whatever the script required. He had become really good at making these backgrounds.

Strains of music came from the main hall, mixed with the sounds of hammering.

That was odd. They looked like Loret's men. They were not supposed to be here until later.

While Sariandra went upstairs, Ellisandra went through the backstage area onto the main stage and found Loret and his team working there. The stage itself was a giant revolving platform, subdivided into three sections that would be turned for each act. Loret and his men were on the section of the platform that would display the setting for the final act.

"What are you doing here?" Ellisandra asked.

" 'S no work when it's snowing like this. 'S too dangerous, so we thought we'd make a start here. Found th' drawings on yer desk. Sorry if I wasn' supposed t' go into th' room, lady."

"It's fine. You're a gem, Loret. You know that."

He grinned a gap-toothed grin.

That was why she liked this team. They needed no explanation or instructions, because they had done this type of work before and they were competent and independent workers.

She and Loret spent some time discussing the building of the fake prison based on Ellisandra's rough sketches: where the main wall needed to go, what the floor should be made out of, because if she went ahead with her interpretation of the play, she wanted the fake blood to pool and drip off rather than be absorbed.

Loret suggested, "We could put a layer of wax on th' boards. That would make them water-repellent."

Then they discussed how many cell doors there should be in the main wall, where the lighting was going to be and how much light the set required.

"It should be fairly dark because we're supposed to be underground. You remember how you did that old house last time with the mossy-looking walls? It would be great if you could make something like that."

Loret said that he could and Ellisandra was happy with progress made here.

At least this part of the production seemed under control.

When Ellisandra was about to go to the office, she noticed a single person sitting in the middle of the many empty rows of audience seats.

It was Vayra.

She froze.

He sat huddled in a thick cloak, one of the heavy, mottled type. His silver hair hung loose over his shoulders. The golden tinge wasn't as obvious in the semidarkness of the hall. There was nothing in his face or clothing that suggested he wasn't a Mirani Endri.

She hadn't noticed him before. Had he been sitting there watching all the time she was on the stage?

Loret must have seen her watch him. "That's jus' our other boss. Youz know him, right? He's got nothing t' do either, what with th' guards crawling all over th' site trying t' find th' thieves who took off with his building materials."

"I heard a bit about that. Were many things stolen?"

"Enough t' create trouble."

"That's terrible. Has anyone been caught yet?"

"No, but some things have already been found, 'cause it was easy t' follow th' tracks of stuff being dragged through th' snow.

Looks like they jus' wanted t' disrupt us. A warning, like. They'd
have been jealous workers, 'cause we got th' good jobs."

That was just one of the possibilities. She could think of many
more disturbing scenarios, some involving both her brothers. "Has
he reported it to the guards?"

"He doesn' work like that. He went t' th' markets to hire some
guards. He doesn' trust th' guards. I wouldn' either, if I were
him."

Did she detect a measure of loyalty to a foreigner in his words?

Loret seemed to understand what she was thinking. "It's a
beautiful house he's building, lady. I'd hate people t' destroy th'
work. Besides, he's doing all th' right things by us. No one else is
payin' us that much, and giving us damn good soup, if youz
pardon th' expression."

Vayra met her eyes across the empty rows of seating. She could
probably have told him that he was going to have trouble.

Ellisandra wasn't sure if she should go to him, or if talking to
him could have any unforeseen consequences. For one, if people
saw her taking to him, they might tell Nemedor Satarin and he
might come back to bother her with questions. Also, she was sure
that Vayra didn't meet the "approved persons" list that Asitho
allowed to come into contact with his daughter. If word got out
that he'd been inside the theatre at the same time Sariandra was in
the building, would she be berated for it?

And then she was angry with herself that she should care about
something like that. This dancing to influential men's orders was
not something she either liked or was very good at.

It wouldn't worry her so much if Asitho Bisumar didn't control
much of the theatre's funding. She'd be happy to jeopardise her
own livelihood by talking back to him, but not that of her
colleagues.

While she stood there in indecision, Vayra solved her dilemma
by rising and coming to the edge of the stage. He gave a little
formal bow. "Good morning, lady." His sand-coloured eyes met
hers. "Good morning." What a strange colour. Any brown eyes she

had seen had been dark brown. His eyes were pale brown in the way Endri eyes were pale blue.

"My apologies if I unnerve you or your workers. Unfortunately, there won't be much work done on the house today with this weather."

Interesting that he said nothing about the thievery. He had to have some idea of the feelings of distrust people had towards him.

He continued, "*Changing Fate* is not an easy play to pull off well." He looked around the stage. "I look forward to seeing the performance. I've seen only a recording."

"Recordings exist?" She had never heard of any.

"Yes, as part of the cultural education program, the Mirani council used to pay for all plays to be recorded. There is an archive of them which you can access if you know where to look. You can watch all the plays. It's a bit old and the quality is not the best. The recording of *Changing Fate* is from before I was born."

"When did you watch this?"

"When I was a boy. My teacher made me watch all the classic plays. I think they show a fascinating side of the history of that time. The fear of *the other* is palpable in those plays."

Hang on. "*You* watched the plays as part of your schooling in Barresh?"

"I had a very thorough teacher." He smiled.

Now that was unnerving. Not even Mirani children watched more than one or two classic plays. They usually did so when the theatre had school days, and they performed an easily accessible play, like *The Invasion*.

"Why?"

"Because they're beautiful. I love Mirani theatre. Is that wrong?"

"Well, no, of course not, but . . ."

"You've always been forced to watch plays as a kid and most people here think they're boring?"

She chuckled. "Pretty much. I like them, though. They're full of drama."

"Of course. You wouldn't be here if you didn't."

Truth be told, she loved *working* in the theatre much more than the actual plays. She loved the independence, she loved completing a production. As far as the art was concerned, she would love to work in modern theatre, but there just wasn't the money in it. The classics were history, the modern pieces were political commentary, and everyone knew what the council had to say about that.

There was a small, awkward silence, in which Ellisandra really wanted to say that she should go back upstairs and continue to work, but was afraid he might consider it impolite. She could ask about the break-in, but he might say something that she didn't want to have to report to the council.

Again, he solved the awkwardness. "I was wondering . . . The weather is going to be pretty foul for the next couple of days. Could you use an extra player in the orchestra?"

"Do you play?"

"I've played quite a lot of Mirani music."

"What instrument?"

"The flute."

Yes! "Are you any good?" She tried not to sound too keen. It would be too much to hope for that his skills were adequate.

"I'm competent."

"Come with me." She jerked her head at the backstage area. He ran to the side stairs and climbed up. Again, she noticed just how tall he was. Easily as tall as Enzo. Very Endri.

In the back room, the orchestra was just taking a break, with most of the players gathered around a trolley where one of the theatre people was serving tea and cakes. The room was filled with chatter and laughter.

Aleyo stood at the conductor's dais, flicking through the score. When Ellisandra came in with her charge, she raised her eyebrows over the sea of empty chairs.

"Can we borrow a flute?"

One of the players put her tea down and went to get her instrument, which she handed to Ellisandra.

Vayra took it from her.

"You want a score?"

He shook his head. He raised the instrument to his mouth, closed his eyes and started playing. Within a few notes, she recognised the solo from the Lover's Dance. The warm notes filled the hall The musicians who were gathered around the tea trolley stopped chatting and turned to watch. Tolaki appeared at the top of the stairs, staring down at him. Her mouth fell open. Even Aleyo, who would normally rather die than admit that someone else did something right, was looking on with more than casual interest. She would know very well that the orchestra had problems.

More and more people were coming into the hall, crowding around others. The builders, the seamstresses, the other theatre workers. Everyone looked on with wide eyes.

When Vayra had finished there was a moment of intense silence in which the last note died in the echoes of the building.

Then one of the orchestra players cheered, and someone else started clapping, and soon, everyone in the hall applauded, including Aleyo.

Vayra gave a flourishing bow, and handed the flute back to its owner. The lady blushed.

Ellisandra knew two things: one, they needed him badly, and two, she had secretly hoped that his playing wouldn't be any good so that she wouldn't have to face the decision of whether it was appropriate to have a foreigner play in a Mirani theatre performance.

He rejoined her. "Do you think I passed?"

"You call that merely *competent*? Where did you learn to play like that?"

"Our teachers made us play music. Playing instruments is very important in Barresh."

"But Mirani music?"

"All kinds of music. Rest assured that we spent enough time being taught *betanka* rhythms as well."

She repeated the strange word. *"Betanka?"*

"It's a five-beat dance rhythm, native to Barresh. It goes like this." He went over to a chair and beat a rhythm on the seat of three beats and then two and then three and two. "And there are variations like this." He made some of the beats shorter or longer, while they still fit in that basic three-two pattern. "Someone beats this on a drum and there is music over the top." He kept beating the rhythm and sang a strange tune with words in a language she had never heard before and that she was sure had never been spoken between these walls. "The trick is to never lose your rhythm, no matter what you do and what happens."

He said all this while still beating the seat of the chair.

"It's Pengali dance music, but it's very popular with visitors, including many Mirani Nikala who work in Barresh."

"Pengali?"

"They're one of the two native peoples of Barresh. They're quite small, nocturnal and have patterned skin and tails."

"Tails?"

Maramarang had tails, which broadened out with flanges in flight. They used them for steering. Tiyuk had tails, but only very short furry ones. They were said to cover the animal's private parts in cold weather. But people with tails?

"They use them for sign language and for picking up things."

It was strange. It was awkward. Here she was, directing the Mirani theatre, supposedly well-educated by Mirani standards, yet she knew nothing of the world beyond the borders, let alone about other worlds. She felt so inadequate and dumb. It was unlikely that he came here to show Mirani people how dumb they were, but right now, she felt like that. Not only that, he was giving everyone a lesson in *How to be Mirani* in the old, honour-based, traditional style, having been taught by a family now considered an enemy of the state.

That was sure to catch the council's attention.

Not only that, employing him would get *her* more attention. There would be outrage. She could already hear the protests. *Why do we have foreigners playing in the orchestra? Aren't there enough competent musicians in our own town?*

And yes, maybe there were, but no musicians that had ever offered their services, because playing in the theatre orchestra was not a very glamorous thing.

Everyone was looking at her, waiting for her to make a decision.

What to do?

Aleyo was looking at her with an intense expression. "Come on, Elli. Let him play."

"Do you want him to?"

"Of course I do. Is there a problem?"

"Come." Ellisandra grabbed the sleeve of Aleyo's dress and guided her to the folds of curtains that made up the backstage area. She was aware that Vayra watched her.

"I'm thinking of what the council is going to say about foreigners playing in the orchestra," she told Aleyo in a low voice.

"What are you talking about? He's Mirani. Everyone can see that."

"Have you seen his eyes? He's not Mirani. He's from Barresh, and he's Aghyrian. I'm pretty sure he dyes his hair and tries to look Mirani. He's pretty convincing, but no one will be fooled. The council is already keeping an eye on him. If we take him on, we'll have trouble."

"What ill can he do on his own, through the orchestra?" Aleyo spread her hands.

Ellisandra wanted to say *Buy everyone's favour and loyalty with really good pay and damn fine soup and a beautiful project* but that would require her to talk about Nemedor Satarin's order to spy on the foreigner and Aleyo might think that *she* was a spy for Nemedor Satarin in the way some people were recruited to give information about their friends that seemed harmless enough at the time, but came back to bite them later.

When she said nothing, Aleyo continued, "Look, I know one thing. If the music doesn't improve, the trouble will be on us after the performance. Those two flute ladies are very nice and might have been competent musicians around the time I was born, but they are no longer. Let him play. We're not doing anything political."

"Guess not."

So Vayra was allowed to stay. Ellisandra still felt uneasy about it. He was very nice and polite and she didn't want him to come to any harm, and she could feel the dark forces move in the shadows. Someone would strike at him, and it might come through her contacts with him. He would not be prepared for it, and he would not have deserved it. Worse, her brothers might have something to do with it.

And she'd promised Asitho Bisumar that his daughter would not associate with undesirable characters and now there was one of those right inside the building. How long would it be before he found out?

For most of the afternoon, Ellisandra sat at her desk listening to the music that drifted up from downstairs. She thought it already sounded better. She hoped. Whenever she went to the door of the office and looked down into the hall, Vayra was either playing or talking to the ladies next to him. He seemed effortlessly popular, as if he'd been born to a high-profile life. He looked so incredibly Endri, down to the little mannerisms. Except for those eyes that kept looking up and meeting her.

So, he was saying that he'd been taught by the Andrahar family? If so, they hadn't lost any of their Mirani habits.

Father used to talk a lot about the time of the great Mirani Traders, when the trifecta of Andrahar, Ilendar and Tussamar families ruled the Mirani chapter of the Trader Guild and when all the merchants flocked to that building every morning to get the best imported deals. These days, only the Tussamar Traders remained, and they had never been quite as successful as the other families. What would life in Miran be like if those families had never left? What would it be like if some of them came back?

Tolaki came to stand next to her. "He's pretty amazing, isn't he?"

Can you stop talking about how wonderful he is? "Yeah. Except I wish I knew what he was doing here. I hope we're not about to be tricked into something or that he's doing it for some reason of wanting to spy."

"Do you always have to think the worst of people?"

"No, but . . ." Tolaki wouldn't understand. Tolaki's father and now her brother had never run into trouble in the council. They had never experienced the force of the men of power gathered against them like Father had. They had never been pushed aside and ignored. They had never had to watch their every step and re-evaluate every friendship. "I prefer to be careful. Be friendly, but don't let anything slip about the council, or money, or the guards, or imports or politics—"

"That's all right. I'm not interested in all that stuff anyway." She giggled. "I think his hair is gorgeous. Do you think he's taken? Oh, I forget that you shouldn't take part in our ogling because my brother might not like it."

Ellisandra had to stop herself rolling her eyes.

Sariandra called that she needed someone to check over her shopping list, and they spent the next while in the drawing room discussing fabrics.

"We can go to the markets tomorrow morning," Ellisandra said, and then cringed because she'd forgotten that Sariandra was not supposed to go out without her father's approval and that she had promised that she would stick to these ridiculous rules.

While they had been talking, it had become silent in the hall downstairs and when Ellisandra came out of the drawing room, the orchestra had packed up and gone home.

Aleyo was just walking out the door in the company of two musicians. Vayra was nowhere to be seen. Ellisandra had toyed with the notion to tell him clearly and unambiguously that by playing the "let's see how Mirani I am" game, he put himself in the path of trouble. Whether it was jealous workers, an overzealous Citizen's Group or something more sinister, there would be more thefts, maybe arson or intimidation. He'd hired guards, huh?

How could he make sure those guards didn't become *part* of his troubles?

By paying them well, said a little voice in her head.

And it looked like he was doing just that.

She wondered . . .

Everyone in the upstairs office had now gone home, including Sariandra. She quickly slipped down the stairs and into the library. In the dark corner, she turned on the reader. It was so cold in the room that her breath steamed by the faint light from the screen.

She sat down clasping her hands together and blowing in them to keep them warm.

When the Accountkeepers' financial system came up, she typed *Ilendar* and waited for the list of accounts to come up.

Earlier that day, a bunch of credits had been taken out of the account. The payment was to a business she recognised as an employment agent at the markets, for construction workers. Also, there was a separate payment for security, for as much as three tirans a day per person. Her eyes almost fell out when she saw that.

Was he trying to upset the labour market all by himself? Next thing it would be impossible to find workers for any less than two tirans a day and the theatre couldn't afford that. No one could.

15

E LLISANDRA WENT home to find both her brothers at dinner. Well, that had to be a first this year. Sometimes she wondered if her brothers ever talked to each other, and then she would be surprised to find out that they did.

They sat at the table and whatever discussion they'd been having stopped the moment she came in. They greeted her with smiles. Jintho's expression looked uneasy. He might say that she was the worst liar in the world, but he couldn't be far behind.

"Did I disturb anything?" That was starting to be the standard greeting when she met both of them together.

"No, we were just having a chat." That chat was probably about her.

She sat down at the table in uncomfortable silence.

It was warm in the dining room, and Ellisandra's cheeks glowed from the sudden change in temperature. "Not having any visitors tonight?"

Enzo gave her a sharp look. "Is there anything wrong with my visitors?"

"No, but you seem to have a lot of them recently, and it's been a long time since I've talked to you."

"Not much has changed since last time. Is there anything we need to talk about?"

"Do we always need to talk about something?"

"Well, no, but . . ."

Another uncomfortable silence.

"You were talking about me."

"Maybe."

Jintho was looking at his plate. Oh, yes, he was such a bad liar.

"So, let me guess: you're talking about me because Asitho Bisumar is on my tail for making sure his daughter only speaks to appropriate people, or because I have access to the Accountkeepers' ledger."

"Actually, we're talking about you because apparently our stranger from next door came to the theatre."

"The weather was bad, and he couldn't work. He came to the theatre out of curiosity. He must have heard the orchestra, and they're truly awful. He plays music, and he offered his services. There was also a break-in and people stole some of his materials."

She stared at him but Enzo's face remained impassive. Jintho continued fiddling with his plate.

"You didn't have anything to do with that, did you?"

"Sister, when are you ever going to listen?"

"Who should I listen to?"

"Your husband-to-be, for example. He told you to avoid this man, didn't he?"

"He came to the theatre of his own accord. I can look after myself. If a stranger comes to the theatre to volunteer playing the flute, that doesn't mean I'm in any kind of risk. Except the risk of a public lynching if the orchestra doesn't improve. You haven't answered my question. Did you or Raedon Tussamar have something to do with materials being stolen from next door?"

Enzo said, "I have no idea what Raedon Tussamar does in the times I don't see him."

"You're deflecting the question. I'm asking about you. *You* were talking about scaring the visitor off. Did you steal from next door?"

"No." He said it in a *what-do-you-think-I-am?* way, but she knew him. He often did that, and his behaviour and actual guilt were two entirely different things. "Why won't you give me access to the Accountkeepers' system?"

"Because I can't."

"You're being stubborn."

"I could say the same of you. I don't want to breach the Accountkeepers' confidentiality and risk my position. Why don't you tell me what's going on?"

"We suspect this stranger is up to something."

"Well, top marks for figuring that out!" She rolled her eyes.

"We still have no idea how he's entered Miran."

"The guards should be able to sort that out."

"We don't know why he's here."

"To rebuild the house. Look, maybe he's gathering information about us, but what is he going to see in the theatre? He's by himself, employs a lot of people locally, pays them really well, so all the businesses will see the benefits when workers have more to spend. He came to the theatre asking if he could play in the orchestra, for crying out loud. The orchestra is full of old ladies who are past their prime. What is he going to learn there that can possibly be harmful?"

"They gossip a lot."

"Oh, come on, Enzo. Whatever he might be doing in Miran that's going to harm us, playing in the orchestra is not it."

He glared at her. She glared back.

"I'm also not sure how rebuilding a house classifies as an act of subversion. I'm as mystified about it as you are, but sabotaging him seems a bit childish."

"What makes you think I've done that?"

"Maybe not you personally, but your Citizen's Group. I don't like Raedon Tussamar. No, I don't know that he was responsible for the break-in, but this is starting to look suspiciously like that break-in at merchant Tamarin's where Raedon was playing hard because the merchant was being stubborn with him. I don't like it that you and Jaeron are involved with this."

"She's right," Jintho said.

Enzo spread his hands and rolled his eyes at the ceiling. "Oh, and what do you know about stubborn customers? The only thing you've ever done is loaf around, telling other people what is or isn't moral to do. At least we protect our nation—"

There was a loud thumping on the ceiling and a muffled voice sounded through the floorboards.

"See what you've done now? You've woken Father." Enzo picked up his cloak and made for the door.

Ellisandra said, "Brother."

He stopped in the doorway.

"I really don't like you and Jaeron being involved with this, and I'm serious. Do whatever you want, but don't rope in Jintho or me. Don't even try."

He spread his hands, looked like he was going to say something and thought better of it, let out a deep sigh and left the room.

After the door had slammed behind him, and his footsteps had faded on the stairs, Riana judged it safe to sneak in with Ellisandra's dinner.

Ellisandra said, "Can you go to see if Father wants anything or if he was just annoyed at us?"

"Darma went up. She said he complained about the noise. He said 'I don't live on top of a rowdy bar'."

They all laughed. That was something Father had said for most of his life.

Riana left the room.

Jintho said, "I'm not sure if it was such a good idea to let this man play in the orchestra."

"We talked about it in the committee and decided there was no harm. We really needed players and he was the only one who offered. He's good. It was a coincidence."

In fact, was it too much of a coincidence? Vayra seemed to

knew an awful lot and managed to turn up exactly at the right time.

And now she was starting to see things, because how in all of heaven's name would he have known that the orchestra had a problem, and even if he had known in some way, why would he bother? What information could he gather that would be of interest to anyone outside Miran?

"He's a spy," Jintho said.

Ellisandra nodded. "Yes, likely, or probably."

"If he listens to you, I would warn him that there might be further action."

She gave him a sharp look. Was he telling her that he and Enzo had been talking about actions to take when she came into the room?

"I already planned to do that."

"Good. If you speak to him tomorrow, tell him to get out of town as soon as he can."

When she finished eating, Ellisandra went to Father's room to wash him and tuck him in for the night.

"Ah, there you are. I thought you'd all abandoned me. I've seen no one all day."

"Darma came up a while back."

His dinner tray, too, stood on the table. He had eaten half of his soup and half a roll. "Do you want some more?"

"No. It's too hard. I can't chew this. It's yesterday's bread."

"I'll ask Riana to bring new bread." It was probably hard because he'd left it to sit uncovered on the plate.

"The girl with the fat arse doesn't have any bread."

"Father . . ."

"Well, she does have a fat arse. I hope Enzo keeps her under control because he doesn't want her to run the house like my wife did."

Oh, he was confused today. Enzo wasn't going to marry Riana
—Ellisandra still hadn't found out who was the unfortunate girl—
and Mother had never been bossy, unless he had somehow
convinced himself that he *had* married Sariandra's half-sister
Mikandra, and that she had run out on *him* instead of her father.
Some days it was really hard to track his thoughts.

As Ellisandra wheeled Father's chair into the bathroom, she
knew that whoever Enzo's wife was going to be, she would never
put up with Father's behaviour. Jintho was right. He had been
getting a lot worse. Part of her had secretly hoped that Enzo would
hold off getting married until Father passed away. That was a
terrible thought, besides being kindest on everyone concerned. She
supposed her own wedding plans had gone ahead too far to annoy
Tolaki by postponing the wedding.

So much still needed to be done, and Ellisandra had concen-
trated on the play. Whenever she thought of the wedding preparations, there was always some other thing that needed to be done
more urgently.

The wedding preparations sucked the joy out of her.

Father, whose arms had once been strong but were now little
more than skin-covered twigs, had taken great care to select a
family and a man who would do the right thing for her.

Was it ungrateful and selfish to say that the whole wedding
thing had her decidedly uninterested?

"I just want to see you happy," Father had said when she asked
him about advice on which of the three boys to choose.

Strangely enough, she had been happy with the prospect of
getting married for a long time, at least until it looked like it was
actually going to happen.

After finishing Father's bath and putting him in bed, Ellisandra
went to her room. Riana brought up some tea. It sounded like
Enzo had gone out—and that worried her. What was he up to with
those friends of his? If he got convicted for something illegal, he'd
lose his council seat.

What was up with this change in Foundation Law?

In her room, she drew her chair close to the fire—why did Darma keep putting it back all the time?—set her tea on the table next to her and continued reading the book of Foundation Law. It was complicated and not very logical in setup. Newer laws and amendments had been interspersed with old ones.

In a chapter on rights, she came across a section with old-fashioned language that spelled out the responsibilities of the Foundation families. She was astonished to find many things that she'd never known before.

Like this:

Heirs of Foundation families shall, at all times, maintain their neutrality in the council. They shall not encourage divisive reasoning and shall not take part in garnering votes for their preferred causes.

Well, they had failed on that score.

Or this one:

If a sufficient misconduct has been perpetrated, the Heir of a Foundation family may, when circumstances justify and when accompanied by the right protocol, invoke the Right of Veto in plenary sessions of the council, specifically related to the matter of voting.

She didn't even know that law was still current. What did this mean about Lihan Ilendar and Iztho Andrahar, the heirs of those families? What even was "the right protocol"?

And this:

Foundation family members shall carry equal responsibility for the wellbeing of all in Miran. This includes the care of the sick, the injured and the disadvantaged.

Fancy that, the work of the Endri women was written into the law, but they got no vote in return?

Even Nikala families had more say. Each registered family had a vote, but Nikala families were more likely to be headed by a woman.

And then this one.

Foundation families shall monitor education and the quality thereof, and shall make sure that children of the population are treated fairly and equally and are educated free of political agendas.

Who ever did that anymore?

Then again, Miran had been very small in the beginning, and in return for being allowed to make money off land and property, the Foundation families had been assigned tasks. Those jobs had been distributed over all Endri and had later also included some Nikala, although they never swore to uphold Foundation Law like Endri did.

Miran was much bigger now. Education was no longer monitored by the Endri. All this was interesting, but brought her little closer to what she was looking for. Although to be honest, she wasn't quite sure what she was looking for anymore. Her list of obsolete little rules and tasks that applied to Endri that no one cared about anymore was growing fast. Did the council really want to abolish all of them?

Fortunately, no further snow fell overnight and Ellisandra had no problems going to the theatre the next morning. Sariandra was already in the drawing room, tracing shapes on huge sheets of waxy paper for patterns.

"If you give me a list of what you need, I'll go shopping for fabrics."

"Can I come, please?"

"Do you think that's all right with your father? I don't really want to get into any more trouble with him."

"I'm . . . sorry about that. He can be really silly about things like this." That was an oddly light-hearted remark given Asitho Bisumar's heavy-handedness. "But the merchants are all Nikala. They don't care about me or my father's rules."

That was true, and it *was* going to be inconvenient not having her there.

"Well . . ." She hesitated. "It *is* a work trip." She should probably risk Asitho Bisumar's displeasure and take her. "All right, you can come."

"Oh, thank you, thank you! Let me get my cloak."

Sariandra ran into the open wardrobe and then back into the drawing room, where she deposited something in one of the cabinets under the large table. Leaving the tracking device here again?

To be honest, the strictness of Asitho Bisumar's rules annoyed Ellisandra beyond pale. His daughter was not a little girl. She could think for herself. Somewhere under that shyness was a certain resolve that Ellisandra thought she could like, if only she found out what bothered Sariandra so, because being caught by her father was obviously not one of those things.

"Here I am, all rugged up." She was, too. Not in her mottled cloak today, but wearing a cloak of lighter fur that had a hood, which she had pulled over her head. Hmm, she'd even thought about going onto the streets without being recognised. That was something to be admired.

"All right then, let's go."

It wasn't far to the markets and fortunately the snow from the previous night had been dealt with. On the way, they talked about costumes, their designs and styles and faithfulness to period.

"And we must also see if we can fit you for a dress," Ellisandra said.

"Me?"

"Yes, we're going to be the stars of the night when the play is performed." At least she hoped that they weren't going to be throwing wet snow and no one was going to walk out because of wrong buttons on the actors' costumes, or about too much blood on the floor. Damn, she still hadn't decided whether she'd go ahead with that gory scene or go the safe route.

"You mean, we go onto the stage?"

"Yes, we do. Usually one of the actors tells us to come up."

"Do we need new dresses for that?"

"I have a couple in the stores, but you may need to get one made if there is nothing suitable. We have to look our best."

"Oh." She looked terrified.

"Don't worry, the theatre will pay for it."

"Oh, all right." But she looked far from relieved. "I don't know that I can . . ."

"Of course you can. I know it's scary facing all these people, but you don't have to say anything. I may have to say something, but you just stand behind me on the stage and smile. That's all."

Sariandra nodded and still didn't look convinced.

They arrived at the markets where they spent a good amount of time looking at fabric at a variety of stalls.

Then they went to merchant Faludin's stall, who sold strong and plain linens. Then merchant Elomin who had a selection of felt and synthetic materials. The cheaper fabrics were out.

"You should consider that you're making these costumes for the rich of Miran," Ellisandra explained. "After the performance, the costumes will be auctioned off."

"Oh. I didn't know that."

"It's how we raise a fair bit of money. The lead actress gets to decide where that money is spent. Tameyo tends to like schools. But the way these costumes are made determines their price. This is why the whole button incident happened, because the rich merchant wives tend to bid a lot more if the costumes are more modern. They tend to dislike laced-up bodices."

Sariandra's lips formed the letter "o". "*Changing Fate* is from the early period. Does that mean you want me to have buttons instead of laces?"

"Well, I wished that we could, because they do sell better. Also, I wish that *some people* got over their issues with buttons, because we use synthetics for the ladies' dresses, where they would have used silk back in those days. But we can't have silk, because it comes from Barresh, and you can't talk about imports unless you want to create even more trouble than if you use buttons. Don't ever mention the term *felt* either."

"Because of forbidden imports?"

"Yes. You had no idea that costume-making was a dance in diplomacy, right?"

Sariandra looked at her with wide eyes.

They bought a good number of fabrics, but there was not much choice when searching for cheap leather to make the prisoners' costumes—those weren't auctioned off. If the play had been performed recently, there would have been prisoners' costumes in the stores, but it hadn't and there weren't, which was a nuisance, on top of everything else.

"You should go to the animal markets," a merchant said. "The tiyuk herders usually have a lot of cheap leather for sale."

So they asked the delivery sleds to take all their purchases from the markets to the theatre and went to the animal markets, which were at the lower end of the commercial quarter. *Animals* meant mainly tiyuk. The building's main function was to provide a base for the pack animal herds and their nomad handlers when they came down from the mountains in the snow months. The building took up an entire block with stables surrounding several courtyards on the ground floor and living quarters above them.

The first courtyard held the public markets where the citizens of Miran could buy animals. There were barking lizards that were said to scare maramarang, egg-laying snakes, and a variety of brightly-coloured butterflies in thick glass cages to protect them against the cold. There were also fish of all sizes, decorative ones and ones for eating. The large commercial fish farmers, of course, would not buy here so these were animals for backyard farmers and for the rich to keep as pets.

There were also a couple of temporary pens with young male tiyuk. Sometimes the farmers on the slopes below the city wanted an animal to get to the steep fields where their machinery could not come. But tiyuk were strong herd animals and tended to mope when they were by themselves, so sometimes they only rented the animal and returned it to the nomads the next time they were in town.

These tiyuk, mostly young males with their neck plates poorly developed, were nosing around in a stack of hay, rattling their neck plates at each other if one got in the way of the other. You did not put female animals with the males, because then they all started fighting.

Ellisandra asked one of the attendants for leather and was sent to the next courtyard, where a number of people were stacking parcels onto sleds. They were mountain nomads, a type of people more ancient than the settlement of Miran. They were fairly short and quite dark-skinned to protect themselves from the harmful sunlight at high altitude. They could climb to heights where a city person died, and spent the summers grazing with their animals, to come to the city when snow fell and there was lots of work in town. They also came to sell their wool and leather and dried meat.

Sariandra stared at all the activity in the courtyard with wide eyes as if she saw all this for the first time.

The leather department was in the far corner of that courtyard, under the overhang of the upstairs gallery.

A woman was working stacking big piles of pelts, mostly the light-coloured variety that belonged to the young animals.

While they crossed the courtyard, Ellisandra noticed someone familiar: Vayra stood talking to an older nomad woman.

She ducked into the shadow of an overhanging gallery. It was probably better if he didn't talk to her or Sariandra, if this expedition was to stay a secret from Asitho Bisumar. But it was too late. Sariandra had already seen him.

"Hey, that's the man who came to play the flute."

"Yes."

"What's he doing here?"

"Organising to get something delivered for his building project?"

That's what she would normally have thought, but Vayra was laughing and the older woman clapped him on the shoulder. She said something and he laughed even harder. He looked completely at ease, not at all the stiff person she had seen.

"He's rebuilding the Andrahar house, isn't he?" Sariandra said.

"I think so."

He didn't seem to have noticed them. Ellisandra wanted to wait until he was gone, but the two were deep in discussion as if they were the best of friends.

And then another thought occurred to her: she knew how Vayra could have entered Miran unnoticed: with the nomads. Every winter, the caravan of animals with their owners walked in from the mountain slopes: a long train of shaggy beasts pulling sleds with men, women and children seated on bales of wool and pelts. The children from the city would often run out and meet them at the high gate. The only other people who used the high gate were funeral processions and sometimes casual walkers and herb collectors. Guard checks at the gate were pretty lax. In fact she didn't think there were guards on that gate at all a lot of the time.

Then another thought: Vayra had planned this. He had researched the best way to come into town without being noticed. He had learned Mirani and Mirani custom. Maybe he had even become a Masterbuilder just so that he could rebuild the house.

If Nemedor Satarin was to be believed, he also held a Trader's Licence and had studied law.

What was the chance that all these things he was doing in Miran amounted to a cunning plan that he had spent years working out?

He was still talking to the woman.

"Need any help there?" This voice was another woman's, a bit younger, but already with lines around her eyes from exposure to dry mountain air.

"We're looking for some cheap sheets of leather."

"Cheap ones or good ones? They're two different things."

"Cheap. It's for the theatre."

She frowned.

"Costumes, only to be worn for one night."

"One night only? You city folk are so wasteful." She tsked, but went to rummage in her wares. She pulled out a pile of cured skins from under the display table and spread out a few over the top of a stack of glorious thick furs. Most skins had faults or were uneven in colour or texture.

"Our rubbish pile," the woman said. "That cheap enough?"

"That will do perfectly."

Ellisandra chose a few of the darker-coloured skins. "We need to make them black," she explained to Sariandra.

The nomads didn't use Mirani's credit system, so she had to pay for the purchases in tiran tokens.

"Is he a friend of the nomads?" she asked while digging in the pocket of her cloak.

The woman returned a deadpan stare.

"He's not a local. We can't work out where he's come from. You people seem to know him well."

"I don't make a habit of talking gossip. Either you want to buy these skins or you don't. I'm not here to talk rubbish."

All right, all right. Ellisandra handed over the money, and handful of little triangular tokens.

"Why not ask him?" the woman said.

"We have, rest assured."

"Ha, maybe he doesn't like your asking."

Well, obviously.

"You know, you're all so afraid in this place. You tremble like a newborn calf when someone does as much as look at you. You worry about what people think. You worry about what people know about you. You worry about what people will do with that information. You worry about what people will tell other people and what they will do with that information." She spread her hands. "By the heavens, how can you live like that? You're very young. Your companion is even younger."

She pointed a crooked finger at Sariandra, who took a step back, her eyes wide. Ellisandra was sure that this woman didn't meet the "Approved Companion" guidelines set by her father.

"You know what you youngsters need to do? You're good girls, and you mean well, but you have to say enough's enough. I've come here many years, and every year I turn up, things have gotten a little worse. When I first came here, as a little girl, I remember staring my eyes out at all the foreign delicacies. Fruit I'd never seen before. Silk! Wood! Someone had to explain to me what that was. And then all the glorious food that you could buy. It was cheap, too. And sometimes it would even be sold by someone from elsewhere. Nothing of that is left. One by one, all the merchants stopped selling the interesting stuff. One by one, all the foreign merchants left. You people don' notice it. You live like the mountain hare stuck in the freezing cave, not noticing how cold it gets until it's too late." Her gnarled finger pointed at Ellisandra. Other shoppers had stopped to stare. "Stop before it's too late. Get off this caravan to madness. Start living again."

Ellisandra quickly gathered her purchases and shepherded Sariandra to safer ground, the anonymity of the street.

"What was all that about?" Sariandra asked.

"Nothing important."

Only a lot of politics. Maybe one day, a long time ago, she would have discussed the nomad woman's opinion, and she would have been able to do so without being afraid to be spied on and have her opinion reported back to the council by a Citizen's Group.

The woman was right, of course. Everyone in Miran was afraid. There was no more pride and no more honour. It was everyone for themselves. Foundation was already dead. It had been dead for years.

"I'M SORRY about that," Ellisandra said when they were back in the upstairs drawing room.

"Sorry about what?" Sariandra frowned at her. She seemed to come out of some kind of deep thought to say that. She had taken off her cloak and hung it over the spare chair, but hadn't sat down yet.

"I only meant for you to come shopping. If I'd known that woman was going to go on a political rant, I wouldn't have taken you."

"I'm familiar with political rants." It sounded a little prim.

Yes. Of course. She would be. Ellisandra hated to think what dinners would be like at Asitho Bisumar's house.

"I'm sorry. Would you get in trouble if someone reported it to your father that you were there? Because I don't want to cause you any trouble." Moreover, she didn't want to have to face Asitho Bisumar again.

"Nothing you could do could cause me any more trouble than I already have."

"But I promised him—"

"You don't understand," Sariandra said. She was hugging herself and not meeting Ellisandra's eyes.

"You left that thing upstairs again, didn't you? The thing that's supposed to tell him where you are."

Sariandra nodded and then looked over her shoulder.

"Why is he so afraid of what you do and who you speak to? These are all just merchants and other workers. You're a big girl. It's not as if they are going to make any difference to your life or will change your mind."

"Look, it's not really important. I'm getting married soon and—"

"Yes, let's talk about that. Did you know you were getting married when you came to join us?"

"I didn't. It has only been arranged recently."

"When is this happening?"

"Soon after the play."

"So soon?"

Her father really wanted to get rid of her.

"It's only big weddings that you need to organise long in advance. We're just having a small one. But *you* should be happy about it."

Me? "Hang on. You're not saying you're getting married to Enzo?"

Sariandra looked down and nodded. Her cheeks flushed with red.

Enzo? With Sariandra?

She tried to imagine there being any kind of spark between those two, and, with all the will in the world, couldn't.

That was awful. If she married Enzo, Sariandra would never free herself from her father's influence, because Enzo was in Asitho Bisumar's pockets. Enzo would treat her like a whore and a slave and Father . . . She didn't even want to think about it. Sariandra was too tiny and skinny to do the heavy work of lifting him, and after he'd leered at her or tried to grab her breasts, she wouldn't want to do it anymore, and Enzo would use her—rightful—outrage to force Father to live as a prisoner in his bedroom cared for by a quick progression of grumpy nurses.

Sariandra shrugged. "Look, don't worry about it. Let's talk about the play."

"I do worry about it. I worry about my father."

Sariandra gave her a *is-he-still-alive?* look. "You think I can't look after him?"

Ellisandra closed her eyes and sighed. "No, I don't mean that at all. It's just that . . . he's not very healthy and sometimes he gets into these moods where he's not very nice." That was putting it mildly. "He might be my father, but I wouldn't wish him on my worst female enemy."

"Good thing I'm worse than your enemy then."

"Stop talking rubbish! Who has been talking this nonsense into your head? Have a bit of confidence. Be proud of yourself."

"You don't understand!"

"Then explain it to me."

Sariandra gave a small sob.

"I understand perfectly. Your father is a first class arsehole. He's got you so frightened that you think you're worth nothing. He's got—"

"It's not like that at all!"

"Then what?"

"It's all my fault! Just leave me alone. You can't help me." She turned and ran out of the office and down the stairs.

"Sariandra!" Ellisandra ran after her, but Sariandra ran across the rehearsal hall, through the corridor to the state door, which she opened—

Ellisandra yelled after her, "It's cold out there!" She didn't even have her cloak.

—the door slammed.

Well, damn it. Ellisandra ran back up the steps, almost crashed into Tolaki who was coming the other way and pressed herself against the wall, eyes wide.

Ellisandra ran into the office, grabbed her own cloak and Sariandra's. She felt through the pockets of that cloak, and dumped their contents onto the desk. She didn't *think* that the listening device was amongst all the assorted debris that bounced over the table.

Then she ran back out the office, again almost crashing into Tolaki.

"What are you doing? What's going on?"

'Sariandra has some kind of trouble. She ran out without her cloak."

"That girl is a lot more trouble than she's worth."

Ellisandra stopped. Met Tolaki's eyes.

A small frown crossed Tolaki's face. "It's true, isn't it? You spend so much effort helping her, you might as well make those costumes yourself."

Ellisandra stared at her.

Her first reaction was, *What, are you jealous that I help someone in trouble?*

The next reaction was, *How dare you say something like that? Have you no idea what sort of arsehole her father is?*

Then the third reaction was that Tolaki probably agreed with the arsehole, and she did not want to go there and lose a friend.

And that brought a deep chill to her insides. She *liked* Tolaki and didn't have the time for a lengthy—and possibly unpleasant—argument, so she said only, "See you later."

But as she ran down the steps, the chill spread. If she ended up going too much against Asitho Bisumar, she risked losing a lot more than just his support.

She ran through the rehearsal room, the corridor and out of the theatre, down the steps and into the alley. It was cold and misty out there. The cold air bit into the exposed skin in her neck.

The form of Sariandra just disappeared around the corner into the street.

Ellisandra sprinted down the alley as fast as the slippery ground allowed. Sariandra had run into the main street and was going downhill towards the lower end of the commercial quarter. She was the only person in the street not wearing a cloak, with just her arms clamped around herself against the cold. Where the hell was she going? It was freezing cold out here, even with a cloak.

Sariandra turned another corner into an alley that led past the back of a number of shops and business buildings. A man came out of a door and down the steps into the alley. He was no more than a shaggy shape in a thick cloak and Sariandra crashed into him—no, she *threw herself in his arms*. He held her in a hug. They kissed, not just a peck on the cheek, but a full-on passionate kiss.

Well, that certainly explained something.

She retreated into a niche next to a stack of packed snow, and watched, her heart still thudding from running down the street. The man drew Sariandra into the warmth of his cloak. His hair slid over her shoulder until his strands of hair mingled with hers. He held her tight as Ellisandra had hoped to be held by her husband, in an embrace of passionate love.

Then he let her go. Hand in hand, the two of them then went further down the alley, down a set of steps and disappeared into a cellar under a shop. Ellisandra followed at a slower pace.

The entrance where Sariandra and her mystery man had disappeared was underneath a bread shop in the lower end of the commercial quarter. She knew the place. A reliable baker, and not too expensive. A lot of Nikala from the nearby high-rise residential area bought their bread there.

She stopped at the top of the stairs. This was one of those old cellars that was half in the ground and half out. They were good for storing things that could not be allowed to freeze, since the warmth from the earth would keep the temperature above freezing point even during winter nights. The sound of many voices—mainly male—drifted into the alley. They were too far away for Ellisandra to hear what was being said.

She slowly went down the steps and put her ear near the door, but although the voices were louder, she still couldn't discern clear meaning. If only . . .

Ellisandra tried the door handle. It turned and the door opened a crack.

The voices continued as if the people inside hadn't heard her. Carefully, she pushed the door further open.

She found herself in a little dank foyer with a bare and worn stone floor where it smelled of mould. Down another set of steps was a larger cellar, in which the ceiling was upheld by rows of columns. On the ground, on cushions, sat a number of people, a mixture of Endri and Nikala. Sariandra was one of them.

Now that Ellisandra had entered the cellar, they stopped talking and all of them looked at the door. Most of the people she had seen before. They were artists, second and third sons of Endri families or merchants. Some of them were associated with the free theatre, the kind that, unlike hers, didn't get a regular audience or pay, but didn't get prescribed which play to perform either. There were about fifteen of them, seated on cushions with their cloaks covering their legs. Her eyes met those of one of the men.

"Jintho?"

Another Endri man rose and came towards her. "What are you doing here?"

"I followed Sariandra. She . . . um . . . forgot her cloak." Ellisandra held out her arm with the garment. He didn't touch it.

"How did you get in?"

"The door was open."

The young man said, "You're going to have to leave."

Jintho said, "It's all right. She's my sister."

The man turned to Jintho. "I know she's your sister. She's also in the council's fucking back pocket. I don't want her here, mate."

"I tell you, she's all right."

This was followed by an intense silence.

Ellisandra noticed the carafe of menisha brew and glasses on the floor.

So this was where he spent all the time he wasn't at home: drinking with a bunch of artists who had nothing better to do.

Sariandra met her eyes, her expression defiant. How had she ended up with a group like this one? Ellisandra had expected better of the High Councillor's daughter. In fact, she expected better from her own brother.

He shrugged, his face sad. "We started meeting here to talk art. For fun, really. You all know how much art gets sold in Miran. We're trying to figure out ways to survive without having to rely on our families. We all want to have our own houses eventually, too."

"That explains the business with the shop."

Did he cringe? Did several people, including Sariandra, cast him a sharp look?

She was involved in it? That made a lot of sense. "What is it about opening a shop that can't see the light of day?"

"Because we're Endri, and because Endri don't have shops," Sariandra said, her voice sharp.

"Because we're planning to sell a wide range of designs, including non-Mirani ones," a Nikala man said. "Young people want to look modern and in tune with the times. They don't want to be dictated what to wear by old-fashioned men with no sense of fashion—"

"All of whom wear uniforms anyway," someone else added.

"We're planning to employ mainly artists. The tailor's association is not going to be happy, because we're not going to adhere to their standards." This was another young man, who could have been Keldon Nirumar's twin brother for all his daintiness. He even wore a jewelled clip in his hair and had his fingernails painted.

Another said, "No one is going to be happy about this, especially not our families."

"How far along is this plan?" Ellisandra asked.

"We've got the designs, we've got the fabrics. We're starting to source people to make the clothes for us."

"What about the shopfront?"

"Working on that."

"And the permit?" She met Jintho's eyes.

"Yeah, that." He looked down. Sariandra glanced at him and the others fell quiet.

What about the permit? Enzo needed to sign it? And Enzo, and Asitho Bisumar, clearly had some sort of hold over Jintho that she didn't understand. Or maybe she did.

She was beginning to think that the man Sariandra had kissed was her brother Jintho. If that was so, why was Sariandra now going to marry Enzo?

"Please let me try this, Elli," Jintho said. "I know you think I'm no good for anything—"

"I never said that."

"No, you haven't, unlike some, but you're very bad at hiding your feelings. Just for once, put away your objections and reasons why this is never going to work."

"Whether it will work is up to you, but I am worried that this is going to fly in the path of the council's import restrictions. Even I run into problems with the theatre. For the last production, we needed silk. The best silk comes from Barresh, so I can't buy it. They also produce some silk in Kesilu, but it's been a bad year, so it's far too expensive for my budget, and besides, that product is substandard and I'm not going to pay what the growers are asking. Do you think I can convince the council to let me import it? If you're going to sell modern, non-Mirani designs, you'll need non-Mirani materials."

"We are working on that."

"I can't see how you can work on it unless you're going to rely on illegal supplies, and if you start selling those in a shop, you'll be on the wrong end of a very hot poker very soon." The council had people everywhere in the form of the Citizens' Groups.

"Trust me, we're working on it."

She stopped asking because she wasn't sure if she wanted to know more. "Be careful, Jintho, because it's not worth getting into serious trouble."

"We will. Don't worry about it. We will be fine."

She wished she could be so convinced.

17

I T DIDN'T LOOK like Jintho knew that his brother was set to marry his girlfriend, and Ellisandra desperately didn't want to be the one who told him. Sariandra obviously knew, but she seemed too terrified to tell him . . . or maybe she had other plans, and Ellisandra desperately didn't want to know about those either. The less she knew, the less she could be accused of not telling people in authority. She had a theatre production to run. It was none of her business.

In the next month, Jintho went into a frenzy of activity. It seemed he had finally found something useful to do. She was still sceptical about the potential for success, but time would tell and it was out of her hands.

Sariandra came back to the theatre. Costumes were made. The orchestra practiced. Snow fell, rather a lot of it. The actors learned their lines. Ellisandra watched the rehearsals, and was still wavering on going ahead with her plan to make the last scene gory, and making up her mind whether the resulting outrage would be worth it.

The blood and gore would be shocking to many people who hadn't done anything that deserved being shocked. There would be children in the audience, and besides the fact that she didn't like the play, what point was she trying to make with that final scene?

This is your country: one of cruel barbarians who kill people just for being foreign.

Could she be jailed for saying that?

Despite the fact that serious progress was being made on the Andrahar house, Vayra came to every practice. He chatted with the players about culture and music, and seemed to enjoy himself. He looked at her often, but Ellisandra stayed away from him, and made sure that she was never in a situation where she was alone with him or where he could tell her anything that she would have to tell Nemedor Satarin.

She dropped into the Accountkeepers' system occasionally to gawk at the huge amounts he was spending. During the day, he had many builders on the site. The roof was almost on, they'd installed windows and were doing the inside. The pace of progress was incredible. When paid and fed well, this team could build an entire city in a month.

At night, at least three or four guards patrolled the site. They were barely recognisable in their strange-looking helmets and dark jackets. When they first started work, a month back, they wore all-Mirani gear, black leather, fur cloaks and crossbows, but there had been a subtle shift to body armour underneath the cloaks, and guns in addition to the crossbows. One by one they ditched the cloaks and donned helmets.

It looked like not only had Vayra managed to get himself into Miran through the back door, but he was still bringing in material. She had thought that he was using the nomads, but they were now staying in town and no longer travelling out of the city.

Often, when she watched the orchestra rehearse, Vayra's eyes would meet hers over the heads of the other players, and he would probably wonder what he'd said wrong for her to be such a cold fish.

She also hadn't decided if she cared that he might think that. She probably shouldn't because of Jaeron, but she was beginning to feel certain that she didn't care much for Jaeron, or for that matter, for Tolaki, after what she had said about Sariandra. Worse, the whole subject of her upcoming wedding made her feel ill. One night, she even dreamed that she sneaked through Jaeron's yard with a knife to kill him so that she couldn't marry him. She was arrested by the guards and taken to the prison—which looked exactly like the set Loret and his team were building for the third scene—where the floor was covered in blood.

That dream was so bad that she woke up in a sweat and had to run to the bathroom to vomit, after which Darma decided that she had a fever and had probably caught something in the draughty halls of the theatre. Ellisandra stayed home by the fire for half a day, already feeling much better, and glad for the rest.

It allowed her to complete the project she had set for herself: to read through every page of Foundation Law. Next to her bed she kept a little notebook in which she wrote all the strange laws relating to Foundation families that she had never heard before and that no one seemed to enforce. Her list grew quite long. She guessed the law was due for an update, but simply getting rid of all these little provisions was not the answer.

Because if, for example, the council wanted to make a top-level decision, like approve a budget, change a law, call an election, oust a misbehaving member, or, for that matter, declare war, no one would be able to stop them. No one would have the authority to step up and ask for a recount, a re-trial or reconsideration. No one could challenge the decision on moral grounds. The council couched the changes in a trivial *just cleaning up the laws* justification, but it was much more than that, and yes, she didn't think many people had an idea of the seriousness of the situation.

That same evening, Enzo came to her when she was about to go and bring Father his meal.

"Elli, do you have a moment?"

"I'm about to bring Father his dinner. You could come."

"I'd rather not. Come with me."

He preceded her into his room, where it was warm and a lusty fire burned in the hearth. He offered her his chair by the fire and sat down opposite her. On the little table between them stood a carafe of brew.

Wow, he really did drink a lot.

"It's about my wedding. I need to get it organised."

She frowned at him. "Why are you asking me? You should ask a planner."

He clasped his hands together. "I should. But you see, they're booked out."

Her frown deepened. "When are you wanting to have this?"

"Next month."

"Next month?" she burst out. "What? Why the hurry?"

"I don't like wasting time."

"No, you're wasting *my* time instead. I've got a theatre production to run. I don't have time to organise a wedding."

"Aw, Elli . . ."

"No. And no, and if you're asking, no. Wait until spring, like a normal person."

"I can't. I promised."

"Promised what?"

He shrugged.

"Enzo?" Her heart thudded. What in all of heavens name was going on? "Where does Asitho Bisumar have his claws in you?"

He looked up, sharply. "Nowhere. He's giving me the best opportunity anyone has ever given me—"

"—Providing you marry his daughter."

"Well, yeah."

"So that's part of the bargain. Does she have any say in it?"

He shook his head, looking down at his hands.

"Damn. He must hate her a lot. You know she's got something with Jintho, right?"

Another sharp look, alarmed almost. Then a nod.

"This is wrong, Enzo, and you know it."

Now he gave her an angry look. "How do you think Jintho is

going to look after her? With this shop that's going to be a failure, even if it actually opens, which I doubt?"

It was a harsh assessment, but unfortunately, Ellisandra agreed with him.

He continued in a calmer voice. "I'm doing it to help Asitho out. Our brother has made an embarrassment of himself, and Asitho has given me an opportunity—"

"What opportunity is worth looking into your brother's eyes for the rest of your life, seeing his anger for taking the girl he wanted?"

He met her eyes, the expression in them hard. He said nothing.

"Do you really care so little about Jintho's life?"

"Jintho is meant to take control of his own life. Since he hasn't done that for the past two years, I will pick up the pieces for him, because I'm his brother, and that's what brothers do. So either help me organise this wedding, or don't speak to me again. Because I've had it with his whining and complaining and his good-for-nothing friends who egg him on. A shop! He could have chosen hundreds of careers, but no, he's got to go all artsy just to make absolutely sure there is no future in what he does. He can apply for the licence, but he's got no contacts and no suppliers, and you know how important those are. No suppliers means no entries in the ledger. It means no credits, no work points. Nothing. How is he supposed to support himself and a family on promises that are nothing but thin air? If his domestic staff can't draw on any of his accounts? Tell me, Elli, because I'm not seeing it."

Ellisandra didn't know what to say to that, because he was right about all of it. She ended up half-heartedly agreeing to help with the wedding, because if he had agreed with Asitho Bisumar, there was no going back. The wedding would be a mere few days after the performance, so if she did the big things now, she could finish it all when the play was done.

"I appreciate it, Elli. I really do. I know you're busy. I don't need a big wedding."

He actually had the gall to look in her eyes while saying this.

Every Endri girl had dreams of the biggest, most showy wedding. It was her one and only way to shine. Asitho was denying his daughter even that?

After she left the room, she felt sick at the thought that she agreed to do it. She was a coward just as much as everyone else was. It would be a long time before she'd be able to face Jintho. She *liked* Jintho. He could be a bit misguided, but his heart was in the right place.

She went down into the kitchen, where she picked up the tray with Father's dinner.

"You must come and eat when you finish, mistress," Riana said, while standing at the stove with her back to the door.

To be honest, Ellisandra didn't know if she could face eating, because Enzo's request had made her feel ill again.

Father sat in his usual chair by the fire and, from the way he looked at her when she opened the door, she knew that his thoughts were reasonably clear today.

"I missed you this morning," he said while she put the tray on the table.

"I was sick."

"Are you better now?"

"Yes." Although the smell rising from the soup when she took the lid off the tray made her feel queasy.

"Did anything interesting happen today?"

"Enzo asked me to organise his wedding."

Father gave her a sharp look. "And, did you tell him to stay away from that Bisumar girl?"

"He seems to have made an agreement with Asitho. I don't like it. She's Jintho's girlfriend."

"She is trouble." Was he again confusing Sariandra with her older half-sister?

Ellisandra used the usual technique with him: half-agree with something he said and change the subject. "Her father is giving us a lot of trouble."

"He's keen to marry his daughter off?"

"It seems so."

"Hates women, he does. Never mind that the Bisumar family seems to be blessed with the most headstrong women in Miran."

"You served in the council with his sister Amandra, didn't you?"

"I did. It was a pity when she resigned. The whole council should have resigned with her over that incident. A pity I didn't see it at the time."

"What happened?"

He flicked up his eyebrows. "What now? My daughter is asking me about politics?"

"Well, I don't know what happened, so I don't know what I'm asking about. Tell me."

"All right, all right." He picked up his soup bowl and raised it to his mouth. Ellisandra helped him steady it.

"No need to do that. I'm not an old man." He sipped. "Ow, that seems to be hot."

He set the cup down without spilling any, and looked at her over the steaming contents. For a moment, Ellisandra was afraid that his moment of clarity had lapsed and he had forgotten her question, but he continued, "It goes back to the time that Nemedor Satarin was army chief of Barresh, when they were still a Mirani protectorate. Some rebel people in Barresh asked for a judgement from *gamra* and they declared that the Mirani protectorate was akin to an occupation and told Barresh that it was their right to order us out, which they did and which led to the Two Day War. People here were pretty angry. We'd spent many years and a lot of money in Barresh. The place was a right mess. Crime everywhere in broad daylight."

Ellisandra was going to say *Like Miran,* but didn't.

Father picked up the soft cloth to wipe his face. She must remember to put some salve on it so that he didn't break the skin and turn those spots into sores.

"The bottom line was that the Barresh council and their lame army were unable to look after themselves. I mean, half the population is running around naked with spears and climbing trees. The city was a hotbed of Coldi influence and only our presence kept that under control. When Nemedor Satarin came back to Miran, people felt sorry for him. He'd been doing all the right things, keeping criminality out of Barresh, and look where it had gotten him. They supported his candidature for the council and they supported him when he was elected. He made the genius move to include a woman on his ticket for the High Council. Amandra Bisumar had a lot of opinions. She was well-spoken, and she was the first and only-ever female Trader in Miran, holder of her own licence. She was very popular. People loved it."

He dabbed at his weeping eye. He didn't do a very good job, because she could still see moisture glistening in the deep grooves of skin.

"But then she started to ask questions, because she was a Trader—still is, I hear. She heard of the stories of foreign Traders being scared out of Miran. *Gamra* had instated boycotts after the Two Day War, mainly because of how they believed Mirani soldiers had treated the locals in Barresh, and they demanded that money was returned. Instead of answering her questions, people in the pay of Nemedor Satarin started blackballing her. She had a Coldi lover—had him for years. He was an all right sort of guy, also a Trader. He came to Miran regularly, but they started putting alerts on his visits and giving him a hard time when he entered. They started making suggestions about her and him and smearing her name whenever she proposed something. *Because she was just a silly woman.* The situation became unworkable, and she resigned. The Ilendar family left at the same time, because the council was restricting imports. Then there was the whole business with the Andrahar family."

"What was with them?"

"Iztho Andrahar took all the family's foreign money out of Miran and put it in an account in Barresh. Nemedor Satarin threatened to suspend council favours to the family unless they brought the money back. They didn't. They invented some scheme that supposedly showed that the Mirani council had blackmailed them and tried to blame the family for crimes they didn't commit. It was all made-up of course, but it went to the Trader Court and they of course sided with one their own and awarded the case to the Andrahars. People in Miran were so angry that a mob of youths burnt down the house that very night."

That wasn't quite how she had heard the story at other times, also from him, but today he was in his bitter stage. It had to be sad sitting here all day by the fire with nothing to do. Father had been a proud man. It was sad to see him like this, and to know that what he said could no longer be trusted to be the truth.

Eydrina Lasko had said that he might still live for years and there was no reason that he would die soon. Who would look after him all that time? People would be increasingly unlikely to take him seriously or want to talk to him.

It was all so terrible, seeing him like this, with his weeping eye, telling stories that mixed up details from several stories in one.

One thing, though, she did realise from his words: in all of the past years, Nemedor Satarin had ruled Miran behind the scenes. He got the praise and the honour. He got other people to do the work that was nasty or dubious.

That person at the moment was Asitho Bisumar. He was trying to pull the last remaining Foundation family into his network.

And women were punished harshly for asking pointed questions.

18

THE PLAY WAS going well. The actors were professionals, and *Changing Fate* was not considered a particularly hard play in terms of learning their lines.

Ellisandra still needed to make a decision about the last scene and it so happened that Tolaki was rehearsing that with the cast.

That particular morning had dawned with a leaden grey sky from which it had started snowing at breakfast time. Loret and his men had come to the theatre. They were meant to be putting on the ground floor roof: that of the kitchen, the laundry and the back of the house, which held servants' rooms. The slate got very slippery with snow, so they couldn't work. Instead, their hammering and happy talk echoed through the theatre building.

Ellisandra went to sit at the side of the stage to watch the rehearsal. There were a few musicians playing to provide the background for the scenes, but not the full orchestra.

Tameyo stood at the back of the stage holding the bars of an imaginary prison cell, and the two men were fighting over her. Despite being both Endri, Liran was a good deal shorter than Keldon and the two had been in training with a real sword master so that they could do a convincing fight. The blunt swords clattered against each other. They were designed to be shiny, so that they would reflect light into the audience. It was done for show, and that fact was overly clear. Despite the fighting training, there was little genuine about this performance. She would have to talk to the sword master to see if he could inject some grittiness in the moves. She didn't want a pretty dance, she wanted a fight.

The curtains next to her stirred, and someone appeared quietly out of the darkness. Vayra.

Oh no.

"Haven't had much of a chance to talk to you," he said. He spoke softly so as not to disturb the rehearsal.

"Yes, well, running a theatre production is hard work. I've been very busy."

"Too busy to give me an opinion on something in the house?"

She raised an eyebrow. "Your house?"

He nodded. "As someone from a traditional family familiar with history, you can perhaps advise me on colours to use in the downstairs rooms."

"Suppose I could. Come and see me in my office at midday. Bring your samples."

"I'd actually prefer if you came out to the house."

All right. So what was this? A ploy to get her away from here? To talk to her alone? "I'm very busy. I don't know if I'll have time for that." If they were seen together, there would be more gossip and she didn't even want to think about what Jaeron would say about it. Or Nemedor Satarin.

"The old Andrahar office will also do, but I am a bit reluctant to take you up there, because I live there by myself. I am aware of how rumours start and spread."

"And you don't want to tarnish my reputation?" That sounded really prim.

He laughed, and she laughed as well.

"I'll come to the house if I can. I can't promise anything."

"It would be much appreciated." He bowed and left again.

Ellisandra remained a bit longer, looking at the actors on the stage who had now progressed to the very final scene. Keldon had thrown Liran to the ground. He lifted his sword, and brought it down. Ellisandra gasped. For a moment there, she thought he was going to hit Liran, but the sharp point of the sword—which was not very sharp at all but could still injure—disappeared in the hollow between Liran's shoulder and neck. To the audience it would look like it went into Liran's neck. Liran lay still.

From the back of the stage, Tameyo called, "Jihan!"

He ran, jumping over the bodies of minor actors who lay as dead on the stage.

This was the part where the play made a major misstep, as far as she was concerned. This was the part where she would have wanted Mariandra to scream at Jihan for killing her lover, where she would have fallen to her knees to check if he was still alive, and where the conclusion of the play should have been *war is an awful thing and makes no one happy* instead of *victors are glamorous people who need to be admired at all times.*

She imagined the stage covered in blood, and felt queasy at the thought of having to ask all those glamorous actors to carry bags of blood under their clothes.

She felt even queasier at the thought of seeing the unsuspecting audience go white in the face. Some ladies might faint. Their husbands would be outraged. Was that something she wanted to have to her name?

This was the part where she could give orders that would change the entire nature of the play. As performed here, the progression of events didn't work. Many of the prisoners had been quite sympathetic characters. This scene spoiled the play. It turned around the interesting development of blossoming relationships between Mirani and Coldi prisoners and killed a number of very decent characters.

Ellisandra turned away from the stage and slowly walked up the stairs while the choir sang the last song of triumph. This type of triumph did not sit well with her at all.

And she still didn't know what to do about it.

She remembered that, a while ago, when sorting the play's

texts, she had come across the little old book with the play's notes. Any political message the author had intended in the play would be in that book.

She went to the library where it still lay as she had left it: in the middle of the large table.

As it turned out, the notes weren't even written by the author, but by some council administrator claiming to speak on behalf of the author, because *the author is not in the right frame of mind and is hell-bent on destroying the reputation of several councillors who she sees as having done her wrong.*

Ellisandra read that passage a few times, focusing on the words *she* and *her.*

Was *Changing Fate* the only play of the classics that had been written by a woman? But why would a woman write such a violent play, unless . . .

Unless she was the woman depicted as Mariandra, unless she had been in love with this visitor, killed by her own kinsmen. Unless this play was about her pain. And seen like that, the story made so much sense. This wasn't about the glory of Miran. It was one woman's protest dressed up as glory of Miran.

It wasn't meant to be performed as it had been in the past. The last scene was supposed to be heart-wrenching and unhappy. She hadn't been wrong about the sympathetic characters of the Coldi prisoners at all. The interpretation of it hadn't changed with the changing attitudes of time. The last scene was horrible because it was meant to be horrible.

Upstairs in the office, a delivery boy had brought a number of large but not very heavy boxes which came from the theatre's stores. While the main actors' costumes were auctioned off after each show, the theatre kept the less glamorous outfits for later use, and it was here that Ellisandra had ordered prison guard uniforms, maid's and other domestic staff's dresses and plain commoner dresses for the ubiquitous "crowd" that was a feature of each Mireni classic play. In the box were also a number of pretty, frilly and colourful dresses. Ellisandra had already decided that she was going to wear the blue one on performance night, blue being the colour of the Takumar family. Tolaki and Aleyo had also ordered their preferred dresses to be taken out of storage, and Ellisandra had ordered a few choices for Sariandra. One of them was a beautiful light yellow number, soft and delicate. There was also a hard pink one, which upon seeing it, Ellisandra thought was too stark, and a green one. Ellisandra hoped that Sariandra was from the branch of the Bisumar family that used the green. She should have asked, really, but that had somehow slipped the net.

She asked Sariandra to come to her office, where she stood looking awkwardly from one dress to the other spread on the table.

"I don't know," she said, fidgeting.

For someone supposedly interested in fashion, she seemed remarkably unenthusiastic. She always wore her thick cloak indoors these days.

"I think the yellow one," Ellisandra said.

Sariandra stared at the dresses some more.

"Or green. Are you from the branch of the Bisumar family that uses green?"

"No. We're orange."

What a bummer. She really should have checked that. "I'll get an orange one brought in. Meanwhile, why don't you try the yellow one on?"

"It's cold," Sariandra said, pulling the cloak closer around her shoulders.

"Just try it quickly. Then I'll know if we need to make any adjustments." She gathered up the dress and dumped it in Sariandra's arms. "Here, use the dressing room up here." She went to the door in the side wall and shepherded Sariandra inside.

The room was tiny and held only one chair and a dressing table which had been without any make-up or hair pieces or wigs since

Ellisandra took over. The mirror made it look much bigger than it was. Apparently it was built as private dressing room for the lead actress, but Ellisandra had never seen it used as such. She lit the lamp with the flame box in her pocket and left Sariandra in the room.

She had been checking the inventory lists of the stores for a while when she realised that Sariandra was taking a very long time.

"And? How is the dress?"

"Fine." Her voice sounded muffled through the door, completely lacking in enthusiasm.

"Do we need to make it shorter?" Sariandra had inherited none of her father's height.

"Um . . ."

"Can I have a look?"

There was no reply to that, so Ellisandra softly pushed open the door. She met with no resistance. With someone in the tiny room, it was warmer inside than out. Sariandra stood before the mirror, hugging herself. Ellisandra had been wrong. The yellow dress did not look good on her at all. Her skin was marked with areas of rashes in the neck and upper arms. The dress was too loose in the shoulders, and the hem . . . oh my, why did it hang uneven like that? It was because . . . it was tight in the waist. In fact, the waist-line hung at least a hand's width above where it should hang at the front, because her lower abdomen showed a very distinct and tight rounded swelling.

Oh.

Well.

That made sense. *Everything* made sense now.

Sariandra met her eyes and there was despair in her expression.

Ellisandra whispered, "Jintho?"

Sariandra nodded. Her bottom lip trembled. A tear leaked out of her eye. She blinked, but now another tear ran out of her other eye. She covered her face with her hands.

"I'm sorry!" She let herself fall to her knees. "I'm sorry, I'm sorry!"

"Stop that." Ellisandra grabbed her under her arms and dragged her to her feet. Sariandra sobbed into her shoulder. "I don't know what to do. My father is so angry."

Ellisandra closed her arms around the poor girl.

No, Asitho wasn't angry. Anger would probably be the first reaction of a parent in this situation. The next reaction, when the first had worn off, would define the parent. They could keep it quiet, give the young couple their blessing and forego the big showy wedding. It happened. With parents being really strict on girls and not telling them about all the things they could do to avoid the situation, it happened rather a lot, actually.

Or they could blackmail the girl, blackmail the poor hapless young man, blackmail the poor hapless young man's brother and make everyone as miserable as possible. And oh, yes, you're getting all this money in return for signing away your rights as heir to a Foundation family. Was there anything else? Could he perhaps have thrown in that Enzo should really seek some medical help for his drinking? We'll give you a job you've always wanted, but you'll have to do all this demeaning shit? Like marry your younger brother's pregnant girlfriend?

Ellisandra caught a glance of herself in the mirror over Sariandra's shoulders. Her cheeks had gone bright red.

"Take the dress off. We'll sort out something. I'll make sure you'll look glamorous," she said to Sariandra. Her voice sounded detached, as if it belonged to someone else.

"I'll resign if you want."

Ellisandra took Sariandra by the chin. "Say that again, and I'll slap you in the face. I'm serious."

Sariandra nodded, pressing her lips together.

"Are you all right? Are you healthy? Do you have any problems?"

"You're kidding? My life is a problem."

"I mean with your health."

"I don't think so. I've been feeling a bit tired, but nothing else."

"Have you seen a Healer?"

Sariandra's eyes widened.

"You know, to check up on your health?"

She shook her head.

"I'll arrange it."

"But—"

"No buts. You will see a Healer. In all of this, *you* are more important than anyone. More important than your father, or the council. That is my little niece or nephew growing in there."

Sariandra changed back into her own clothes, and for the rest of the day, whenever Ellisandra walked past her, she smiled.

Even Tolaki noticed it. "What did you do to her? She seems completely changed."

"She enjoys the theatre," Ellisandra said, and she felt a twinge of guilt about not sharing what she knew with Tolaki. In the past they'd shared everything. But this was beyond gossip and she wasn't sure that Tolaki would understand. Tolaki's family was very traditional, agreed with the council in a no-nonsense kind of way. They were serious business people, and with Jaeron in the council, the men had no idea about the other world out there, the world of artists and women and other people who were irrelevant in Miran.

Poor, poor girl.

She had badly underestimated Sariandra, even though she prided herself on being a good judge of character. She knew nothing, especially not about love. Sometimes she would dream of a man sweeping her off her feet with his kisses. Old rules said that there would be no interaction between a couple until they married, but many couples went out and kissed, and sometimes more. Jaeron had never shown any interest, and damn it, she wanted the affection that everyone said was part of marriage.

Eariandra was not unfortunate; she was *lucky* to have that affection.

The bad weather of that morning cleared up in the afternoon. Loret and his team, who had come to the theatre in the morning, asked permission to go to the Andrahar house. The orchestra had also just finished practice and Ellisandra realised that she had left some of her production notes at home, so it was a large and mixed group of people who walked from the theatre up the hill to the Endri quarter.

There was much talk and laughter, and somehow, she ended up walking next to Vayra. With a certain amount of dread she realised that she now had no excuse not to go with him to the house and look at those colours that he asked her about.

He and Loret were talking about a stonemason specialising in old-fashioned stone carving, and he'd also employed a panel-maker who constructed custom-made resin panels with inlaid stems of grass. It was how the magnificent doors to the theatre had been made.

"I didn't know anyone could still make those," she said. It still surprised her that he knew so much about Miran, and why he'd been so keen to learn. Seeing the welcome they had given him, she would have left long ago.

"It wasn't easy finding someone, but he's amazing."

"I can imagine." She'd seen pictures of the hot rooms where the panels were made, where people arranged every stem of hay by hand so the reflection off the stems made a pattern once the resin had been poured on top.

"I'll show you how he works."

She followed the group into the yard.

Much progress had been made on the house in little time. Most of the exterior had been completed. The only thing missing were the roof tiles on the rooms that were built around the main section of the house: the laundry, the staff rooms and the front porch. Stacks of roof tiles sat in big piles for this purpose.

The main section of the house looked almost finished, except for the front door. A couple of workers were walking in and out, carrying tools and stacks of tiles.

"Wow, did the house really have wooden window frames?"

"Yes. They're harder to come by than the resin ones, but wood has better insulation. The whole house has been built to retain heat."

Under the canvas shelter against the side wall stood a dome-shaped tent that hadn't been there before, a strangely unearthly-looking glowing white thing.

"Have you been sleeping here?" she asked Vayra when they were crossing the yard.

"No, I normally stay in the office. The tent is for the resin-maker. The resin dries better when it's warmer."

A heated tent?

"Come and have a look." He opened a flap at the tent, and they went inside a little tunnel that connected to a second dome-shaped structure that glowed like a light pearl. The sound of a sanding machine came from inside.

"What is this thing?"

"It's a miner's tent, from Hedron. It's what they use to house exploration miners on the surface at Hedron. See how it's got two walls with an air chamber in between? That insulates the living area inside. Pretty impressive, isn't it?"

He opened a flap which let them into a heat lock and then into the inner tent where a pungent smell of resin hit her in the face.

Inside the structure stood a table where an old man was working. It was so warm inside that he needed to wear only a shirt and trousers. On the table lay a half-finished panel. The man bent over it, carefully arranging stems of straw with a pair of tweezers.

He looked up when Vayra and Ellisandra came in.

She recognised him. When she was young, he used to sit at markets plying his trade. She hadn't seen him for quite some time.

He'd been one of these people who had quietly disappeared and their trades had disappeared with them.

"Old Jasep is one of the best in resin-making," Vayra said. "Apparently some people have been ordering a lot of these doors."

"They're very traditional," Jasep said. "But the councillors want them in all the places where they don't belong."

Such as Asitho Bisumar's house.

"Still, the money is good, so I keep quiet, but it pleases me so much that I get to make some doors that are not to be put in some modern monstrosity. It is so nice to work here."

His hands had resumed arranging stems of straw in intricate layered patterns. Already with the light in the tent, you could see the patterns in the different ways in which the stems reflected the light.

He rose from his seat and went to the back wall, where a pot bubbled on the stove. He took it off with two stained rags, and carefully poured molten resin over his designs. The pungent smell of it filled the tent. He used a brush to spread it evenly over the straw. "You want to be careful, because you don't want bubbles to form."

"It's beautiful," Ellisandra said.

"The patterns in the door represent mountain flowers. Each panel maker has their own designs. That why the cheaper versions are rubbish. They're put together quickly and with poor materials."

"We'll leave him to work," Vayra said.

Old Jasep laughed. "Ha, he pays me too much to spend my time chatting."

To one side of the tent stood a smaller table with three chairs. They were very old, beautifully-made and didn't suit the modern tent at all.

"Where did you get these?"

"They're from the office. Sit down. Want some tea?"

She laughed. "You even have tea in here?"

"It that odd?"

"This whole tent is such a strange combination of foreign and traditional Mirani things."

"These are all traditional things from many places. The mining tents have been used at Hedron since their first settlement, and the design has changed little in the last hundred years. I only like beautiful, well-made and good things. I don't care where they're from, as long as they've been made with skill and craftsmanship."

He rummaged in a cupboard and took out two tall mugs. He filled these with water, added powdered tea and put them inside a box which produced a slight hum. Vayra waited.

Ellisandra looked around the tent. Apart from a device with a screen on the table, there was a bigger machine on a stand next to where Vayra stood. It had a screen at the front, where occasionally lines of blue text appeared and scrolled out of sight. The writing ran from right to left, and she figured it was Coldi.

Once, Vayra glanced at the screen, raised his eyebrows and typed something. This line appeared on the screen in yellow. A blue line responded and he replied something else.

Where did the blue text come from? This did not look in any way like it came through the Miran Exchange.

The box stopped humming. Vayra took out the two mugs.

He placed them in front of her on the table. Steam rose from the tea inside. She picked up her mug. It was made of a very strange metal that wasn't even warm. After the cold of the theatre, she was also starting to get nice and warm so that she had to take off her cloak.

"It's very nice in here."

"This is what Miran could be like in the future."

"What do you mean?"

"You could have all these things to make your lives more comfortable."

"We're already pretty comfortable."

But she realised that was an Endri view of things. Many of the Nikala lived in cramped, cold and damp conditions. Too many people had no homes at all and slept in porches and hallways. "These tents . . . are they expensive?"

"Depends on your definition of expensive. Why?"

"Because housing is a problem for many of the Nikala. Short of the empty Endri houses being converted with apartments, there is no quick accommodation available . . ." She was going to add something like *for women who want to escape violent marriages* or *young people who flee abusive households*. A lot of the older apartment blocks were very cramped and cold. If they had windows—which many didn't—they were draughty. People got diseases that were entirely preventable. These tents were easy and comfortable. You could quickly build an entire city out of these.

"And how did you get all this here? Illegally?"

"Why would I do that when there is a legal route available? It has come overland from Barresh to Bendara and then via air to Miran. Nothing illegal about it."

"Is there still a land route between Bendara and Barresh?"

"There used to be a main road. A lot has overgrown with jungle, but the Barresh side has been cleared. The Mirani side is only really bad between the border and the start of the Bendara agricultural zone. I would like to re-open it. I would like to build a train line from Miran to the western coast. Transport would be easy then."

It would. Ellisandra dreamed of sitting in a cabin—trains had cabins, didn't they?—and being brought drinks while looking at the landscape slide past outside the window.

Then she sighed. "Like that will ever happen."

"Why not?"

"Because of the boycotts, because of the import restrictions. We can only dream of things like that. As soon as the council finds this legal loophole of yours, they'll close it."

"Then you stop them."

She frowned at him. "Are you serious?"

"Of course I am. People tell me I have no sense of humour. I think I inherited that from my father."

"How should I stop the council? They don't listen to me."

"Then you make them listen. That's part of their tactics, too. They do whatever they want because no one challenges them, because you're complacent."

"I think there's a bit more to it than that." She tried to keep the indignant tone out of her voice, but didn't think she succeeded.

He fixed her with an intense look and pointed a finger at her chest. "Because you're complacent. They treat you Endri women like shit, because you let them."

"Because they hurt some of us."

"They can't hurt you when you as a group stand up for yourself. Because there are more of you than there are of them."

"You want to try and face Asitho Bisumar and tell him to leave his daughter alone? Do you want to face my brother and tell him that he can't marry this girl, because she is my younger brother's?"

He shook his head. "I don't want to *try*. I want you to *do* it."

She snorted. "That's not how Miran works."

"No. It isn't. But it is why Miran is a backwards hole, and other nations have freedom, are connected and have proper hospitals and housing. Because people stood up and protested. It's your choice."

"Maybe it is, but it's my life, too, and I only have one."

She was making excuses, and she knew it. He knew it, too, and he continued to meet her eyes until she had to look away, and even when she did, she could feel his gaze on her.

I'm a coward. We're all cowards. We could make this place so much better.

"Anyway. I really want your opinion on wall colours in the bathroom."

She looked up sharply. He was saying all these insulting things about Miran and wasn't even going to apologise?

He smiled. "So, you *can* get angry."

"What's that supposed to mean?"

"You're complacent."

"You would be, too, if you were in my situation."

"I probably would—"

"See? There you go. Because of Father, I can't—"

"—for a while. Until I saw that being complacent doesn't work, that people take advantage of it. And then I would make a plan."

"You can plan as much as you like, but if the other side has all the resources and the power—"

"—I wouldn't execute the plan until I was certain that it was going to work."

"That may be easy for you, but how do you argue against everything you've grown up with? You've had an easy life, studying at the Trader Academy and Masterbuilders Guild and *ganra* Law."

He laughed. "I see Mirani intelligence is not as bad as it's made out to be."

She smiled awkwardly. Probably she should not have let him know that the council knew those things.

"In all honesty, what else do you know about my life?" He met her eyes, his expression honest and open.

She shrugged. "Nothing, really."

"It's easy to assume that other people's lives are easier than your own. But I am very familiar with standing up against the only life you've known." He managed to sound kind, but she was sure that she had insulted him.

"Sorry, I didn't mean to assume—"

"Don't worry about it. I'll tell you." He picked up his cup and sipped. "I'm the oldest of five children. I have three brothers and a sister. The man I considered my father when I was little isn't, in fact, my father. My stepfather and my father almost killed each other once. That should be indicative of my stepfather's feelings towards me, although he'd rather die than talk about feelings. He's an awkward, dysfunctional man prone to violent mood swings, who is so absorbed in his project of creating an Aghyrian community that he's forgotten how to be part of that community. When I was young, my mother was so ashamed of me that she used to dye my hair black, so that people wouldn't ask questions."

"What colour is it normally?"

"It's golden brown, a bit darker than Nikala hair. My stepfather has black hair, and all my brothers and sisters do, too. They're studious little kids who are completely under his influence. But I fought a lot with him, and he doesn't handle fights very well. He's got this . . . ability to store energy inside him, and has a lot of trouble controlling it when he's angry. I made him angry a lot. I was a shitty precocious little kid."

She laughed. She could relate to that.

Then he lifted the left leg of his trousers. A shallow scar ran across his shin. "This happened one day when his ability got out of control. I did something wrong, I can't even remember what, and he flew into a rage. He was pacing around in the downstairs room that he used as library and trails of lightning were coming off him. It was fascinating. I wasn't scared and didn't realise I'd been burned until much later. He was so shaken that he avoided me after that. My mother tried to apologise for him at first, but she gave up."

Vayra's expression had changed to one of pain. "The Andrahar family was my home. I often watched my mother look out the window if the Andrahar kids were playing in the yard next door. I only realised later that my mother should never have married my stepfather. I didn't fully understand that until Rehan Andrahar gave her the box that contained the wedding armbands that my real father had made for her. The armbands had both their names engraved. At the time, she didn't know that my real father was still alive. When Rehan gave her that box, he had to physically stop her from snapping the armband shut around her wrist. She cried so much I thought she would die. My mother is a strong woman, but that broke her." He sipped again. His eyes glittered. "And then she received a letter from him. She sat in front of the window for a whole afternoon staring at the marshland. You can see aircraft arriving from that direction. I don't know what she was thinking. Maybe that he was coming for her? Later I overheard her talking to one of the domestic staff. 'But I have to think of the children,' she said. And the maid said, 'Take them.' But she didn't think she could do that. And then the maid said, 'I'll look after them.' That scared me so much, because I was only young at the time. My mother didn't leave, out of duty to us and out of duty to her teaching work. That knowledge has always weighed heavy in my mind. So this house is for her so that she can finally leave my step-father. My brothers and sisters are old enough to look after them-selves. I want this to be a safe place for her. I want my real father to come here."

"Have they seen each other since?"

He shook his head. "Not since before I was born. But they'll be together again. I will go to my parents' wedding. I know you have all kinds of theories about me, but this is why I've done all this. I want my parents to be married."

That comment brought her back to Nemedor Satarin and his request for information, requests that would turn into threats if she couldn't deliver. The more she spoke to Vayra, the more she didn't *want* to deliver. His story was so sad and beautiful and so personal. She had no idea why the Endri families had thought his story so important that they had given him the use of their money, but the things he did were to the benefit of the people of Miran.

She didn't want to hear more details of his plans, because she couldn't guarantee that no one would get those details out of her, given enough pressure. And the whole thought of protecting him against the council gave her the chills. In the past, people who had gone against the council had been driven out of Miran. She didn't want to have to leave. This was her home. She only had one home.

"What did you want me to look at in your bathroom?"

He gave her a curious glance—did he sense why she changed the subject?—but got up from the table. Behind the table stood an old-fashioned cabinet made from beautiful mountain pinewood that came from gnarled trees that grew on the western slopes. Just below the tree line, the environment was still very harsh, and the wood was dark, knotted and twisted. Fashioning it into furniture was a delicate art that required soaking the wood to straighten it.

There used to be a cabinet like this in her grandmother's formal dining room, and it was odd to see it in this modern tent.

He opened one of the carved front doors and took something out, which he placed on the table: a flat metallic disk. He ran his hand over its surface. A three-dimensional projection sprang into the air.

It depicted a house, vaguely recognisable as the construction site at the moment.

"I'd take you inside the house, except they're putting in the floor and we can't walk on it." He moved his hand over the screen, and the projection turned around so that she faced the main door. Then it enlarged, and enlarged.

"Whoa!" All around her walls had appeared, as if she were in the house. The walls were made of dark resin panels with flower patterns. The door had six little square windows of coloured glass. The floor mosaic was like the ones on the floor in the council building, depicting geometric patterns. There was even a coat stand with cloaks hanging on it, and a shoe rack with house shoes. To the left was the kitchen—with a wooden table and a stove. It looked so real that she expected the cook to come out any moment.

"This is the entrance hall." He traced his finger over the screen. Slowly, as if they were walking, the projection moved so that they went through a door into a corridor. It was fairly narrow, with no windows and a couple of doors on the right-hand side, but only one on the left.

"See, this is the original flooring that was put in soon after the house was built." The projection focused on the black, grey and white mosaic of small hexagonal stones. "These stones are all handmade and hand-polished. The walls are the original river clay render. It's off-white naturally, and it was not until much later that people started to add colouring in the cement."

The rendering was green in her house.

They "walked" to the door in the left-hand wall of the corridor. It opened at their approach and they entered the bathroom. It was huge, rectangular, with a huge pool in the middle. The water was still and clear, with faint wisps of steam rising from the surface. There were benches against both of the walls, as well as a dressing table next to the door.

"Wow," Ellisandra said. She looked around. It was as if they were both standing in the room.

He smiled. "The walls and floor are all covered in baked tiles. I've made them white, but I'm not really sure if that is the colour they would originally have been."

"The tiles in our bathroom are creamy white."

"Your house was built fifty years later. Except white, the other option is pale blue." He touched something on the screen and the entire room around them changed. The tiles became blue, and now there were decorative tiles at certain intervals depicting flowers in dark blue and gold paint.

Ellisandra looked around. "This is just like the bathhouse."

"Good. That's what I wanted to know."

"You wanted to know what the inside of the bathhouse looks like?"

"Exactly."

"You could have gone to the bathhouse for that."

"I can't, because I'm not allowed in."

"Why?"

"I'm a foreigner."

Coming from his mouth in unaccented Mirani, it sounded ridiculous. But he was right, there was that rule, especially when applied to the old bathhouse in town, the one he'd wanted to visit.

"You could have told them what it was for."

"I could, but everyone is too edgy about my being here already."

That was right, too.

He flicked off the projection, and the house disappeared around them. Once again she sat at the table in the tent. She blinked to adjust her eyes to the sudden increase in light level. The light above the worktable, however, was off, and the resin-maker's seat was empty. Her heart jumped. When had he left? Had it been Vayra's plan to get her alone?

She rose from her seat. "Thank you for the tea, but I've got to go—"

"Ellisandra, wait."

Her heart jumped even more. He still sat at the table but she felt like he had physically grabbed her arm.

"You know that you're in danger, right?"

Me?

"They're targeting you to spy on me. If you don't deliver what they want, they'll start to put pressure on you."

How did he know that?

"It's already happening, isn't it? This is how they work. I have seen long reports of why families left Miran."

"Those reports are all part of the *gamra* propaganda against us, right?" She'd said it before she could stop herself. This was what the council always told the citizens of Miran. But lately she had started to wonder if it might be better to put all the claims and counterclaims on the table, have an inquiry and big discussion about it and be done with it.

"Nothing to do with propaganda. They are accounts recorded as the best approximation of the truth, witnessed and signed by independent Peacekeepers who have no interest in Miran or any connection with it. It's true that the retelling may have introduced some bias, but they're people's personal stories as they remembered them." Like a true Trader, he was measured and gracious in his reply.

Ellisandra dragged a hand over her face, stifling a groan. She and her big mouth.

"They're the stories told by Amandra Bisumar, who was blackballed, ignored and ridiculed for wanting to clear up the council's reputation in the missing persons case. They're the stories of Iztho Andrahar, how he went from being the celebrated heir of Miran's most powerful Trading family to outcast. You should read that."

Vayra rose from his seat. From the old cabinet behind him, he took a bunch of paper, which he gave to her. "This is his story. I'd give it to you on file, but I wasn't sure what devices you'd have to read it, so I'm playing it safe."

"We're not *that* backward."

"You'd be surprised."

She looked around the tent. Yes, probably she would be.

"Read it, and burn it. Don't let anyone find it. You don't want to fall out with the council and I'd hate something to happen to you." His expression was so intense that it gave her the chills. He'd said that like he cared about her. But to him, she was just another dumb woman to be used for his aims. These men in power were all the same.

She swallowed. "I was going to warn you that *you* were in danger. There are rumours that some of the young men are planning to disrupt your work and harass you until you leave." Enzo was likely to be one of those men.

"I have no illusions but that they will do that. In fact, I would have been disappointed had they not made those plans. I'm prepared. I've got guards and they have weapons. I pay them well, and they will be loyal to me if I ask them to defend this house. In fact, every one, to the last person I have working here, will defend this house, whether they're a guard or not."

Was that a threat, or some sort of warning?

She laughed, uneasily, clutching that bunch of paper that felt like a hot fire poker in her hands, a thing she wanted to throw away as soon as possible as far as she possibly could. "What is this? Some kind of declaration of war on the council? Who are you really? What are you doing? Why are you here?"

"I told you: to rebuild a house. Rebuild a country that I've grown to love, if I may help a little bit. If you understand what I'm talking about, come and see me again. If you don't, I'll just play the flute. But do know that I can get you a lot more musicians for your orchestra."

19

E LLISANDRA WALKED back to her house, clutching the papers under her cloak.

That last statement of his, *I can get you a lot more musicians for your orchestra,* chilled her deep inside. He didn't mean real musicians or real orchestra. He meant to say that he was building a rebel group of people loyal to him by paying them well and showing them the future they could have if they supported him.

His plan included having asked all the families who left Miran for the pass codes to their Mirani credit accounts so that he had a lot of money to do all this. It was not the action of one man, but the silent action of many. She'd been wrong in assuming that the families who had left didn't care about Miran. They'd left Vayra their entire Mirani wealth to support his plan.

What had he said again? *I wouldn't execute the plan until I was certain that it was going to work.*

Would she take a part in the plan and if so, what part would that be? She knew the power of theatre to motivate people and to provide social commentary with little risk. This was why the council watched the theatre so closely: because the political messages were strong.

She walked up the veranda and into the house. It was quite

early. The smell of cooking drifted from the kitchen, but the only sign of dinner was a pot bubbling on the stove. Riana must have turned it to simmer and gone to her room. It was too early for Father's dinner.

Ellisandra went up to her room where she stacked a couple of firebricks on top of waxed straw kindling in the hearth and used a coal from the fire box to light it. While the flames devoured the kindling, she unfolded the bunch of paper Vayra had given her. There were two columns: The right-hand one was in Mirani and the other in Coldi. She stared at the curly script. Coldi was written from left to right because most Coldi people were left-handed. Ellisandra couldn't even begin to imagine what all those curls meant.

The Mirani text said,

Statement provided by the claimant to the Gamra Law Office, witnessed and sworn under oath.

The date on it was in *gamra* notation, in *gamra* years, which she hadn't needed to convert into Mirani years since leaving school. She wasn't sure if she got it right, that one Ceren year was 1.7 *gamra* years and that 8457 in *gamra* years was the same as 4439 in Mirani years, or was it 4425? Which was a rather large difference and didn't help her much in determining how old this was.

She started reading the declaration.

In the schools in Miran only the Mirani version of events was given: that Iztho Andrahar had not held to an agreement he had with the council and had responded by taking all the family's money out of Miran, much of which was, according to the council, Mirani because Andrahar was a Foundation family and could not sell their assets. The council had tried to recover the money by going to court, but because the family were Traders, they had to go through the Trader Court. It, of course, protected one of their own.

That was the Mirani version.

This version started out when Barresh was still a protectorate and Iztho Andrahar would go there for work. Iztho Andrahar's statement said, about Nemedor Satarin,

I became friendly with him, because he is an intelligent man and we share a love for history. I had long been interested in the history of the group of people called the Aghyrians, who are said to be the forefathers of all human types. They are known to be long-lived, hyper-intelligent and some are said to possess an ability to absorb energy into their bodies and release it at their command.

That was what Vayra had said his stepfather could do.

Without my noticing at first, Nemedor Satarin became interested in this latter ability. He found out that there were several of these people on Hedron and set about recruiting them. He wanted to breed a group of these people and use them in the production of a defence system. I wasn't happy about this when I first heard of it, but he assured me that all people were in Miran by their own choice.

They were all male and when he heard of a single female Aghyrian, he asked me to bring her to Miran. It was supposed to be a simple job.

The lady was the most delightful person I have ever had the pleasure of meeting. She was strong-willed, nobody's fool, but ignorant in the ways of our world. She also had no idea of Nemedor Satarin's plans for her and wouldn't have agreed with them if she had. It was my absolute moral duty to protect her. I refused to bring her to Miran.

For this, the Mirani council and, most notably, our competitors the Tussamar Traders invented a scheme that connected the Andrahar Traders with the illegal import into Barresh of several bags of menisha *fungus. At the time menisha brew was a huge problem on the streets of Barresh, linked with gang warfare and criminal behaviour.*

When I refused to appear in court, they chased me. When I escaped, they went to my family. But I prepared my family and gave them the tools to refute the accusations, which the Trader court has seen to be absolute nonsense.

There were paragraphs of detail on how the false accusations were made to seem genuine, all with a level of detail she had never heard before.

Maybe, just maybe, he was right. But even if he wasn't, the people of Miran needed to know the truth, whatever the truth was.

Someone called in the hall.

Ellisandra gasped. She had forgotten about Father, and dinner. But it wasn't dinnertime yet. She rose from her chair with the paper in her hand and flung the pages in the fire. The flames licked over the paper, curling the edges and turning it black.

In the hall, Riana stood at the bottom of the stairs. "Oh, I thought I was going to have to come up to get you, mistress."

"What's the matter?"

"There is someone here for you."

Ellisandra wasn't expecting anyone, at least she didn't think she'd made any appointments. She went down to the living room, where it was warm and smelled of tea and sweet cakes.

In the chair by the fire sat . . . Jaeron.

"Oh, good afternoon. I . . . wasn't expecting you." Why did he always unnerve her so much?

"I can't come to visit unannounced?"

"You can, but . . . I haven't made myself pretty." She was going all hot in the face again and she hated that. His penetrating eyes looked as if they could see straight through her and he knew what she'd just been reading.

"You're always pretty to me."

She smiled at him, and he returned the smile, albeit a bit stiffly.

At the little table next to the hearth stood a tray with a teapot and two cups as well as a plate of dainty cakes. She poured two cups of tea. One of them, she gave to him, as well as a plate with two cakes, which she set down on the table next to his chair. His hands didn't touch her at all when she gave him the cup, but his gaze followed all her movements in a detached, unemotional way.

She nodded at the little stool next to his seat. "Do you want me to sit there?" Mother used to do that, and then Father would put a hand on her shoulder and she'd lean into him.

"You're not a servant, are you? There will be no need for you to crawl on the floor."

She sat on the couch, straight-backed, with her own tea clutched on her lap, but she didn't trust herself to pick it up and drink. He would notice that her hands trembled.

He clutched his cup with long-fingered hands and she wondered how it would feel if those hands massaged her shoulders. She sort-of wanted him to, just to show her that he was actually interested in her as a person rather than a checkbox in his life achievements to be ticked.

Get a wife: tick.

He picked up one of the cakes and bit off half. "Hmmm," he said with his mouth full, and when he had swallowed it, he added, "Excellent. Do eat some. I don't want my wife to be skinny."

Those two words, *my wife*, sounded so chilling. Ellisandra took a cake, but didn't think she'd be able to eat one bite.

He ate the rest of the cake and then the other one. She looked at his lips as he chewed. They were quite broad and a little bit raw from the cold.

Then he was finished eating and set his plate down. "I have a request to make of you."

Oh? That didn't sound like he'd come here to kiss her. It sounded like business.

"This is really quite important for me and it will be important for you, too." He fixed her with a stern look. "A Nikala man came into one of our tenants' shops this morning. He bought a brand new male tiyuk cloak for himself and one for his wife. He was not an old man, quite young, in fact. Young enough not to have children."

"Your tenant had a good day, I presume?" Where was this going?

"Yes, a very good day. Then another man came in, wanting a cloak also, and boots. Then a third customer came in, and my tenant was out of quality cloaks."

"Why are you telling me this? The shopkeeper must have been happy."

"Of course he is."

She still didn't get what the problem was.

"The customers are all people who are working for our friend next door."

Vayra.

"He's paid them more than any local employer can afford, and they like it."

Why didn't he just tell her what his point was?

"He's *buying* the workers' favours. They've never been paid this much before and they'll do anything for him. He's using the Ilendar account. I could ask for council action to have it blocked, but chances are that he's got other accounts as well. For years, the rich families have hoarded credits in their accounts. It's why things have become cheaper, because there are fewer credits in circulation. It looks like he's dumping all this money on the market."

"Isn't that a good thing?" She'd heard that those accounts were a problem. Because credits were directly linked to the available land within the city boundaries, the council couldn't simply respond to the problem by releasing more credits, or at least not without seriously affecting people's old age livelihoods.

"He's buying their loyalty, telling them where to buy. The amount of money involved in this could potentially be staggering. He could potentially bring all of Miran to its knees."

"So what does this have to do with me?"

"We need to know how much cash there is in these accounts."

"So you want me to give you access to the system."

"Yes."

In one chilling moment, she understood: this was not about the information at all. If the councillors really wanted to get that information, and Jaeron was on the council, they could get it through their own channels. To suggest that the safety of Miran hung on her access to the Accountkeepers' system through the theatre was just ridiculous. Either he needed to have access for something illegal or, more likely, this was a test of her loyalty to the council. The blood roared in her ears.

What would happen if she refused?

What would happen if she agreed?

Oh, she wanted to tell him what she thought of these tactics and the intimidation that had been directed at her, and oh, by the way, do you know the wedding is off? But her mouth was too dry to speak, and she was too scared to say those things, because she had nowhere to go that wasn't controlled by the men in power.

"Ellisandra."

She froze.

"As my future wife, you have sworn loyalty to me."

She nodded, but she felt like she was about to faint.

"Give me those figures."

"I . . . don't have access to them from here." Which was actually true.

"Tomorrow." His expression was hard. "I'll come to the theatre."

When he left, Ellisandra ran up the stairs. It smelled like dinner was almost ready, but her throat felt so tight that she couldn't have eaten anything had she tried.

She stood in the middle of her room, her heart racing. This room where she had dreamed of getting married in a big beautiful ceremony.

She was not the crying type, but her eyes pricked. It had all been an illusion, carefully built for her by the people around her. But now, nothing was the same.

Nothing would ever be the same.

She sat at her desk and pulled out a sheet of paper with dainty flowers. With her best pen from the inkpot on the desk's corner, she wrote in neat letters:

I, Ellisandra Takumar, of the Takumar Foundation family, withdraw my consent of marriage to Jaeron Hirumar.

She blew on it to dry the ink, folded the paper, put it in an envelope and stuck on a seal.

This she put in the pocket of her cloak.

20

ELLISANDRA DIDN'T touch that letter for a number of days. The next morning, it seemed such a rash and risky decision. What would happen to her if she backed out now? Would she ever find a husband? More worryingly, was there a future for her without one? Enzo would inherit the house, and she would have no income.

She had always known that Jaeron wasn't interested in her as much as in being associated with her family. That was a common thing in Mirani marriages. But if the notion that she should love, or even like, her future husband was just a silly idea, why then did she feel this ache inside when she thought of Sariandra and Jintho, or Rana and Mariandra?

Being jealous didn't suit a Mirani Endri lady. They were quiet and obedient, and above all didn't cause trouble.

She would probably never send the letter, and would obediently marry Jaeron in the spring. After all, he meant well and she would have a very comfortable life.

But she kept the letter in her pocket just in case.

Two days later word came that Gisandra had given birth to a baby girl, so Ellisandra went to the markets to buy a present. Browsing at the stalls for little romper suits, she noticed what

Jaeron had said: a lot of the merchants had less stock than usual, and whatever they had left was inferior.

"It's all been sold," a woman told her when she asked. "A lot of people with a lot of money around these days."

Most notably, when she left the markets, the group of beggars that usually hung out at the shuttered door to merchant Ranuddin's shop was gone. Not only that but the shutters were open and people moved in the dark and dusty interior. Ellisandra already knew what they were before she could see: more builders.

Gisandra and her husband lived on the lower part of the Endri quarter, only a few blocks away from the markets. It was a decent house with a nice yard. Today, a couple of sculptures lined the path: Little snow men sculpted from compressed snow. They had rounded, fat bellies and little short legs. They were mountain cherubs, said in the myths to bring babies.

These types of mythical sculptures would be put up in yards if a significant event happened in the house, and would stay there until they melted or were snowed in.

A maid let Ellisandra into the house and pointed her to the main bedroom.

Gisandra sat propped up against cushions in the huge bed.

When she saw her friend come in, she cried out. "Elli!" She spread her hands.

Ellisandra ran to the bed and hugged her friend.

"Ow, ow, my backside." And then she laughed. "Don't look at me like that, I'm fine unless I lean forward."

"Oh, sorry. Was it bad?"

"I was in agony for two days and nights. I don't know how often I begged for the midwife to cut me and rip this thing out of me. I sat pushing my guts out on the damned chair for half a day and when she finally came out, it felt like I was ripped apart. There was so much blood. It just shot out with her, like whoosh, all over the floor."

Ellisandra shivered, but remembered that Gisandra always liked to spice up stories with gore.

She peeked in the little cot that stood next to the bed. Under the embroidered blankets lay a tiny baby. Her head was bald except for a soft layer of fuzz. Her tiny eyes were closed.

"Oh, so cute."

"A girl," Gisandra said and there was a tone of disappointment in her voice.

Ellisandra turned sharply and gave her a questioning look.

"It means I have to do all this again until he has his heir. The oldest son of the oldest son."

True, and nothing could be done about it. Ellisandra sat down on the chair next to the bed. The maid came to bring tea. She set Gisandra's on a small tray on the blankets.

When the maid had left, Gisandra said, "So, I understand that you were landed with having to stage *Changing Fate?*"

Ellisandra nodded.

"That's such a weird play. I wouldn't know what to make of it. It doesn't seem to have a point except all the nice people die."

"I think it's a message."

"What do you mean?"

"I've found out that the author of the play was a woman, most likely the one depicted as Mariandra."

Gisandra's eyes widened.

"I think it's likely that the author would have been made to write the play as punishment for her evil transgression of having fallen in love with a foreigner."

"I just can't believe that the council would do that. Imagine seeing your lover killed before your eyes and then to be forced to write about how it was a good thing."

"That's what I think happened. It's pretty obvious from the play that she was still in love with Rana. She was facing a loveless arranged marriage and she had something beautiful . . ." Her voice wouldn't cooperate. All of a sudden, she thought of Sariandra and Jirtho. They should marry, preferably before Sariandra gave birth. She thought of the sad story Vayra had told her of his parents. The image of his mother almost snapping her armband shut around her arm, thinking that her former lover was dead, brought tears to Ellisandra's eyes. So many young women were being forced to marry against their wishes.

"Elli? What's wrong?"

Ellisandra swallowed hard. "I'm all right. Just exhausted. We should be talking about your beautiful girl."

"You're not all right. What's the matter?"

Ellisandra hesitated. Out of all the many women she knew, Gisandra was the most down-to-earth, the most honest.

She said in a low voice, "I don't want to marry Jaeron."

Ellisandra had expected an outcry of *What?* but instead her friend just looked at her. Her eyes glittered with tears.

"Gisi?"

She whispered, "Go, while you're still free." She wiped at her eyes. "Run away, Elli. Run."

"What's the ma—"

"If you don't want to marry him, don't. Please. Don't do anything because some man says you have to."

"Are you all right?"

Gisandra nodded. "I'm fine. Just a bit emotional. And we had a fight. Because he wants a son, he wanted to . . . you know, last night."

"After you've given birth? He's got to be kidding."

"No. And I told him to go to hell."

"You did? What did he say?"

"He just sort-of shrugged and left. Haven't seen him since, but that could be because there is some sort of thing going on with the council, so they're very busy."

"He didn't hit you or anything?"

"Oh no, he's too much of a softy for that. We'll be fine when it's settled. I don't mind, you know, pleasing him, and having another child, apart from the gory end-bit. But you know . . ." She looked aside where her little daughter was still fast asleep, a tiny hand resting relaxed on the sheets. "You know her life is worthless, just like mine is worthless, and yours?" Her voice cracked.

The anger Ellisandra had felt building for days was clawing its way to the surface. It wouldn't be long before she had reached that point of no return. Vayra had said that Mirani women were too complacent. Well, she was done with being complacent.

"No, none of our lives are worthless," Ellisandra said. "I have a plan. We're going to do something about it."

"But how? I can't see what we can do."

"Make sure that you get out of bed on the day of the play. Come to the hall and bring your drums, cymbals and bells. We're going to form an orchestra."

Ellisandra walked past the Andrahar house on the way home. It was uphill from her, and she needed to walk around the block to pretend that she was coming from that direction. Even this late in the afternoon, there was a lot of activity at the house. Builders were just packing up their tools, walking out the front door and stowing their tools on the porch.

Vayra had ordered blue tiles, she noticed.

While the builders walked out of the gate in small groups, other men came in. These were taller and broader, mostly in grey clothing. They took up position in the shadows, blending with the snow. Did she imagine it or were some of them not Mirani?

The open metalwork gate into the yard was no longer rusty. Flaking paint had been scrubbed off and replaced with a shining coat of black.

A very eager person had shovelled a broad path from the gate to the front porch and the tent. The piles of stones now formed the wall, the slate was on the roof. The windows had been put in. She wondered how close the house was to being finished.

While she stood there, a man came from the tent—where the cock and resin maker had already gone—and crossed the yard to the gate.

She recognised Vayra about halfway to the gate.

"I see you chose the blue tiles."

"Yes. We can have a quick look if you want."

Ellisandra glanced up at her house. The light was on in Father's room, as well as Jintho's room and in the downstairs rooms on this side of the house. If she just went quickly, no one would know, right?

Vayra led her over the shovelled path, up the new steps to the porch and into the hall. The floor was still rough. Crates of stone pieces stood against one wall, a couple of doors against another.

"Wow, is that real wood?" She ran her hand over the surface. It felt rough and warm.

"Those are the doors for the living room, the kitchen and the front room. This room next to the front door used to be Iztho's room."

She peeked into the space. The ceiling beams were still exposed, and the wall panels hadn't been put up yet. A couple of workmen walked past with bags of cement.

"They're for the bathroom. We'll be starting on that tomorrow."

He guided her into the corridor that was familiar to her because she had seen it in the simulation. The bathroom seemed smaller than it had appeared in the simulation because the walls were still rough stone, and the piping and ductwork was exposed. The water heater would sit in a little room at the far end of the pool.

The workmen walked out, leaving behind an uneasy silence. Outside the bathroom and upstairs, men talked and laughed and hammered.

"It will be nice when it's finished," Ellisandra said. "I'm sure your mother will appreciate it."

"This is not only about my mother." He faced her. His eyes were intense and she couldn't continue to meet them. "This is about us, the younger generation of Miran."

She stood within reach of him, and all of a sudden, she was afraid that he had only invited her here so that he could grab her and kiss her.

She glanced at the open door, as if seeking for a way to flee. Her heart hammered against her ribs.

"Do you still think it looks good?"

"It's hard to see without the tiles." Her heart thudded so much that she could barely hear him. She was starting to feel hot under her cloak and wondered if he would notice beads of sweat on her upper lip.

"I suppose." He looked around, craning his neck. "I need to get them to fix that duct."

A few more moments passed in uneasy silence.

Then she said, "I could use some players for the orchestra."

He turned sharply to her and smiled. She had never seen him smile like this, never seen much emotion on his face. That was to be expected, since he'd been to the Trader Academy, but it shook her. Had he waited for a reply like this from her?

"I'm sorry that I didn't—"

"Shhh." He put his finger on her lips. The skin was cool. "Not a word. Talk to your conductor. I'll bring some players for her to audition."

She nodded, taking deep breaths. The first step had been taken. The next step was . . . registering for the council election?

At home, she went upstairs to look after Father. She had hoped that she could have another talk with him about politics of the past, but he wasn't very good today, and started making remarks about Darma's big tits the moment she came in the door.

So she helped him eat and washed him without saying much and then went for her own meal.

But as she was just coming down the stairs, two things happened at once. The door to the living room opened and Enzo came out in the company of Asitho Bisumar.

Also, the front door opened and Jintho came in from outside, his cheeks red from the cold.

The three men faced each other, Enzo and Asitho Bisumar on one side, Jintho on the other. The atmosphere in the hallway turned colder than outside.

Jintho's cheeks went even redder than they already were. He balled his fists by his side.

Ellisandra realised the terrible thing. *He knows.*

Jintho very calmly took off his cloak and hung it on the hooks on the wall. His hands trembled.

"Still working on your idiotic shop, are you?" Asitho Bisumar said.

"Yes." Jintho whirled around, his chin raised. "We're going very well. Expecting to be able to employ the first workers soon."

"You didn't sign that permit, did you?" Asitho turned to Enzo, who looked decidedly white in his face.

Jintho replied for him. "He didn't, but we found a way around it. Hiron's father signed, and we expect to be fully independent and able to support ourselves soon. This will be happening. Your daughter will be joining us."

"No, she will not."

"I'll leave that up to her to decide."

"How dare you talk to me like this after what you've done?" Asitho's voice was an angry hiss.

Enzo stepped between them, raising his hands. "Please, everyone, let's talk this over."

"There is no talking over," Asitho Bisumar said. "Except that a good-for-nothing artist destroys my daughter's life, and my reputation."

"You're much more worried about your reputation than your daughter's life. If you cared about her, you wouldn't force her to marry my brother. Because she does not want to marry my brother, even though he fits your ideal of a nice young man. But the choice is not yours, and her life is not yours—"

Jintho had come forward and Enzo pushed him back. "Jintho, please leave it. Don't do anything stupid."

'He's already done plenty of stupid things," Asitho Bisumar cut in.

Enzo turned to Asitho again. "Please calm down, let me deal with him."

"No, brother of mine," Jintho said, "there won't be any dealing, because this has got to stop. Don't you see how he's trying to ruin your life as well as mine and his daughter's? What an insufferable arsehole he is?"

Asitho Bisumar stiffened. He took in a sharp breath through flaring nostrils. His face went white. He lifted his fist and pushed Enzo aside—

Ellisandra screamed, "No, Jintho, watch out!"

She jumped off the stairs and threw herself in front of her brother.

Asitho Bisumar's eyes widened, but he could not deflect his momentum. His knuckles, adorned with rings, hit Ellisandra's left cheekbone.

She screamed. Enzo yelled.

Pain exploded in her face. She reeled on her feet, seeing black spots in her vision. Someone held arms around her. Jintho, she thought.

There were running footsteps of people coming through the house.

Darma yelled, "Oh, mistress, you're bleeding."

Ellisandra brought her hands to her face. They came away covered in blood.

Jintho said, his voice cold, "How dare you hit my sister."

Ellisandra straightened her back. Her head was pounding and she felt decidedly ill, but pushed Jintho aside. Blood trickled from her face down into her neck.

She met Asitho Bisumar's eyes. She did not care what he could do to her. She no longer cared about reputation, his or hers, or about council rules or unspoken rules of behaviour.

"Get out of our house." Her mouth hurt when she spoke and blood crept into the corner of her lips.

"I'm . . . I'm awfully sorry, lady. I . . . I didn't mean to . . ." His face had gone pale.

"Get out of our house! Don't ever dare set foot in here again."

Enzo said, "Elli, be careful."

"I'm done with being careful! Jintho, run, get your girl out of there."

Jintho's eyes went wide. Then he ran to the door. He didn't put on his cloak, he didn't change out of his house shoes. He didn't even close the door behind him.

Asitho Bisumar ran after him, but it was clear he was no match for a young man, and halfway down the yard he must have realised this, and the fact that running didn't look dignified, so he slowed down to a fast walk.

Ellisandra staggered a few paces, feeling dizzy. She wiped her cheek and her hand came away covered in blood.

Enzo put an arm around her shoulders. "Let us look after you, sister."

He accompanied her to the living room, where Darma brought out a box of bandages which they used for Father, and proceeded to clean the cut on her cheekbone. Riana brought a chunk of ice wrapped in a cloth, which she pressed against the wound. Water ran down her face mixing with the blood that had already seeped into her collar.

"My dress is getting dirty," Ellisandra protested weakly.

"Don't worry about that, mistress." Riana rummaged in her box and held a few bandages up for size and rummaged again.

Enzo sat by the hearth, fidgeting and letting out nervous sighs.

Ellisandra pushed away Darma's hands. "Really, it's only a cut. I don't need all that stuff."

"But this is going to be a bad bruise tomorrow, mistress."

She was probably right about that. "I don't care, Darma. You've done well. Go and put Father in bed for me, please."

"Certainly, mistress." Darma bowed and left the room, leaving behind a woolly silence.

Riana left as well, declaring that she needed to do something in the kitchen.

Ellisandra waited for Enzo to speak, to offer his apology, but he didn't, so she said, "There is no way you are marrying Sariandra. There is no way he will ever set foot in our house again, or that he'll give you any kind of job—"

"Elli, you have no idea what's going on."

"Then enlighten me, and I want no more of this *women-are-not-interested-in-politics* nonsense."

He nodded, once. "He's got us by the throat. He's got me, and he's got Jintho. He's got a lot more power than you think. He'll probably fire you from the theatre *for being incapacitated* or some stupid thing."

"Let him try. The performance is two days from now. We're ready for it. Let him try to find other actors, or another committee and get this play performed to the standard that the council expects, or lose his face."

"Do you really think any of the actors and the committee will be brave enough to walk out if he dismisses you?"

He had a point there. Sariandra would, but Tolaki wouldn't, and Aleyo certainly wouldn't. Keldon would like to, but he could ill-afford to lose his job, and Tameyo would be too frightened. But the rest? Probably not. Too many people had gotten into too much trouble for speaking out, or even for buying the wrong things.

Enzo sighed. "He has his claws in all of us. The whole council has its claws in us, especially those of us who still have power. They monitor us, they record what we say, they check what we spend money on."

"The whole thing started because we're a Foundation family, right?"

He nodded and stared at his hands.

"What have they promised you in return for your vote in favour of abolishing the laws that give us the power to stop them?"

To be honest, she had never seen Enzo like this. She got off the

chair and crawled over to his chair, looking up into his down-
turned face. "Hey, Enzo. Courage, remember how Father used to
tell us this? You remember when he took the library home when
the council was going to discard it? He stood by his principle."

"And suffered for it. He was never promoted into a position of
influence in the council."

And that was true.

"I'm afraid, Elli. Asitho Bisumar knows that he needs the
support of the Foundation families to change the law. We're the
only ones left. He was going to offer me a high position in
exchange for our support. A high position meant that I could carefully influence the high council. We're young. Asitho Bisumar and
Nemedor Satarin will retire or become too old to function in the
High Council. That is when we can make things better. I can't say
no, and I can't go back, because they'd do the same to us that
they've done to every family they wanted to get rid of. And they
do want to get rid of us. Or they want us to be in their immediate
influence. I'd prefer to stay in Miran."

"It's like the nomad woman in the markets said and I've been
thinking about since. Everyone is frightened into silence in this
place. Father's generation of people travelled to Kedras and
Damarq. We've closed the borders and progress has passed us by.
What are we doing, Enzo? We're the younger generation. It's up to
us to kick Miran back into life. To stop this decline into fear."

"It's easy for you to say."

"Why? Because I'm a girl and I have no influence anyway?"

"No, because no one has influence over you."

"Is that how you see it?"

"Yes, because if you want to do something, I have to sign. I will
because even if you don't believe I do, I love you. If I want to do
something, other people hold power over what I can do."

"Then stop letting them have that power."

"Can't, Elli. Can't. If I do, I'll lose all my friends. I need their
support."

Somehow, she didn't have much confidence if Raedon

Tussamar was going to be one of those friends. "Wouldn't the solution be *not* to give up our position as Foundation family? When the changes of the law are being voted in, we vote against. Do we still have the right of veto?"

He shook his head. "Only for those in possession of the Foundation stones. Anyway, if we voted against, they'd kill us or drive us out."

He let a long silence lapse. The fire popped and crackled in the hearth. The wind whistled past the window. There would be snow again overnight.

It didn't look like he would say any more, so she rose, stiff-legged, from her uncomfortable position on the floor. "I'm going to get something to eat." She reeled. Ouch, her head.

He said nothing.

Ellisandra walked to the door.

"Elli."

She turned.

"I know you've been wondering about this: go to Father's room. Open the window. You'll find it on the outside windowsill."

What the *hell* was he talking about?

"The thing that Father was so upset about a little while back. Don't tell anyone that I told you, all right? You found it because Father wanted the window opened."

Father, of course, was already asleep. Ellisandra went to her room, found the emergency light, went downstairs, got her cloak and crept into Father's room. It was pitch dark with the curtains drawn, and she bumped into a chair. Father was a deep sleeper and his hearing was not what it used to be, and he didn't wake up. She pushed aside the curtains and put the emergency light on the windowsill where it spread an eerie white glow. As quietly as she could, she lifted the latch on the window. A flurry of snowflakes drifted in. Great. More snow. And damn, it was cold. Using her bare hands, she scooped freshly-fallen snow off the windowsill and found that in the far corner, some impressive icicles hung from the sill. In this spot, her icy fingers met a spot of warmth, where the snow had melted. On the very edge of the sill sat a little device. Ellisandra yanked at it, and the glue that had been used to attach it came loose. The little object felt warm and metallic in her hands.

She quickly shut the window, put the light in her pocket and retreated behind the curtains in the darkness of the room, where her breathing sounded loud in comparison with Father's soft snores. Ouch, her hands stung from the cold. Her head pounded. She tiptoed back across the room, found the door and went back into the corridor. By the orange glow of the oil lamp against the wall at the end of the corridor, she could see that the object was a box with a little microphone at the top.

21

S O THAT WAS the state of affairs. Asitho Bisumar had placed a spying device on the windowsill not to spy on the house next door, but to eavesdrop on Father's conversations.

What did they think they could learn from a forgetful old man?

Nothing from him, Ellisandra realised, but they could learn from what she said to him about the theatre, about the council's choice of play, about the other people in the committee, heck, even about the council.

What should she do about it?

Tell someone?

If she went to the guards, they'd report it to the council.

If she went into a council sitting . . . who knew what would happen. Most of the council were Endri heads of families in support of the current High Council. A third of the council were Nikala who probably couldn't care less about Endri spying on Endri, or just didn't care about Endri full stop. They cared about their businesses and any upset in the status quo damaged their sales and any favours they had won from people higher up the decision-making slope.

And she was only alone, only a woman, and was likely to be

dismissed by the major heads of families as *deranged*. They would have to deny her allegations, lest the same thing happen to them, because to fall out of favour was their worst fear.

They feared the truth.

They feared the High Council.

They feared each other.

She put the device on the little table next to her bed. Of course she made sure that she'd taken out the tiny little energy pearl inside and blocked the microphone of the thing with a piece of tape just to make sure.

She crept under the blankets and lay there looking at it. She had no illusion that she would fall asleep. Her heart was racing, her mind was racing, and now that the shock of what had happened was worn off, her face hurt like hell. But most of all, she hurt inside. She worried about Jintho, because he hadn't come back home yet. Maybe Asitho Bisumar had hired thugs to look for him. She worried about Sariandra, who would be scared. In her condition, she should not be sleeping on the hard ground in cold cellars. She should not be running from men hired by her father to bring her back. She wished there was a way to contact him. If the High Council hadn't been stupid and backward for so many years, then there would be a local network . . . actually, there was Sariandra's device, which she would probably not have taken with her.

And there was Vayra's machine.

Ellisandra might have slept briefly, but it wasn't long before she jolted awake with a shock. Between the curtains, the sky was starting to go blue. She sat up, and almost yelped with the pain. Her head throbbed. She raised her hand to her cheekbone. Her fingers met warm and swollen skin. The edges of the cut felt rough and tender.

She stumbled out of bed and checked in the mirror. One half of her face was swollen. Her eyelid had gone puffy and burst blood vessels in the outer corner of her left eye socket made for a momentous black eye, with areas of blue, red and purple spreading down her cheekbone.

Very pretty.

She dressed herself and went downstairs. Riana's eyes widened at the sight of Ellisandra's face.

"Oh my, mistress, you look terrible. Does it hurt?"

"Only when I smile. But I shall not be doing too much of that today."

"You're not going to work like this, are you mistress?"

"I sure am. Jintho come back yet?"

"No, but a young man brought a message from him." She handed Ellisandra a folded-up note.

Ellisandra unfolded it and read. *Safe. Will probably not see you for a few days. Sariandra will come to work if possible. Don't try to look for me.*

Well, that was something at least.

Eating soup hurt, and she didn't even try the bread. Riana protested, but she left the house not much later, with her head throbbing dully, but with plenty of determination.

First, she went to the markets and looked at the stalls for baby clothing. She chose a little jerkin, a romper suit with feet attached, a tiny hat and fur-lined booties. They were so cute, she couldn't stop smiling. But smiling hurt her face. Ouch.

She gave them to the merchant. "Put them in a nice box. It's a present."

The merchant gave her a strange look. "You don't look too good yourself, lady."

"No. Asitho Bisumar hit me."

His eyes widened.

"I was trying to protect my brother, because he's been blackmailing both my brothers. Do you know that the council intends to abolish all the powers held by Foundation families?"

The man was too stunned to reply.

Ellisandra went to a few other stalls. She bought a cake for the theatre people, a bottle of pills for the pain and a handful of pens, which she didn't really need. Everywhere she told people her story, whether they asked or not.

A fairly large group of people followed her around, mainly out of curiosity.

Eventually, some people started making comments, always carefully looking around, probably for guards or anyone they didn't know and found suspect.

I've heard rumours about how he used to hit his first wife.

He probably hits his second wife, too.

I always thought there was something odd about him.

We should write a formal complaint to Nemedor Satarin.

"Do you think he doesn't know?" she said to the maker of that last comment.

The man looked taken aback. Others raised their eyebrows.

"Nemedor Satarin is not a bad man," a merchant said. He looked defensive, with his arms crossed over his chest. "You only need to look at how he cares about his ex-soldiers."

"Yes, but what about everyone else? Which society allows the oppression of women, the blackmail of young people by the government? This is what they do to you when you protest." She pointed at her bruised cheekbone.

There were some mumbles of agreement, and some uneasy looks.

"Anyway, what I was going to tell all of you is that we're performing a never-seen-before interpretation of *Changing Fate* in two days' time. The theatre is free and it's warm. And . . ." She got an idea on the fly. ". . . there will be free food for everyone in the interval."

She could do what Vayra did, even if she could only do it for one day. One day might be all it took.

Ellisandra left them to digest those statements. The rumour mill would do its work and hopefully it would come to the conclusion she wanted it to reach. They would come. They would bring their friends and neighbours.

In the theatre, she found Tolaki on the stage with the actors, and Aleyo must have gone out, because the orchestra was not rehearsing. She was pleased to find Sariandra upstairs in the office. Her eyes widened when Ellisandra came in.

"You're all right?" she asked, staring at Ellisandra's bruised face.

"Fine, as long as I don't smile. Not much risk of that happening today."

"That really does look horrible."

"It hurts."

"I'm so sorry that you had to get involved. There is going to be so much trouble."

"Where are you staying?"

"We slept in the den."

"Isn't it cold in there?"

"Yes. Very."

"I'll see if I can arrange something else."

"I'm so sorry for all the work it's causing you."

"I'm not sorry. I think that maybe we should have had this confrontation a long time ago. Anyway, I've brought you this." She handed her the package.

Sariandra pulled the ribbon and looked into the box. Her mouth fell open. She set the box on the desk and took out the cute little booties.

"Oh, look at them! They're so cute." Her eyes glistened. "You're so kind to me. I don't know that I've deserved it, especially with what happened."

"You have deserved it, because everyone is entitled to a safe life. Also, in all of this trouble, has anyone thought of you and the little mite or are they all too busy arguing over what's appropriate and raking snow over this scandal? 'Woman has baby,' what a scandal that is. Last I looked, the Endri had a fertility problem."

A tear ran over Sariandra's cheek.

"Healer Lasko will be here later today. No need to go home, ever, anymore. You and Jintho will be married as soon as possible."

"Thank you so much. What have I done to deserve this?"

"You've got the bad luck to have the biggest arsehole in Miran as father."

"Thank you. Thank you so much." She hugged Ellisandra—

"Ouch." Her face bumped into Sariandra's shoulder.

"Oh, I'm sorry. I'm so sorry what has happened. If I could tell my father what I think of this . . . but I can't. No one can tell my father anything."

"Yes, we can," Ellisandra said. "You wait and see. I think we can."

She left Sariandra in the drawing room and went downstairs to the stage where Tolaki and the actors were rehearsing the final scene. She sat down on a stool between the folds of the curtains of the backstage area.

Besides Tolaki and the main actors, there were a lot of people fighting on the stage: the prisoners who had broken out of their cells, the prison guards and soldiers. Shouts and thuds echoed in the empty hall. This was the final scene in the play, and it lacked . . . emotion. There was lots of fighting, but no one screamed.

"Stop, stop!" Tolaki yelled, holding her hands high.

The noise dimmed. People stopped acting out fights. The only sound was that of the actors' panting.

Tolaki said, "I want you to spread out more. Use the entire stage. This is a large battle."

Ellisandra got off the stool and walked onto the stage, to gasps and wide-eyed looks of the actors. "This scene isn't working at all. I want more drama. I want death screams. There will be blood. You will all be covered in blood."

Tolaki looked at her, her eyes wide.

"What did you do to your face?"

"Asitho Bisumar hit me."

There were some gasps after this statement, too.

"You're kidding."

"I wish I were."

Tolaki raised her hand to her mouth. "It was an accident, right?"

"Well, he did mean to hit my brother." Ellisandra told her what had happened minus the fact that Sariandra was pregnant. As she spoke, Tolaki's mouth fell open. When Ellisandra finished, she opened and closed her mouth several times, but said nothing. Then her expression closed. "Well, you were obviously in the wrong place at the wrong time, and Jintho must have done something that made him really angry."

"Enough to hit him in his own house?"

"That's not for me to judge."

"It is, Tolaki. Do we let people from the council get away with this kind of behaviour? Do we let them rule our lives?"

"What are you suggesting?" Her tone sounded hostile now. "You do know that my brother, your future *husband* works for Asitho Bisumar, right? Your own brother, too. Why are you telling everyone this? Why are you even here, making a point of showing your face to everyone?"

"Because we have a show to run and I can't afford a day off. And because I'm sick of not saying anything about stuff like this. We're all so afraid that we don't dare to speak up. We obediently allow these people to bully us into silence. We are afraid to find out what they're deciding over our heads because we don't want a fuss. We are complacent. We're silent witnesses to everything the council decides. It's time that we stood up to be heard."

"So showing your face like this is somehow going to make a difference? Or covering the stage in blood?"

"Yes, it does, because this is what they do to us. The play is not about the victory of Miran, it is about Mariandra. She is horrified that her kinsmen kill defenceless prisoners, and she says she loves Jihan only because she is afraid that he will kill her, too. The writer of the play isn't writing about the greatness of Miran. She was Mariandra. This play is a plea for help, but for many years, they misinterpreted it as a heroic play. It isn't, it's a protest play. It shows the prisoners as human beings. It shows that they're sympathetic and could have been our customers, trading partners and friends if only we had listened." All of a sudden, she felt like she was on fire. Yes, she knew for certain that she was right about this, but that everyone, even the council, had missed this message because they assumed that the author had been a man whose motive for writing the play had been literary accolades. And covering the stage in blood was absolutely the right thing to do.

Tolaki's cheeks had gone red. "You call the invaders sympathetic? After they killed so many of our people?"

"They were hungry. The war was a misunderstanding because their technology frightened the Mirani. Everyone knows that."

"You suggest that all our people have died for nothing? That is an insult." She threw the text onto the ground with a great flutter of paper. "I'm done here. I've tried to accommodate your strange ideas for the sake of harmony in the family, but I'm finished. Maybe my brother can get some sense into you."

"He won't, because I'm not marrying your brother."

Tolaki froze. Her mouth fell open. "What did you say? After all the effort we've put into the wedding?"

"My life is not about a wedding. It's about a marriage, and it's never going to work. I don't get along with Jaeron, and I don't think he likes me."

"You dare reject my brother, who is a respected businessman?"

"I'm not marrying his career, I'm marrying a person, and he's not the type of person who would happily be married to me." She had to make a great effort not to say the words *bully* or *authoritarian prick*. With a trembling hand, she pulled the letter out of the pocket of her cloak and handed it to Tolaki. "Here."

Tolaki ripped the seal and opened the letter. Her eyes widened. "What? You're serious about this?"

Ellisandra nodded. She had never been more serious about anything in her life.

Tolaki's eyes were full of anger. "You're a self-absorbed brat! You selfish harlot! I never want to have another thing to do with you."

She turned and marched into the corridor.

A moment later, the side door slammed.

Somebody behind Ellisandra said, "Wow."

She turned around to find all the actors and all the members of the orchestra staring at her. "What are you looking at? Carry on."

Nobody moved.

"You can gossip about me all you like, and I don't care. I'm done with being an obedient little woman. Done with keeping quiet about things that worry me. If that means that I'm not going to get married then I'm happy with that. I don't want a husband who thinks that he can bully me. We Endri women are deliberately being kept out of decision-making. We don't own anything, we have no rights to anything except finding a husband, and we need our husband's approval for anything we'd like to do. These men are deciding things on our behalf, and don't want to tell us what they're changing and what is being decided. Because supposedly, we're *not interested* or *politics is boring* or *you're much better off talking about the theatre*. Well, guess what? This woman would like to know what changes the council plans to make to Foundation Law. This woman would like the council to present a solid case for their changes. This woman would like to read the arguments, heck even vote for or against the changes. Because I am sick of bullying men speaking for me and saying that they know what I want, and that I cannot possibly have any interest in how the country is run. I have news for them: I'm not impressed with how they run the council. I want to see all the information on the table. I want to know what our precious family heirs are voting for."

Everyone in the hall had fallen quiet as she spoke, but now a woman in the orchestra applauded. She was an older Endri woman, of that age that she was too young to be an elder, and too old to still have dependent children at home. She played the lute in the orchestra, wasn't a flamboyant or outstanding player, just someone who was always there, always learned her part and always listened to instructions. Ellisandra was ashamed that she had forgotten the woman's name.

Others joined in the applause, some of them standing up from their seats.

Her eyes met Vayra's across the heads of the orchestra. He smiled.

Half the orchestra had risen and some people were cheering or had even climbed on their seats. More and more people joined the applause, on the top of the stairs and in between the curtains of the backstage area. Ellisandra didn't quite know what to do or say. She hadn't said anything so outrageous to deserve this reaction, had she?

Eventually, the tumult died down.

Ellisandra said, "Play that scene again. Make it violent. Scream as if you're really trying to kill someone, or if you're really dying, whichever applies to your character. Tameyo, let me see your fear. When you go down on your knees to Jihan, make it *sound* as if you're begging him to spare your life, even if your text says something else."

"But what about . . ." Tameyo glanced at the corridor where Tolaki had disappeared.

"I'll carry on supervising the rehearsals. My part of the work is almost completed anyway. If she comes back, she comes back. If not, then she doesn't. I'm not going to worry about it." Her cheeks glowed with the emotion.

The group resumed, timid at first.

Ellisandra stopped the action. "I want more emotion. Can't you scream? Can't you cry? I want none of this civilised melodrama. I want raw emotion. I want the ladies in the front seats to squirm."

Tameyo nodded. She looked slightly horrified, but kept her lips pressed together in determination.

"You are going to scream when Jihan kills your lover, like any normal woman would. You . . ." She indicated the actors playing the prisoners. "You're going to give a good fight. When you're fatally wounded, you'll scream. I want to hear screaming, and crying and wailing. Start again."

Everyone went back to their positions. The people who played the prisoners went to the far side of the stage, the ones who played the guards gathered in a group on Ellisandra's side of the stage. Tameyo went back to the imaginary cell.

Ellisandra called, "Everyone ready? Let's do it!" Her head throbbed, but she ignored it.

The escaped prisoners sneaked onto the stage one by one.

"How do we get out of here?" one said.

"Rana, do you remember?" another asked.

"Don't leave me here!" Mariandra called from the cell. "I know I can't live where you come from, but if I stay here, they'll kill me!" Her voice cracked with the emotion.

"Good, good, keep going," Ellisandra called.

Rana ran across the stage, but at that moment, the guards burst in.

"Halt!"

He turned around.

"Show fear!" Ellisandra yelled.

He scrambled back until he stood almost against the imaginary cell door. He held up his hands to show that he had no weapon.

"Stop!" Ellisandra called. "We need Rana to say something in Coldi. Can anyone here translate something?"

"I can." Vayra came from the orchestra with the instrument under his arm. "He can shout, 'You betrayed me!' "

"That will do. Can you teach him?"

Vayra retreated to the side of the stage with Liran, who produced his copy of the text. Vayra wrote something at the top of the page, first with his left hand, and then with his right.

Liran read it aloud.

Vayra corrected him until he got it right.

"Let's do it again," Ellisandra said.

Everyone resumed their positions.

Keldon proclaimed in his loud stage voice, "Behold, the first time real Coldi is spoken inside the Mirani state theatre!"

Someone in the orchestra said, "Our mistress is breaking all the rules."

Someone else said, "We want our mistress in the High Council!"

"You would be elected by a landslide!"

Far too many people clapped and cheered. It made Ellisandra feel sick with worry. The fact that she would run in the public section crept ever closer. She had even come to the conclusion that if she wanted to change Miran, she should nominate herself. That would risk *her* life, but she didn't want all these good people to put themselves into the path of the current council. She *hoped* Nemedor Satarin wouldn't use the army against his own people, but he would never just resign his position. He would fight. It would be ugly, and a genteel Endri woman was probably not the right person to lead that fight.

The prisoners went to the side of the stage again and the guards to the other side.

The guards had swords, but Rana was unarmed. He yelled his Coldi line—Ellisandra had no idea if it sounded genuine—and the group launched into a fight.

"Remember that Coldi people are much stronger than us!"

He lashed out at one of the approaching guards. The man fell down.

"Good, let me see some more of this. I want real fights. I want the audience to wonder if perhaps the prisoners are going to win. I want them to *hope* that the prisoners might get out alive."

The other guards had gotten into a fight with the remaining prisoners. The fight surged back and forth over the stage, with shouts of victory and pain.

Mariandra screamed and cried from her cell.

When Liran put his sword through Rana's heart, she let out an ear-piercing scream that made Ellisandra's skin break out in goose bumps.

"Yes, like that."

The fight was over. All the prisoners were on the ground, and Mariandra had fallen to her knees, sobbing.

Jihan went to open the cell. Mariandra scrambled to her feet and retreated against the wall.

"My love, I will never harm you." Jihan's line came out with a chilling undercurrent of meaning. It was perfect.

Mariandra sobbed into her hands.

Jihan stepped into the cell. She shied away from him.

"My love, I will protect you against all future invaders." He pulled her out of the cell, still sobbing. She stumbled along with him and let herself be guided off the stage.

There was silence.

"Yes!" Ellisandra called and her voice echoed in the silence. "This is how we will perform it. With blood. Lots of blood."

Someone in the audience clapped, and then another one. These were the theatre people, who usually turned up at the end of rehearsals to sweep the stage, collect the food trays and get everything ready for the next day.

One of the actors playing the guards cheered and started helping the "victims" to their feet. There were claps on shoulders and congratulations.

As all the actors walked off the stage, chatting, Aleyo came to Ellisandra.

"Is it really true that Asitho Bisumar hit you?"

"It is as true as I'm standing here. And I'm not going to keep quiet about it."

"I guessed as much. Still, I think there will be a lot of trouble. Not sure if the end result will be something you're happy with."

"What am I supposed to do? Let myself be abused like this?"

"Guess not . . ." Aleyo said, but she didn't look convinced. "But standing against Nemedor Satarin in the elections? No one has done that for years."

"Someone has to be the first." She let a silence lapse. "Anyway, I haven't decided if I will do it. I don't know if I'm the right person to do it."

"You will," Aleyo said. "I know you well enough. You will and you should. As for being the right person, isn't that what we've waited for, a man to stand against him? The men of Miran have no courage. It will take a woman to get this done. I will vote for you."

"You will?" Ellisandra was speechless. Was this Aleyo speaking, who she had always considered traditional and unsupportive?

"Of course I will," Aleyo repeated. "Sometimes I wonder what you think I am."

Someone very different from what Ellisandra had judged her to be. She hugged Aleyo—ouch, her cheek. "You're a good friend."

"You silly. I'll see you tomorrow."

Her head still reeling, both from the recent developments and the blow to her cheek, Ellisandra collected her cloak upstairs. It was dark and empty in the office. Sariandra must have left while she was on the stage. She hoped Healer Lasko had been to see her.

She walked down the stairs through the empty hall where her footsteps echoed against the high ceiling. One of the theatre staff had already started cleaning. "See you tomorrow, mistress."

"See you tomorrow."

She went down the corridor with the clothes stands with the ancient costumes.

Brrr, it was cold in here. Her breath steamed in the light of the lone lamp that hung on the wall halfway down the corridor.

The moment she realised that the echoing footsteps weren't all hers, somebody grabbed her from behind.

Ellisandra gasped and turned around and looked into the face of . . .

Nemedor Satarin.

"Oh. I didn't know you were here." Her voice came out as a squeak.

"You're in a great hurry."

"I'm cold." Her heart thudded against her ribs. How much had he seen of that final scene? Did he know about the fight with Tolaki?

"I think it might be time that we had a little chat."

"A chat?" *What about?* Ellisandra did her best to look undisturbed, but she was sure she failed miserably. Her heart was thudding so loudly that she could barely hear anything except the roaring of blood in her ears. Why was he here? Did he have nothing better to do than snoop on her? Did he already know of her fledgling plans to get into the council?

He led her into one of the dark rooms off the corridor, leaving the door open. The light from the oil lamp on the opposite wall cast long shadows on the fold-up tables and chairs that leaned against the wall.

He forced her to face him. The light side-lit his face, showing the canyons around his eyes and the pockmarked surface of his cheeks. Like this, he looked old and ugly. There was a time she had respected him, but that time had gone.

His eyes fixed hers.

'I was under the impression that you would provide us with information about our mysterious stranger. You were seen talking to him, but I got no information."

He let a silence lapse to let that sink in. Ellisandra did her best to keep meeting his eyes, and tried not to swallow or show any signs of fear.

"Next thing I heard that he was in the orchestra, and I still got no information. You sure must have talked to him at some point? I don't remember that this is what we'd arranged."

"It was just chatter. I haven't had a chance to talk to him about anything important." It was a cowardly reply and she knew it the moment the words were out of her mouth. What she needed, what the women of Miran needed, was courage.

"While he's been in the orchestra for some time?" His voice was cold and emotionless.

She said nothing. Her heart thudded so loudly that she was afraid she was going to faint.

"You were spotted going to the Andrahar yard twice, once going into the tent with him. All that time he's told you nothing?"

"Nothing worth reporting." *If you know all that, why don't you spy on him yourself?*

"You are wrong there." He came so close that his breath made a warm spot on her skin. He smelled of soap with a hint of perfume. "*Everything* is worth reporting. Who he is, what he wants, how he entered Miran. No, he's not going to tell you outright. I thought you would be smart enough to understand that."

She was smart enough to understand that this wasn't about getting information about Vayra, this was about testing her, and it possibly had been so ever since his first visit to the theatre.

"Do you understand that?" His voice was soft. He *had* to know that she was planning to make a political point with the play.

She returned his stare and said nothing, but her heart was racing. Any moment now and he was going to hit her in that same spot where Asitho Bisumar had hit, or he was going to tell her that she was relieved of the theatre job, or that the performance was cancelled.

He did not.

"I think I'm a kind man," he continued in a too-soft and too-patient voice. "Support Miran and Mirani people, and you will receive all the support you need from the council."

"Explain to me what am I doing wrong?"

He laughed. "You jest, certainly. Do you think I would have missed your political comments, your stabs at the council, and me? How you went across the markets recruiting voters? If you think you can undermine me, I'm warning you now: you're wrong. I am far stronger than you think. I do not hesitate to act. I'd hate to do anything to a reputable lady of our society, but if I'm forced to act, I will. I understand that this . . ." He pointed at Ellisandra's cheek. ". . . was an accident. When I act, there will be no accidents. Do you understand this?"

Still, she said nothing but held her face in what she hoped was a defiant expression.

He laughed, not in a nice way. "We can keep playing this game for a bit longer, if you want. I have no problem with that, because I always win in the end."

"Suits me," she said. "I quite like games and theatre."

She yanked her arm out of his grip and strode out of the room.

Behind her, he said, in a mock-cheerful voice, "Run home, little princess, run home."

22

ELLISANDRA WALKED out of the theatre as quickly as she could without running, down the steps, into the alley. Around the corner, in the main street, she leant against a shop wall to catch her breath. Her heart was still thudding like crazy and her cheekbone gave sharp stabs of pain. She brought her hand to her face. It was bleeding again.

She could still hear Nemedor Satarin's voice behind her.

Run home, little princess, run home.

What was that supposed to mean? Run home and be spied on by others? Enzo even? Or did he have spies in the other houses surrounding the building site? Was he using the Citizen's Groups to intimidate people into obeying him?

You know what? She *wasn't* going to run home, as he so obviously expected. She wasn't some kind of delicate flower who'd run to her family crying if something bad happened. And she wasn't going to let one other person bully her into anything, not even if that person was Nemedor Satarin.

She remembered the way to Jintho's den, but walked around the block to make sure that no one was following her. She only went into the alley when she decided that all was clear.

The door of the cellar under the baker's shop was closed this time. She listened against the door, but could hear nothing. She held her breath and listened closer, but either everyone there had heard her come and was quiet or . . .

She knocked softly.

Nothing.

She knocked again. "Jintho? Please let me in."

She dare not call any louder. There was no one else in the alley, but she couldn't be sure if no one saw her. The shops had living quarters above them, and some windows looked out into the alley. Miran was full of eyes and full of people who reported things to their masters.

"Jintho!" A bit louder.

There was no answer. She tried the door handle. It didn't open. Damn it. Did that mean that they had all moved or that it wasn't a meeting day?

There was nothing for it, she had to go back home. There was Father to be looked after as well.

Her hands in the pockets of her cloak, she walked back. Darkness fell quickly in Miran, and the light had already gone blue. The shopkeepers were taking in their wares, packing up their displays and helping the last of their customers. At the bakery, a group of scruffy men waited for the baker to come outside with today's unsold rolls.

She had rounded the corner when someone came to walk next to her: a man hidden deep within the hood of a very scruffy and matted cloak. Ellisandra glanced aside. *Shoo!*

She had no time for being accosted by beggars. He turned his head briefly, and kept walking.

Ellisandra stopped. He kept walking. She turned aside to a shop window which displayed tableware and waited until he disappeared.

Except the beggar slowed down and then stopped, too. He put his hands in his pockets. His head was turned so that he could still see her in the reflection of a shop window.

Ellisandra took a few steps back down the street. The large

group of vagrants with the breadbasket was coming up behind her. They were talking and laughing, and completely ignored both her and the beggar.

That's because he's an undercover guard.

Someone employed by Nemedor Satarin or Asitho Bisumar to check where she went.

What now?

She breathed in deep gasps, staring at the tableware in the shop window without really looking. Her cheek hurt. In the window's reflection, she could see people walking down the street. More were walking in the direction of the Nikala quarter than uphill to the Endri quarter. The man stood uphill from her.

She went to the next shop downhill. It sold—of all things— baby clothing. She feigned interest in the wares and went to the next shop. It was a tattoo parlour. The owner must be doing administration, because only one light burned at the back of the shop, casting a faint glow over a couple of benches along the walls and hundreds of prints of tattoo designs. Many of them depicted flowers or local animals. A corner was dedicated to family crest tattoos that men from Endri families put on their shoulder blades. Enzo and Jintho both had one. She'd wanted to get one as well, but Father said she couldn't, so she got a tattoo of flowers on her left shoulder.

One of the family crests lay on the table next to the workbench. A scrunched towel indicated that they'd just had a customer. That crest was . . . Andrahar? Were there any young men of the minor Andrahar branches old enough to be getting their tattoos?

She glanced into the street.

Damn, the beggar still stood there.

She was already shivering with the cold and nerves and she really needed to start moving, so she went further down the hill. There were a lot of alleys in that area of the commercial quarter, and maybe she could lose him in one of those. The first alley she glanced into was a dead end. Maybe a practiced thief could climb up on the bins at the end and scale the wall, but, clumsy as she was, she would probably hurt herself.

The next alley looked more promising. She walked down at a fast pace, rounded the corner and waited in a shop entrance.

The beggar appeared in the entrance to the alley.

Damn it.

She had come quite a way downhill. This was the Nikala section of the commercial quarter and because many Nikala worked during the day, the shops here were still open. Many people strolled up and down the street, talking and carrying purchases.

Ellisandra's sleek Endri hair stood out here. She pulled her cloak's hood over her head and started uphill. She walked as fast as she could, with brief sprints when a group of people came between her and her follower, who—she checked several times— still followed at a distance, a fuzzy outline in a disgusting matted cloak.

The street led back to the Endri section and from that into main square, a huge empty space in the darkness. She definitely wasn't going to cross that with the guy following, so she stuck to the perimeter and walked past merchant Ranuddin's shop, the guest-house next door, the office of the Mirani Chapter of the Trader Guild and then the markets. From the corner of her eye, she kept watch on the dark shadow following her at a distance.

Damn it, he was really determined.

The only thing she could do was go home as quickly as possible and hope he wouldn't catch up with her on a deserted stretch of street. But the only street that linked the markets to the Endri quarter was a dark passage, with the market building on one side and a tall wall surrounding the council compound on the other. The other pedestrians became mere shapes in the darkness, as the world around her contracted to just the pools of light cast by the few streetlights. Of course the scruffy man chose this alley to come closer.

Ellisandra increased her pace, but the man was fast closing the distance between them.

Never mind the fact that it was unladylike to run, she broke into a sprint. Pain spiked in her cheekbone. She slipped and almost fell, but kept running. The man came closer and closer. He was right behind her now . . .

He grabbed the back of her cloak and yanked her to a stop. She slid into the hard wall that was the side of the market building.

"Stop running away from me." It was too dark in the street to see his face, but his voice sounded familiar. It was . . .

"Jintho?"

"Why did you keep running away from me?"

"What are you doing here? You're supposed to be in hiding." Her heart was still thudding.

"Shhh. Don't talk to me like that. I'm a dirty beggar and I'm harassing you."

"You *were* harassing me and you *are* dirty. Where did you get that disgusting thing? You just about frightened me to death. Nemedor Satarin—"

"Shh. Tell me later. Come to the alley at the back of merchant Ranuddin's shop."

Then he was gone again, sprinting down the side of the market building and into the open area of the square.

Ellisandra waited for a while in the darkness, regaining her breath and her nerves. Damn Jintho. Why hadn't he called earlier before giving her the fright of her life?

She walked back downhill past the market. Some market building attendants were pulling shutters closed. She met the bunch of vagrant men carrying a basket of bread rolls between them going uphill. They were far too busy eating to take any notice of her.

Merchant Ranuddin's closed shop was on the corner of the square and the main street through the commercial quarter.

It was very dark in the alley behind the shop and hard to see where to put her feet. Twice, she stepped on an ice mound and sank up to her knees into the underlying soft snow. Because merchant Ranuddin's shop had closed, no one had kept the ground free of ice. Eventually she reached the shop's back door.

It opened a crack as she approached.

"Come in, quickly." That sounded like Jintho.

Ellisandra climbed up the steps, stamping snow off her boots.

Inside the shop, it was very dark but surprisingly warm. Jintho pulled her into a hug that made her face bump into his shoulder.

"Ouch."

"Oh, I forgot about your face."

"How have you been? I was worried about you."

"No reason to worry about me. We're fine. Vayra's guards are patrolling the entire block and warn us if there's trouble coming. We're safe and warm."

Ellisandra hadn't noticed any guards when coming in.

Vayra's guards? How many did he employ? Was he staking out his own safe patches in the city? In fairness, this building belonged to him.

Jintho led her through a dark passageway with doors on both sides to another room where a lusty fire burned in the hearth. It was warm here, and a couple of people sat on old couches around the fire.

Sariandra was one of them.

"Elli!" She rose and came to Ellisandra at the door. "I can call you that, right?"

"Of course." All manner of people called her Elli without asking.

It was so warm here that Sariandra had taken off her overdress. Underneath she wore a proper maternity dress, made of silky grey fabric with a couple of pressed pleats at the front, and belted under the distinct swelling of her belly. Apart from the red blotches on her skin, she looked radiant and gorgeous. Her eyes were bright, her hair done up in a neat bun with a jewelled pin.

How far along was she? A lot further than Ellisandra had first thought.

"That dress is really beautiful. Did you design it?"

Sariandra nodded. "This is an example of the things we're going to offer. We're trying to get this shop for when we open for business. Most of our stock is here."

"The shop belongs to the Andrahar family. Does Vayra have anything to do with this?"

"He sleeps upstairs. He's happy for us to have the shop."

"Are you going to hire it from him?"

"At some point, probably, but he wants no payment for now."

Ellisandra looked at the racks of clothing along the walls. There were many different types of dresses, cloaks, trousers, skirts, men's and women's shirts, and a whole rack of pretty party dresses.

"You've made all this?"

"Us and the three tailors we've hired."

Ellisandra met Jintho's eyes. "It seems I misjudged you. I thought this was just a whim. I'm sorry."

He smiled. "It's all right, sis. I've given you enough false alarms to make you think that. But now I'll have a family, and I need to support them, because I'm sure as hell not going to ask Enzo for money."

"You're entitled to some, and he'll give it to you."

"He can give it to me *after* I've proven that this will work."

Except the shop would never work if the boycotts remained in place. "How much of this is legal?"

"The Mirani stuff, totally legal. The imported stuff . . . let's not talk about that too much. Not illegal, but not totally legal either."

"You're bringing in stuff overland to Bendara and flying it in from there."

The sharp look he exchanged with a man across the room told her that she was right. "Vayra told me about the land route. Honestly, I can't see why you should have to do this. All of this only because the council is too stubborn to allow a *gamra* investigation into things that happened when we were toddlers. That tells me that the council has something to hide, and they want to hide it even further by taking away the Foundation families' rights to question and demand investigation. We must stop this law, and we must again allow foreign imports and exports. When the council goes into session after the play, it will be our last ever chance to send the council home. We must use it."

' What do you mean?"

' I read all of Foundation Law. Foundation families can veto decisions made by the council."

'"Only if they're in possession of the Foundation stones," one of the young men said. "I studied law."

She met his intelligent eyes. *Then what are you doing starting a shop?* But she knew why he was here. He didn't agree with the ruling forces and therefore was denied employment with Miran's Lawkeepers.

"We can worry about the protocol later. Let's start with trying to get the Foundation families together and back to Miran for this meeting. Does anyone know how to contact the Ilendar family?"

One of the young men nodded. "They were our neighbours."

"Andrahar?"

The young man shook his head and others did the same. "Not sure even if they still have an heir. Iztho was the oldest and he went missing. Not sure if he's still alive. He wasn't married."

Ellisandra was beginning to get very sick of this oldest son of oldest son requirement. The family representative should be the person most apt to do a good job. Maybe she could claim herself the heir of the Takumar family and act in Enzo's stead. This was one of the first things she would change if she went into the council. "There were three other sons. I'm sure one of them has a son." Vayra would be able to tell her. "What about Velisar?"

"They live in Kesilu. You could find a contact for them. They're probably the easiest to reach."

"Then," someone said, "you must ask your brother. He's the only Foundation family heir we still have in Miran."

"Enzo is pretty much lost to us. He's too involved with Asitho Bisumar." Too scared, too.

The fifth family, Calthunar, had probably died out, but then again, there had been four Foundation families for a long time, so four would have to do, or however many people from the four she could bring together.

Sariandra asked, "What are you trying to do? Why should these people who have left Miran long ago make any difference?"

"Because they're Foundation families and according to the law, they still have a say. The council sits the day after Theatre Day to vote for these law changes. If we get members of Foundation families—preferably heirs, but anyone we can get—in the audience, we can make a stand, and we have the law on our side to defeat the proposed changes. If the law says that we need the stones, I know where they are. We simply get them."

Jintho's eyes grew wide. "You mean steal them?"

Her cheeks grew hot. "I guess Father would know how to get them out of the cabinet without smashing it, but at this point, I don't care."

The young man who had studied law said, "I'm not sure that will be worth the trouble, because Foundation Law isn't clear on the point of whether the right to veto still holds. It would probably give you more trouble than it's worth."

"How can you say that? How can all of you just sit here, complain and do nothing? This is our one chance to stop the isolation of Miran. Your entire business model depends on it. The stones are ours anyway. I don't care how we get them. Last I looked, uprising and rebellion was never legal anyway! We need a team. We need people to support us. You are it. Stop being complacent." She was fully aware that she borrowed that word from Vayra.

The Lawkeeper student asked, "That's all very well, but how do we get into contact with the other Foundation families? The Exchange will know if we try. They can listen in on anything we tell them."

"I think I know a way to get around that," Ellisandra said.

"But the Ilendar family lives in Damarq. Nothing is secret about off-world communication."

' I know. I still think I can contact them without anyone noticing. I just have to ask Vayra. He's got a lot of modern devices. Is
there a way I can get upstairs from here?"

'There's the fire stairs," someone said.

Jintho rose. "I'll show you."

By the time Ellisandra had followed him into the cold corridor,
her burst of energy had faded. Why hadn't she noticed how
hungry she was, and how much she trembled?

"I have to hand it to you, sis, you're an excellent politician."

"You jest, certainly."

"No, I'm serious. You scare me. The way you get people to
believe in what you say, and to feel that you can really improve
our lives, that's a rare gift. Nemedor Satarin had it, once when he
was young and angry. He is going to be scared of you."

"Already is. He tried to rough me up this afternoon after our
rehearsal."

"What? You're serious? Nemedor Satarin himself?"

Ellisandra nodded, thinking back to that frightening encounter.
The shock and concern on Jintho's face made tears prick in her
eyes.

"You should go into hiding," Jintho said, his voice low. "You've
become a target."

"I can't. I have to look after Father."

"Darma will look after him."

"Really?"

She met his eyes and saw in his expression that he didn't
believe his own words either.

Then he said, "Ask Vayra for protection."

"Since when do we need help from foreigners to stage
rebellions?"

"I get what you mean, but having money makes it a lot easier.
He's got limitless supplies. You ask him, and he'll put a guard on
you. It will be a Mirani man, paid with Mirani money."

"Don't you ever think of what Vayra's aims are? Don't you ever
worry that he's buying your favours or leading you into a trap of

dependency. I know he looks Mirani, but he's not. I know he genuinely loves Miran, but he remains a foreigner. The central issue remains that we still don't know who he is."

Jintho returned her stare unflinchingly. "That may be as it is, but the other alternative is to ask Enzo for money or try to get a loan to start a rebellion. Between the three, I know which option is going to deliver the goods."

True.

"I wish I knew Vayra's full story," she said.

"It will be an interesting one, and we'll probably discover it sooner rather than later."

And that was true, too.

23

E LLISANDRA AND JINTHO had arrived at the far end of the dark corridor, where there was a narrow door, which, when Jintho opened it, led into a dark maw where just the first few steps of the emergency stairs were visible.

Ellisandra swallowed. She did not like tight and dark spaces, and to be honest, she was beginning to feel very shaky. She peeked into the darkness. "They're on the first floor, right?"

"Yes. There's two more floors above the office, but they can't use these stairs."

Ellisandra started up the stairs. It was dark inside the tight space and her footsteps echoed muffled between the heaviness of the stone walls. The air smelled stale with a faint tang of decay. She was halfway up when a wave of dizziness hit her.

Damn it.

She held tight onto the railing, waiting for the feeling to subside. Coloured spots danced before her eyes, accompanied by a sharp stab of pain in her cheekbone. She thought she heard music, but that had to be her ears ringing. Warm fluid trickled over her face and when she touched the spot where Asitho Bisumar's rings had hit her, her fingers met the stickiness of blood.

On the first floor landing she found a heavy door held shut by a spring. She had to pull with all her weight to open it, while covering the wound on her cheekbone with one hand.

The door came out in a kitchen area. A faint glow of light fell in through the door, showing a couple of cups sitting on a clean bench. Outside the kitchen was a neat hallway with a traditional mosaic floor.

As soon as the door clicked shut, the sound of footsteps came from elsewhere in the apartment, and voices. A man appeared in the doorway backlit by the light. Squinting against the light, she could just make out that it was Vayra.

"Lady Ellisandra! Are you all right?"

"I think so." She staggered an uncertain step.

"You don't look all right. Come, I'll put something on that cut." He supported her with an arm around her shoulders.

He led her into a large room between rows of desks to a smaller room with a desk and two chairs. On the far side was a window which looked out over the main square.

The chair closest to the window was occupied by an older man holding a Mirani style metal lute on his lap. He jumped up as soon as Vayra guided her in, putting the lute on the desk with a faint musical thump. He was very tall like Vayra, and had a sleek curtain of black hair. His eyes were very dark, but his skin pale.

Vayra said something to him and he left. Vayra guided her to the closest chair.

"Wait here. I'm going to get my kit." Vayra left, too.

Ellisandra leaned against the back of the chair. It was quite warm in this room and it would be nice if only the room would stop spinning.

"You should go to the hospital," Vayra said, returning with a sturdy pack which he set on the desk next to the lute.

"The hospital has better things to do."

"Really? I think he hit you a lot harder than you'll admit. If nothing else, you'll get a nasty scar." He flipped off the lid of the pack. Inside was a full medical kit.

He selected a little bottle with a long tip and a pointy lid that cam⊃ off when he twisted it. He dabbed the wound with a ball of fabr⊏c.

"Ow, that stings."

He squirted fluid from the bottle onto her cheek and used a spat⊔la to spread it. "What is that? It makes the skin feel warm."

"It speeds up the healing process. It glues the sides of the wound together to reduce scarring. Have you met my father, by the way?"

"Your father?"

The older man leaned against the doorway. He was tall and gangly like Vayra, but the eyes that met hers were eerily dark. Did eyes even get that dark? She could see clear similarities in the faces of father and son. He nodded at Ellisandra and asked Vayra something in a language she didn't recognise. Vayra replied.

"What's that language you're speaking?"

"Trader Coldi."

And he expected the council to have no trouble with this man and his mother living in Miran? "Were you just playing music?"

"We were practicing. I said I'd get you players for the orchestra. My father has been a professional musician for many years."

Ellisandra looked at the man in the doorway. Something about him didn't quite seem right. Maybe his hair was too dark, maybe his face too Endri, maybe he understood every word she said. Maybe she was becoming entirely too paranoid about Vayra. "Is your mother Mirani?"

"My parents are both Aghyrian." Which wasn't really a reply, because according to the definition of some, Endri were an Aghyrian race.

He now took a bandage from the box and some tape. With a knife from the kit he cut a square piece from the bandage, as well as a few lengths of tape. The square he carefully deposited over the wound, and then affixed it with the tape. His touch was gentle and professional, but it occurred to Ellisandra that it was the first time that a man who was not a family member had touched her, or at least since she had become an adult.

That was a strange thought. All her life, she had expected that man to be Jaeron, and she had waited and hoped in vain for signs of Jaeron's affection. Now she'd made a definite decision that this wasn't going to happen. She was free. She could flirt if she wanted, not that she wanted to do that now, but the freedom was there.

It was a strangely liberating thought.

She met Vayra's sand-coloured eyes and smiled.

He returned the smile. "You know, people don't normally smile when they've been almost knocked out."

"I'm too scared to act unhappy. I have stopped caring for my safety. When we stage the play, I expect it will be total mayhem after the genteel audience sees the final scene. We're interpreting the play as it has never been interpreted before, and many people won't like it. I'm scared out of my mind of what the council's reaction will be."

"Hold on tight. You have more supporters than you think."

He finished putting the bandage on the wound and then went to bring her some tea, leaving her in the room with the man he said was his father. He still leaned against the doorframe, and observed her with a cool gaze.

She tried not to stare, but didn't know where to look.

He wasn't supposed to speak Mirani, but she wondered what would happen if she said something rude or provoking. How good an actor was he? Or did he really not understand Mirani? She had trouble believing that, although there did seem to be a foreign feel about him. His clothing was certainly strange enough. The trousers were a thick blue, a dirty-looking, unevenly dyed fabric. There was a little hole in them, too, on the side of his thigh. Maybe the fabric had worn there from carrying things in his pocket.

The lute on the desk, though, was a most magnificent Mirani instrument, with patterns beaten into the metal panels and little glass-stone beads on the knobs to tighten the strings. You couldn't buy an instrument like that in a shop. This was custom-made. It looked like a Darumin-made instrument, and merchant Darumin had died about ten years ago. This was not something he would have sold to the first random customer who walked into his work-shop. Had merchant Darumin ever sold his lutes to foreigners?

When Vayra's father noticed her looking at the lute, he picked up the instrument. It had a strap which he slung over his shoulder. He set his fingers on the strings and started playing.

Within a few bars, Ellisandra was completely lost in the music. This man couldn't just play the lute; he made the lute perform magic.

She barely noticed Vayra come back into the room carrying a tray with a teapot and cups. He sat next to her on the desk.

They listened.

When his father stopped playing, there was a moment of silence before Ellisandra applauded. He bowed his head in acknowledgement.

"That was amazing!"

"I said I'd get musicians for the orchestra," Vayra said.

"We need to let him play a solo." She'd said it before realising that an obviously foreign man in the orchestra was going to create a lot of protest. She could get away with Vayra because he looked somewhat Mirani, but . . . "Do you think he could bleach his hair? I don't want any trouble—or any more trouble than I'm already going to get." Who was she kidding anyway? There would be so much trouble over this play. "I'd like everyone to stay calm until the very end of the play."

Vayra nodded. "I'm sure we could arrange for both of us to look very Mirani. Don't worry."

He distributed the tea and they drank in silence for a while.

"Anyway, the reason I'm here is because I think you have a way of contacting people outside Miran without using the Exchange."

Vayra gave her a critical look.

"I saw that screen in the tent. You were replying to someone outside Miran."

"That's just going to Barresh, using the satellite."

The army had satellites. They were built in a factory near the airport and taken up in military aircraft. They were said to spy on remote mountain regions and Barresh. She couldn't imagine Vayra's machine using these satellites. "Does Barresh have satellites?"

"Barresh doesn't, but the Trader Guild does."

And he was a member. Another reminder not to trust him too much.

A wave of doubt hit her. Did she want to use a non-Mirani satellite to contact people about a Mirani problem?

Well, she couldn't use a Mirani satellite.

But everyone in *gamra* would know what she was doing.

That might not necessarily be a bad thing.

On the other hand, how would she know? Miran could be overrun with foreign interests if she did this.

Damn it, wasn't that why they'd got into this problem in the first place? The Mirani fear of foreigners? That fear had been drilled into everyone from birth. It was not just the council, it was embedded in all the people, Endri and Nikala both, in the council, the merchants in the markets, the workers, everyone, even her. And she needed to *get over* it.

She licked her lips and nodded to Vayra. "I will use it." *I will use it and suffer the consequences, because we cannot go on living like this.*

He put his cup down. "Come with me."

She followed him into the main room of the office—whoa, her head—where there was a central communication hub. Much of the equipment was at least ten years old and probably had been abandoned when the family left Miran. Vayra had hooked up some more modern-looking equipment to one of the screens.

"You sit here and type on that. I presume you know how to use a local hub?"

She gave him a *what-do-you-think-I-am?* stare.

"Do you know the *gamra* codes of the people you want to contact?"

"I need to look those up. Not all of them are outside Miran."

Next he would want to know *who* she wanted to contact, and once she told him, there would be no way back, and this whole avalanche would be in motion with no way to stop it.

'I'll help you."

She'd been afraid of that. Asking to figure this out in a private room by herself would have been too much to ask, right? It was now or never, another moment for a choice. Live like this, or try to make life better.

She spoke in a low voice. "I have to warn you, to allow you to back out if you can. This is not an innocent chat I want to have with these people. I want to contact all surviving members of all Foundation families. I want as many as possible to come to Miran for the council session where the new laws are being voted on. I don't know if the current laws still give us the right of veto, or if they do, if the council will honour it, but I want to try."

His eyes fixed hers. "I realise that. We can help."

"Is this why you've come to Miran?" On dangerous ground now.

"This is *your* idea. We just . . . make it happen."

He showed her how to search for the people she needed. The hub was so much more modern than the simple thing she used for the theatre's finances.

The Velisar family proved a lot harder to track down than she thought. They had left Miran so long ago that it was no longer clear who was the family's legal heir. She spoke to a man in Kesilu who seemed to have little interest in the situation as she explained it. He told her he'd ask around and get back in contact with her.

That didn't look hopeful.

The Calthunar family lived in Bendara. Ellisandra spoke to a woman who seemed a lot more interested than Velisar.

Then came Ilendar, the first important family, also the first time ever Ellisandra spoke to someone off-world. Vayra helped her make the connection and after a lot of strange beeping and clicking noises, a gruff man replied in a language she didn't recognise.

Vayra nodded at her, whispering, "That's him."

"This is Ellisandra Takumar of Miran. I need to draw your awareness to proposed changes to the Mirani Foundation Law. The council under the leadership of Nemedor Satarin wants to abolish those sections of Foundation Law that give Foundation families the power to dismiss the council, giving the current High Council effective absolute rule. We, the younger generation in Miran, want to stop this. I'm contacting all Foundation families to see if you can provide some assistance."

There was a silence in which Ellisandra was afraid that the connection had been broken.

Then the same male voice said, "What form would that assistance take?"

"I'm aware that you have already made your Mirani account available, and I thank you very much for that. There are a lot of people in Miran who have well-paid jobs because of this money. However, this issue will be decided by a vote in the council. Foundation members have a vote. Do you still have the right to veto council decisions?"

"Not that I know. We used to, with the Foundation stones, but we have lost ours a long time ago. Andrahar was the only family who kept theirs, but as far as I know, it was destroyed in the fire and has never been found. Those stones are a relic of the past and I wouldn't hold much faith in the council's commitment to this part of Foundation Law. They'll do as they please unless they meet serious opposition."

"I may be a woman, but I have many people behind me. I am serious opposition."

"I never meant to suggest that you didn't, lady."

Oh yes, he did. She'd been warned that Traders could be pompous. She should not let him rile her. She needed him too much.

"What is it that you would like us to do?"

"I would be happy if you could send a representative to the council session. Even if we no longer have the right to veto, our presence would give them pause."

"Let me know the details, then I will see if we could spare someone."

Not someone, we need you.

She gave him the times of the council session, and didn't hold out much hope that he would be there.

When the conversation clicked off, she let her shoulders slump. "I was silly to think that these people are still interested in what happens in Miran."

'You've got one family left."

Andrahar. "I'm almost too scared to speak to any of them. The Mirani council treated them badly. I don't know which is the truth, but they're doing fine without Miran. Why would they support us?"

"Because they are Mirani?" His eerie light brown eyes met hers in an intense expression. "The Andrahar family would like to re-establish part of their business in Miran. They will be there."

"We'd like the heir to come."

"He will be there."

Ellisandra would have stayed with Jintho and his group, but she needed to go home to give Father his dinner and get him ready for bed.

Vayra offered to walk her home. Jintho protested and said that he should do it, but Vayra subtly shifted aside his cloak, showing the glint of a gun which he wore, Coldi-style, on a bracket on his upper-arm.

Oh. Jintho and his friends nodded. Yes, they understood. And it was chilling that it had come to this, that a respected Mirani citizen needed to walk through the streets with an armed companion.

They left the building through the proper entrance of the Andrahar office, the one next to merchant Ranuddin's closed shop. Normally, there would be a vagrant sleeping on the steps, but there hadn't been anyone for days, and while no one appeared to have missed the scruffy men, Ellisandra realised where they would have gone: Vayra had given them a job on the building site, as guards or workers.

A soft drizzle of snowflakes drifted from the sky, appearing out of the darkness in little bubbles of glow around the street lights. Vayra took her arm and led her across the square. The streets were quiet and the last people were leaving the markets. A couple of guards stood idle on a street corner. They glanced at her and Vayra, but didn't move.

"They'd have one of their fellows following us," Vayra said.

Ellisandra looked over her shoulder, but saw no one. "Are you sure?"

"Either that or they've got enough guards to cover every corner."

"I don't think they would—"

"They've been doing this for years. It's not new. It's a system they used in Barresh, too. They call this *Mirani surveillance* in security circles. On every corner, there is either a guard, a street seller or another civilian in the pay of the military, or a camera. They will know what happens on every street."

"They're afraid."

"Possibly."

When they entered their street, a dark figure came down the hill. He was nothing more than a black form with light reflecting in the helmet's visor.

"All quiet?" Vayra asked.

"As quiet as it's going t' get," the man said inside the helmet. The Nikala accent sounded very much out of place with the modern gear.

Ellisandra noticed another man with a similar helmet at the corner of the alley that ran on the lower side of her house.

She laughed nervously. "Are you trying to take over this part of the city?"

Vayra's light brown eyes met hers with an intensity that made her shiver. "I'm protecting my house, and anyone who wants to be protected. I know that those fellows who stole building materials weren't after the stuff they stole. If I do nothing, they will be back. They might even try to light another fire. As we know, the house burns quite well and I haven't been able to change much of the design. I'm not about to waste my money and time, and all the work that the builders have put in. These are all Mirani guards. I haven't brought in many people from outside. I've just given them better equipment to work with."

"But . . . they've all got weapons."

They stopped walking in front of the gate to her house. The glow from the street lantern side-lit his face, making him look older and tired.

"They've got nothing that can't be bought locally. I had a local company make these helmets for me. They're very basic, but allow the men to carry communication equipment inside."

"Is it really necessary to put them in the street?"

"You're the last Foundation family left in Miran and you ask me that question?" His breath steamed in the space between them. "You are the only family that can do serious damage to the council. Of course you need protection. I've included your house in the guards' protection zone. Nemedor Satarin probably suspects that you're planning to run for council against him."

She burst out, "How do you know these things?"

"Well, you are, aren't you?"

"That doesn't answer my question."

"People talk."

"I've only spoken about it with a few people. I haven't made a decision."

"The decision is written on your face."

"With this?" she pointed at the bandage he had just put on.

"Ha, ha, ha."

"Stop making fun of me. How do you know these things about me? Are you spying on me?"

He retreated a step, his expression disturbed. "I'm not a spy. I don't know any more about you than I am able to guess, quite accurately, as it turns out. I apologise for that. I've been honest in my interactions. I'm sorry if I've offended, because it was not my intention."

"Then why are you always looking at me?"

He let a small silence lapse. "Does that disturb you?"

"Yes!"

His expression softened. "You . . . interest me, as a person. I find you strong, with solid opinions and willing to fight for them. And you're beautiful. It's probably not appropriate that I look at you a lot. I'm sorry."

What?

She looked up into his eyes, and couldn't see any suggestion that his words were anything but the absolute truth.

There were a hundred replies that went through her mind, most of them full of snark.

Isn't it normally the girls that do the flirting?

You barge in here thinking to pick off one of the most eligible women in Miran?

Who even says that I'm interested in getting involved with another man?

But his expression was much too sincere for all of those things. After having worked on the play and having seen the relationship between Jintho and Sariandra, she knew that love was not a trivial thing to be joked about, never mind that Mirani Endri marriages were seldom, if ever, about love.

Not that she had ever expected a declaration of love from anyone, least of all a foreigner.

And you know what? It touched her deep inside.

She was used to having to fight and snipe or tread carefully around people.

She didn't think anyone had loved her for a long time.

Mother died a long time ago, Father was too far gone to express love, her brothers said they loved her, but acted like they didn't care. The one friend she *thought* cared, Tolaki, turned out not to care. Sariandra had become a friend, but her affection was reserved for Jintho, and the theatre people just expected her to be a professional.

Vayra continued to meet her gaze unwaveringly.

She said, in a low voice, "Thank you." Her eyes pricked. It was as if her insides had all turned to mush, as if her thoughts were tangled in an impenetrable knot.

Damn it, she wasn't going to cry in front of him, was she?

"I'm sorry if it upsets you." He reached out, but let his hand hover above her arm without touching her.

She turned her hand palm up. He gently lowered his hand on top. His skin felt warm and dry. She squeezed his hand gently and he squeezed back.

"I'm so scared." Her voice cracked. "Tomorrow is the beginning of what could be the last free days of our lives." She could end up like the poor woman who had written the play, living in fear and being forced to write about all the things she had supposedly done wrong. They might even put her in jail.

"Or it could be the beginning of the rest of our lives, remember that. You must have hope that whatever you do will make the world better."

"I don't know who you are or why you care so much, but thanks."

He raised his hand to her cheek, but stopped short of touching it. "You'll be fine. I'll help."

They stood like that for a moment that seemed to last an eternity.

For a while she thought he was going to kiss her, and she thought that she probably wouldn't mind if he did, but the tenseness passed, and he let his hand sink.

"I care so much because I want to see my parents get married at the Foundation monument. I want them to have the big springtime wedding they've been denied for so long. I care so much because of all the stories I've heard of Miran for most of my life, and I want the city to be like that once again."

"You care because of the Mirani blood in your veins."

He nodded, once.

When all this was over, she'd ask him which Mirani family was in his ancestry.

She went through the gate into her yard, still feeling the warm spot of his touch on her skin.

The same time tomorrow, the play would be over and she would be either in jail or a hero.

She was Mariandra. This time, it was up to her to make sure that the foreigners made it out alive.

24

E LLISANDRA STOOD between the curtains of the backstage area.

In the next section stood the three men who played the beggars, dressed up in rags, with their faces dirty. They were the first actors to go onto the stage. Behind them stood the members of the theatre "crowd". All of them were silent, staring into nothingness while going over their lines one last time.

Liran and his group of fake Coldi negotiators waited a bit further. They wore their leather costumes, and every bit of their ample exposed skin—they were barbarians after all—had been rubbed in brown oil. Behind them waited the members of the orchestra with their instruments.

Ellisandra met Vayra's eyes. She heard that he had called a special meeting of the orchestra that morning where apparently details had been discussed about a slight change in the musical program to accommodate his father.

Vayra's father, however, was not yet here, but that didn't seem to bother anyone.

Stop worrying.

She was scrunching up the fabric of her dress. Sariandra was checking all the orchestra uniforms. She wore her own glorious grey dress that came with a shimmering overdress embroidered with little beads. She looked very pregnant. She kept looking over her shoulder, as if afraid that her father would turn up in here. He wouldn't, because Vayra's guards stood at all the doors that connected the backstage area to the rest of the building or outside.

Her father would be in the audience that was the source of the many buzzing voices on the other side of the main curtain. The door attendants had confirmed that the hall was full and they'd had to start turning people away.

Ellisandra felt sick. The hall hadn't been full for any of the plays she had arranged. Last year, there had been a lot of empty seats at the back, even though the council normally filled empty seats with school classes, but that wasn't necessary today.

She peeked through a gap between the curtains.

All the important councillors sat in the prime seats in the lower middle part. She could see Asitho Bisumar with his wife. Next to him sat Nemedor Satarin and his wife, a grey-haired Nikala woman with her curly hair in a bun. She might have been pretty had it not been for the scowl permanently etched on her face. Then again, being married to such a manipulative man would make her scowl, too. His two daughters were with them, seated on the other side of their mother. Both were a number of years older than Ellisandra, and both were married. Neither of them looked as if they wanted to be there.

Next to them sat one of the other two High Councillors, who dealt with the internal city affairs and commerce. The fourth High Councillor sat on the far side of Asitho Bisumar.

Behind the High Councillors and their families sat the other councillors. She spotted Jaeron's father, and Jaeron next to him. Jaeron's mother was there, too, a woman with a face that was round for an Endri. They certainly wouldn't be here out of support to Ellisandra's theatre work.

"Oh, there she is," someone said behind her. She turned her head.

Aleyo had come up from behind. She wore her beautiful dress, with her hair in a bun and held by a jewelled net. Tolaki was with her, her appearance demure.

What was this?

"Tolaki?"

Tolaki held her hand over her mouth and stared at Ellisandra's face. Thanks to Vayra's bandage, the wound was not as sore, but if anything the bruising was worse. She had removed the bandage this morning, and the make-up women had put some extra colour on her cheek.

'I'm so sorry about what's happened to you." Tolaki's voice sounded unsteady. "I've come to apologise. I like you. I'm sorry for what I said. I didn't really mean it. I don't agree with what was done to you. The past few days have been really bad for me. I missed you all so much."

"It's all right," Ellisandra said.

"No, you're too forgiving. It isn't all right. I see that now. I understand what you're fighting for. I want you to succeed. I was just jealous that it couldn't be me, that I didn't have the courage to do what you are doing. Here. You should have this."

She gave Ellisandra a piece of paper. It was an official document. At the top, it said, *Declaration of Candidature.*

The election.

"Stand for election. I want you to succeed."

"Thank you." She wondered what had brought Tolaki's sudden change of heart. "We should all stay together and stand up for each other, especially the women."

Tolaki nodded. "I'm sorry. I thought you were selfish, but I can see that I was selfish."

She hugged Tolaki. "It really doesn't matter. You were shocked by what I was doing. I asked a lot of you."

Vayra looked over the heads of the orchestra, most of whom were Nikala women much shorter than he was. There were more people than there had been at any rehearsal. His father was still nowhere to be seen, but Gisandra was there with her drums and bells, and so were a group of other women who had left the theatre to have families.

The clock jumped. Starting soon. Liran was checking the bags of red dye he had taped under his shirt. Then he checked the bags of the other players. One leaked a little bit and he asked for some tape to fix the hole.

Then the clock jumped again.

Aleyo hefted the baton. The curtains started moving apart. The audience fell quiet and the orchestra walked onto the stage. In the expectant silence, they took up their positions in the orchestra pit. Aleyo asked for attention and they started playing.

The first act went off without a hitch. Tameyo stuffed up one of her lines in the second act, but Vayra's flute solo in the Lover's Dance was beautiful. As they had decided, he stood on his chair for it so that everyone could see him. People in the audience were whispering to each other and frowning at him.

She could almost hear the voices. *A foreigner? Playing Mirani music?*

They had decided to lengthen the Lover's Dance. Liran, with his hair dyed black, led Tameyo across the stage. Both were excellent actors and although the characters in the story couldn't understand each other well, their love came out beautifully. They kissed passionately, for real, something that had also never been done in the state theatre.

Ellisandra studied the faces of people in the audience. The younger ones watched with wide eyes. Traditional plays were high on melodrama, but real, true emotion was not usually part of a play. An older lady whose name Ellisandra didn't know held her hand to her mouth. This woman would have seen the play the previous time it had been performed and would know what was coming.

At the break between the second and third act Ellisandra went to her upstairs office and pulled open the curtains that covered the window. Downstairs in the hall, the councillors stood in the special area clutching drinks. Most were not talking. Several of them were glancing at each other or at the other people in the hall, who all stood clustered around the tables with food and drinks provided that morning by Vayra's cook.

Sariandra came up and let herself drop into the seat behind Ellisandra's desk. "I'm so tired. I think I could sleep for a whole day."

"The babe is slowing you down, right?"

Sariandra put her hands on the lower curve of her belly. "He kicks me in the insides a lot. It hurts. I can't breathe."

"You kept this secret for a long time, didn't you?"

Sariandra looked down. "We were hoping to have left Miran when I started showing. But then my father found out. I was terrified at first, but now I don't mind. We'll fight. We'll get a couple of us in the council. We'll defeat my father."

Ellisandra wished she could be so optimistic. "How long have you got?"

"Healer Lasko says two months at most, probably less." Sariandra smiled. "The world will be changed when he's born."

Ellisandra nodded. Every one of her muscles was tight with fear. So many people expected so much from her.

What if the council cracked down on the actors after the play was finished? What if she and the other Foundation families wouldn't be allowed into the assembly hall? What if none of them came?

What if everyone would withdraw their support from her at the last moment?

The fear made her feel weak. "We better go back downstairs. The interval is almost over."

When she pulled the curtain shut, she spotted a couple of familiar faces in the audience: Jintho and his friends, right down the back where the tiered seating met the theatre's wall.

What were they doing here? There were guards all over the audience. Did Jintho want to get himself arrested?

The bell heralding the beginning of the last act rang while they were going down the stairs. The tail end of the orchestra was about to disappear between the curtains, and the actors were all ready, the prisoners in their leather gear and the guards in uniforms.

The third act was full of action. Fights, Mariandra's arrest—beautifully acted with heart-rending screams that made a number of the ladies in the audience squirm.

Then a musical version of the Warrior Song, where Jihan goes to gather his mates to *drive the foreigners out*. Keldon looked so much like Enzo when he said those things.

There was a failed attempt at negotiation, led by Rana, who successfully escaped while his fellows were put in prison.

Could he get them out? There was hope on young faces in the audience and a measure of unease in the older ones. They saw him hug Mariandra through the bars of her prison cell. They knew he'd done nothing that justified the killing that was to come.

That embrace through the bars of the cell was a short musical interlude. Normally it was a trio between two lutes and a drum. But Ellisandra only needed to hear one haunting chord that made the strings twang to know who was playing this instrument. Vayra's father rose from amidst the orchestra. The light glinted on his black hair and the panels of his lute.

Ellisandra raised a hand to her mouth. Whatever happened to making sure he looked Mirani?

For a breathless moment, he played alone. He played rough, unrefined, sliding his fingers over the neck of the instrument so that one chord seamlessly segued into another while his skin squeaked against the surface of the strings. Then he broke into the well-known melody.

The music was lilting, it was haunting, it was spine-chilling. When he finished his solo and the trio took over, a good number of people cheered in the audience. They ended the piece, not with the genteel sounds typical of the Mirani theatre music, but with a loud dissonant chord.

Some people in the audience gasped.

The escaped prisoners sneaked onto the stage one by one.

"How do we get out of here?" one said.

"Rana, do you remember?" another asked.

"Don't leave me here!" Mariandra called from the cell. "I know I can't live where you come from, but if I stay here, they'll kill me!" Her voice sounded raw, as if she had really been crying.

Rana ran across the stage, but at that moment, Jihan and his guards burst in.

"Halt!"

Rana whirled around and shouted his line in Coldi. Numerous people in the audience turned to each other.

Rana scrambled back until he stood almost against the cell door. He held up his hands to show that he had no weapon.

Jihan pulled out his sword. Both men had trained extensively and not only were they healthy and skilled, the weapons had been improved so that they made big clanging noises. Several ladies in the audience winced. The first prisoner was wounded. The actor burst the bag of dye under his shirt. As it spread across the floor, a murmur rose up in the hall. More prisoners fell. Fake blood turned the white tiles on the floor red. Loret had done an excellent job in polishing the stage so that it ran off. Loret stood on the viewing platform in the backstage area. He had not been around when they had rehearsed the final scenes and had never seen the play.

The fight between Jihan and Rana was in full swing and then Jihan tripped Rana up and without a thought stabbed him through the heart. Blood went everywhere. The practice with the paint bags paid off. Splatters landed even in Jihan's face and all over his white shirt.

Mariandra let out a heart-wrenching cry.

A woman in the audience started screaming.

Jihan freed Mariandra from the cell, and she walked like a prisoner with him off the stage.

Then there was an intense silence.

The curtain shut.

And a roar broke out from the audience. Some people shouted, some cheered or clapped, or stamped their feet. Others cried.

Behind the curtains, the theatre staff worked quickly to turn the set around. The big turning platform left a trail of red paint.

All the actors got to their feet and clasped hands.

Ellisandra called for the others of the theatre committee. She held hands with Sariandra, whose palms were sweaty with nerves. The whole building shook with the thundering tumult in the hall.

The curtain opened again.

The people in the audience were on their feet. Guards were shouting for calm but the people ignored them. Some surged up to the stage, others tried to get out of the hall. A huge cheer went up for the actors. Keldon and Tameyo opened up the chain of hands and gestured for Ellisandra and the committee to come forward. They did.

The cheers were deafening.

Ellisandra noticed some people turn to each other, no doubt gossiping about Sariandra's status. Not only were women supposed to marry before they fell pregnant, they had to stop all their public activities when they did so.

Ellisandra spotted Asitho Bisumar in the audience, his lips pressed together with anger. His poor wife was wiping her cheeks.

She motioned for calm. Slowly, the crowd fell into a hushed silence.

"Thank you," Ellisandra said when it was quiet enough for her to do so. "I took a risk with this very different interpretation of *Changing Fate* and I am glad that you enjoyed it. The play is unusual, but I hope that the messages it contains make you think about the value of life—"

In the back of the hall, a male voice shouted, "We want elections, now!" It might even have been Jintho. "Ellisandra for the High Council!"

A good number of people cheered.

A tense moment followed, in which Ellisandra was afraid that someone would call the guards into action.

Then someone else shouted, "Down with the tyrants!"

"Elections now! Let the people speak!"

"No more blood, no more repression."

"No more spying on our own citizens."

"Down with the Citizens' Corps."

"Elections, elections!"

"Ellisandra! Ellisandra!"

Soon others took up the chant. Everybody stood on their seats, clapping and chanting her name.

At the front of the stage, a number of guards gathered, one of them a higher-ranking officer.

Nemedor Satarin sat unmoving in his seat, his lips pressed together. He was looking straight at her.

Then he smiled, a mean grimace that made her insides turn cold.

'Come on, quick," Ellisandra said. She herded the girls into the curtain folds of the backstage area, where it was a mess of soaked clothes and costumes and props hastily discarded between acts.

"Don't worry about cleaning up just yet," Ellisandra shouted.

From here, the shouting and chanting in the main hall sounded muffled. There was also a lot of rumbling of people trying to get out, shouts of people to let women with children through.

"Take off your costumes as quickly as possible and go home. Be safe."

"I'm not going home," Keldon said in his loud stage voice. "That's what we've always done: run home whenever there is trouble, so that the men in power can continue to do whatever they've been doing for years."

"Agreed," Liran said. He *had* to be cold in his skimpy outfit and covered in wet red dye. "If we want change, we should be out there helping the young guys call for an election."

"Please. They're not going to concede. There is too much at stake," Ellisandra said. "Tomorrow, the council will be voting to change part of Foundation Law to make it harder for council decisions to be challenged. They're repealing a whole raft of small provisions in the old law that on the surface look quaint and outdated, but that allow challenges to proposed new legislation, or election results, or anything the council does. Without them the council can do whatever it wants."

"That power was in the hands of the Foundation families," Keldon said. "And only you are left."

He didn't mention the important part: that Enzo, who had voting power as oldest son of the oldest son, was in the other camp.

"I've tried to bring the Foundation families together to veto this law change. I've contacted the other Foundation families, but none of them have sent anyone. My brother supports the law change. We can't wait for any of the other families to arrive. We have to stop this change going through on our own. I don't care if my family loses its powers in the council, but *someone* should have the power to block proposed laws. If this law goes through, only civil war can stop a power-hungry council. We need to go into that meeting tomorrow and make our concerns heard."

"We'll come," Tameyo said.

Keldon said, "I think we should go to the council and demand to be let in now. We'll have a sit-in protest in the hall and then go into the session tomorrow. That's what used to happen with protests in the past."

That was true. Ellisandra remembered that from history books.

"Yes, let's go!" someone said.

There were a good number of agreeing noises, so after a quick change into more practical clothing, Ellisandra led the group through the corridors of the theatre building.

In one way or another, the guards had managed to calm the crowd down and ushered most of the people out of the theatre. A few stragglers still hung around, while theatre staff had started the task of cleaning up.

"Good night, lady Ellisandra," one of them called. There was laughter in his voice. The theatre would get paid by the council for the number of people in the audience. Theatre Day was always good for them, but today would give them a bumper payout.

In the foyer, one of the orchestra's drum players had been holed up by a merchant.

"You're sure you don't know his name at all?" the merchant was saying.

"Not a clue," the woman said. "He was never at any of our rehearsals."

'If you see him, tell him that I organise weddings and I have quite a few customers who would pay handsomely for good music . . ."

The orchestra member responded, but by then Ellisandra had walked too far to hear the reply.

The merchant's voice was louder. "I don't care, frankly. If he can play like that, that's all I care about."

The column of actors and other artists went out the theatre up the hill. The night was blustery, with low clouds chasing each other over the city, but no snow fell.

Ellisandra walked with Tolaki and Aleyo.

Jntho and Sariandra were behind them, holding hands.

But when they arrived at the council building, they couldn't get in because the gates were closed. Ellisandra had never seen those gates closed.

The group bunched up in the place where you could normally walk through into the main entrance that led into the foyer of the assembly hall. That foyer where they had planned to camp overnight.

"They're already in lockdown," someone behind Ellisandra said.

Ellisandra felt cold. The council could have ordered all their councillors to come here straight after the performance had finished and no one would need to go in or out of the building until morning.

A lone guard walked across the entrance porch, in between the columns.

"Let us in," Keldon called out. He rattled the gate.

"The hall opens tomorrow morning." The guard went into the main door.

Tomorrow morning, they would open the little gate to the side, and there would be such a long queue to get in that surprise, surprise, a lot of people wouldn't make it to the council session.

Ellisandra glanced at the fence—it was not that tall—and noticed Keldon also looking at it. He probably had the same thought.

She jerked her head. "Come."

The main group of actors who had followed them here stood mulling in the square, hands in their pockets and collars turned up around their necks. More still came walking up from the theatre. They clumped together, huddled in their cloaks for the cold. Keldon put on his acting voice and explained what was going on.

"You can go home if you wish," Ellisandra said. "Come back tomorrow morning when the gates open."

"We're going to stay with you." A man who had played one of the prisoners said. His face was still tinted with oil.

"I don't know where we can go." She also realised that someone at home would need to look after Father if she wasn't there to do it. Were they even free to go or was the square surrounded by guards?

Ellisandra walked up the steps of the Foundation monument to look over the heads of the people. There was no sign of any more guards than usual, or at least it was too dark to see any, but as Vayra had said, people would be watching.

She leaned against one of the five pillars, the stone rough under her hands.

This was where, many, many years ago, her family and the other Foundation families had gathered to sign an agreement with the Nikala people about the division of tasks in Miran. The laws had worked for many years. There was a line in one of the later classics, where Esintho Andrahar, High Councillor says, "Whatever happens to Miran, we have this document." She said it aloud to herself. "We have the agreement that safeguards us against destruction, both from outside and within. We must not stray from it, or doom will come to us, because we are a nation of two halves, and we are bound by honour to keep it this way."

Her voice had risen while she spoke, and a number of people had followed her up the steps to the platform. One of the minor actors had brought a storm lamp from the theatre.

Now Tameyo came forward, and spoke in her loud theatre voice. "The chaos is of our own making. We were greedy and complacent and more interested in bettering our own lives than the wellbeing of Miran as a whole."

These were lines directly from that play, *The Days of Pain and Love*, which was the final instalment of the Classics and dealt with political upheaval caused by a group of power-hungry councillors. This was set in the time that the five High Councillors were still those from the Foundation families, but there were disturbing passages that resonated today. The theatre had performed it a few years ago.

Speaking in the role of Esintho Andrahar, Ellisandra said, "We challenge the people of Miran: if anyone breaks the agreement, speak up. If forces gather to silence groups in our community, speak up. If men in power, even if they are in the High Council, try to push out or overpower other groups, for all that is dear, if you love our fair city, speak up!" She raised her fist, as the script required.

The entire group of actors had gathered on the steps of the monument. Someone at the back shouted, "Speak up!"

Others joined in the chant.

"Speak up, speak up, speak up."

Over their heads, Ellisandra could see the guards at the gates to the council building. They had been joined by a group of colleagues and stood in a group arguing.

"Speak up, speak up, speak up!" The sound of many voices echoed over the square.

From the shops, the apartments in the commercial quarter, from the markets came small but steady streams of people. Many

carried lights. A small group came even from the building of the
Mirani chapter of the Trader Guild. They were Nikala, they were
Endri. They were shop owners, business owners, Lawkeepers,
administrators, account keepers, domestic staff. They were . . .
Loret and his men, Aleyo's younger sister, workers from the place
where they often bought the midday meal—

A male voice in the crowd yelled, "Out of the way, people, let
us through. Out of the way!"

People moved aside and a sled with a big male tiyuk stopped
at the bottom of the steps. Next to the nomad driver sat Vayra with
his musician father, and a couple of packs wrapped in white material lay on the tray.

Vayra jumped off, unlashed the netting on the sled and rolled
one of the packs onto the ground. He jumped after it and undid
the fastening. The bundle unfolded itself into one of those white
Hedron miners' tents.

He said, "We have six of these. We have heaters, too."

Within moments a camp had sprung up around the monument.
Vayra and his father set up the tents and turned on the heaters.
The eating house's owner left and came back later with a sled
containing huge steaming pots of beans in fish sauce. Another
brought tea.

As the night wore on, the actors played scenes from the classic
plays that were about the fairness of Mirani law and about the
importance of Foundation.

Others came with books and read passages. One man even had
a copy of the same version of Foundation Law that lay next to
Ellisandra's bed at home.

Guards hung around in the square, but they seemed uncertain
as to what to do.

In the middle of the night, when most people had retreated
inside the tents, Jintho, Liran and a couple of others went to half-
saw through the hinges of the gates to the council complex.
Ellisandra pleaded with him to be careful, but he said one of his

fellows was an ex-guard and knew their way of patrolling. Jintho came back not much later.

People in the tents told each other stories, and daydreamed about what they wanted to do or buy when finally the borders again opened. Under much cheering, Ellisandra signed the application to join the council at the next elections.

Some time very early in the morning, there was word that Lihan Ilendar had arrived. He was, according to the rumour, staying in one of the guesthouses. Ellisandra sent a couple of her actors to chase up which one.

Not much later, the tent entrance opened and the young actor returned in the company of a middle-aged man. His height and shape of his face clearly marked him as Endri, but he had cut his hair to shoulder length and wore it tied up in a ponytail, held together with an embroidered ribbon the ends of which hung down both sides of his neck and down his chest. He wore a dark blue robe with a red cloak, fastened with a gold clip. On his chest he wore the medallion that marked him as member of the Trader Guild.

"Lihan Ilendar?"

He nodded. "A pleasure to meet you, lady." She recognised the overly formal speech from Vayra. Was that a Trader thing or just a peculiarity about Mirani speech from around the time she was born? "You're Ellisandra Takumar?"

"Yes."

"I'd thought your brother would be here."

She gave him a sharp look. "And as a girl I can't speak for my family? I speak for my father, my younger brother and myself."

"No, no, but it would be much easier if the family heir supported this action."

"Well, at this point in time, he doesn't."

"I see." He seemed disappointed.

She went on in a calmer voice, "I'm sorry, we still have some respect as Foundation families."

"Which other families are here?"

Ellisandra let her shoulders slump. "I've contacted all of them, and had hoped that the Andrahar family and the Velisar family would come."

"But?"

"But I've been unable to get any response from either of them."

"I would have expected the Andrahar family at least to be here. Their departure from Miran was ugly, but they've not sold their property, and I can only guess that this is because they're planning to return at some point, or at least resume their business interests. Velisar stopped caring about Miran a long time ago."

She nodded. "It's a sad thing."

One of the theatre staff came in with tea. Ellisandra took the hot cup and cradled it in her hands. She felt incredibly tired. Contacting the other families had been a good plan, but stupid men with stupid self-interests had thwarted it. Hadn't Vayra said that Andrahar would be there? Where was Vayra anyway?

She let out a sigh. "We'll still go into the meeting regardless. There won't be another time to raise these issues. All of us with the theatre will probably lose our jobs anyway. There is nothing left to lose. If they dismantle Foundation Law, we're going to have to leave as well, painful as it will be for Father." She had to keep her voice in check. She didn't *want* to leave Miran. She didn't *want* to stand by the sidelines while the nation she loved was being dismantled by idiots. She wanted the boycotts gone. She wanted the Traders to come back. She wanted the life to come back to Miran.

"You are very brave, lady."

"Thank you." But braveness alone would not make the plan succeed.

25

ONE THING the stories never tell you about rebels is that they have family chores to fulfil. In the stories, the heroine does not have to take time out for feeding her children, or, in Ellisandra's case, look after her elderly father.

Jntho had said that Darma would look after him, and often they'd had arguments that she should just trust the staff to do a good job. The thing was, she didn't. Much as she liked Darma, Ellisandra didn't think she did a good job of looking after Father. That was not Darma's fault; he made it hard for anyone to do a good job, and the staff members were too timid to tell him to stop being stupid or keep his hands to himself.

So Ellisandra put on her cloak, gloves and scarf.

While they waited for the council building to open, many of the protesters caught some sleep, huddled on the comfortable inflatable mattresses, leaning against each other covered by cloaks. The heater blew warm air across the people. Even in this tent, it was hard to believe that it was freezing cold outside.

She opened the entrance to the air tunnel and slipped out of the heated space. It was already so much colder here, and became colder still when she opened the outer entrance.

An undisturbed carpet of snow greeted her, twinkling in the

light from the street lamps like little gemstones. Snow had capped the columns of the monument and the stone slab between them.

There was no sign of guards, although she had no illusion that they watched the group's every move.

"Where are you going, sis?"

Ellisandra gasped. She hadn't heard Jintho come up behind her.

"I need to look after Father."

"I'll come."

The two walked across the square in silence.

When they were in the alley between the markets and the council compound, Jintho said, "Thank you."

"For what?"

"For taking that hit for me. For not telling me how stupid I am."

"Well, you *are* stupid, but I'm sure you don't need me to tell you that. Of all the girls in Miran to get pregnant, Asitho Bisumar's daughter has to take some special idiot award."

"Thanks for reaffirming that."

She laughed. "The hide of you."

"It was Sariandra's idea."

"Don't tell me you planned this."

"I didn't. She did."

"Guess you were a willing participant?"

"It was fun, if that's what you're asking."

Brothers! She rolled her eyes. It was said that all the Bisumar women were strong-willed. Sariandra seemed to be no exception. She clearly had one aim in mind: to get out of her father's house. Short of running away—and cutting herself off from her inheritance—a family of her own was probably the safest route.

"So that was what the thing with the shop is about: getting your own income."

"Yeah."

"Well, I hope I can make that happen. I really do. We should talk to Enzo to see if he has changed his mind about supporting us.

We would stand a better chance if we have at least two of the official heirs."

"Do you think we'll get much support from Lihan Ilendar?"

"I don't know. He seems like . . ." She wanted to say *a bit of a pompous prick* but he *had* made the effort to come, even if he expected to take part of the credit for it. Or something.

"Nothing yet from the Andrahar family?"

She shook her head. "Vayra said there would be someone here. I don't know how he knows. He's friendly with them, so I can gather that he's asked them. Now I wish I'd talked to them myself."

"What can we do?"

"Well . . ." She hesitated. "Theatre is all bluff and show. The best we can do is put on a show. Did you go to the library as a kid and see the Foundation stones in the little glass cabinet in that dark room in the tower?"

"I did."

"Father has the keys to that room."

Jintho frowned at her.

"If the council considers the Foundation families and the stones worthless, let them state that this is the case, clearly, in the open, while members of the Foundation families are holding the stones."

"That's . . . kind of . . . confrontational."

"I'm sorry. It's the only thing I can think of doing. The council is good at avoidance. When we're all standing there demanding that they make a decision, they can't avoid us. They can talk, or they can send in the guards. It's up to them, but eventually, they're going to have to prove which sections of the law allow them to abolish the safeguards."

"All right," Jintho said, but he sounded petrified.

They found the house warm, but Enzo wasn't there. He'd gone out, Riana said. They quickly ate some soup and bread in the kitchen and then went up to Father's room.

He turned his head to the door when both of them came in.

"Ah, at least you're not leaving your old father to sit alone by himself."

"Did Enzo come in?"

"He wanted to know where you were."

"When was this?"

"This morning." That made no sense. It was morning. That would have been yesterday. His perception of time was muddled sometimes and it might have been yesterday. "He was very angry with me about telling him not to marry that girl."

No, definitely not a good day today.

Ellisandra quickly made Father comfortable and then followed Jintho out of the room. "Where do you think he would have left those keys?" she asked him when they were in the hallway.

"In the library desk?"

Indeed, they found several key bundles in the desk drawer. Ellisandra took all of them.

Getting into the library tower was a lot trickier. The library's entrance was next to the council building, at the top of the same set of stairs. The library remained open throughout the night so that students could use it before and after class. Because vagrants tended to sneak in and sleep in the building, guards were everywhere: in the foyer, in the halls, on the galleries.

A group of them stood in the courtyard which held the only entrance to the tower. Jintho went to ask them something and Ellisandra managed to quickly slip into the door, and shut it behind her. In the small space of the staircase her breath sounded muffled.

She waited until the voices outside had faded.

Phew.

The staircase went around the tower twice. At the top was a small door. She had to try at least ten keys before she found one that fitted. For a moment she thought the door was rusted shut, but the key turned.

Inside the room the smell of disuse met her. The light from the staircase glinted on glass. The cabinet looked smaller than she remembered it being, and the fabric was a lot more dusty and faded. She tried opening the sides, but there was no door.

Jintho would have said, *Try lifting the top.*

She did and the glass cover came off, releasing ages of dusty air. She gathered up the four chains. The velvet underneath showed narrow dust-free trails where the chains had lain for many years.

She stuck them in her pocket and went back down the stairs, where she found Jintho still talking with the guards. She slipped into the overhang of a gallery and stood behind a post to listen. He passed himself off as a student of the stars, and had asked the guards for that section of the library.

Brother, you are so full of nonsense, you should have been an actor.

He left the courtyard, thanking the guards profusely, and Ellisandra joined him on the way back towards the square.

They stopped in a little niche where an oil light hung on the wall above a cushioned bench.

"You got them?" Jintho asked.

Ellisandra dug in her pocket and showed him the stones with the silver chains all tangled up.

Each stone was different, but they were all plain water-polished river pebbles. Each had a silver band encircling the widest point. Engraved on the silver were tiny letters.

"The Andrahar stone is missing," she said.

"It was lost in the fire. I remember how people from the council spent days and days combing over the ruins and digging up the top layer of soil. They never found it. An expert said the river pebble would have exploded in the fire, and the silver would have melted in unrecognisable globs and would have been taken away with the rubbish or the spare stuff for sale."

She pulled one out. "Look, this one is ours. It even has our name engraved."

Jintho took the stone from her, undid the clasp on the silver chain and hung it around her neck. "This probably has no more than symbolic value, since these stones were taken from their families."

But having the stones still felt good.

By the time they made it back to the camp, it was fully light and the group of protesters had left the tents and lined up in front of a small side gate that the guards had opened, just as Ellisandra had predicted. They were processing entrants one by one, and taking their time to do it, too. She had been afraid that they would use this tactic.

Meanwhile, the councillors arrived through another gate and went into the building unhindered. Ellisandra pushed to the front of the queue.

The guards gave her a strange look, as if they'd written off the protesters as "rabble" and weren't expecting to see someone like her.

"Can you let us in? We're lawful citizens and we're entitled to attend the council meeting."

"We need to do ID checks on everyone in the public gallery."

"Then call a few more guards, so that we can be inside when the meeting starts."

"They're all busy. We didn't anticipate this many people."

"Why is this gate closed anyway? It never is."

"It's necessary for security."

"What's changed since yesterday? As far as I know, we're still all Mirani citizens and we have a right to be inside."

A couple of young men next to her started to push the gate. They, of course, didn't know that the hinges had been sawn through and were hanging by the merest thread.

Then Ellisandra spotted a familiar face on the other side of the fence. "Enzo!"

He stopped, searching the crowd and found her. His expression turned uneasy. Raedon Tussamar and Jaeron stood on either side of him, about to go into the building as councillors. Jaeron's eyes met hers with such contempt that a chill touched her. He would never forgive her. She had probably made a mistake in handing that letter to Tolaki rather than him. To get the bad news through his sister would have added even more embarrassment.

Enzo strode to the gate. "Elli, what are you doing here? You're making a spectacle of yourself. Why haven't you been home all night? I worried about you after that horrendous mauling of that beautiful play."

"Mauling? Didn't you hear the cheers. Tell me that the people didn't like it."

"Nemedor Satarin is furious."

"Anyone else? Asitho Bisumar maybe? Did you notice that most people in that hall stood on their seats cheering for us? Most people in that hall called for elections. Most people in that hall have had enough of being isolated as a nation, and kept ignorant as citizens. Join us. Make a stand with us. I know you're a good man because I've seen your good side. This is not it. Open the gate."

"It's for your own protection. The High Council will order you killed before conceding."

"Let them try."

"You can't stop them."

"Maybe we'll have trouble stopping them, since we're only artists and *women*, but *you* can stop them legally. You, and Lihan Ilendar. He's with us."

He said nothing.

"Come on, let's go," Raedon said.

Enzo gave her one last look, worried more than angry, and turned around.

"Enzo, you know it's the right thing to do. Father would have wanted it this way."

"Oh, shut up, woman!" Raedon called.

Ellisandra would not be silenced. "I won't shut up until I know what you're using to bribe my brother. By law, he's the only one who can still block the law changes. You know it's wrong, Enzo! Do the right thing. Help me, help your brother."

Enzo said nothing and joined his colleagues. The three of them disappeared into the building.

Ellisandra turned her attention back to the guards. "Let me through. It's our right to attend the meetings."

"Be patient, please, we're required to check everyone's ID. Stand in line! Move back from the gate."

A man shouted, "We're legal Mirani citizens. There is no need for this nonsense." He kicked the gate, and several of the others, also actors, grabbed the bars and pushed. That was the last bit of force the hinges needed to fall apart.

The big metalwork frame toppled inward—both guards just managed to scramble out of the way—and fell onto the ground with a big clang that echoed over the square.

The protesters cheered and surged into the courtyard. In the crush, someone took Ellisandra's hand and led her through at the front of the crowd. It was Keldon.

They went up the steps into the foyer, where they were met by the next group of guards standing defensively in a line. These ones all carried their crossbows across their backs.

The council wouldn't really order them to attack their own citizens, would they?

Ellisandra stepped forward. She drew the chain out from underneath her clothes. "I'm Ellisandra Takumar. I'm here as a member of Miran's last Foundation family. By law, you are required to not only let me into the meeting, but to let me speak in the council." Never mind that this only applied to the family heir. Two people joined her from behind: Jintho and Lihan Ilendar.

The doors to the hall were open and in the glimpse it gave Ellisandra of the stands, it looked like the council hall was already almost full.

The guards looked from one to the other. Oh no, maybe they'd been ordered to do so, but they didn't look like they wanted to use those crossbows.

One who appeared to be a superior motioned for Ellisandra and the two men to walk through. "Only you, then."

Lihan said, "Us three and as many of us as the hall will seat. The others will wait here patiently."

Ellisandra followed him through the resin-panel doors into the assembly hall. The councillors sat along three sides of the hall in tiered benches. The fourth side, on both sides of the door, was for the public and claimants. A red-carpeted aisle led from the door to the centre of the hall, where the High Council's table stood. It was empty right now.

The guard found some unoccupied benches. Besides Lihan Ilendar, Ellisandra chose Aleyo, Sariandra and Tameyo to come with her. A handful of others, mostly actors, also found seats, but most of the protesters had to stay outside. The buzz of voices that drifted in from the foyer suggested that they weren't happy with this

Ellisandra wasn't happy with it, either. All the council meetings she had ever been to had been poorly attended. Who were all these people in the audience if not supporters of the changes in law?

In the aisle, the guards were attempting to shut the doors. "Step back, all, we need the doors closed or we can't start the meeting."

"We have a right to be here," a man said.

"Sorry, the hall is full. You'll have to wait outside."

This was met with unhappy grumbles, but eventually the guards managed to close the doors.

The High Council came in from the door at the other side of the hall. Everyone rose.

Nemedor Satarin walked first, followed by Asitho Bisumar and then the other two, Eldan Hirumar and Jelindor Temanin. The latter was a bent old man with a walking stick and he took his time to walk around the table and sit down.

Everyone in the hall remained silent and standing.

Finally, the old councillor was seated and Nemedor Satarin gave the signal that people could sit down. He made a show of walking up to the speaker's dais which stood in the very centre of the hall. He motioned for silence.

"Welcome to our first session of the council's legislative sitting. We have a number of items to get through today. The most important item is the changes proposed in Foundation Law. It is the first time in twenty years that the law is to be upgraded, and it has become necessary for the sake of keeping our legislation up-to-date with modern practices and reflecting the current values of society."

He read out a long list of sections of the law that they proposed to update. Most of those Ellisandra had also identified as being the ones that gave Foundation families powers that could limit the council's decision-making.

While he spoke, Ellisandra found Enzo's gaze in amongst the councillors, next to Raedon and a few rows behind Asitho Bisumar. He looked unhappy.

Nemedor Satarin finished with, "But look where these laws have taken us. Most of our hallowed Foundation families no longer live in Miran. This document pre-dates the Invasion and does not account for the possibility that a family would even consider leaving Miran. It does not account for Miran being at the beck and call of foreigners."

There was some applause following this.

Ellisandra rose. "You call me a foreigner?" She trembled all over with nerves and excitement, and had to steady herself by putting her hands on the back of the seat in front of her.

Nemedor Satarin's gaze found her in the crowd. "Ah, lady." He bowed and gave her a playful smile. "You are not a foreigner, but you are also not a Foundation family heir."

"But I am." Lihan Ilendar rose next to her.

His appearance caused some talk and commotion.

Nemedor Satarin's eyes widened briefly. Had he not known that Lihan Ilendar was in Miran? "You chose to leave Miran. You have no business getting involved in internal affairs."

"The law sees it differently."

'If we are going to stick to the letter of the law, it also says that you should be in possession of a Foundation stone."

Lihan pulled out the silver chain. "I have this." He held it up so that the stone dangled on the chain.

"Where did you get that? The stones were repossessed. That stone was illegally removed from the council premises."

Ellisandra said, "My father, librarian of Miran, authorised their removal. The law proposals are illegal. You need to consult with us."

"And we have." He gestured to Enzo. "We have agreed that the Foundation families will be compensated for the loss of influence—"

"I'm not interested in compensation. I want to live in a country where someone can send the council home if they've lost the trust of the majority. I don't have to be that person, but I want someone with integrity and with understanding of the responsibility to have this task. Someone who has sworn not to act in self-interest."

"Unfortunately, lady, the deciding power lies with the family heirs—"

"And not with silly, deranged women? Because you have never listened to half the Mirani population—"

Some people cheered in the hall. Others protested. Someone shouted, "Calm down!"

There was a lot stumbling and thudding up in the audience stands, but because those seats were higher up, she couldn't see the reason for the noise.

Nemedor Satarin cast an impatient look in the direction of the noise. "Can we take those troublemakers outside? I'm sure there are plenty of people who could sit here without creating a disturbance."

"I will not be silenced!" a man shouted.

"Remove this rabble from the hall."

Guards came from behind the council seating.

In that terrifying moment, Ellisandra realised that she had misjudged the council. They *would* use guards against their own citizens. Wasn't that the definition of civil war? This was going to be a repeat of *Changing Fate*, only the victims would be Mirani.

"This is wrong!" she yelled, but her voice was lost in the shouting and stumbling. People were now trying to get out of the public gallery. Sariandra's face had gone white. "They're sending in the guards to remove us."

All was lost and she would be Mariandra, forced to write about the council's victory.

Traders were allowed to carry arms, and Lihan had taken his gun out of the bracket on his arm, under his cloak. "This is ridiculous," he said. "Stay with me, ladies."

Why did he say that? Why did every Endri man think that it was his moral duty to protect women as if they couldn't look after themselves?

Ellisandra was going to protest, tell him that she wasn't going to flee, that she wanted no violence, that she would climb over the partition that separated the audience from the assembly hall's floor and talk to the High Council herself.

But the double doors to the hall burst open. One of the doors hit the wall with a loud bang. People fell silent.

A guard protested in the foyer. "But you can't all just—"

A large group of people walked into the hall over the main aisle that led between the two halves of the public stands. Backlit by the glare of sunlight from outside, it was hard to see who they were, but the first were all guards dressed in sleek, dark grey, modern gear. Ellisandra couldn't see their faces because they wore helmets, but by their shapes and sizes, these were definitely not locals.

Following them were a varied group of people young and old, some of whom wore traditional Mirani clothing. With a shock she recognised Vayra at the front, dressed as Endri, as well as the man he had introduced as his father. Except he had washed the black dye out of his hair. It was now white, Endri white. And his eyes were no longer black but Endri light blue. No doubt remained in her mind that he was pure Endri.

Several people gasped.

"Hell, that's Iztho Andrahar," someone said behind her.

The man who had gone missing, the heir of the Andrahar family. He'd been here all along and Vayra had said nothing about it? He'd even sat beside her when she tried to contact the families? His father? The oldest son of the oldest son?

Behind the pair were two more Endri people, a couple, the man with his hair in a most peculiar hairdo, with a mixture of little plaits, glittering beads and loose strands cut at different lengths. He was accompanied by a woman with short hair and tattoos on her neck. Those had to be Rehan and his wife Mikandra Bisumar, Sariandra's half-sister. Both of them wore Trading uniforms, not the khaki Mirani ones, but shirts and trousers of blue-green fabric that were much too thin for Mirani weather.

With them were two adolescents, girls both, wearing a simple version of the uniform but without the Trading medallion. One was Indrahui, with skin velvet black and copper-coloured hair, the other . . . was lithe and small. She had huge eyes and dark hair, patterned skin and . . . she had a tail, which waved behind her.

Behind them was an Endri man with long hair, a little bit wavy, and he walked next to a leather-clad Coldi woman who visibly carried two guns, one on each arm. This had to be Braedon and his Hedron guard wife Izramith Ezmi. There were two girls with them, the youngest one holding the woman's hand, the older one adolescent. Both had almost luminous orange hair. Since when did Endri and Coldi have *children*?

Behind the family walked the elderly Endri matriarch, Isandra, her back straight, wearing a magnificent mottled cloak and a Mirani Trading uniform. Behind her was another Mirani couple, the youngest son Taerzo and his wife Calliandra Azthunar, with two young Endri men, identical twins, a young woman and two younger girls, also identical.

The group came to a halt, but Vayra progressed to the speaker's dais in the middle of the floor in the company of the man he'd said was his father, and others said was the missing Andrahar heir. He pulled at something from under his clothes and held it up to the light. A plain river stone with encircling silver band.

The missing Foundation stone.

It was so quiet in the hall that you could hear people cough.

"On behalf of the Foundation families of Miran, on behalf of the people of Miran, on behalf of fairness and peace, I, Vayra Perling Dinzo Andrahar, veto the changes to Foundation Law. On behalf of the Mirani people, on behalf of my parents, Iztho Andrahar and Anmi Kirilen Dinzo and my entire family, I, Vayra Perling Dinzo Andrahar, dismiss the council, declare all seats vacant and up for re-election."

A murmur of talk went up from the council benches.

Can he do that?

Is that still legal?

The murmur rose to voices of protest and consternation.

Vayra held his hand higher and the stone dangling from the chain caught the light. He had to shout over the talking to be heard. "Behold the Foundation stone you thought lost! We cherished this treasure from the day Foundation Law was signed and have never lost it from our sights. Nor have we ever truly left Miran. The Andrahar family is back!"

The audience broke out in shouts. Councillors got up from their seats. Guards approached Vayra, but his family's guards closed around him. He continued holding up the Foundation stone so that everyone could see it. While he slowly turned around, his eyes met Ellisandra's.

A wave of anger came over her.

He had deceived her and deceived all of the people in the theatre. He'd come here with only one aim in mind. He probably had led his entire life with that aim. Nothing else mattered to him. No wonder Isandra had given him the house: he was their weapon and Ellisandra had been nothing more than a tool.

The Mirani guards gathered on the aisle behind the family, and also around the councillors. A higher-ranking man was speaking to Nemedor Satarin. He then walked to Vayra and asked to see the stone. He went back to Nemedor Satarin. Several of the councillors spoke in angry voices, but there was too much noise in the hall to hear what they said.

When the family had come in, they had left the door to the foyer open, and the crowd that waited outside had entered the hall. These were the actors, the merchants, the builders who had camped out in the square overnight in the company of many newcomers.

Some guards were trying to get these people to leave, but there were too many of them and they simply ignored the orders.

Lihan Ilendar touched Ellisandra's shoulder. "Let's go."

"Go? Why?"

"You got what you wanted."

"I haven't gotten anything yet. Nothing is resolved and the High Council has not yet stepped down."

"They will sort it out. It's likely to get nasty."

"Nasty suits me fine. I'm used to nasty."

He took a step back, and looked genuinely puzzled. "I don't understand. I'm concerned for your safety."

"Yes, and thank you for that, but you don't live here, and it's not your fight anymore. The fight is ours, the younger generation."

"What do you mean—not yours? Don't you think that I would have preferred to stay in Miran if I could have?" He sounded so hurt that she felt sorry for having raised this. Lihan Ilendar was a respected man and it seemed he genuinely didn't understand her anger, and genuinely thought he was doing the right thing by protecting the delicate ladies.

Which meant that once again, the important men expected to make the decisions over her head.

And no, she wasn't going to smooth it over, and she wasn't going to be quiet, or run to safety.

She shrugged off his hand and went down the steps, pushing onlookers aside. Some people were going the other way, trying to get out of the hall.

"Come with me," she said to any of the theatre people she passed.

There was still a big argument going on in the centre of the hall.

Asitho Bisumar's voice sounded over the noise, "You have no right to come here and tell us how to run our council. You have no legal right. Yes, we will fight this in whatever court you choose to bring it. We don't recognise *gamra* law. Don't even try."

She felt cold. Nemedor Satarin wasn't going to concede, even based on Mirani law. He would hold on until someone physically removed him from office. The only way he knew to hold on would be with violence.

The Andrahar family had brought enough guards to do damage, and she knew they had performed one raid into Miran before. They were here to remove the council with violence. And she was determined not to let this become another bloodbath.

"Let me through, let me through." She pushed the guards aside.

A councillor gave an indignant cry. "But, lady, behave yourself."

Ellisandra was through with behaving. She pushed right through to the speaker's dais where the main body of the argument was taking place, and a scuffle had broken out.

Someone said, "You will step down from office, or I will remove you."

That was Vayra, and he faced both Nemedor Satarin and Asitho Bisumar.

And a guard shouted, "Stop that, or suffer the consequences." He lifted his crossbow.

Several of the Andrahar family's guards pulled weapons.

Ellisandra didn't think and didn't hesitate. She launched herself at the guard. He hadn't expected that, and tried to fend her off with one hand while keeping hold of his weapon with the other. Mirani crossbows were extremely heavy and it became unbalanced in his free hand. Ellisandra pushed past the dais and took up position in front of Nemedor Satarin and Asitho

Bisumar, looking directly into the business end of Rehan Andrahar's gun.

Everyone froze.

'Don't even think about it," she said, glaring at Rehan. "Lower
that thing."

Rehan didn't move. The years that had passed since the picture
had been taken from which she recognised him had made his face
harder and more angular.

Mikandra gently touched her husband's elbow. He lowered the
gun slightly and studied Ellisandra over the top.

"I have no weapons but words," she said. "I am the director of
the state theatre. There is a play that we've just performed,
Changing Fate. No one has understood it very well up till now, but
it is the only play in the classics that shows the horrors of armed
conflict. In the last scene of the play all the bad things happen to
good people, because that is what conflicts are like. There is death
and destruction, and many families are hurt, and things never go
back to normal for these people. This is *not* going to be one of those
conflicts."

The circle had widened to include a couple of others, including
Enzo, who stared at her with wide eyes.

She addressed Rehan. "The people in the sitting council may be
bad in your eyes, but death is never a good punishment for
misdeeds of the past. Death leaves widows and makes enemies."

'This man is responsible for the deaths of many."

'This man is our legally voted leader. I don't defend him, but I
want to defeat him in the regular way."

Rehan jerked his head up, and stuck the gun back in the
bracket under his cloak. A smile ghosted over Mikandra's face.

Nemedor Satarin said, "I'm not going to run against a mere
girl."

"Then don't run. I am standing for election. Anyone is welcome
to stand against me. We let the people speak, not weapons. No
more blood will be shed over this issue. The day Mirani people
start fighting each other is the day that Miran truly dies."

He glared at her, but said nothing. He didn't need to. There were far too many of her supporters in the hall to try to hustle her out. Her nomination would already have been processed. His time in the High Council was finished and he knew it. He could retire gracefully or be defeated. It was all the same to her.

She gave a mock bow to Asitho Bisumar. "See you in the elections." She turned her back on both men and faced . . . Vayra. All the anger of learning who he was came back to her.

"I trusted you. I trusted your words and your support. What do I get in return? Betrayal."

"Everything I told you was the truth. I did not lie to you."

"The Andrahar heir will be there. Was it really so hard to tell me that you were the Andrahar heir?"

"I couldn't. People knew that we still had our stone, or at least that it was not in the library with the others."

She continued her angry glare. Excuses, excuses.

"I gave you all the clues. I told you the story about my parents. I told you about my special bond with the Andrahar family. I even went to get my family crest tattoo in the hope that the gossip would reach you and you'd figure it out."

And she'd seen that tattoo in the shop. Ellisandra spread her hands. "If you knew me so well, you'd know that I'm impervious to gossip. And I'm a stupid woman to boot."

"You're anything but stupid. I understand why you're angry, but I'll prove to you that I'm a good man."

"Just leave me alone. I've got an election campaign to run."

She turned away from him and walked towards the door. The members of the extended Andrahar family made way for her, and so did all the other people who had followed them. By the time she was at the door, the cheer in the hall was deafening.

In the foyer, someone caught up with her from behind. It was Enzo. He said nothing, but swept her up in a hug so tight that she could barely breathe.

26

MANY THINGS happened that long winter.
Mirani law required a two-month minimum period to call an election so that all parties could prepare. And prepare, they did.

Ellisandra got together with a large group of people involved in the arts and theatre and set up the New Miran party, which listed no less than twenty candidates for the public section of the assembly. Ellisandra went to all the other Endri families to lobby for their support, and she got it from many.

Ellisandra spent much of the rest of her time either in Father's library or in the council archives or in many meetings. Her team consisted of theatre people, and included Aleyo and Jintho. Vayra started turning up at their meetings not long after the formation of the party. Ellisandra debated telling him that he wasn't welcome, but could find no ground to refuse him except her own hurt over his betrayal. He did know a lot, and he made himself very useful.

Ellisandra dealt with her anger towards him in the usual way: by avoiding him. But eventually even the anger seeped away. He was probably right. She wouldn't have liked to have known who he was for fear of someone getting that information out of her. And she should stop being stupid and apologise to him. But with every day she didn't apologise, the need to do it seeped away, until it became like an annoying pain in her elbow: something she only noticed when performing one particular action, and risking a fight with him wasn't worth destabilising their new party.

The sitting High Council kept remarkably quiet, and neither Nemedor Satarin nor Asitho Bisumar were seen much in public anymore.

Most of the Andrahar family went back to Barresh, but Iztho stayed in the house. At night, from the window of her room, Ellisandra often saw father and son sitting by the fire talking or playing music. Sometimes she wished she could be with them, because it looked like they were having fun. Braedon and his family were regular visitors to the house, and rumours went that he wanted to open the Andrahar Traders office.

Ellisandra happened to be in their dining room talking elections with Vayra and his father when the family turned up. This time, they had brought a visitor.

As soon as the woman entered the room, Iztho froze.

The woman stopped in the doorway.

She was tall, and had very dark eyes. She looked . . . regal, and far too young to be Vayra's mother.

She whispered, "Iztho?"

He rose from the table with such speed that his chair almost fell over, ran to the door in a few steps and swept her up in his arms.

She cried and he cried, and they kissed without regard for Braedon's two daughters who had also come into the room. Vayra hugged both of them, and so they stood for a long time, a family reunited. The sight of the three of them almost made Ellisandra cry. Lately, she had been closer to her brothers, but it had become painfully clear that Father might not see spring, and might not even see his first grandchild.

Then the cook brought tea and cakes, and there was much happiness and talk about organising the biggest spring wedding that Miran had ever seen.

Sariandra had moved in with Jintho. They decided to hold off the wedding until after the baby was born, because it was far too late to organise it before. Indeed, it was a bit over a month later that she went into labour.

Sariandra was a slight girl and Jintho quite sturdy. Healer Lasko said that the baby was "big and healthy" and took its time arriving. The first day, the pains were mild and Sariandra spent much of that day in the bath being rubbed by various people, including Ellisandra when she could get out of her meetings. The second day was much more stressful. On Sariandra, because she was exhausted and the pains started in all earnest, and on Jintho because he couldn't stand his girlfriend suffering. He walked in and out of the room, getting hot water, getting ice, getting tea or whatever to keep her comfortable. Eventually, he realised that there was nothing he could do about her pain.

Even after having looked after Father's most unpleasant episodes, Ellisandra found it hard to be in the house, let alone in the room, with Sariandra's distressed cries.

If this was how much pain a woman suffered, she wasn't sure she wanted children, ever.

She sat in the kitchen—which was the room furthest from Jintho's bedroom—when Vayra came into the back door and sat at the table.

From upstairs came an almost inhuman-sounding howl that, even through the floor and several walls, chilled her.

"Still at it, huh?" He looked a bit uneasy, too.

"Healer Lasko says there are no problems. She says first children often take a while."

He nodded, letting the question *Does she have to scream like that?* hang between them. Apparently some women liked to yell.

She got up to pour some tea. He cradled the cup in long-fingered hands.

They drank in silence for a while. Previously, he might have said something about the cold, but it was always cold in Miran and that fact was no longer new to him. He became more Mirani with every day that passed.

Another beastly howl, louder than the last. There was no longer any emotion in the cry. It was just . . . sound, and a really awful sound at that.

"Really getting serious." She felt sick.

They tried to make some small talk, but Ellisandra couldn't concentrate.

Then there were footsteps on the stairs and the door opened. Darma came in. "Mistress, the baby is almost there, if you want to come . . ."

Ellisandra really wasn't sure that she wanted to, but it was customary for family members to attend. It was just that there had been no births in her family for as long as she would have been considered old enough to attend, and she never had.

"I'll come," Vayra said.

Darma didn't question it, but led them up the stairs. Ellisandra turned and whispered to him, "Thank you."

It was hot and stuffy in the room upstairs. Jintho's bed had been moved to the window so that the centrepiece of the room was the padded birthing chair placed on a sheet with towels spread around it.

Sariandra sat on it, naked, slicked with sweat, her head leaning forward to gasp for breath. She was too absorbed in her task to notice people coming in. Jintho stood to the side of her, holding her shoulders. Healer Lasko sat on her knees between her spread legs. Riana stood behind the healer, holding a towel. Healer Lasko said something. Sariandra nodded.

While Ellisandra and Vayra went to sit on the bed to be out of everyone's way, Sariandra breathed faster and started howling again. It was not from pain, Ellisandra realised. It was effort. When she howled, all her muscles went tense. Her white-knuckled hands gripped her knees. The skin on her face and chest went red.

A little spell for a breather, and again.

Healer Lasko made encouraging sounds. "Good, good, keep going."

The atmosphere in the room was tense. Ellisandra subconsciously leaned into Vayra, who put an arm on her shoulders.

Sariandra started howling again. And then all of a sudden, there was a rush of action. Darma and Jintho tilted back the chair with Sariandra in it. Riana knelt next to the Healer with the towel. Healer Lasko eased the baby out while Sariandra pushed. The head, shoulders, the rest of the body, and a rush of fluid that spilled onto the floor. The baby cried before it was fully free, a little contorted red face and open mouth. The little arms went up, shivering.

"That is a big boy," Healer Lasko said.

Riana cheered.

"Oh, look at him!" Sariandra cried in an emotion-filled, hoarse voice. "I knew it was a boy. I knew it!"

The boy her father had wanted so badly and never got. Healer Lasko wrapped him in the towel and put him in his mother's arms, and Sariandra stroked his little cheek going, "Oh, oh, look at his hands. Look at his feet." Her eyes glittered with tears. Her hair hung in wet strings down the sides of her face. Her skin was pale and her thighs bruised and blood-stained. She looked utterly spent, but her eyes were bright with happiness.

Jintho hugged her. He looked a little worn out himself.

Ellisandra wiped at her cheeks. She was crying, too. That was stupid, because she never cried. This was beautiful. Hard and painful, yes, but beautiful.

"I'm glad I came," she whispered to Vayra.

He nodded, with a knowing expression as if he had seen a good number of babies born.

When most of the cleaning up was done and Sariandra sat in bed with her son, Ellisandra went to get Father. He had deteriorated badly in the past few months and barely spoke anymore, but he seemed to understand who the little baby was that Darma gently lowered in his arms.

He cried, too, and that made Ellisandra cry again.

Her family was due to undergo some big changes.

The biggest change would come a few days later, when Ellisandra went to give Father his breakfast. He had always been an early riser and did not react to her entering the room.

"Father?"

He lay in his bed, very still.

It looked like he was asleep, but his face was strangely pale. She rushed to his side, but knew what had happened before she felt the coldness of his skin.

She sat down on the edge of the bed, crying, holding his cold hand until Darma came in wondering where she was. Vayra was with her, and he prised Ellisandra off the bed and let her cry into his chest. He understood, he said in a soft voice, of grieving for family members with serious faults. About loving someone as they were and hating what they had become.

A few days later, they buried Father next to Mother in the family plot in the cemetery that lay uphill from the Endri quarter, just outside the city walls. Many people came, most out of respect. The day was beautiful and crisp, and the sunlight made the snowy mountain flanks glitter. Again Vayra was there, standing quietly in the background while Ellisandra was forced to talk to visitors. He seemed to be determined to be part of her life.

"You are the most beautiful woman I know," he said when they walked back home.

"Beauty alone does not make a good person."

"I mean beautiful on the inside. Have I ever told you how much I admired you staring down both sides in the conflict at the council meeting? Any other person would have stood by and let the fight happen."

The united New Miran Party won the election by a landslide. Nemedor Satarin ended up being surprisingly gracious in defeat. He said he'd remain in the assembly, but retired a few days later. He left town a few days after that. To his estate in Bendara, people said, but everyone agreed that it was right for him to go. He was no longer a young man.

The elections were big news in *gamra*.

The new High Council, the youngest ever, agreed to an ordered plan to reopen the borders.

Five new posts were established to take the place of Foundation families and check on the council. From now on, families had to nominate an heir for legal purposes, and that heir could be a woman. Gisandra caused great consternation by nominating her daughter, who had started to crawl.

The big wedding that took place on a beautiful day of spring symbolised many things.

The love between Vayra's parents made a warm spot in her heart. It was in the way she smiled at him, in the way she would touch his shoulder when walking past, and the way he played music for her.

"It's almost embarrassing," Vayra said to her on the morning of the big day. "Couples that age aren't supposed to behave like that."

But they did, and they walked arm in arm through the streets of Miran in a traditional parade while having only eyes for each other. They stood through the ceremony at the Foundation monument never taking their eyes off each other.

When the marriage celebrant snapped their armbands shut, which Iztho bought before Vayra was born, they kissed for such a long time that people thought they'd never stop. Then the marriage celebrant detached the chain that linked the armbands, called Vayra up on the platform and hung it around his neck.

The three of them hugged.

Vayra came back to Ellisandra. "For the first time in my life, I'm a legitimate child." His voice was so filled with emotion that she put a hand on his knee. He took it and held it for a long time.

Enzo was looking at her from where he sat. Since when had he started to spend so much time with the oldest of Braedon Andrahar's red-haired daughters? She was much too young for him, only barely out of adolescence, which was . . . the time Endri women often married. Maybe she was older than Sariandra, who carried her son in a sling.

The girl's name was Riget. Maybe she needed to start paying attention to her.

When it was all done and people had gone home, Vayra and Ellisandra shared tea in Ellisandra's kitchen.

Vayra was not someone of many words, but he had been more quiet than usual. Ellisandra asked him about it.

He said, "I got a message this morning. I've been asked to fulfil a position at Trader Guild headquarters."

That little statement opened up a hole inside her. Trader Guild headquarters was at Kedras, and he would have to leave.

"And? Are you taking it up?" Her heart was thudding so loudly that the blood roared in her ears.

No, no, please!

He shrugged. "It's a good opportunity. Good pay, too."

No, no, nooooo!

"I thought I'd ask you what you thought about it."

She heard in his words *since you leave me hanging and won't commit* and it was not like that at all, and if he thought that, it was not what she intended. There was no way she would live without him. And in all that, she left a terrified silence.

"Well?" He spread his hands.

The words that always came to her quickly failed her now. She pushed herself up from her chair so abruptly that it fell over. He gave a *whoa* cry of surprise when she dropped herself on his lap. She kissed him on his lips. She had no idea how to take it any further, but between the two of them, and clashes of noses, they worked it out. Big, wet, hungry kisses. His hands on her back pressing her against him. Feeling his chest expand and contract against hers with his fast breaths.

Jintho came into the kitchen carrying his son in one arm.

He stopped in the doorway and simply said, "Oh. I was wondering how much longer you'd take to get to that stage." And left again.

"I guess this means I'll stay," Vayra said when Jintho had gone. His lips were still wet from kissing.

"Please?" And when he said nothing, she repeated, "Please?" She slid off his lap and dropped to her knees on the floor. Leaning on his knees and holding his hands in hers, she said, "I, Ellisandra Takumar, ask permission to take Vayra Perling Dinzo Andrahar as my lawful wedded partner."

He smiled. The look in his eyes made her heart sing.

A Word of Thanks

THANK YOU very much for reading the Return of the Aghyrians series. While this is the end of the series, the Ambassador series is set in the same world, a hundred years in the future.

ABOUT THE AUTHOR

Patty Jansen lives in Sydney, Australia, where she spends most of her time writing Science Fiction and Fantasy.

Her career started in earnest when her story *This Peaceful State of War* placed first in the second quarter of the Writers of the Future contest and was published in their 27th anthology. She has also sold fiction to genre magazines such as Analog Science Fiction and Fact, Redstone SF and Aurealis, before making the move to independent publishing.

Patty has written over fifty novels in both Science Fiction and Fantasy, including the *Icefire Trilogy* and the *Ambassador* series.

pattyjansen.com

BOOKS BY PATTY JANSEN

MORE INFORMATION:

PATTYJANSEN.COM

Books by Patty Jansen

For a complete list of books, scan the image below with your phone.